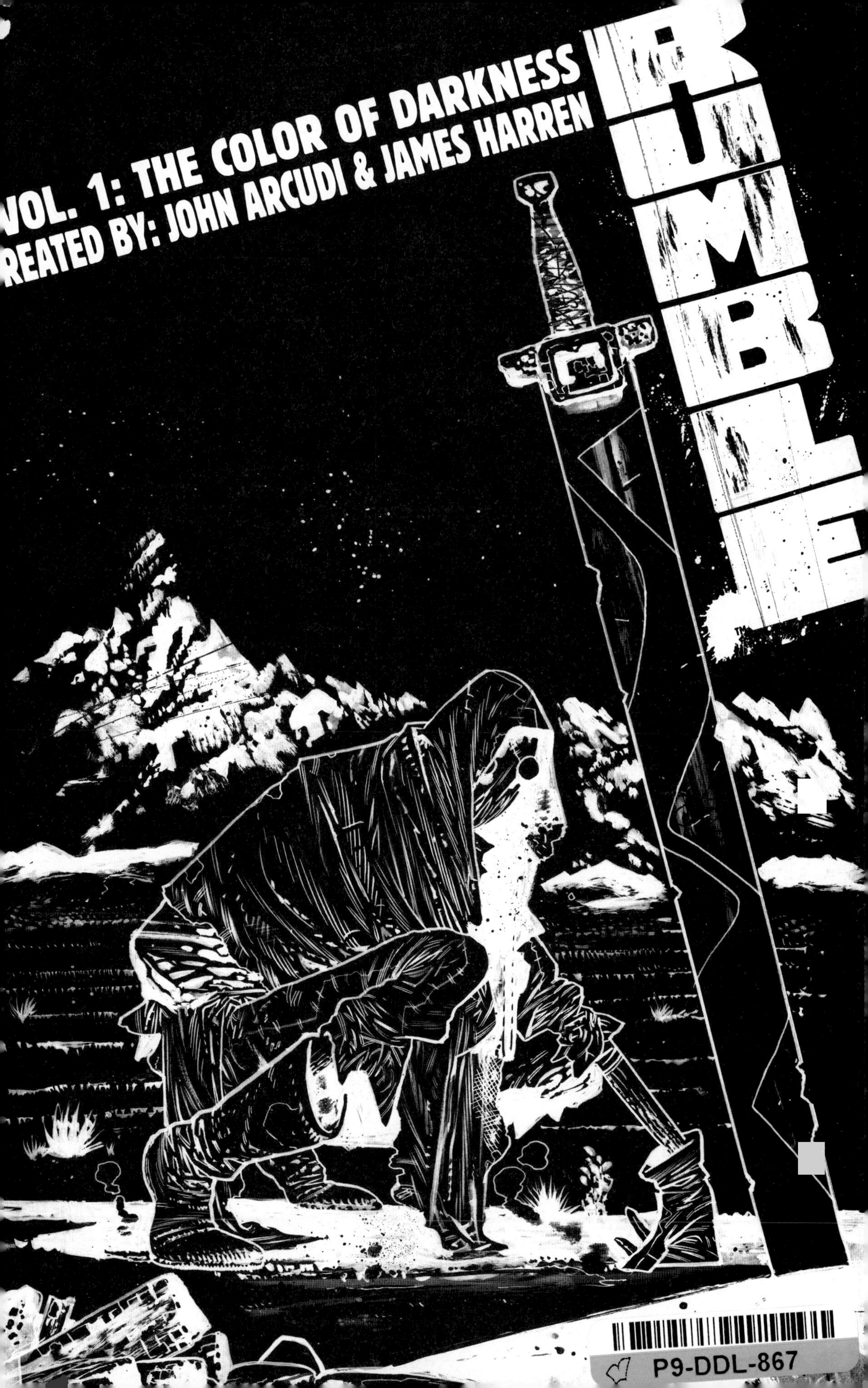
RUMBLE
VOL. 1: THE COLOR OF DARKNESS
REATED BY: JOHN ARCUDI & JAMES HARREN

RUMBLE, VOL. 1: THE COLOR OF DARKNESS. SECOND PRINTING. JULY 2017. Published by Image Comics, Inc. Office of publication: 2701 NW Vaughn St., Ste. 780, Portland, OR 97210. Copyright © 2017 John Arcudi & James Harren. All rights reserved. Originally published in single magazine form as RUMBLE #1-5. RUMBLE™ (including all prominent characters featured herein), its logo and all character likenesses are trademarks of John Arcudi & James Harren, unless otherwise noted. Image Comics® and its logos are registered trademarks of Image Comics, Inc. No part of this publication may be reproduced or transmitted, in any form or by any means (except for short excerpts for review purposes) without the express written permission of Image Comics, Inc. All names, characters, events and locales in this publication are entirely fictional. Any resemblance to actual persons (living or dead), events or places, without satiric intent, is coincidental. PRINTED IN THE U.S.A. For information regarding the CPSIA on this printed material call: 203-595-3636 and provide reference: RICH#– 747518. FOR INTERNATIONAL RIGHTS, CONTACT: foreignlicensing@imagecomics.com.

JOHN ARCUDI
JAMES HARREN
Co-creators

DAVE STEWART
Color Art

CHRIS ELIOPOULOS
Letters

VINCENT KUKUA
Book Design

Special Thanks to
PAT REDDING SCANLON

FOR IMAGE COMICS, INC.

ROBERT KIRKMAN - chief operating officer
ERIK LARSEN - chief financial officer
TODD McFARLANE - president
MARC SILVESTRI - chief executive officer
JIM VALENTINO - vice-president

ERIC STEPHENSON — Publisher
COREY MURPHY — Director of Sales
JEFF BOISON — Director of Publishing Planning & Book Trade Sales
CHRIS ROSS — Director of Digital Sales
JEFF STANG — Director of Specialty Sales
KAT SALAZAR — Director of PR & Marketing
BRANWYN BIGGLESTONE — Controller
SUE KORPELA — Accounts Manager
DREW GILL — Art Director
BRETT WARNOCK — Production Manager
LEIGH THOMAS — Print Manager
TRICIA RAMOS — Traffic Manager
BRIAH SKELLY — Publicist
ALY HOFFMAN — Events & Conventions Coordinator
SASHA HEAD — Sales & Marketing Production Designer
DAVID BROTHERS — Branding Manager
MELISSA GIFFORD — Content Manager
DREW FITZGERALD — Publicity Assistant
VINCENT KUKUA — Production Artist
ERIKA SCHNATZ — Production Artist
RYAN BREWER — Production Artist
SHANNA MATUSZAK — Production Artist
CAREY HALL — Production Artist
ESTHER KIM — Direct Market Sales Representative
EMILIO BAUTISTA — Digital Sales Representative
LEANNA CAUNTER — Accounting Assistant
CHLOE RAMOS-PETERSON — Library Market Sales Representative
MARLA EIZIK — Administrative Assistant

IMAGECOMICS.COM

image

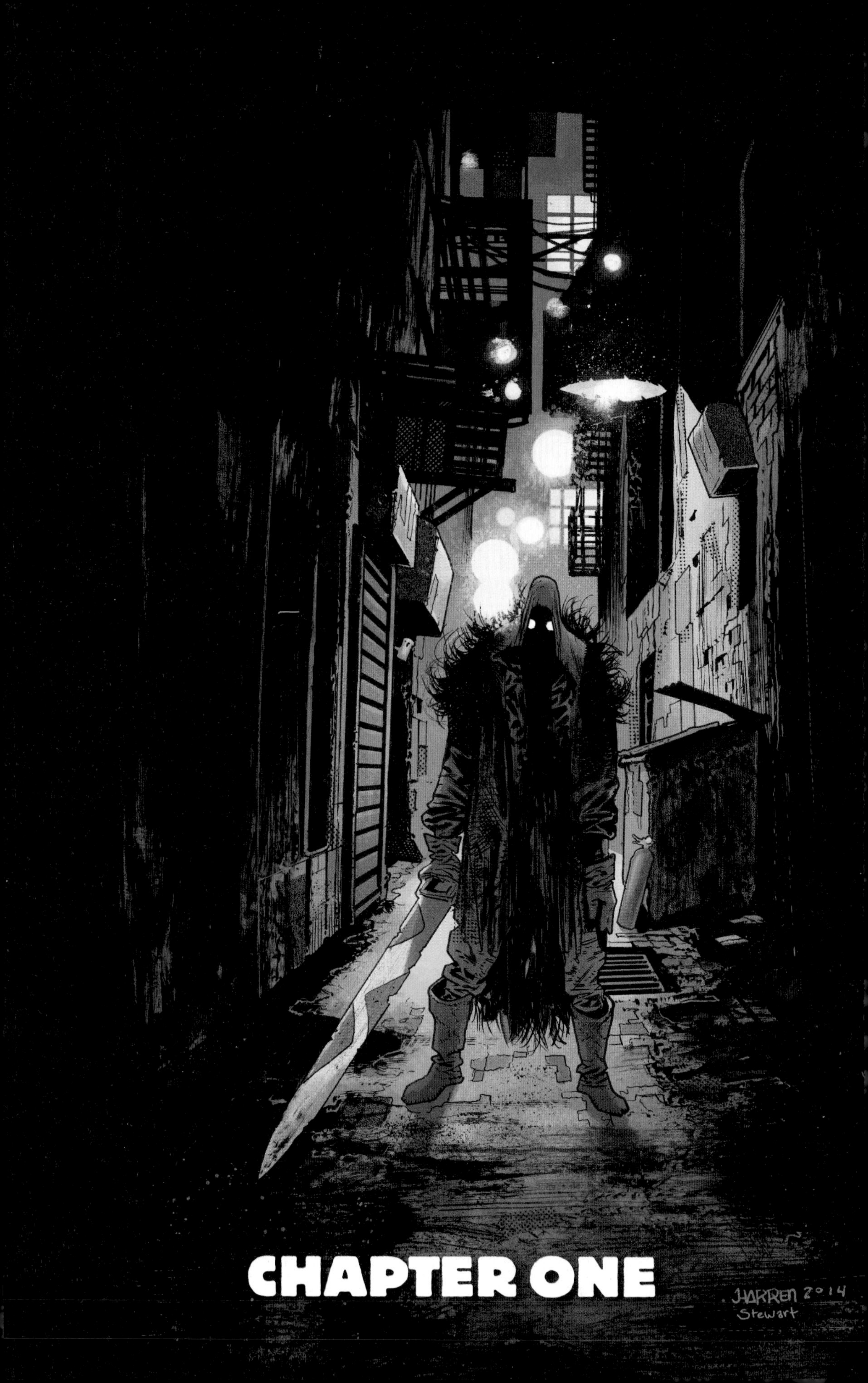
CHAPTER ONE
JHARREN 2014
Stewart

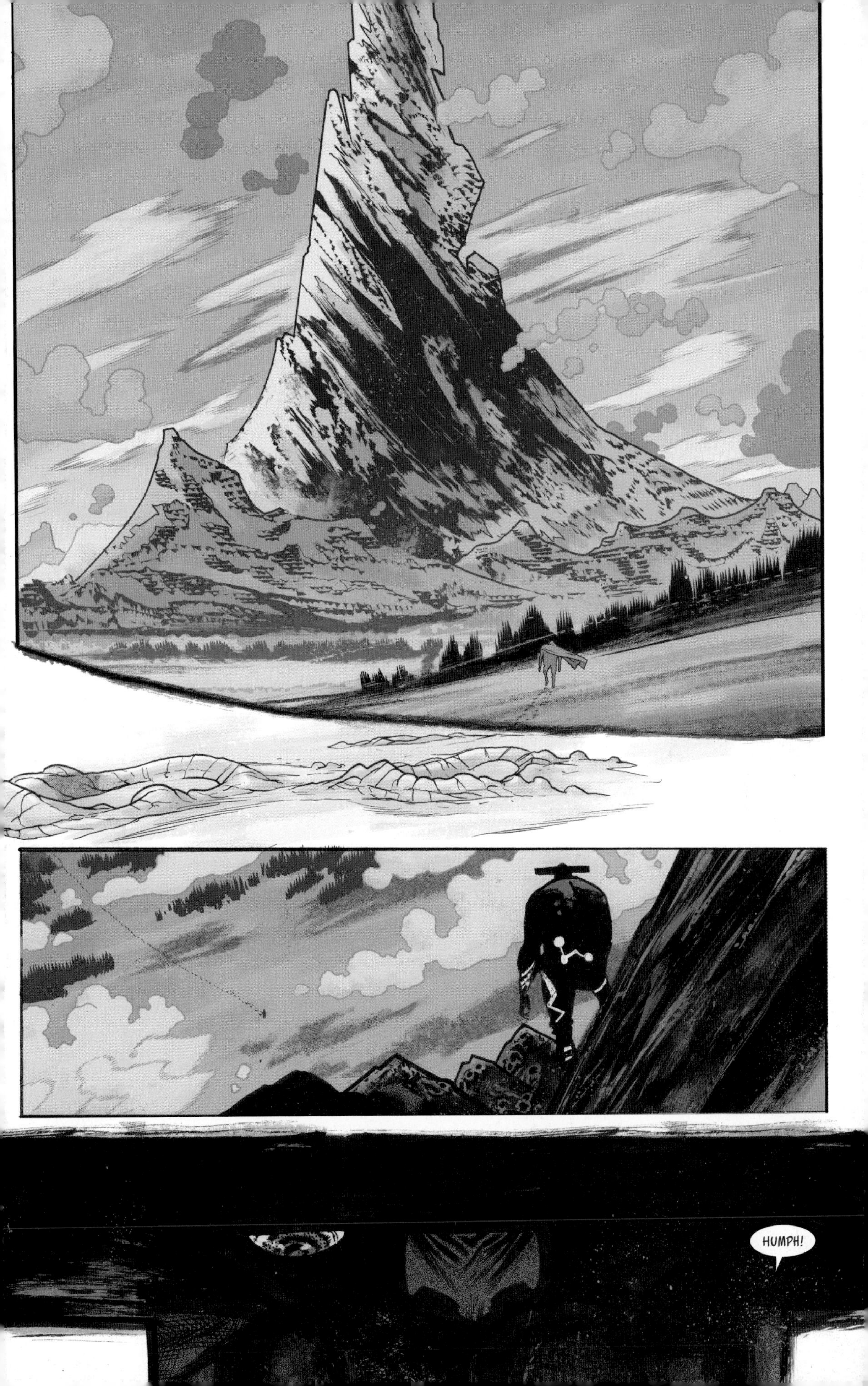
HUMPH!

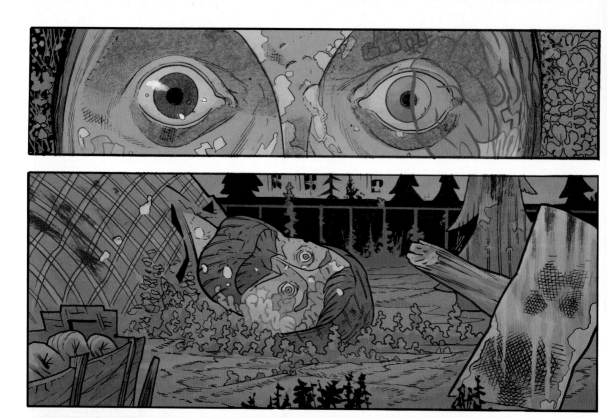

What variety of emptiness is this?

What color of darkness that makes blind the eyes of a caring God?

What is the full quantity of nothing?

NUNNUN N UNN NNUNNUNNUN NUN NUNNUN NUN NUN NUNNUN

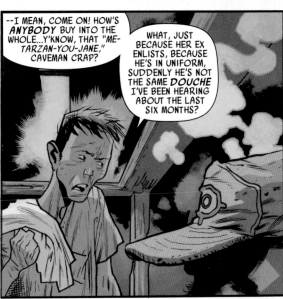

--I MEAN, COME ON! HOW'S *ANYBODY* BUY INTO THE WHOLE...Y'KNOW, THAT "ME-TARZAN-YOU-JANE," CAVEMAN CRAP?

WHAT, JUST BECAUSE HER EX ENLISTS, BECAUSE HE'S IN UNIFORM, SUDDENLY HE'S NOT THE SAME *DOUCHE* I'VE BEEN HEARING ABOUT THE LAST SIX MONTHS?

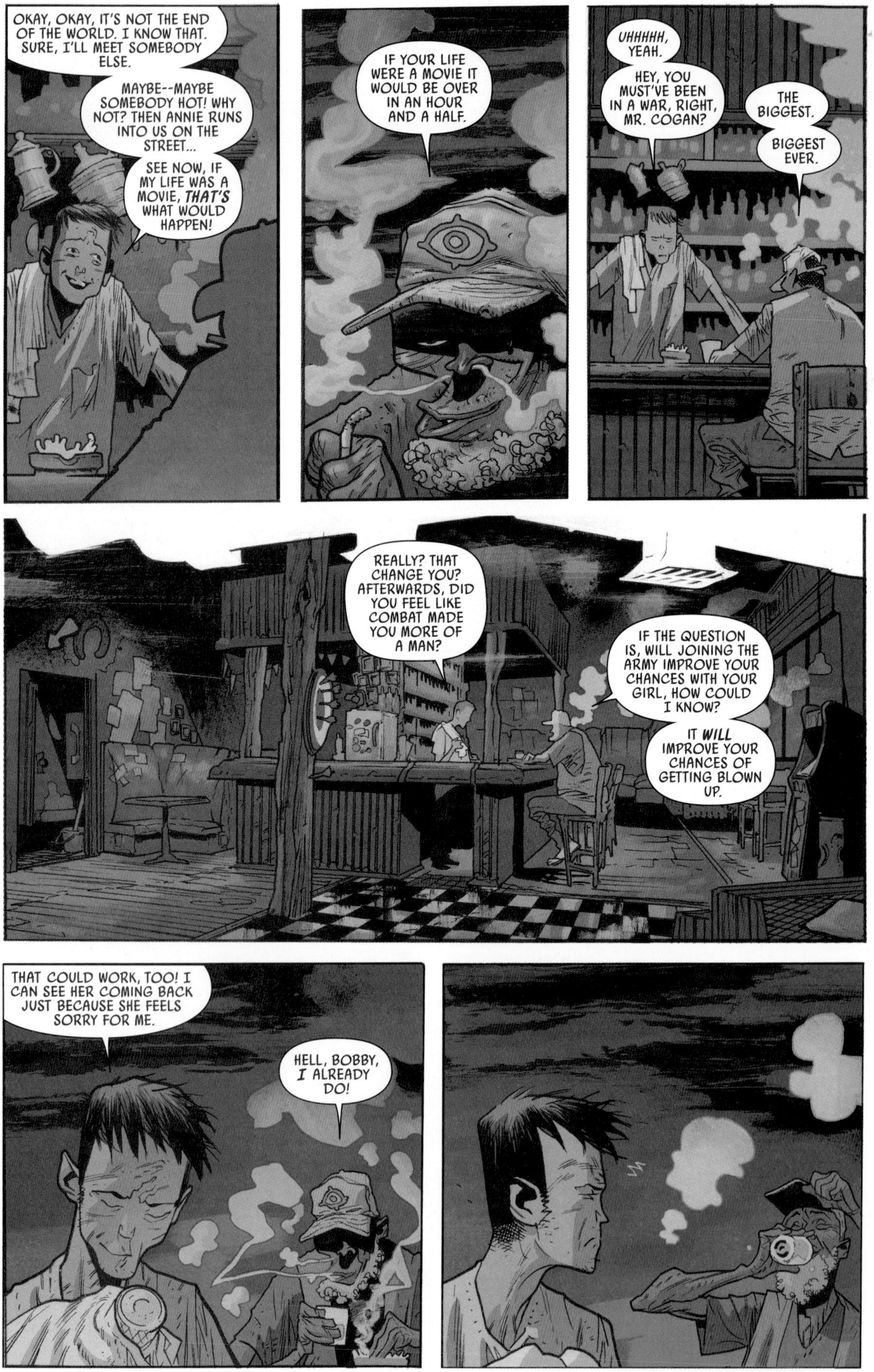
OKAY, OKAY, IT'S NOT THE END OF THE WORLD. I KNOW THAT. SURE, I'LL MEET SOMEBODY ELSE.
MAYBE--MAYBE SOMEBODY HOT! WHY NOT? THEN ANNIE RUNS INTO US ON THE STREET...
SEE NOW, IF MY LIFE WAS A MOVIE, THAT'S WHAT WOULD HAPPEN!
IF YOUR LIFE WERE A MOVIE IT WOULD BE OVER IN AN HOUR AND A HALF.
UHHHHH, YEAH.
HEY, YOU MUST'VE BEEN IN A WAR, RIGHT, MR. COGAN?
THE BIGGEST.
BIGGEST EVER.
REALLY? THAT CHANGE YOU? AFTERWARDS, DID YOU FEEL LIKE COMBAT MADE YOU MORE OF A MAN?
IF THE QUESTION IS, WILL JOINING THE ARMY IMPROVE YOUR CHANCES WITH YOUR GIRL, HOW COULD I KNOW?
IT WILL IMPROVE YOUR CHANCES OF GETTING BLOWN UP.
THAT COULD WORK, TOO! I CAN SEE HER COMING BACK JUST BECAUSE SHE FEELS SORRY FOR ME.
HELL, BOBBY, I ALREADY DO!

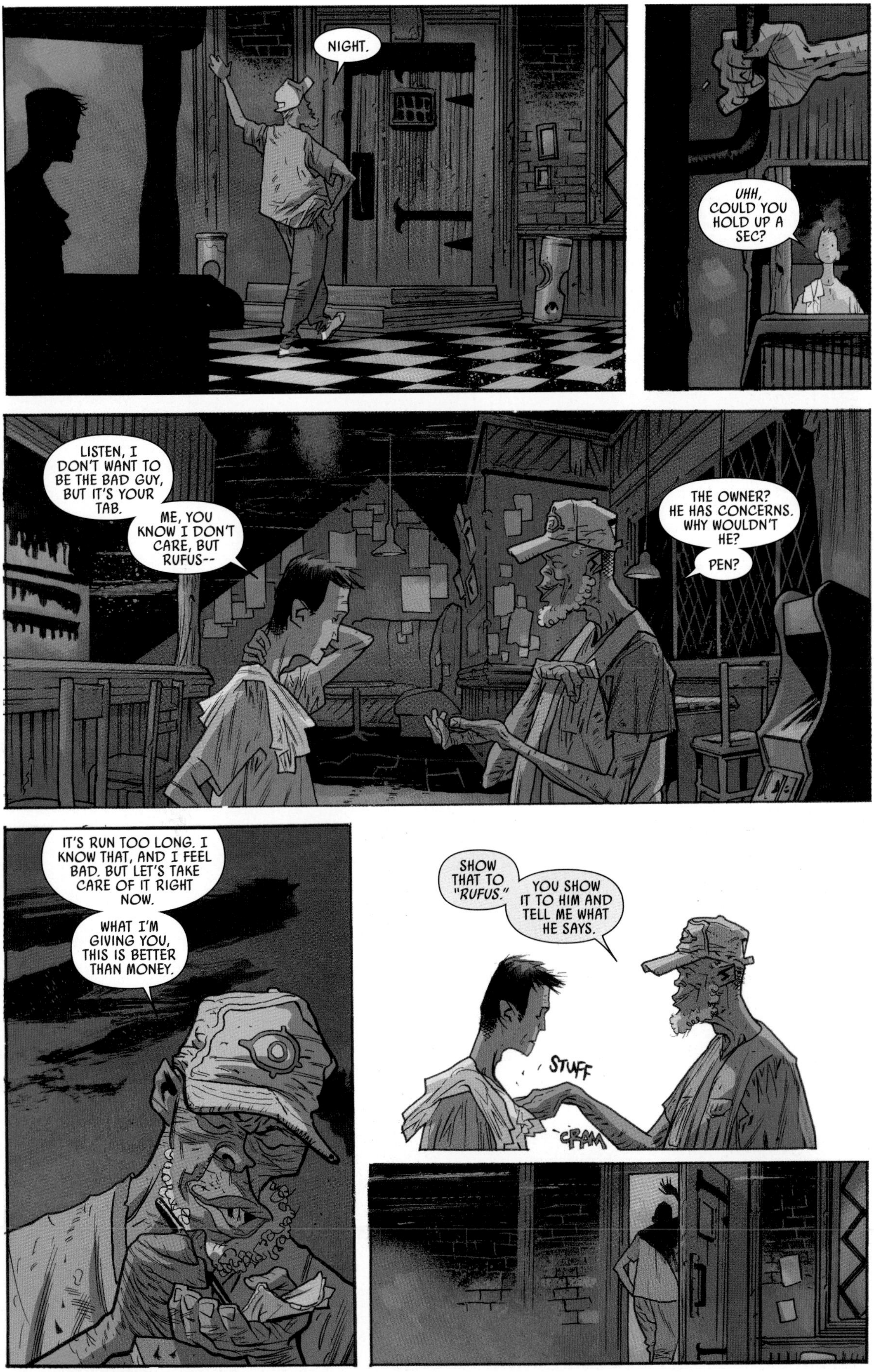
NIGHT.
UHH, COULD YOU HOLD UP A SEC?
LISTEN, I DON'T WANT TO BE THE BAD GUY, BUT IT'S YOUR TAB.
ME, YOU KNOW I DON'T CARE, BUT RUFUS--
THE OWNER? HE HAS CONCERNS. WHY WOULDN'T HE?
PEN?
IT'S RUN TOO LONG. I KNOW THAT, AND I FEEL BAD. BUT LET'S TAKE CARE OF IT RIGHT NOW.
WHAT I'M GIVING YOU, THIS IS BETTER THAN MONEY.
SHOW THAT TO "RUFUS."
YOU SHOW IT TO HIM AND TELL ME WHAT HE SAYS.
STUFF
CRAM

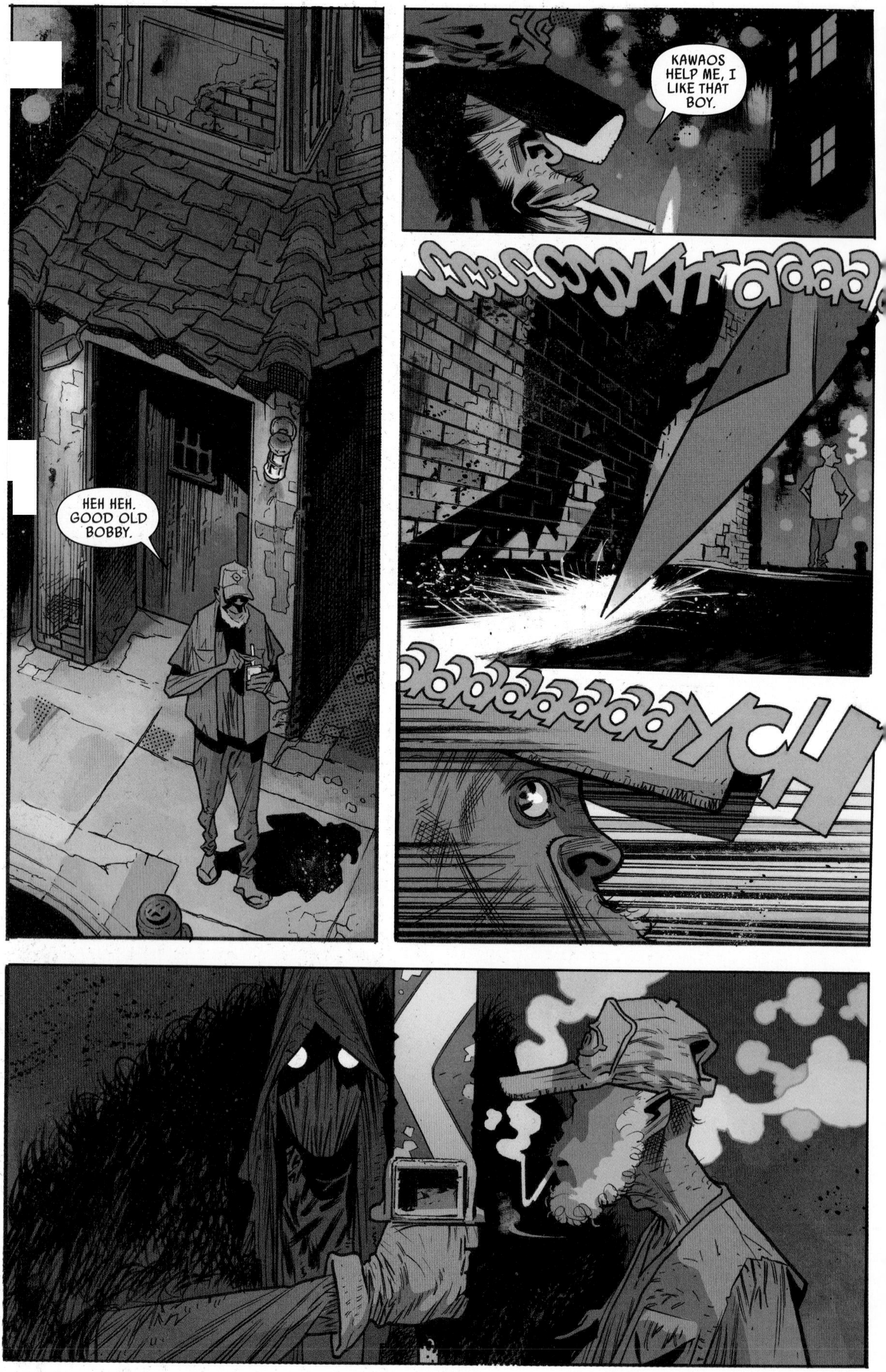
HEH HEH. GOOD OLD BOBBY.
KAWAOS HELP ME, I LIKE THAT BOY.

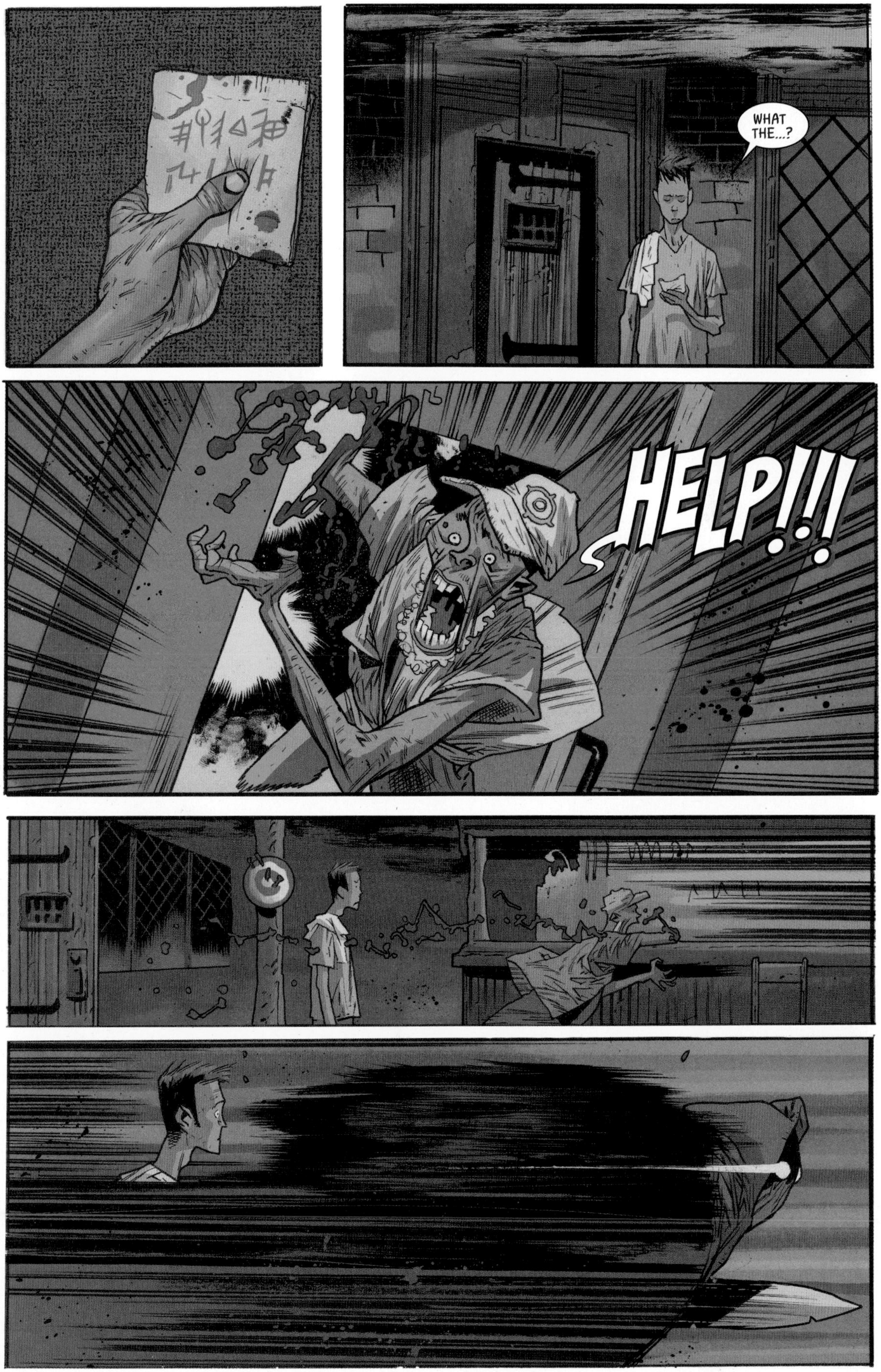
WHAT THE...?
HELP!!!

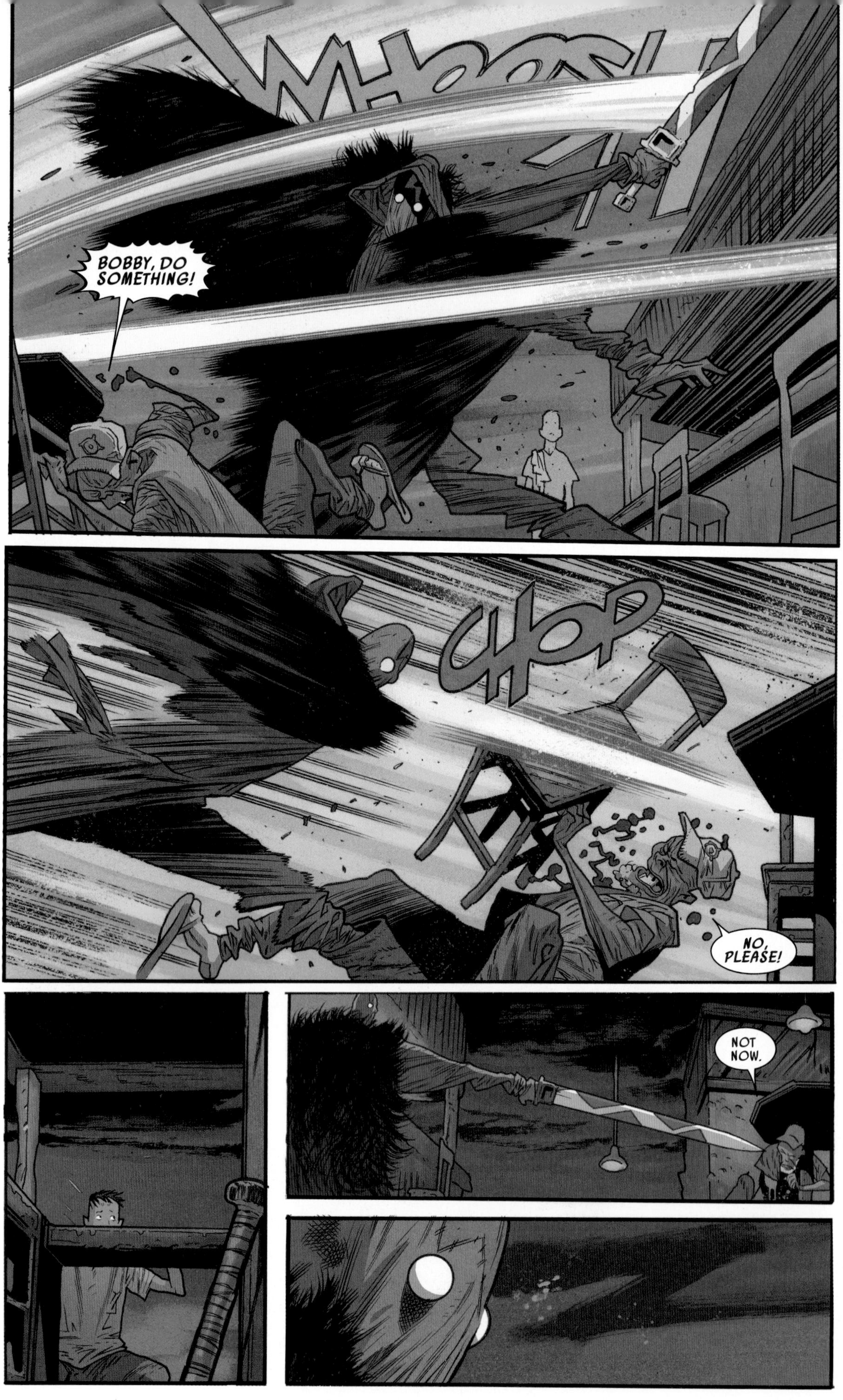
WHOOSH!
BOBBY, DO SOMETHING!
CHOP
NO, PLEASE!
NOT NOW.

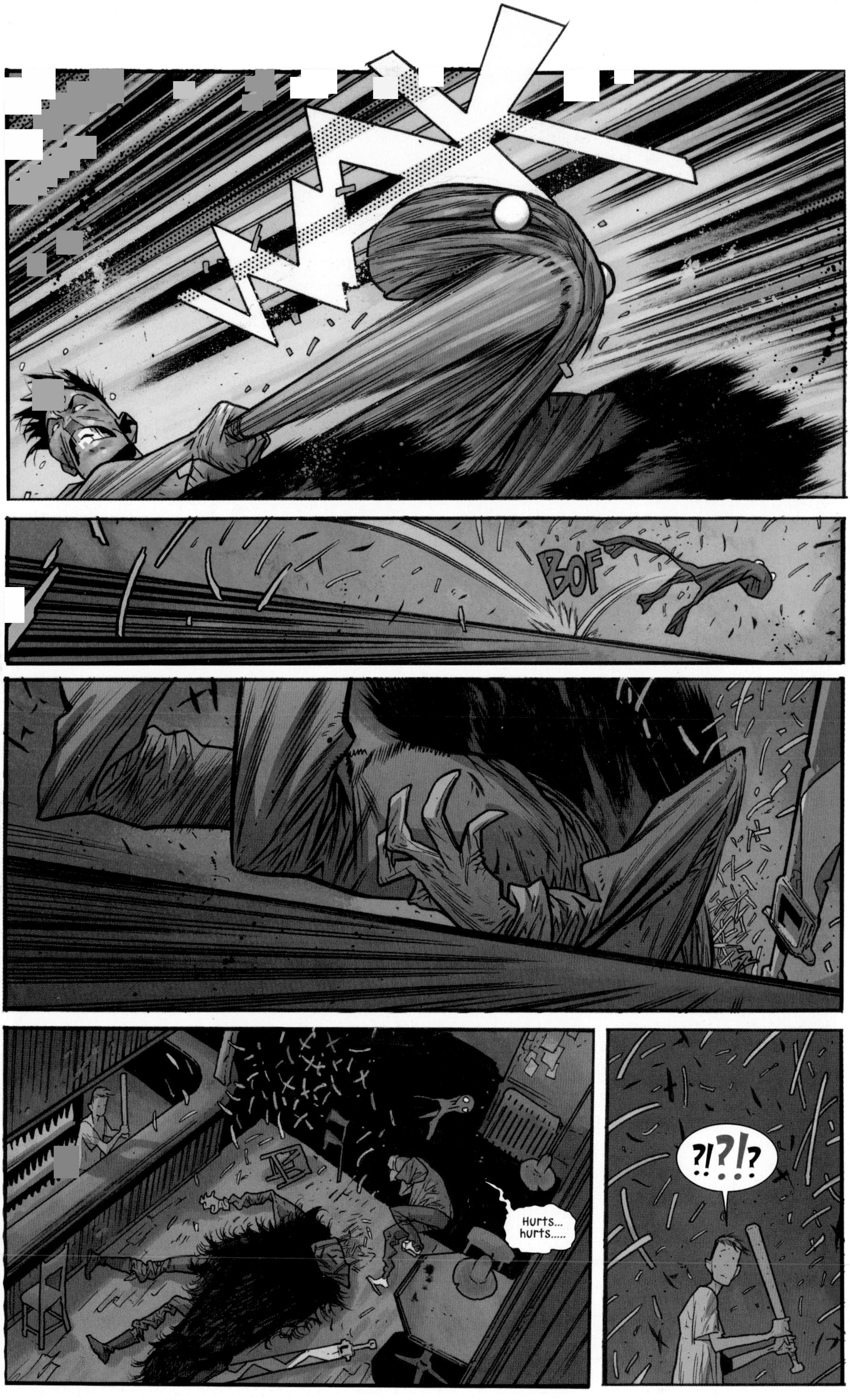
BOF
Hurts... hurts.....
?!?!?

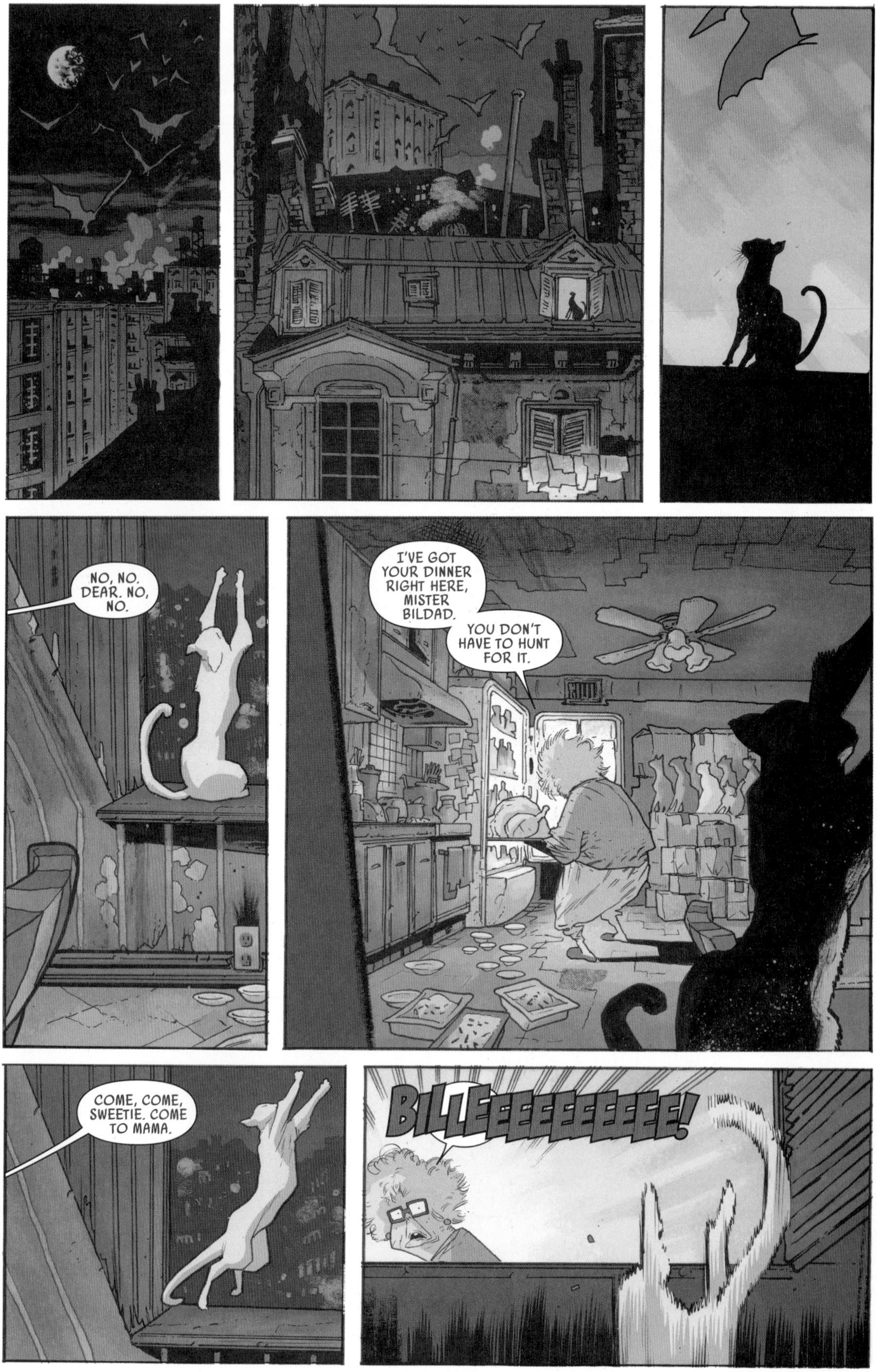
NO, NO. DEAR. NO, NO.
I'VE GOT YOUR DINNER RIGHT HERE, MISTER BILDAD.
YOU DON'T HAVE TO HUNT FOR IT.
COME, COME, SWEETIE. COME TO MAMA.
BILLEEEEEEEEEEE!

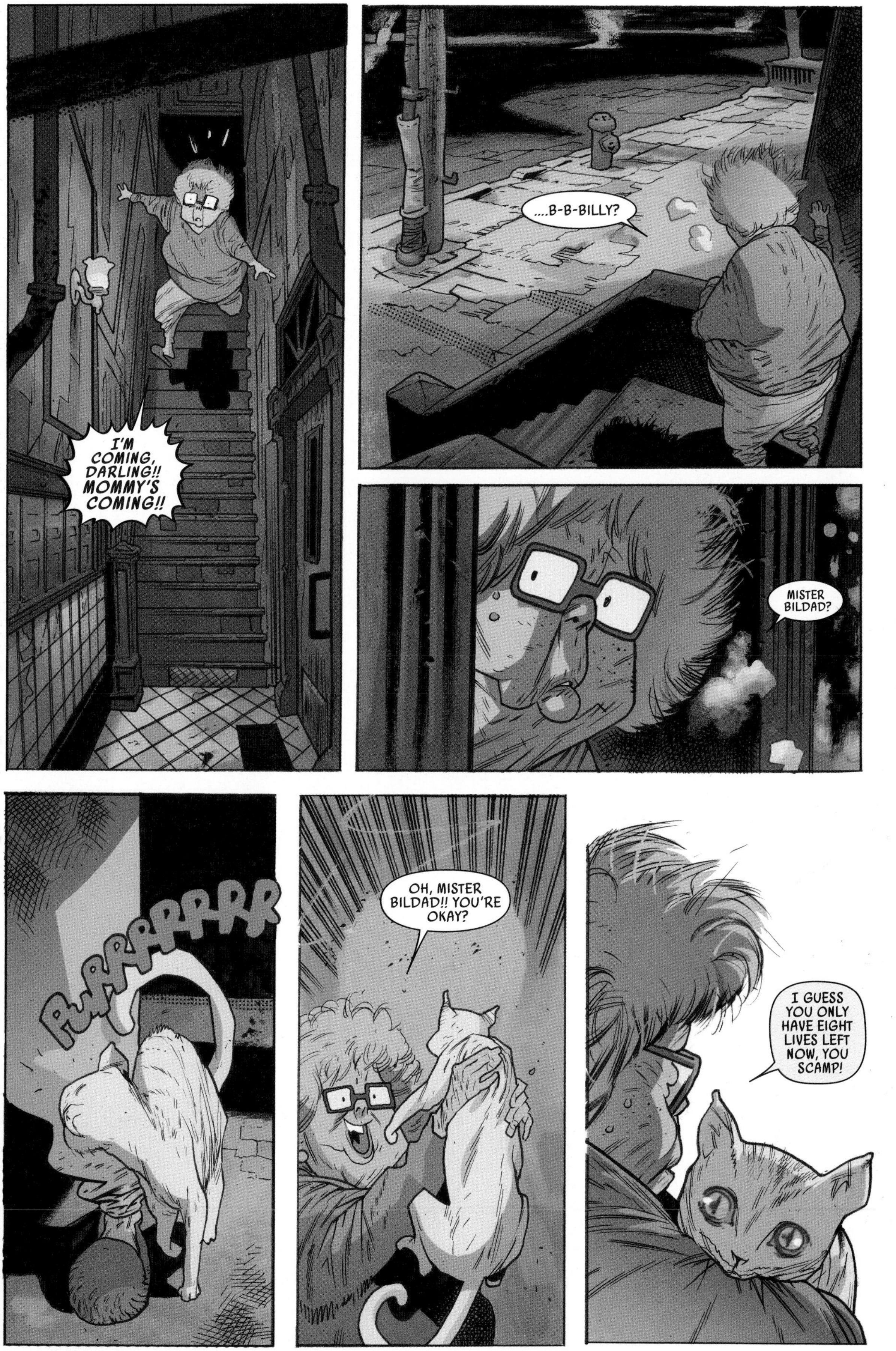
I'M COMING, DARLING!! MOMMY'S COMING!!
....B-B-BILLY?
MISTER BILDAD?
PURRRRRRR
OH, MISTER BILDAD!! YOU'RE OKAY?
I GUESS YOU ONLY HAVE EIGHT LIVES LEFT NOW, YOU SCAMP!

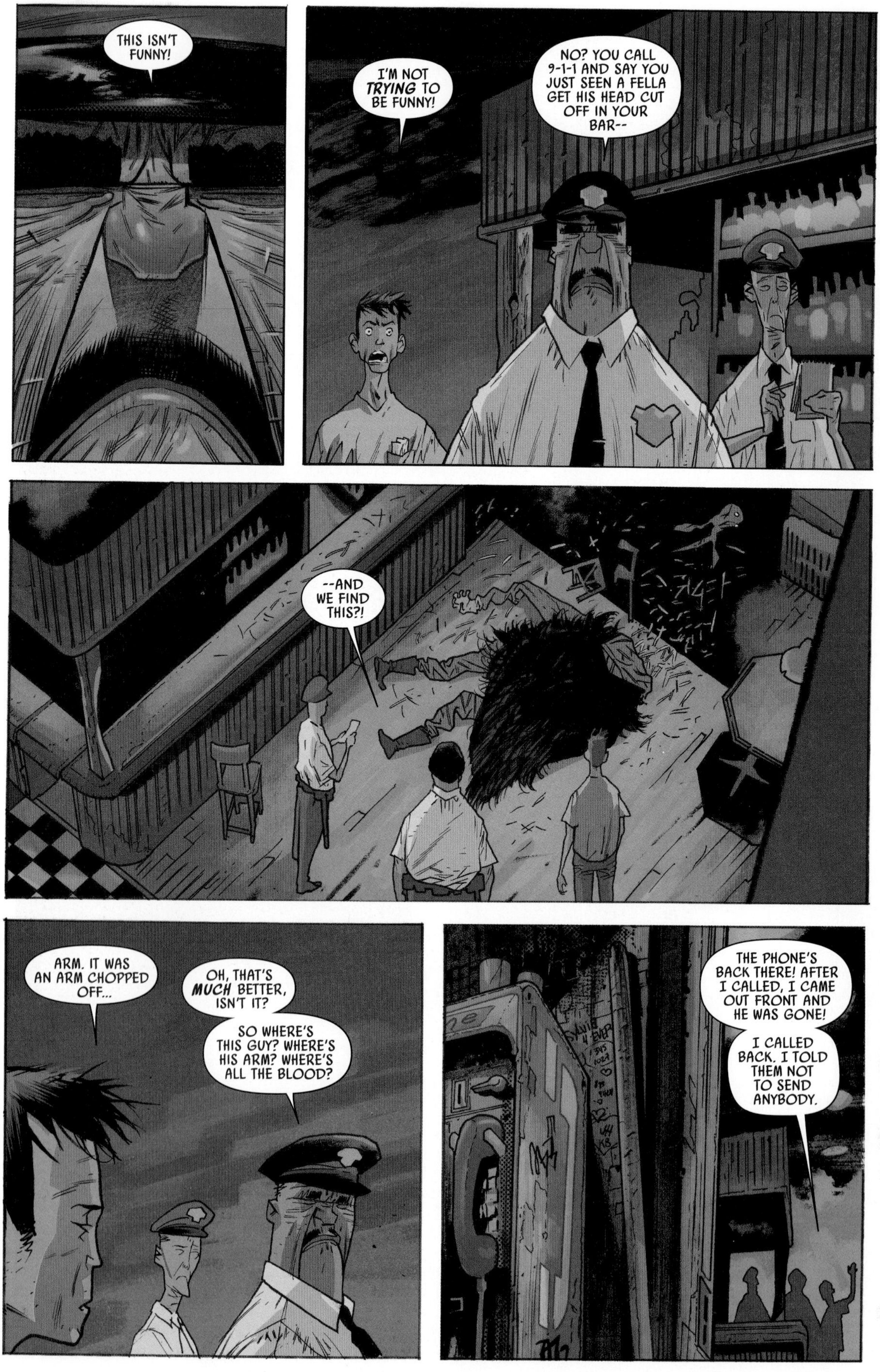
THIS ISN'T FUNNY!
I'M NOT TRYING TO BE FUNNY!
NO? YOU CALL 9-1-1 AND SAY YOU JUST SEEN A FELLA GET HIS HEAD CUT OFF IN YOUR BAR--
--AND WE FIND THIS?!
ARM. IT WAS AN ARM CHOPPED OFF...
OH, THAT'S MUCH BETTER, ISN'T IT?
SO WHERE'S THIS GUY? WHERE'S HIS ARM? WHERE'S ALL THE BLOOD?
THE PHONE'S BACK THERE! AFTER I CALLED, I CAME OUT FRONT AND HE WAS GONE!
I CALLED BACK. I TOLD THEM NOT TO SEND ANYBODY.

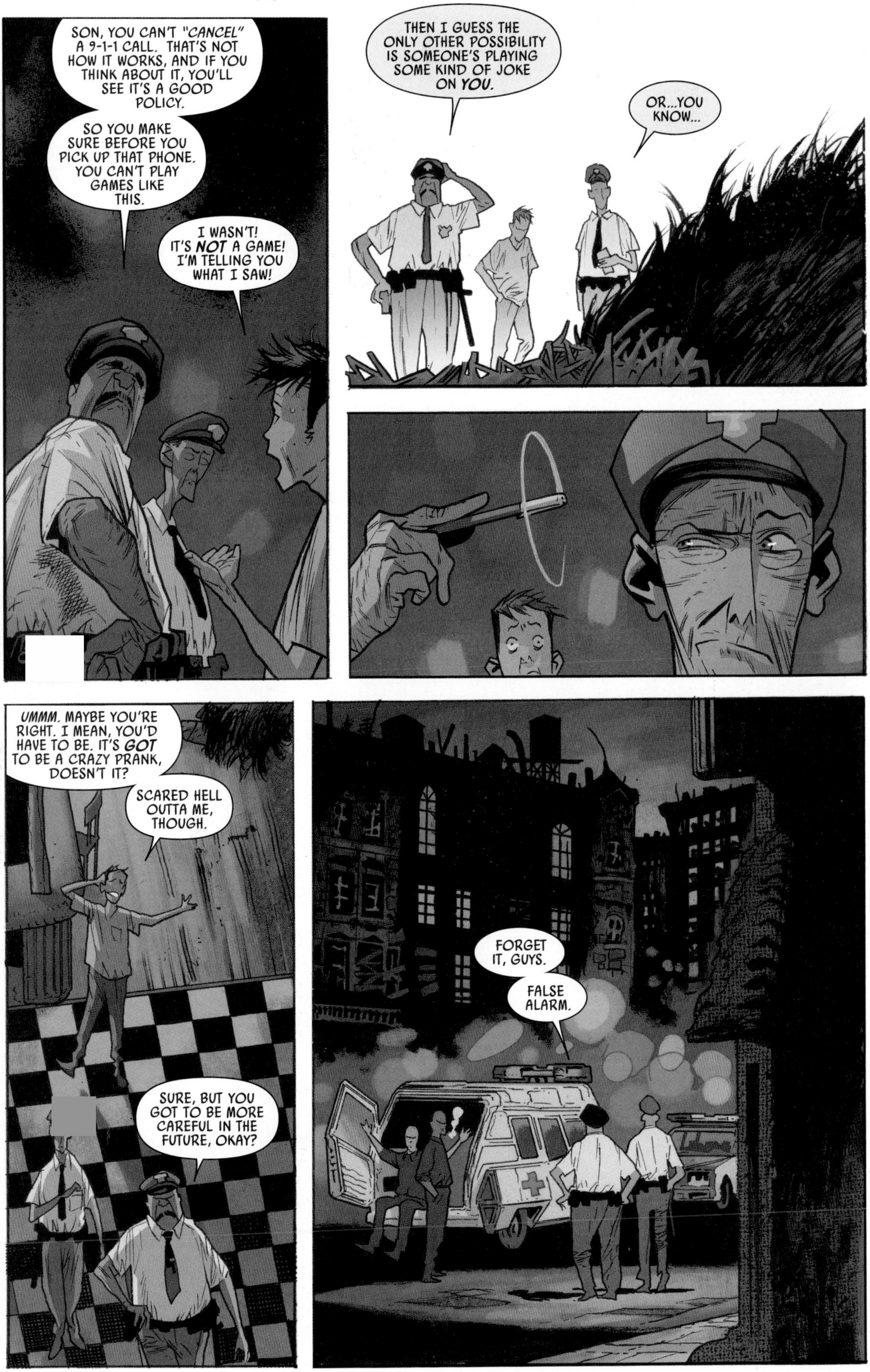
SON, YOU CAN'T "CANCEL" A 9-1-1 CALL. THAT'S NOT HOW IT WORKS, AND IF YOU THINK ABOUT IT, YOU'LL SEE IT'S A GOOD POLICY.
SO YOU MAKE SURE BEFORE YOU PICK UP THAT PHONE. YOU CAN'T PLAY GAMES LIKE THIS.
I WASN'T! IT'S NOT A GAME! I'M TELLING YOU WHAT I SAW!
THEN I GUESS THE ONLY OTHER POSSIBILITY IS SOMEONE'S PLAYING SOME KIND OF JOKE ON YOU.
OR...YOU KNOW...
UMMM. MAYBE YOU'RE RIGHT. I MEAN, YOU'D HAVE TO BE. IT'S GOT TO BE A CRAZY PRANK, DOESN'T IT?
SCARED HELL OUTTA ME, THOUGH.
SURE, BUT YOU GOT TO BE MORE CAREFUL IN THE FUTURE, OKAY?
FORGET IT, GUYS.
FALSE ALARM.

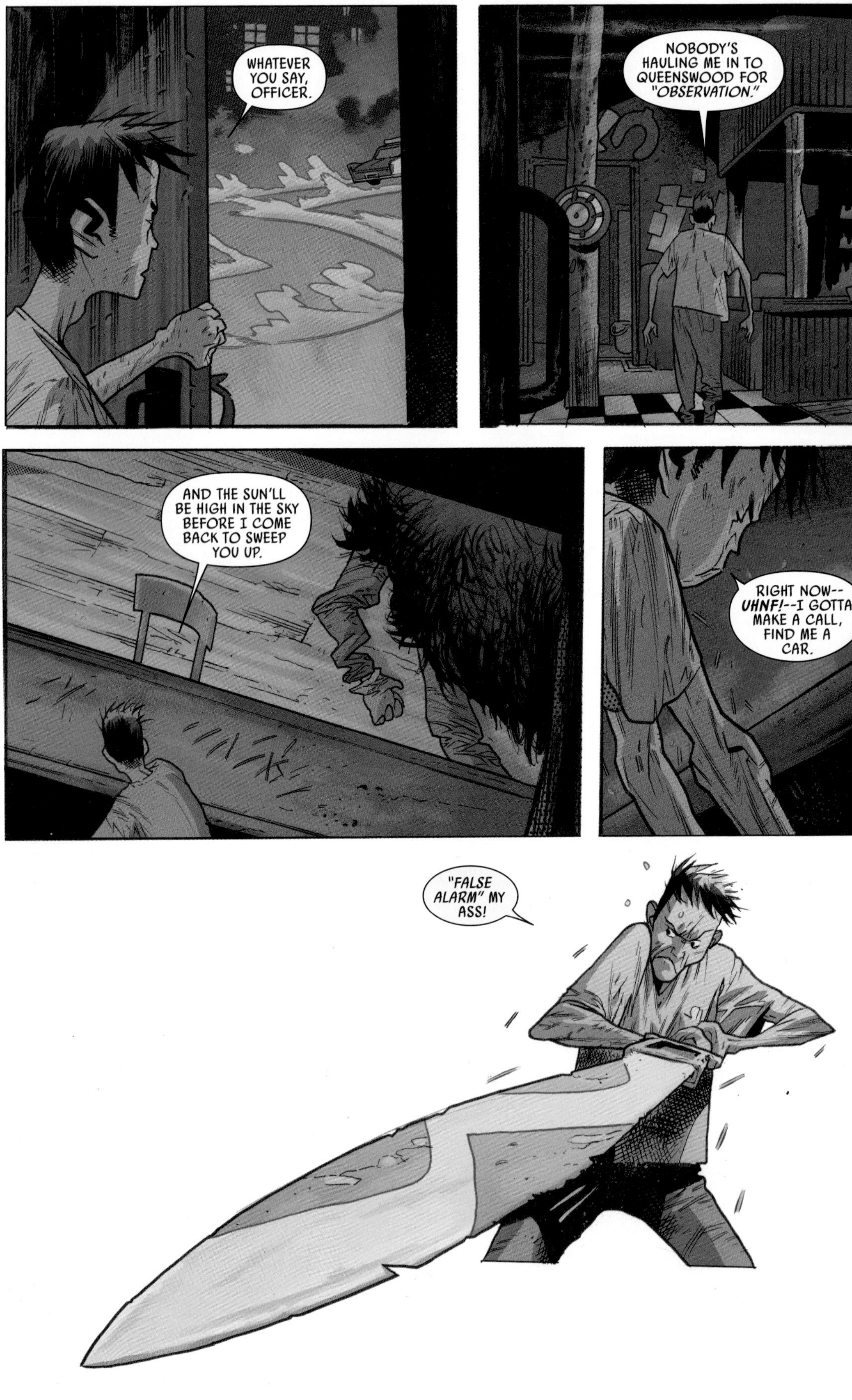
WHATEVER YOU SAY, OFFICER.
NOBODY'S HAULING ME IN TO QUEENSWOOD FOR "OBSERVATION."
AND THE SUN'LL BE HIGH IN THE SKY BEFORE I COME BACK TO SWEEP YOU UP.
RIGHT NOW-- UHNF!--I GOTTA MAKE A CALL, FIND ME A CAR.
"FALSE ALARM" MY ASS!

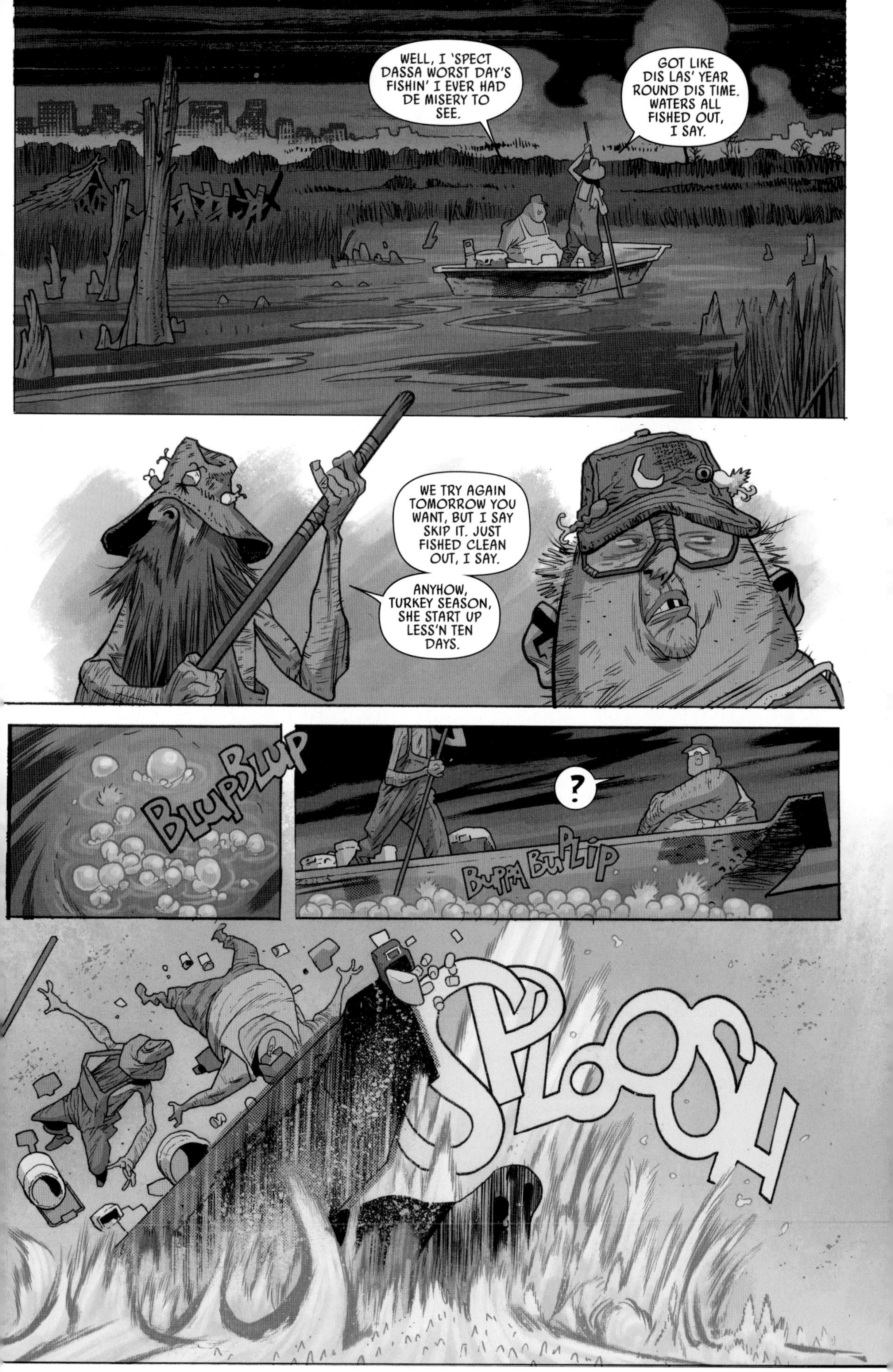
WELL, I 'SPECT DASSA WORST DAY'S FISHIN' I EVER HAD DE MISERY TO SEE.
GOT LIKE DIS LAS' YEAR ROUND DIS TIME. WATERS ALL FISHED OUT, I SAY.
WE TRY AGAIN TOMORROW YOU WANT, BUT I SAY SKIP IT. JUST FISHED CLEAN OUT, I SAY.
ANYHOW, TURKEY SEASON, SHE START UP LESS'N TEN DAYS.
BLUPBLUP
?
BUPPA BUPLIP
SPLOOOSH

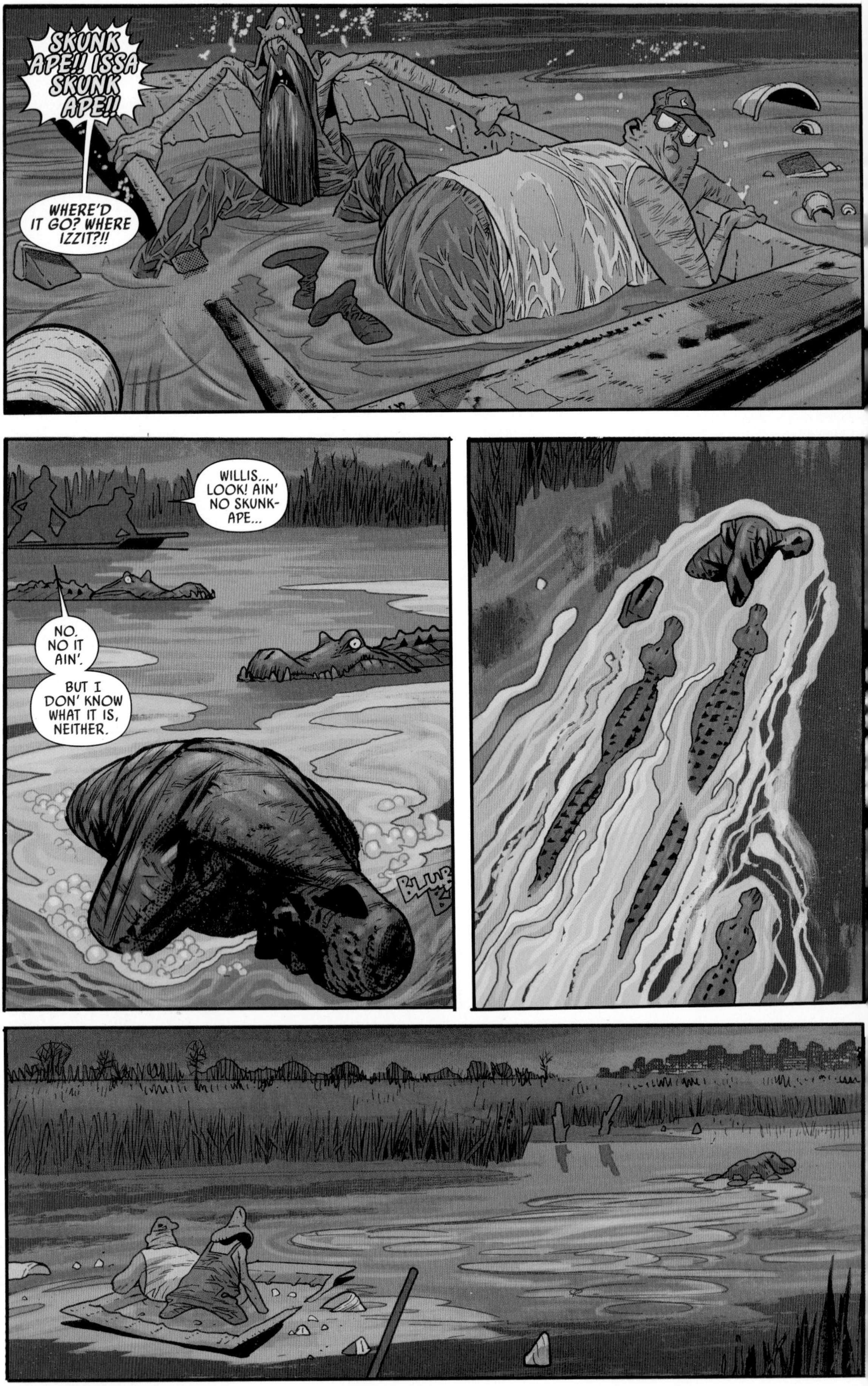
SKUNK APE!! ISSA SKUNK APE!!
WHERE'D IT GO? WHERE IZZIT?!!
WILLIS... LOOK! AIN' NO SKUNK-APE...
NO. NO IT AIN'.
BUT I DON' KNOW WHAT IT IS, NEITHER.

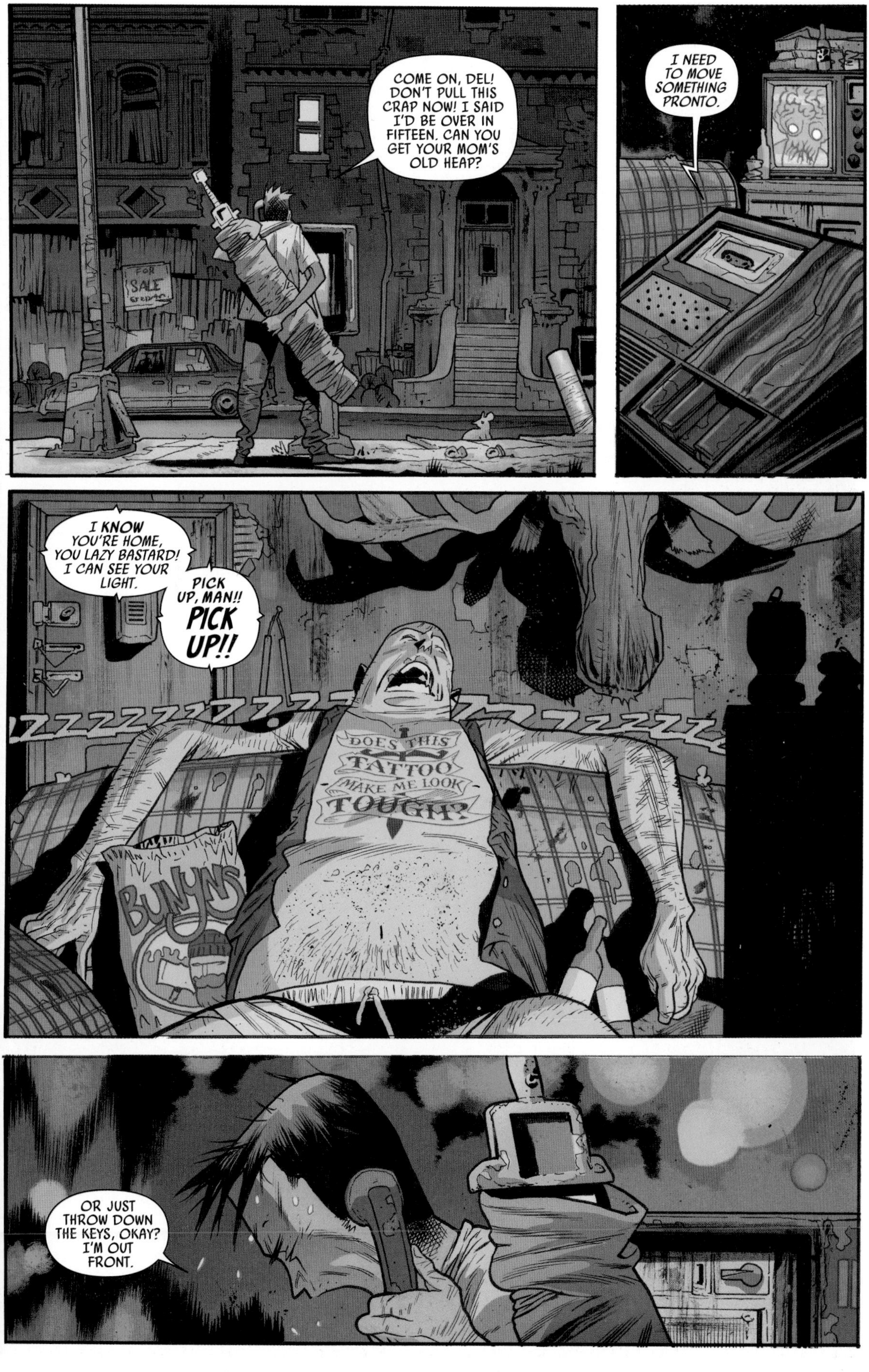
COME ON, DEL! DON'T PULL THIS CRAP NOW! I SAID I'D BE OVER IN FIFTEEN. CAN YOU GET YOUR MOM'S OLD HEAP?
FOR SALE
I NEED TO MOVE SOMETHING PRONTO.
I KNOW YOU'RE HOME, YOU LAZY BASTARD! I CAN SEE YOUR LIGHT.
PICK UP, MAN!! PICK UP!!
ZZZZZZZZZZZZZZZZZZZZZZZ
DOES THIS TATTOO MAKE ME LOOK TOUGH?
BUNYNS
OR JUST THROW DOWN THE KEYS, OKAY? I'M OUT FRONT.

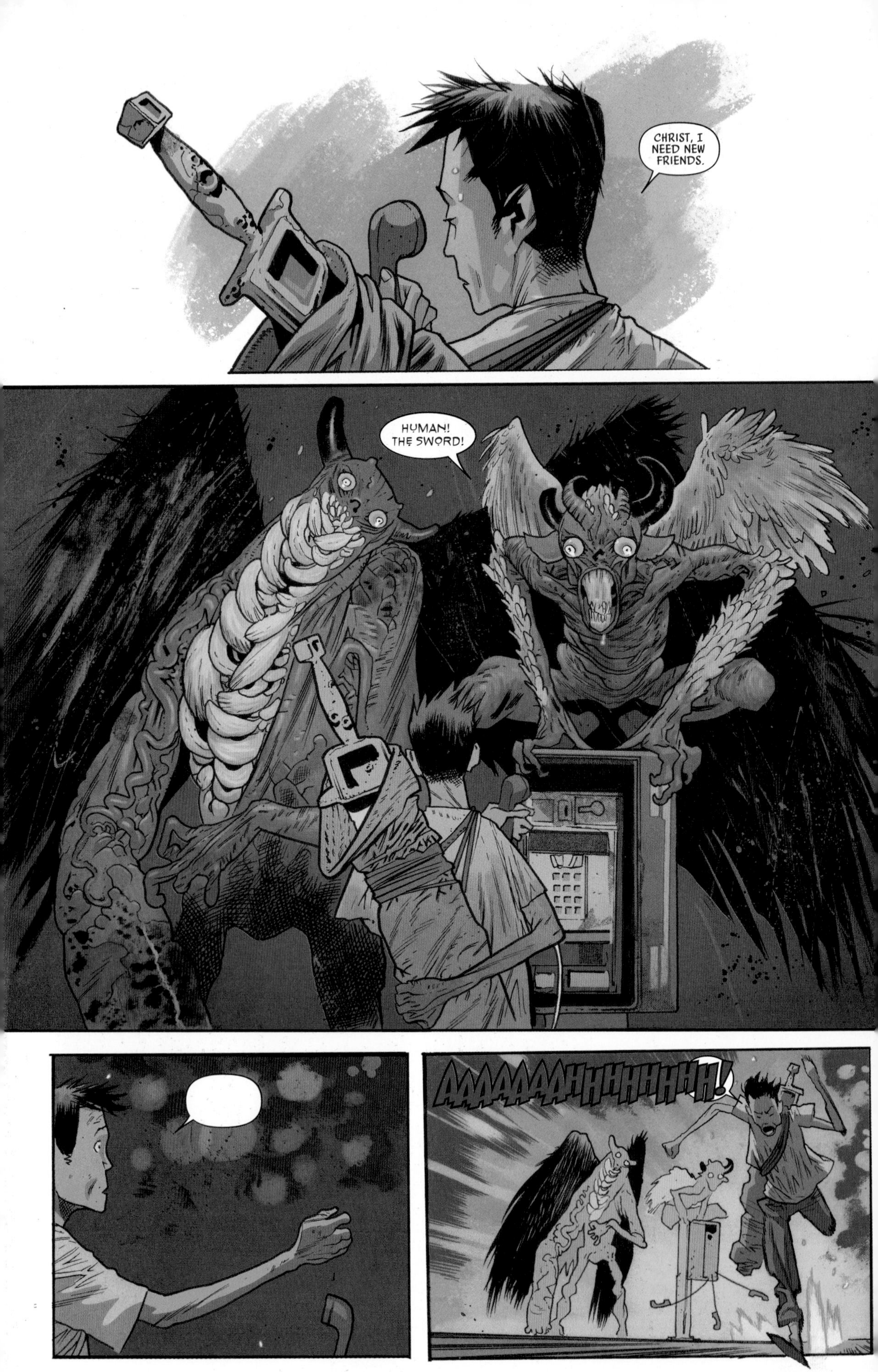
CHRIST, I NEED NEW FRIENDS.
HUMAN! THE SWORD!
AAAAAAHHHHHHHH!

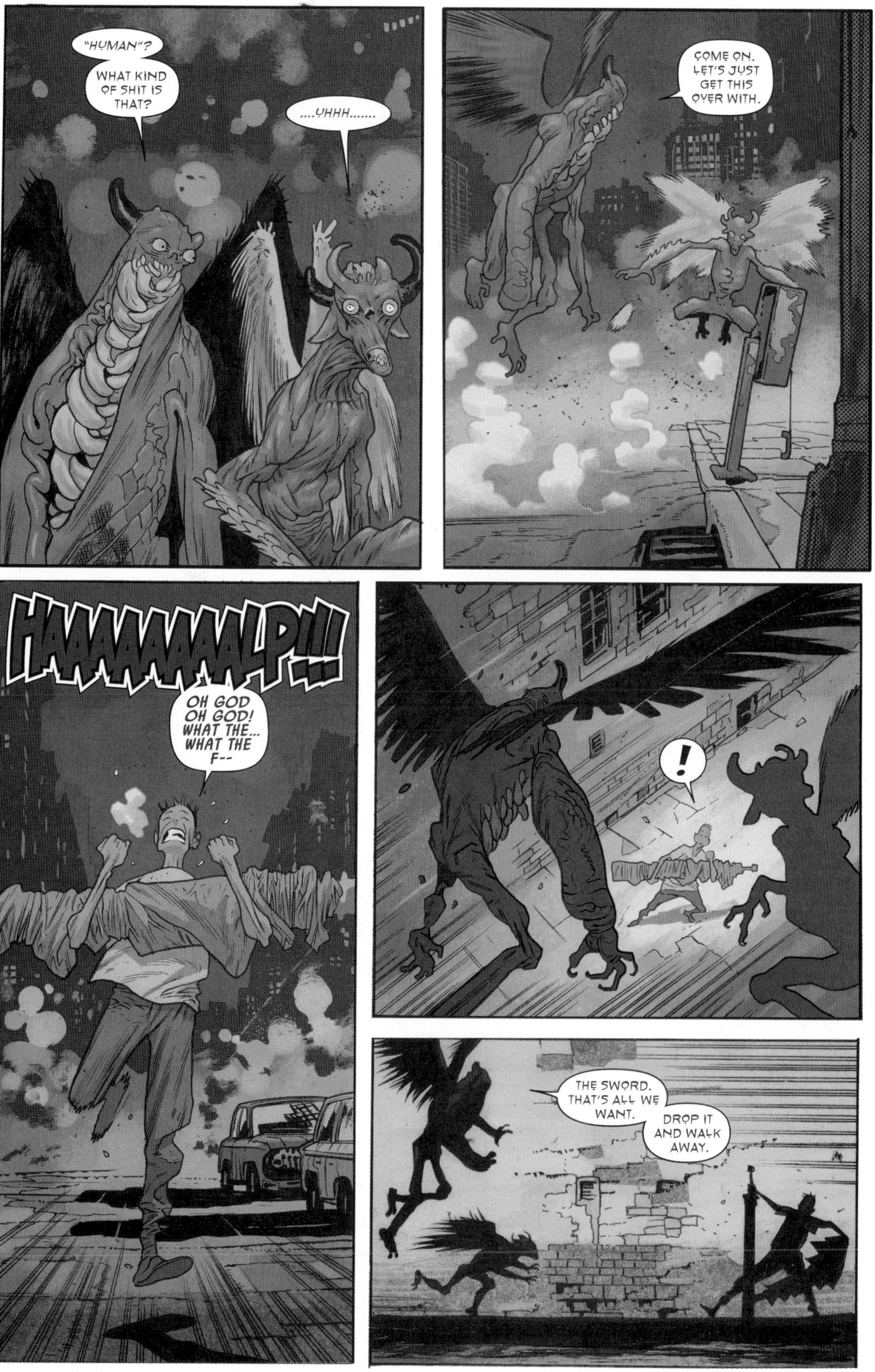
"HUMAN"?
WHAT KIND OF SHIT IS THAT?
....UHHH.......
COME ON. LET'S JUST GET THIS OVER WITH.
HAAAAAAAALP!!!
OH GOD OH GOD! WHAT THE... WHAT THE F--
!
THE SWORD. THAT'S ALL WE WANT.
DROP IT AND WALK AWAY.

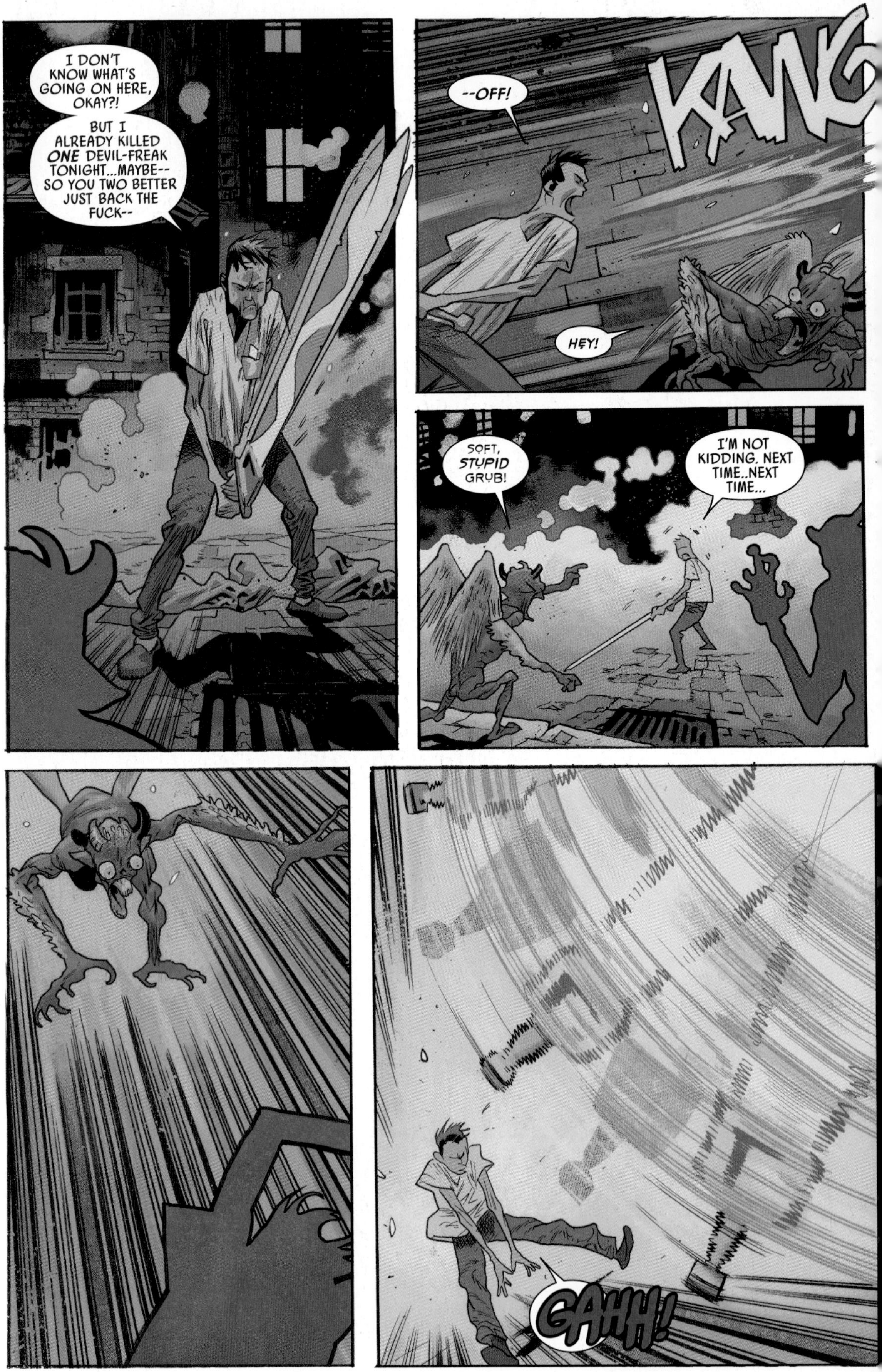
I DON'T KNOW WHAT'S GOING ON HERE, OKAY?!
BUT I ALREADY KILLED ONE DEVIL-FREAK TONIGHT...MAYBE-- SO YOU TWO BETTER JUST BACK THE FUCK--
--OFF!
KANG
HEY!
SOFT, STUPID GRUB!
I'M NOT KIDDING. NEXT TIME..NEXT TIME...
GAHH!

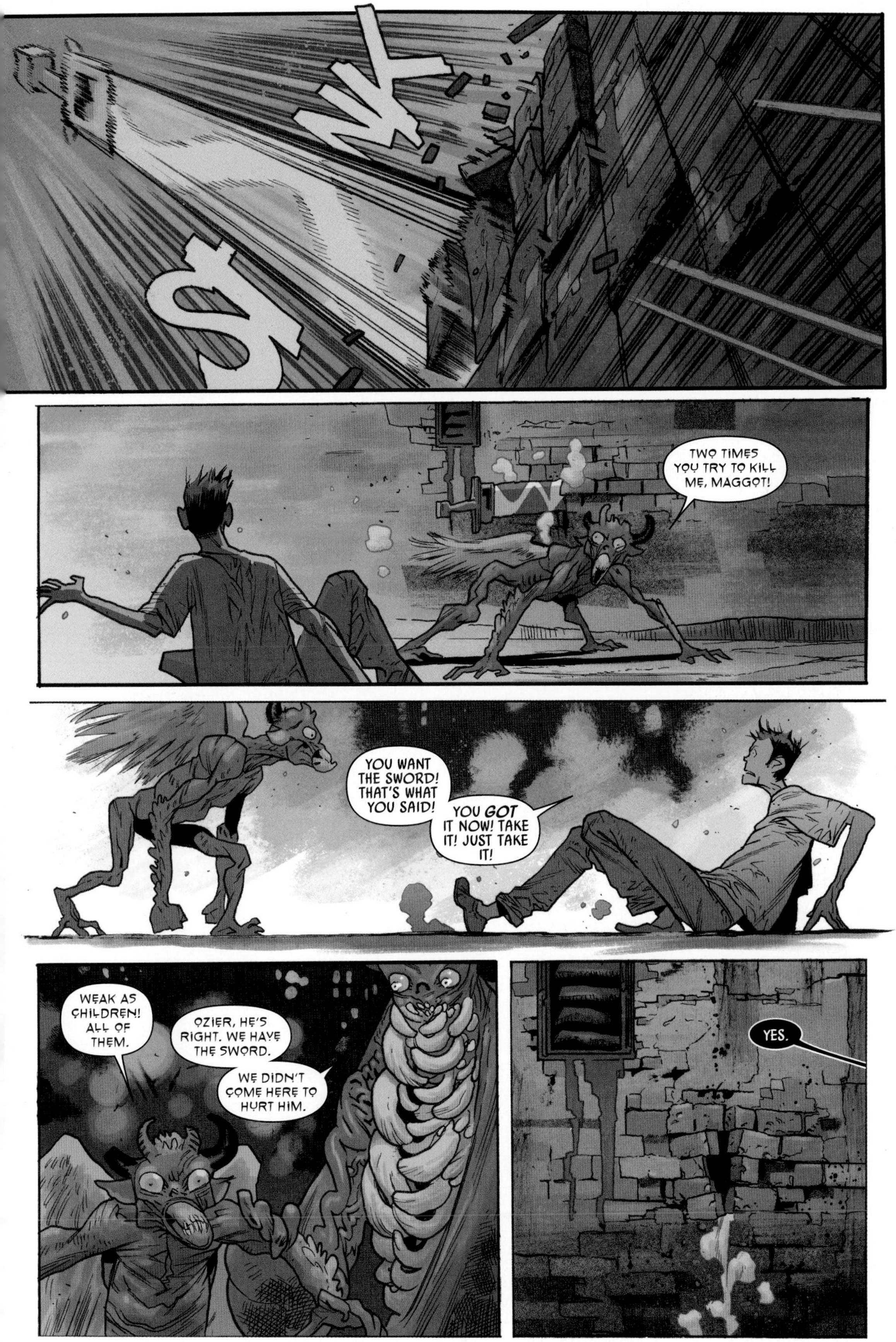

SK
TWO TIMES YOU TRY TO KILL ME, MAGGOT!
YOU WANT THE SWORD! THAT'S WHAT YOU SAID!
YOU GOT IT NOW! TAKE IT! JUST TAKE IT!
WEAK AS CHILDREN! ALL OF THEM.
OZIER, HE'S RIGHT. WE HAVE THE SWORD.
WE DIDN'T COME HERE TO HURT HIM.
YES.

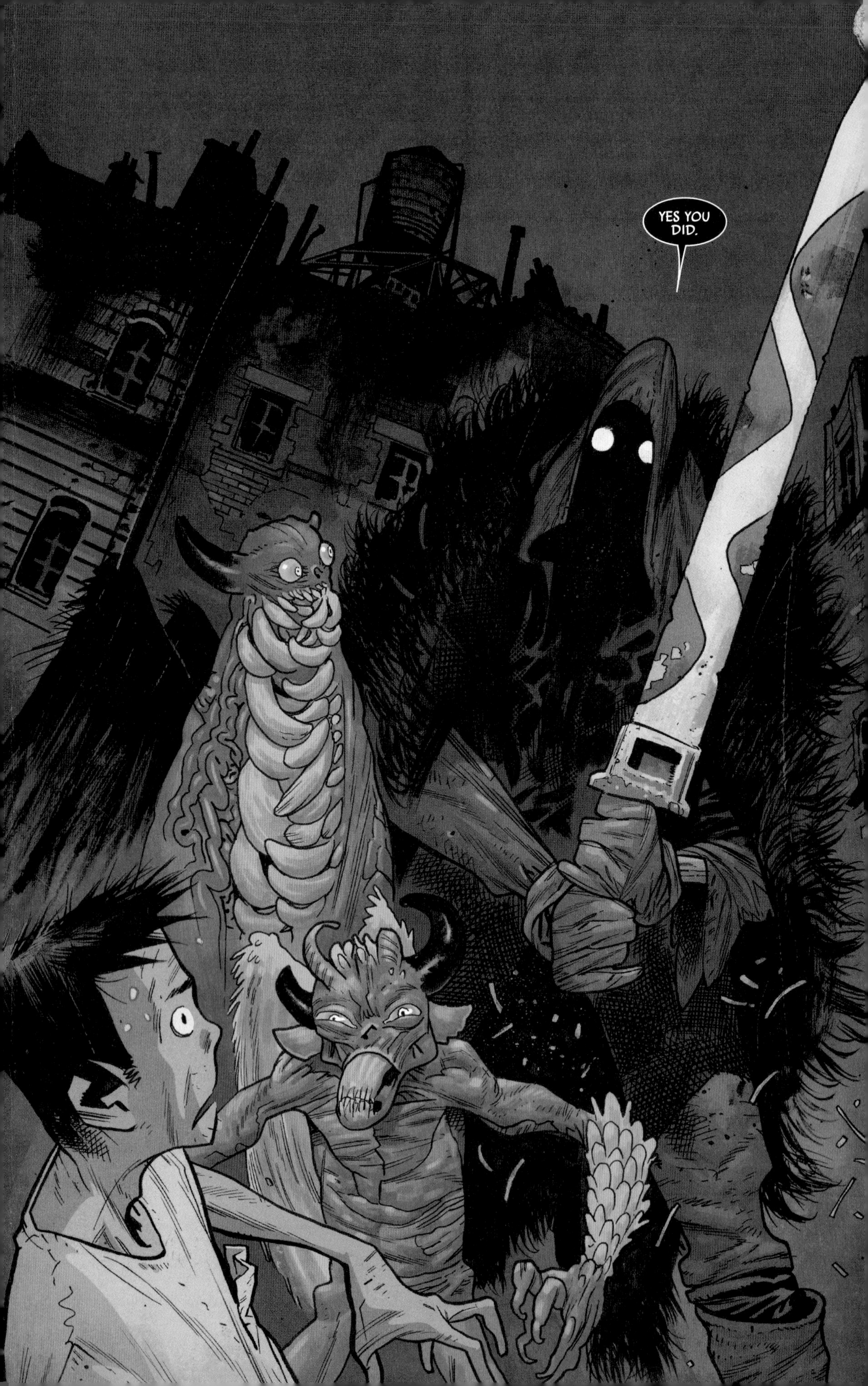
YES YOU DID.

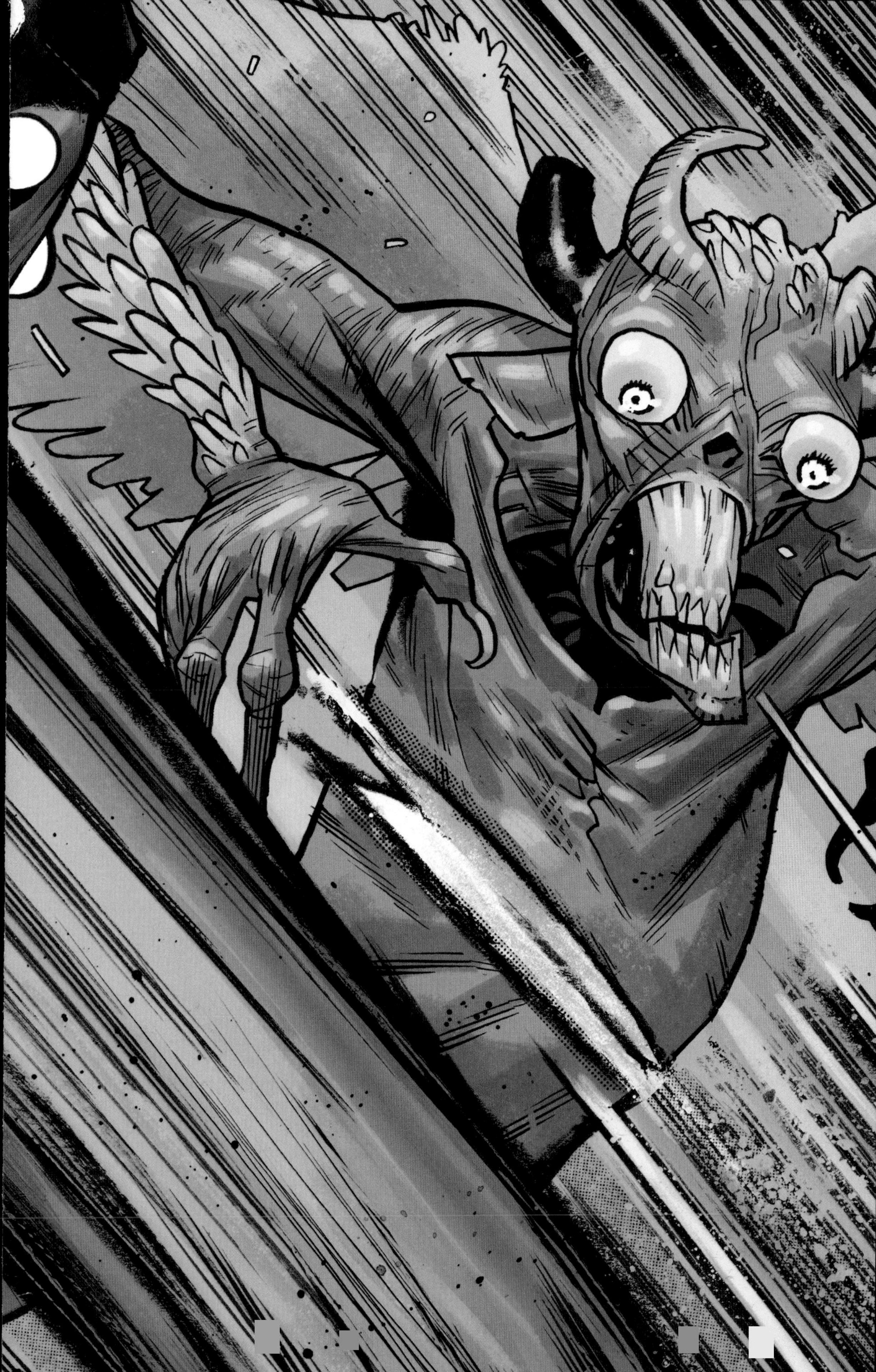

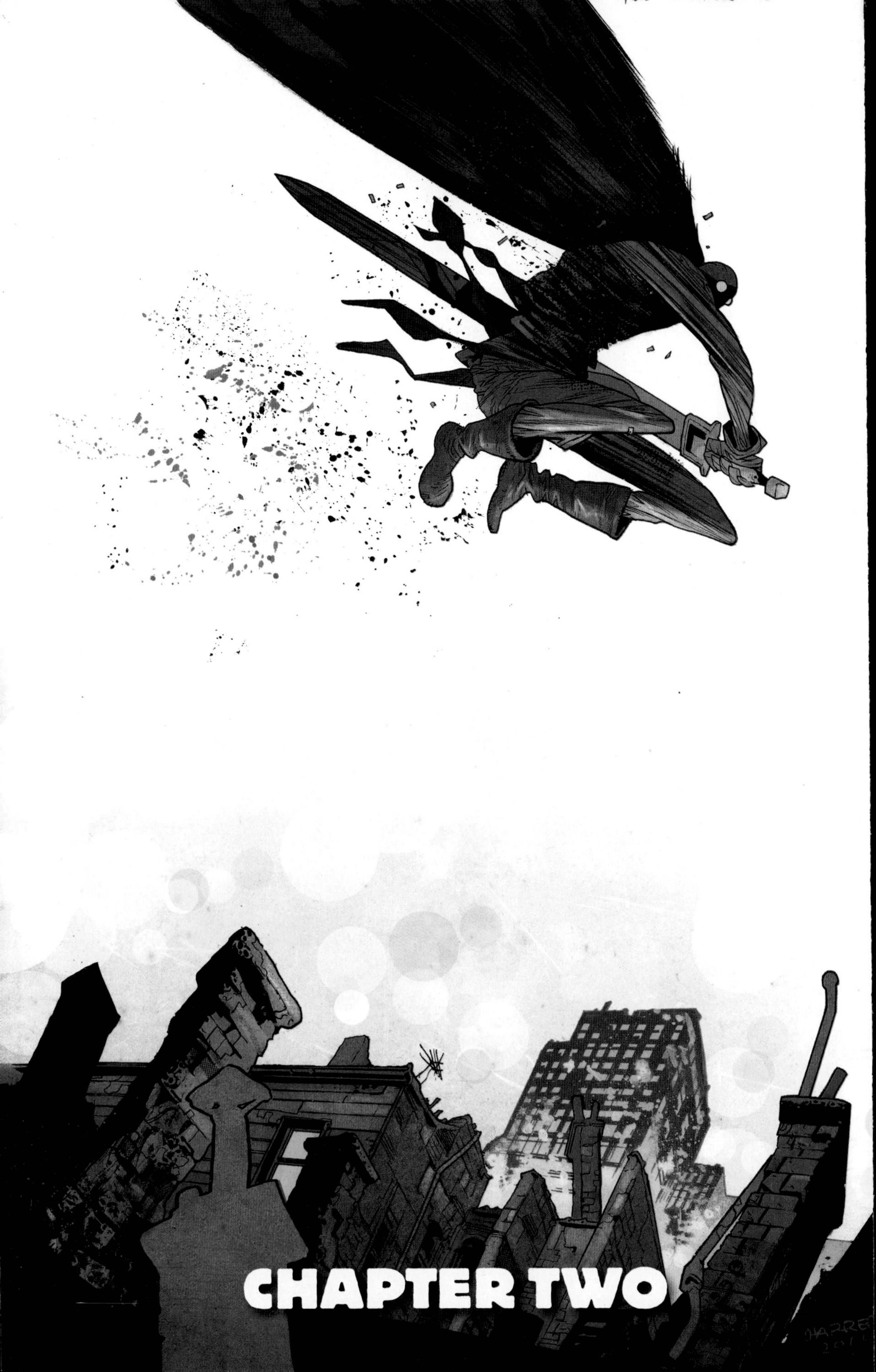
CHAPTER TWO

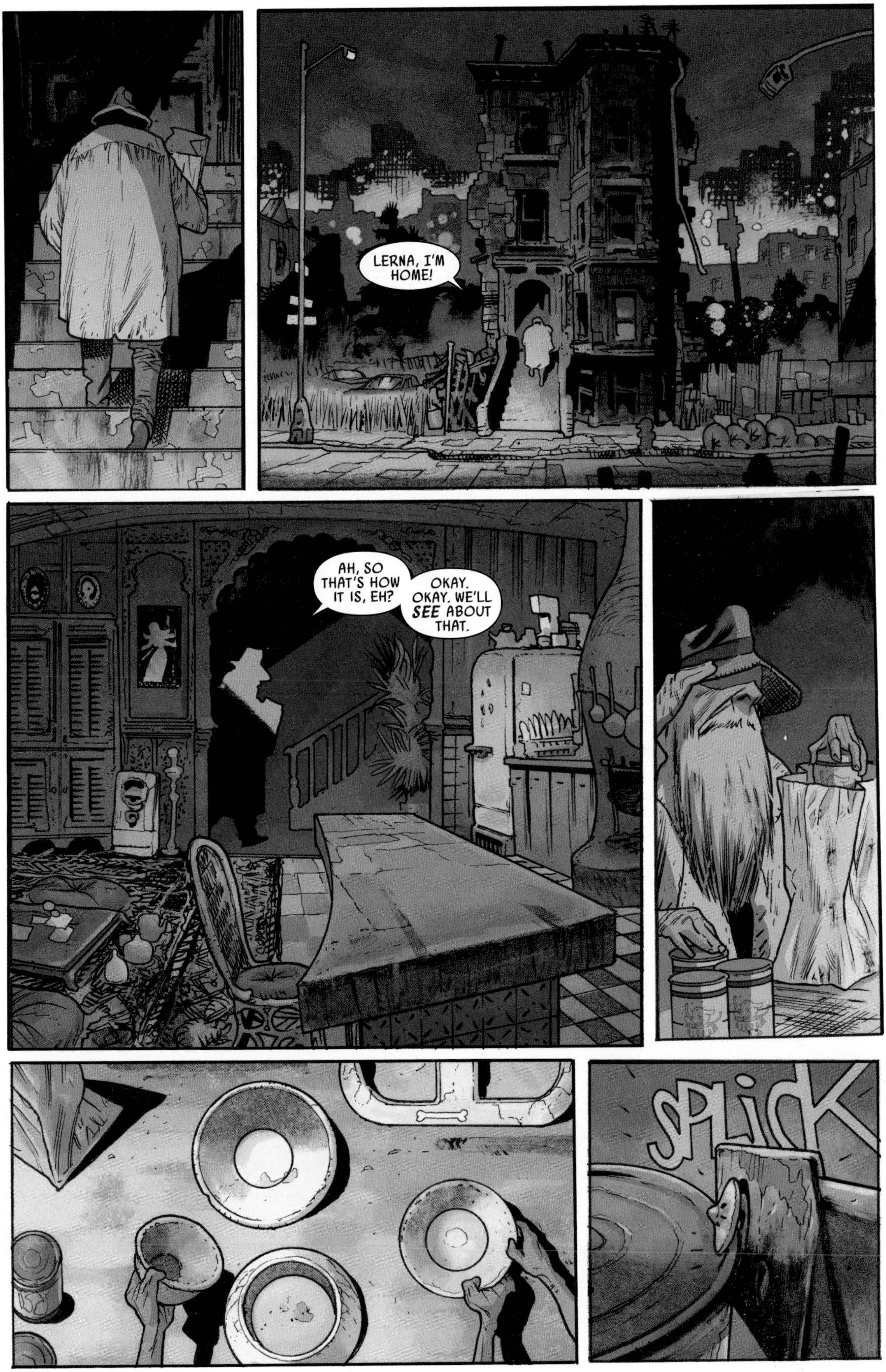
LERNA, I'M HOME!
AH, SO THAT'S HOW IT IS, EH?
OKAY. OKAY. WE'LL **SEE** ABOUT THAT.
SPLICK

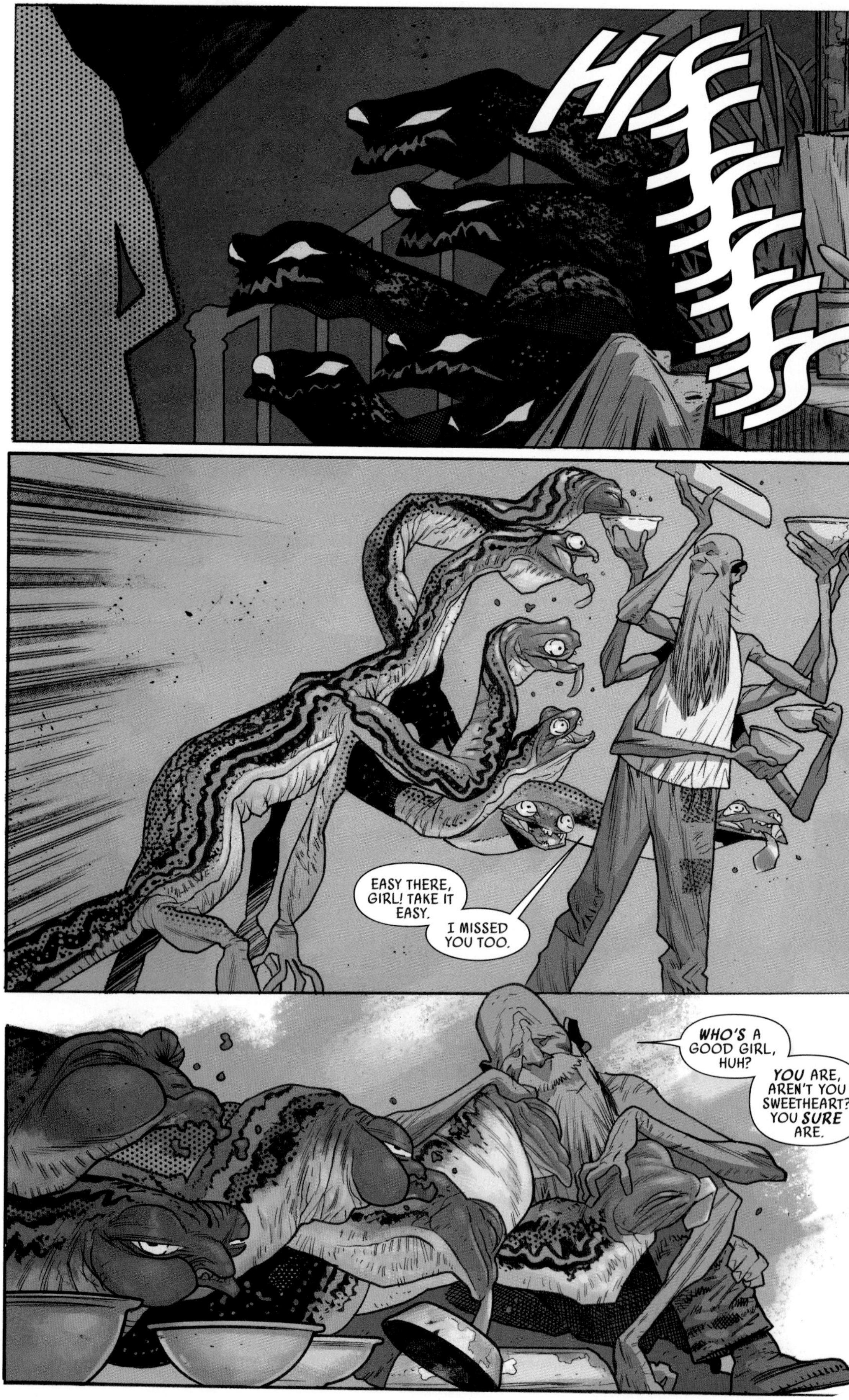
HISSSSSS
EASY THERE, GIRL! TAKE IT EASY.
I MISSED YOU TOO.
WHO'S A GOOD GIRL, HUH?
YOU ARE, AREN'T YOU SWEETHEART? YOU SURE ARE.

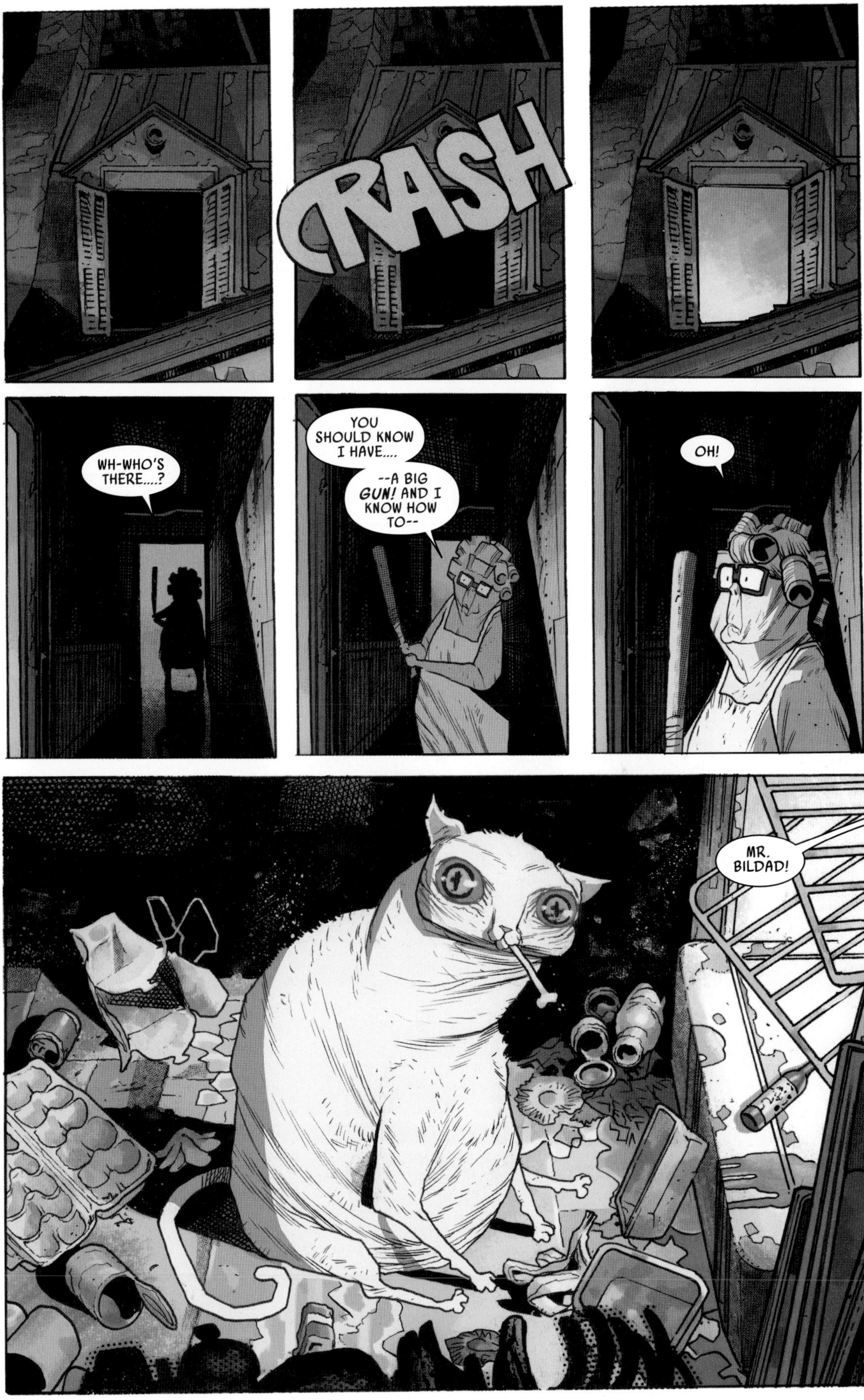
CRASH
WH-WHO'S THERE....?
YOU SHOULD KNOW I HAVE....
--A BIG GUN! AND I KNOW HOW TO--
OH!
MR. BILDAD!

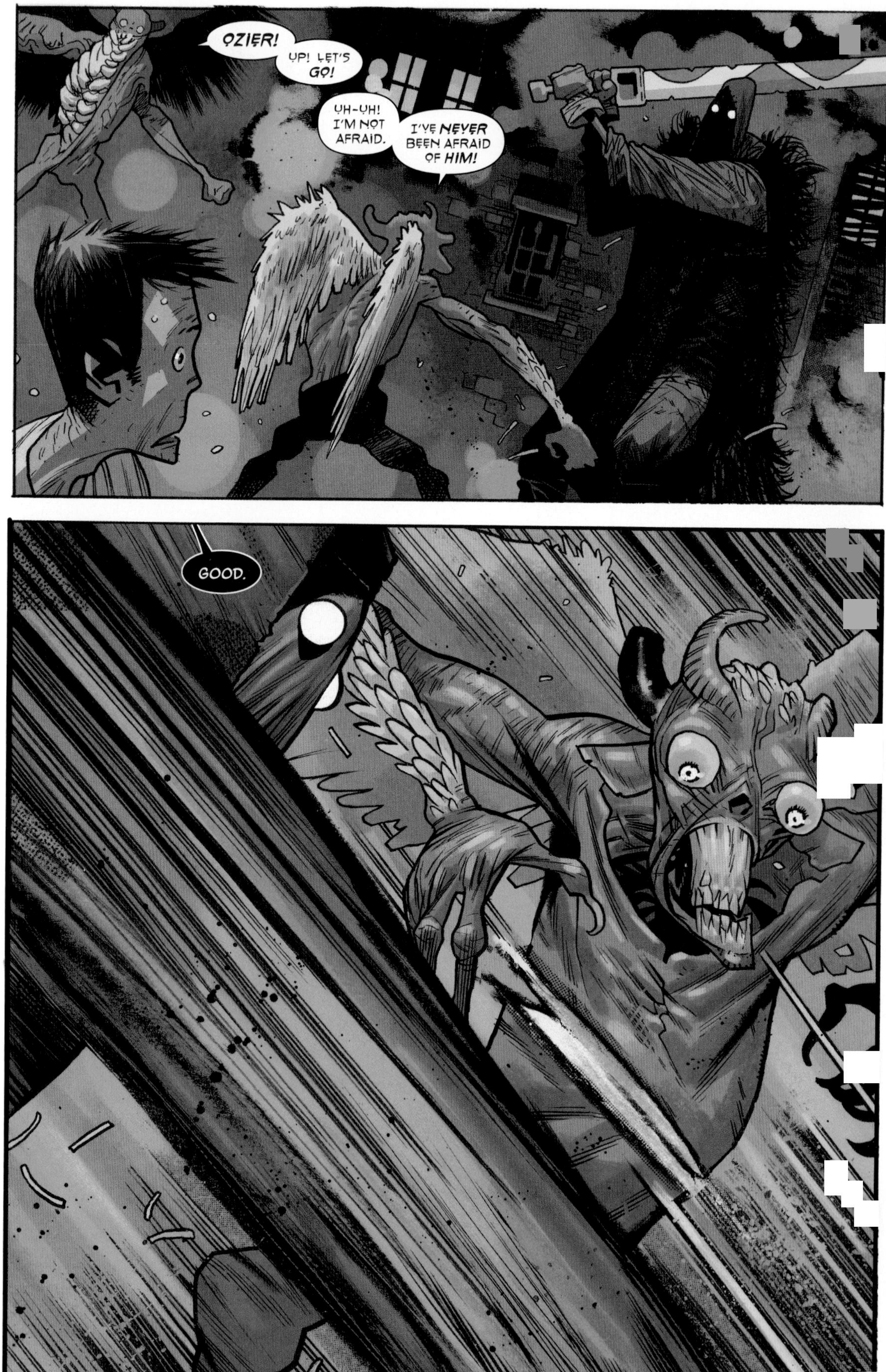
OZIER!
UP! LET'S GO!
UH-UH! I'M NOT AFRAID.
I'VE NEVER BEEN AFRAID OF HIM!
GOOD.

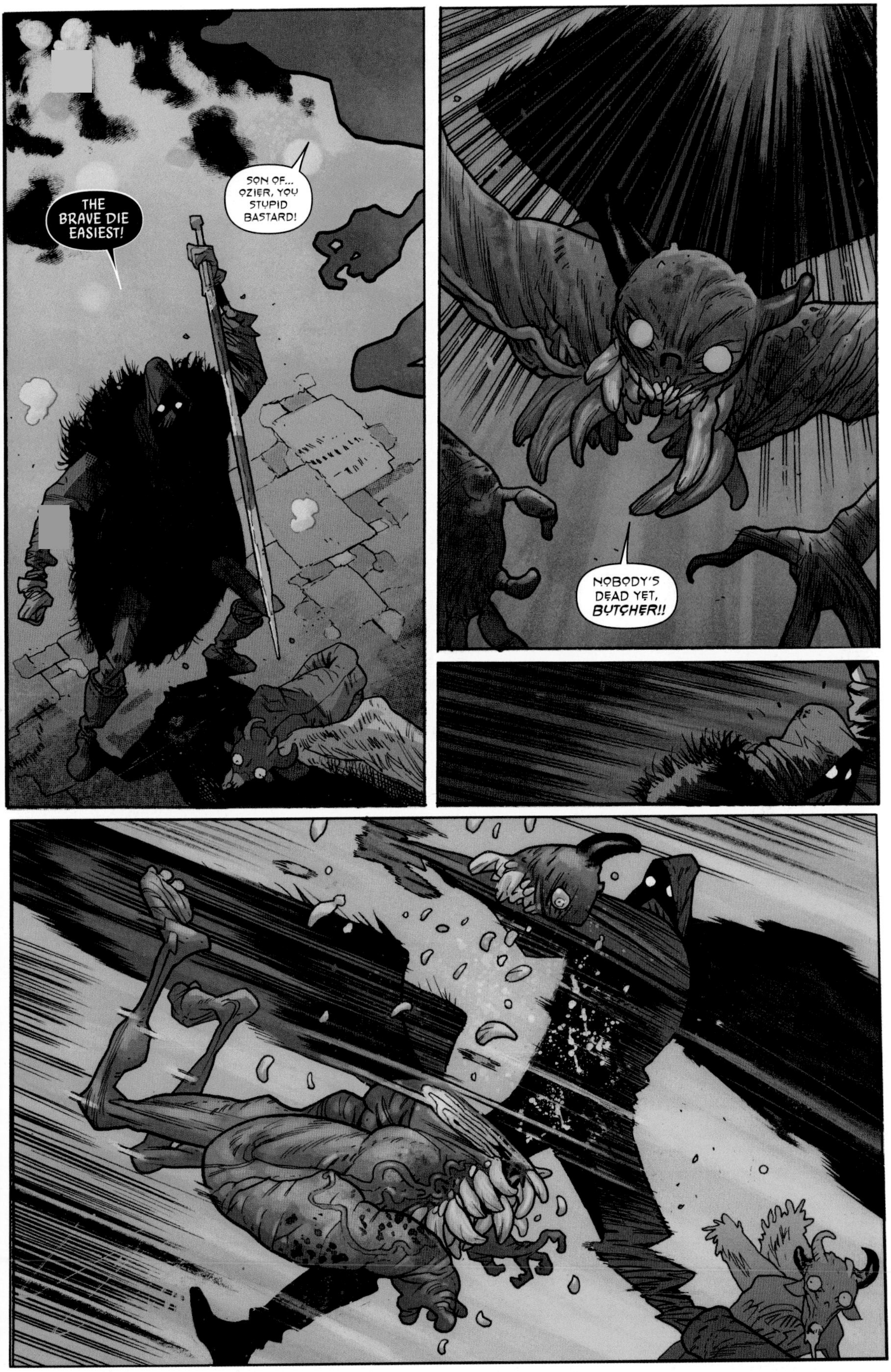
THE BRAVE DIE EASIEST!
SON OF... OZIER, YOU STUPID BASTARD!
NOBODY'S DEAD YET, BUTCHER!!

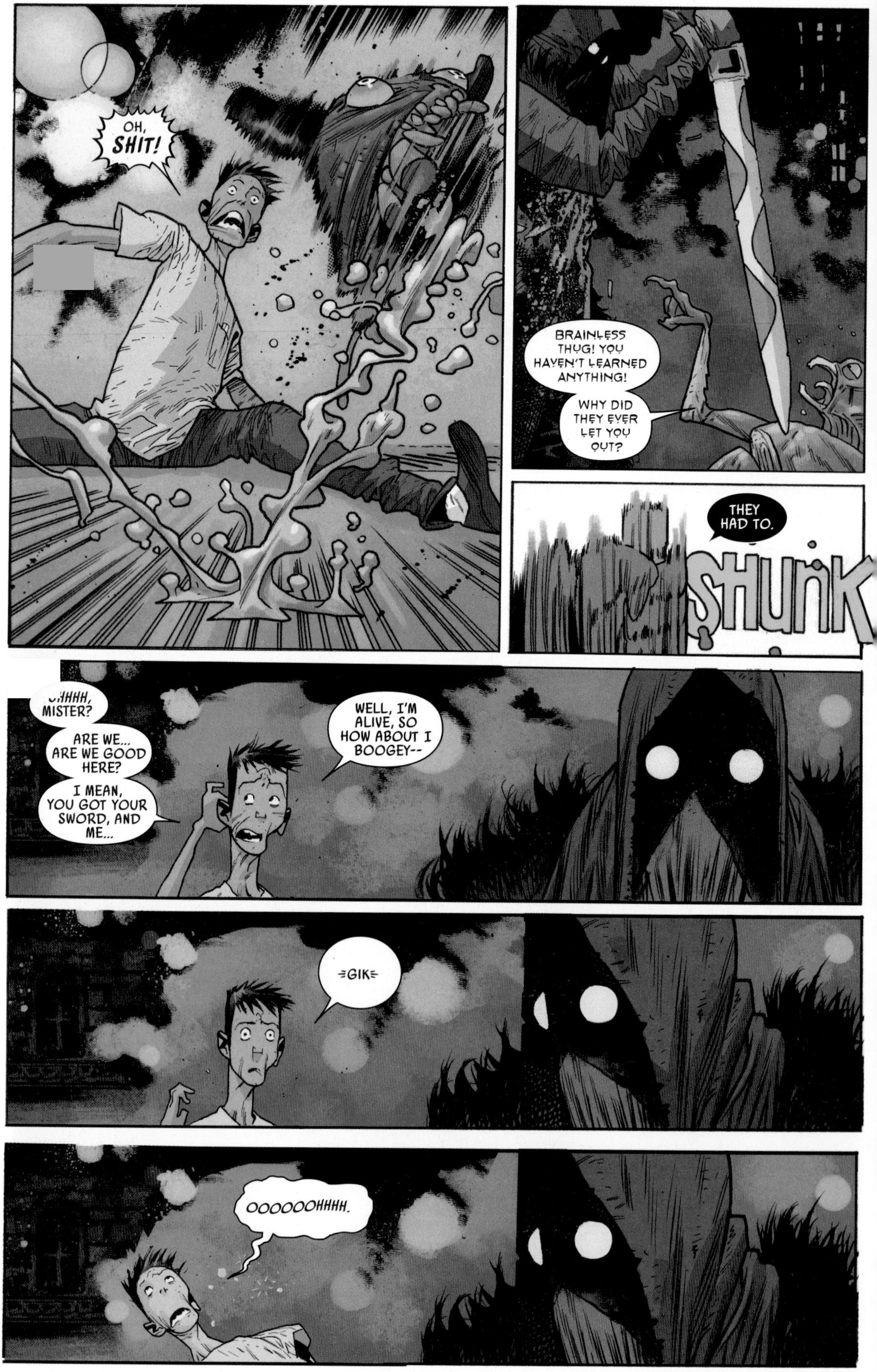

OH, SHIT!
BRAINLESS THUG! YOU HAVEN'T LEARNED ANYTHING!
WHY DID THEY EVER LET YOU OUT?
THEY HAD TO.
SHUNK
HHHH, MISTER?
ARE WE... ARE WE GOOD HERE?
I MEAN, YOU GOT YOUR SWORD, AND ME...
WELL, I'M ALIVE, SO HOW ABOUT I BOOGEY--
GIK
OOOOOOHHHH.

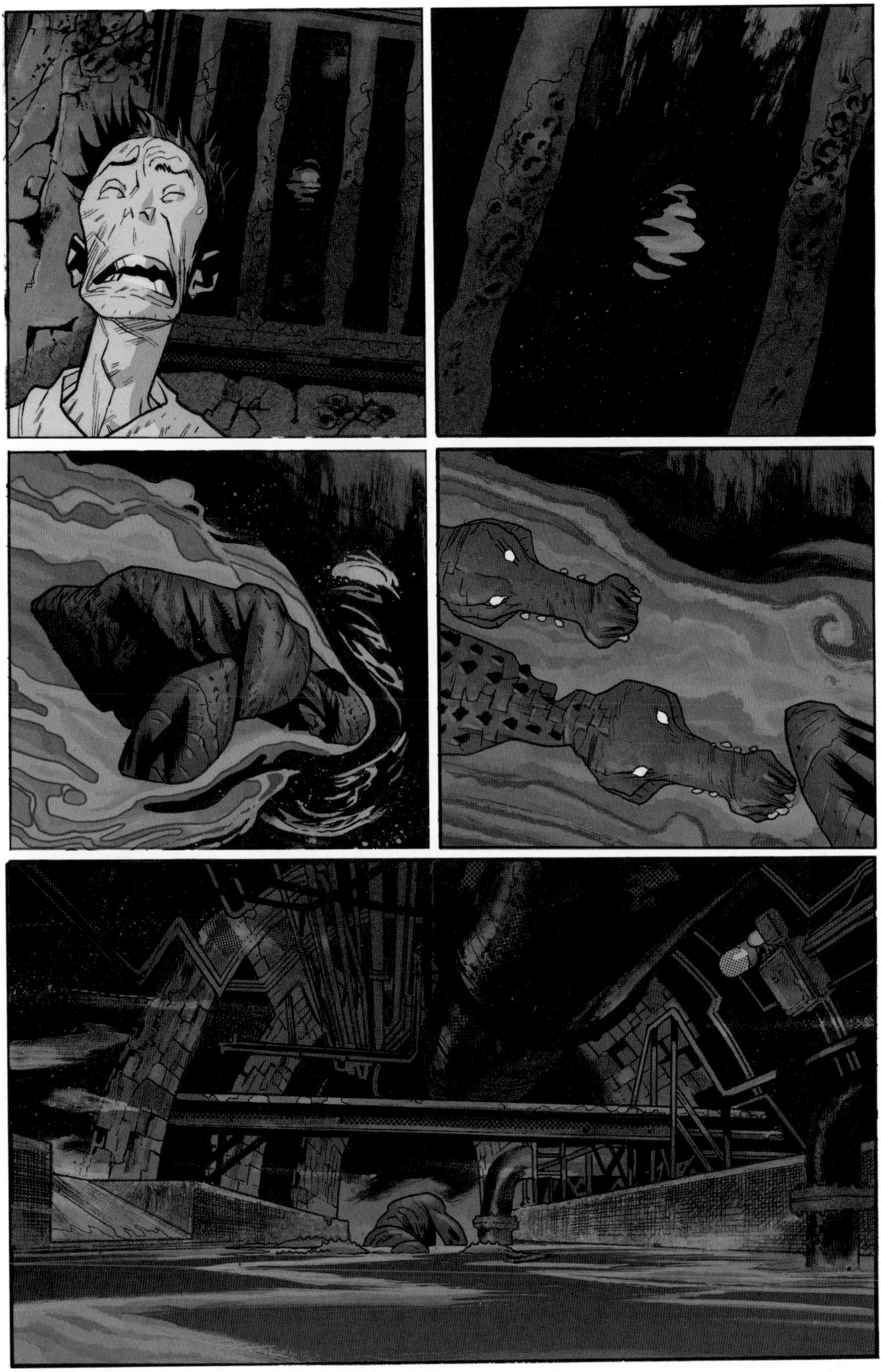

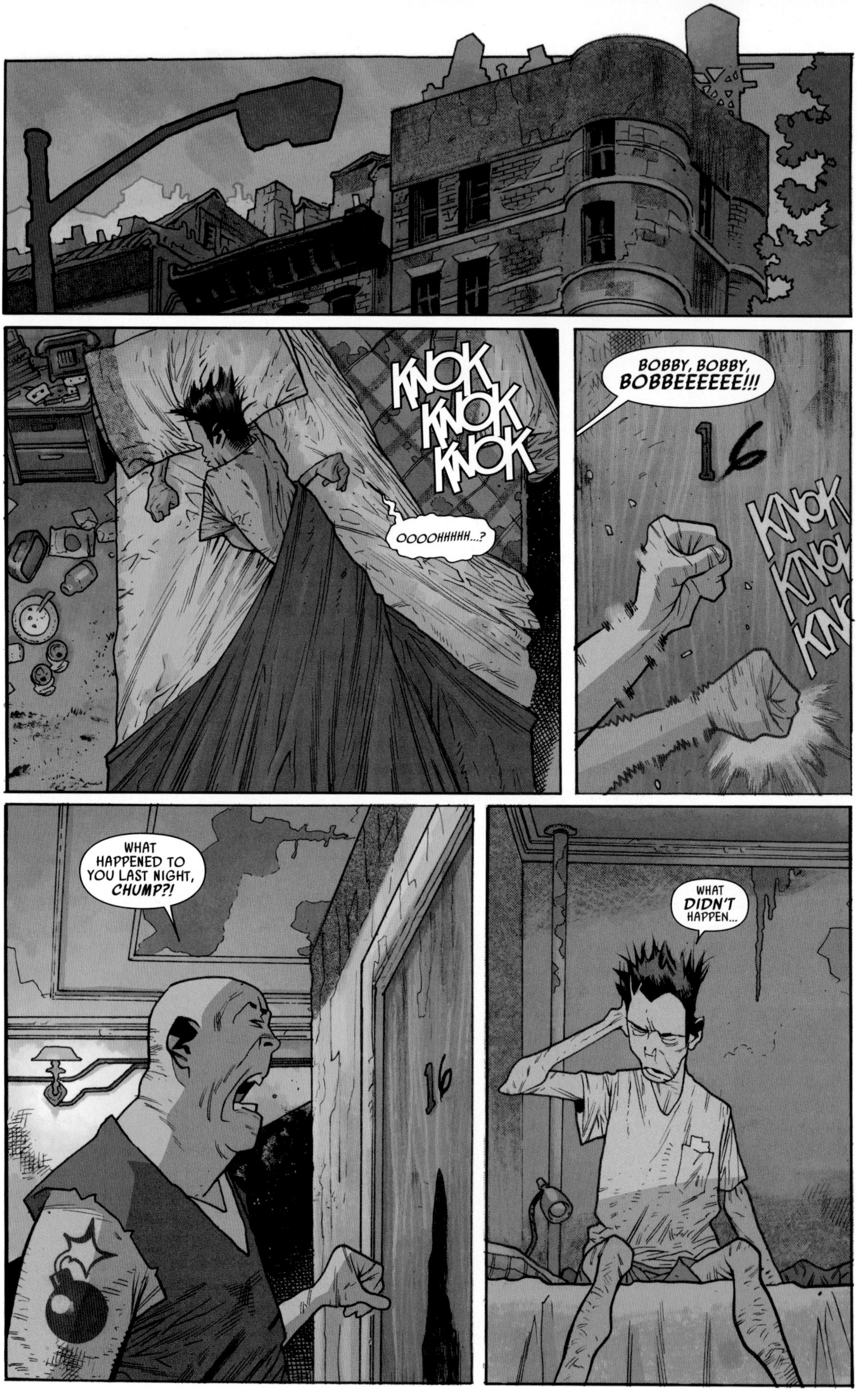
KNOK KNOK KNOK
OOOOHHHHH...?
BOBBY, BOBBY, BOBBEEEEEE!!!
KNOK
WHAT HAPPENED TO YOU LAST NIGHT, CHUMP?!
WHAT DIDN'T HAPPEN...

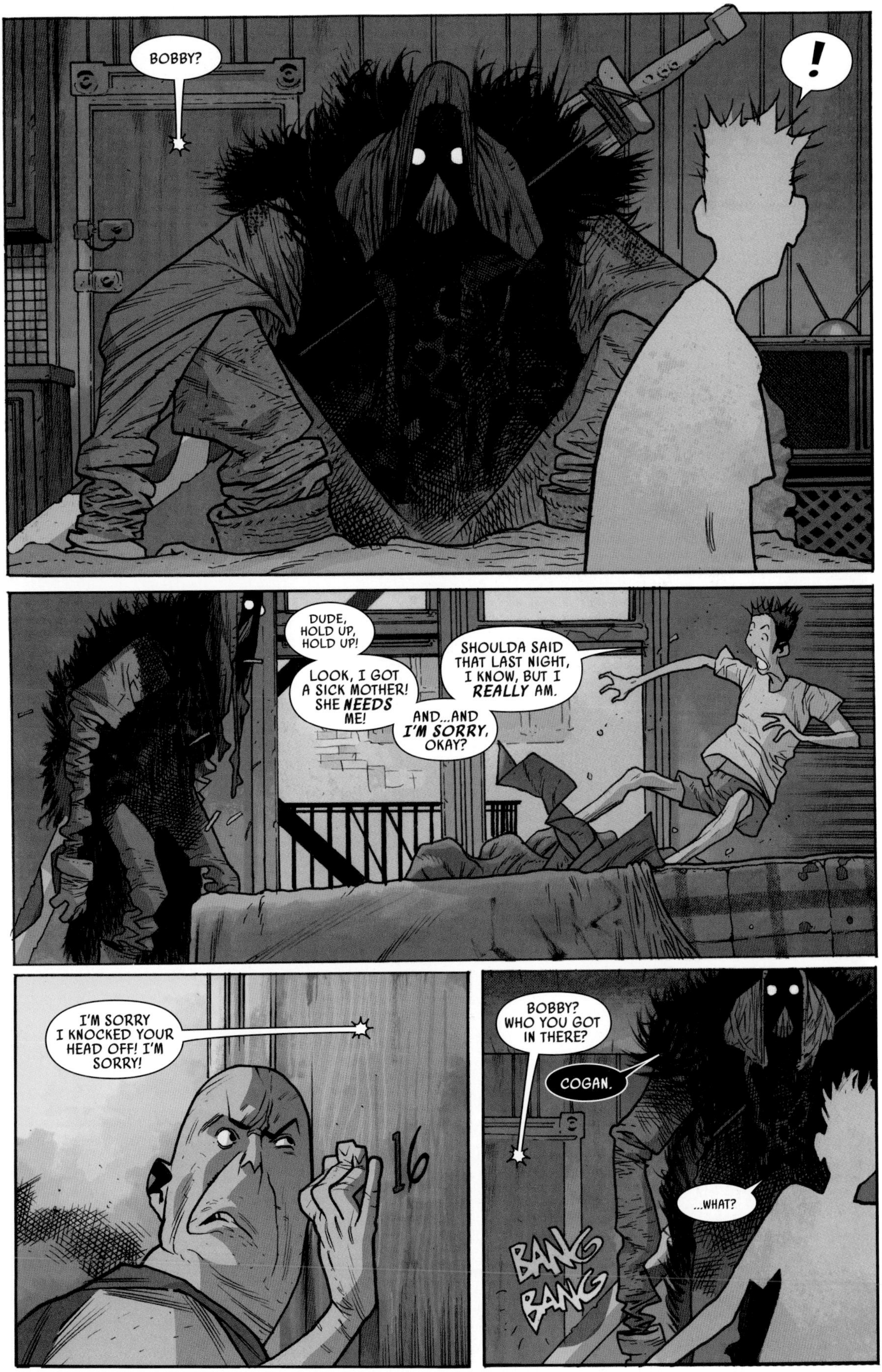
BOBBY?
!
DUDE, HOLD UP, HOLD UP!
LOOK, I GOT A SICK MOTHER! SHE NEEDS ME!
SHOULDA SAID THAT LAST NIGHT, I KNOW, BUT I REALLY AM.
AND...AND I'M SORRY, OKAY?
I'M SORRY I KNOCKED YOUR HEAD OFF! I'M SORRY!
16
BOBBY? WHO YOU GOT IN THERE?
COGAN.
...WHAT?
BANG BANG

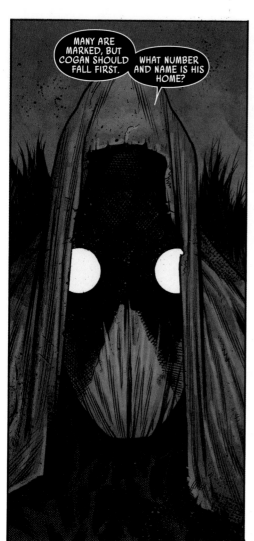

MANY ARE MARKED, BUT COGAN SHOULD FALL FIRST.

WHAT NUMBER AND NAME IS HIS HOME?

YOU FIGURED OUT WHERE I LIVE, MAN. WHY YOU NEED MY HELP?

YOU HAD *THIS* IN YOUR GARMENTS.

MY LICENSE...?

MY PANTS!

WHERE'S MY PANTS??!! WHAT'D YOU DO TO ME?

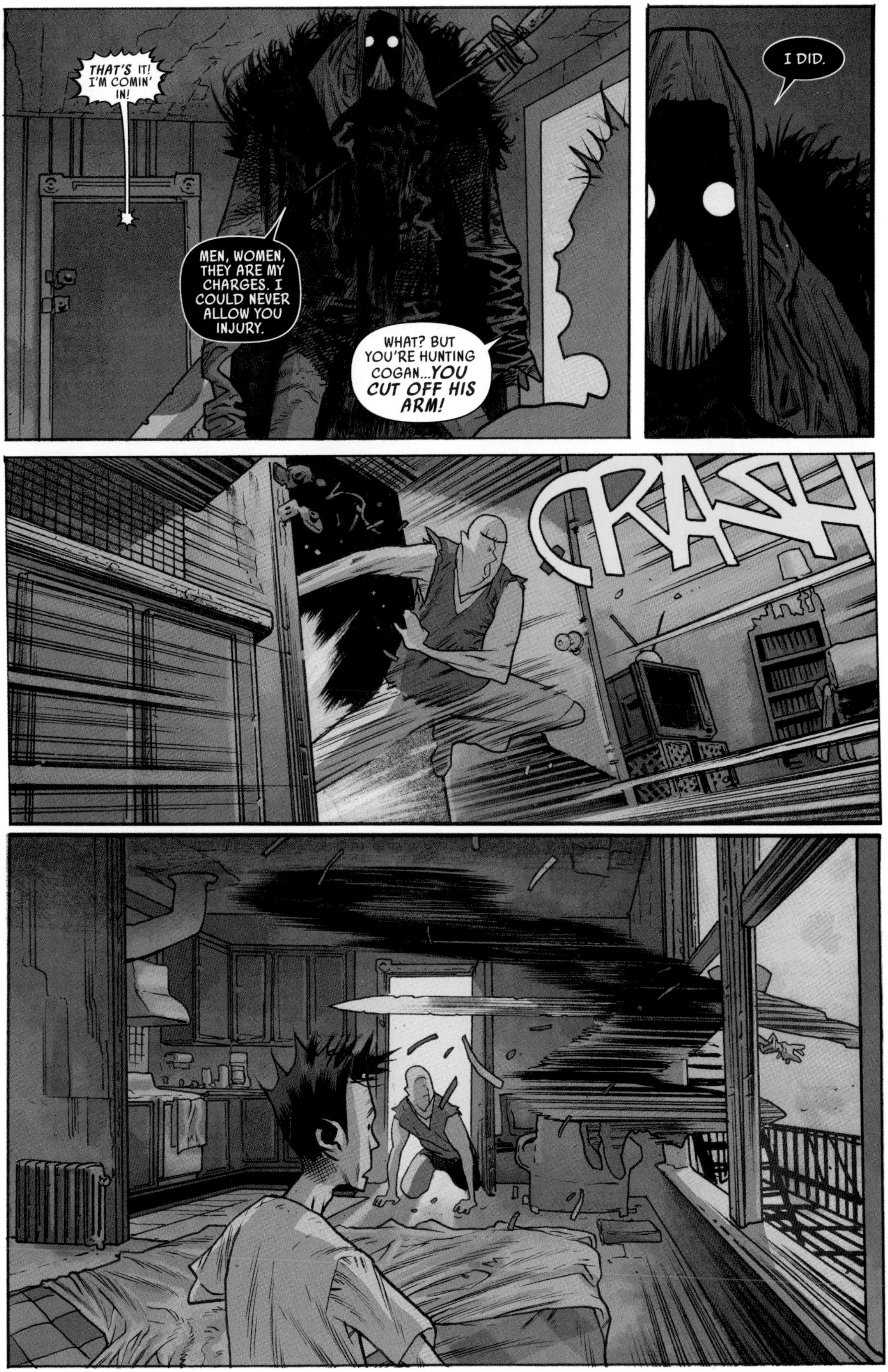
THAT'S IT! I'M COMIN' IN!
MEN, WOMEN, THEY ARE MY CHARGES. I COULD NEVER ALLOW YOU INJURY.
WHAT? BUT YOU'RE HUNTING COGAN...YOU CUT OFF HIS ARM!
I DID.
CRASH

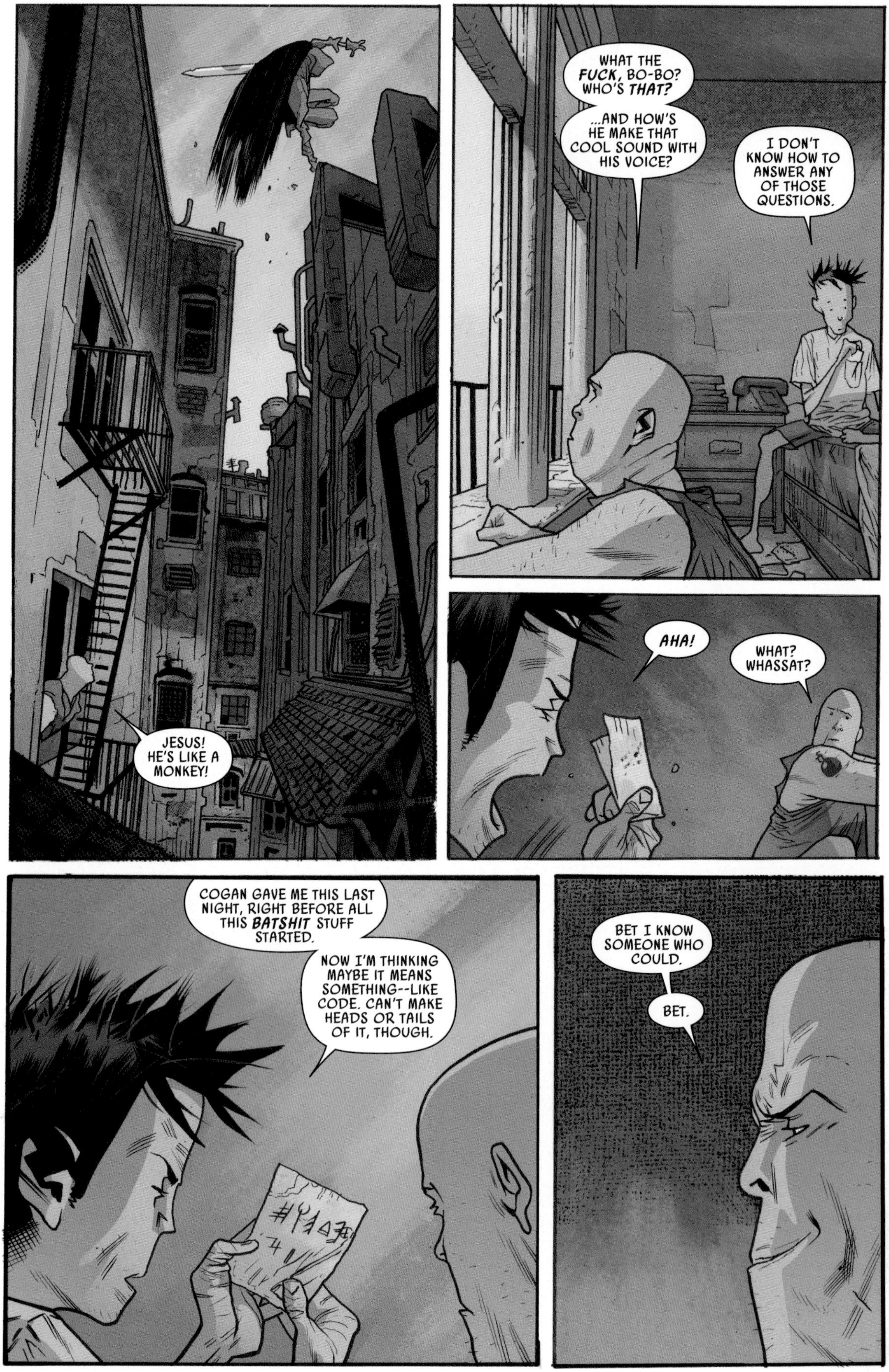
JESUS! HE'S LIKE A MONKEY!
WHAT THE FUCK, BO-BO? WHO'S THAT?
...AND HOW'S HE MAKE THAT COOL SOUND WITH HIS VOICE?
I DON'T KNOW HOW TO ANSWER ANY OF THOSE QUESTIONS.
AHA!
WHAT? WHASSAT?
COGAN GAVE ME THIS LAST NIGHT, RIGHT BEFORE ALL THIS BATSHIT STUFF STARTED.
NOW I'M THINKING MAYBE IT MEANS SOMETHING--LIKE CODE. CAN'T MAKE HEADS OR TAILS OF IT, THOUGH.
BET I KNOW SOMEONE WHO COULD.
BET.

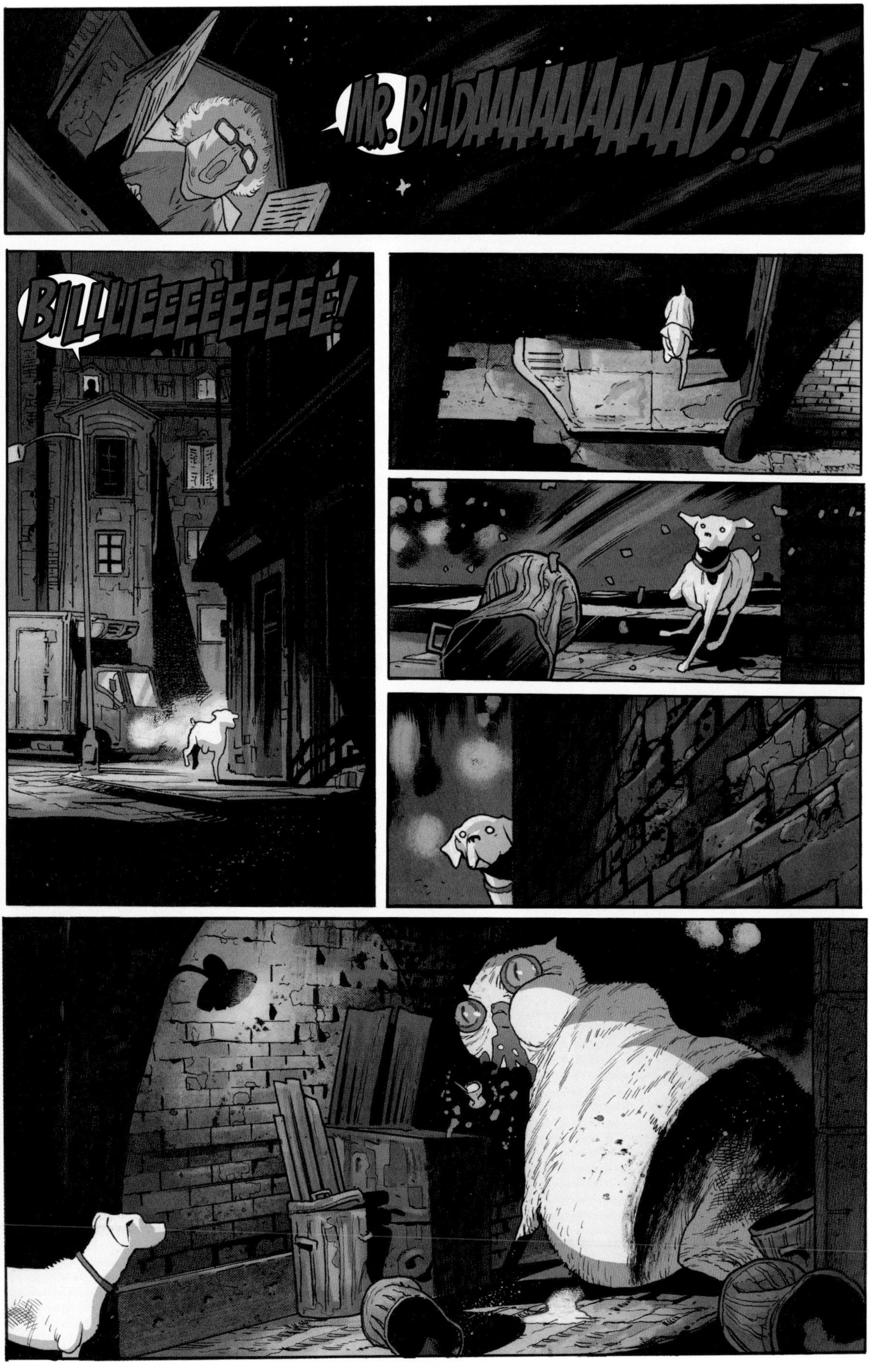
MR. BILDAAAAAAAAAD!!
BILLLIEEEEEEEEEE!

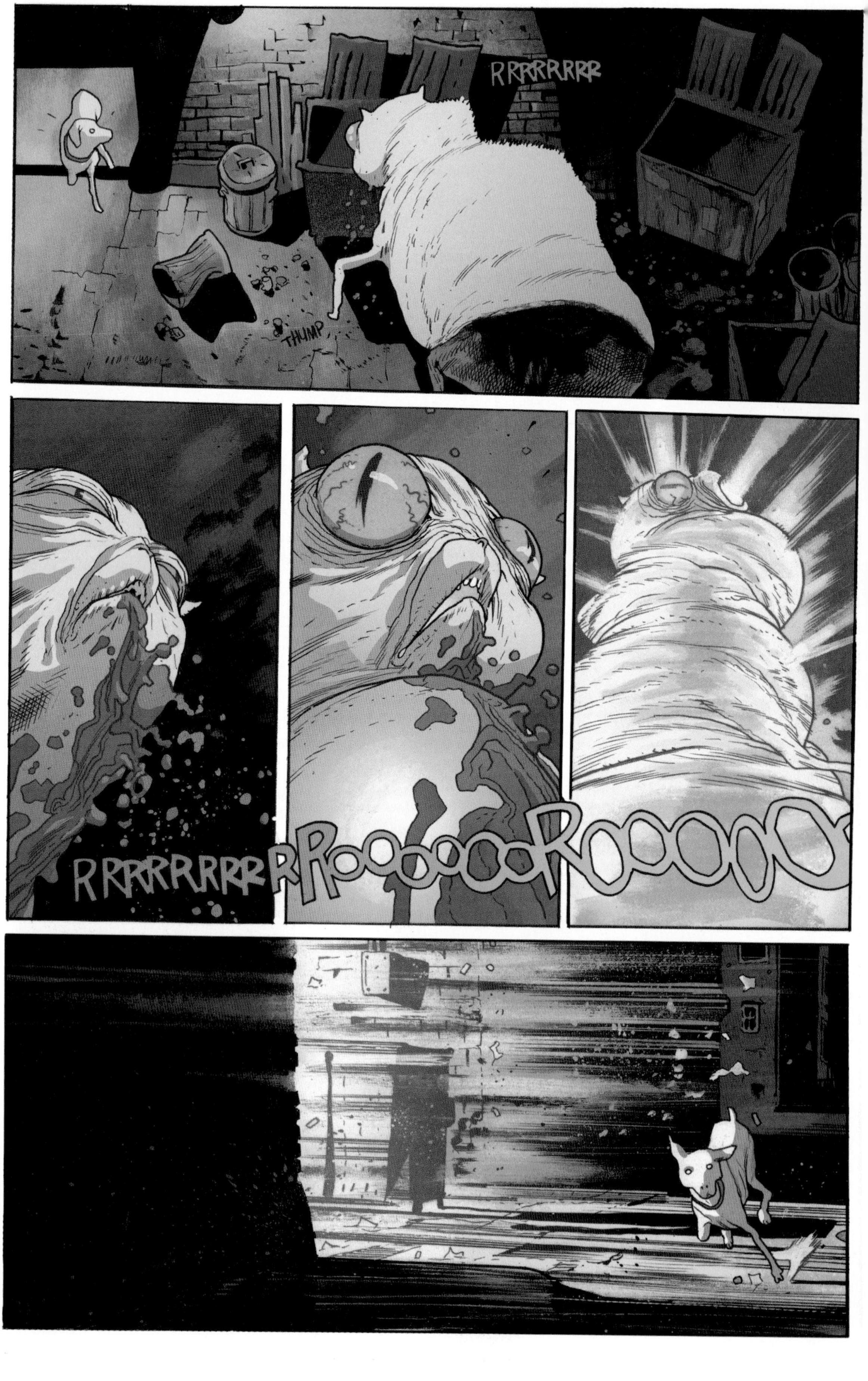
RRRRRRRRR
THUMP
RRRRRRRRRRRoooooooRooooo

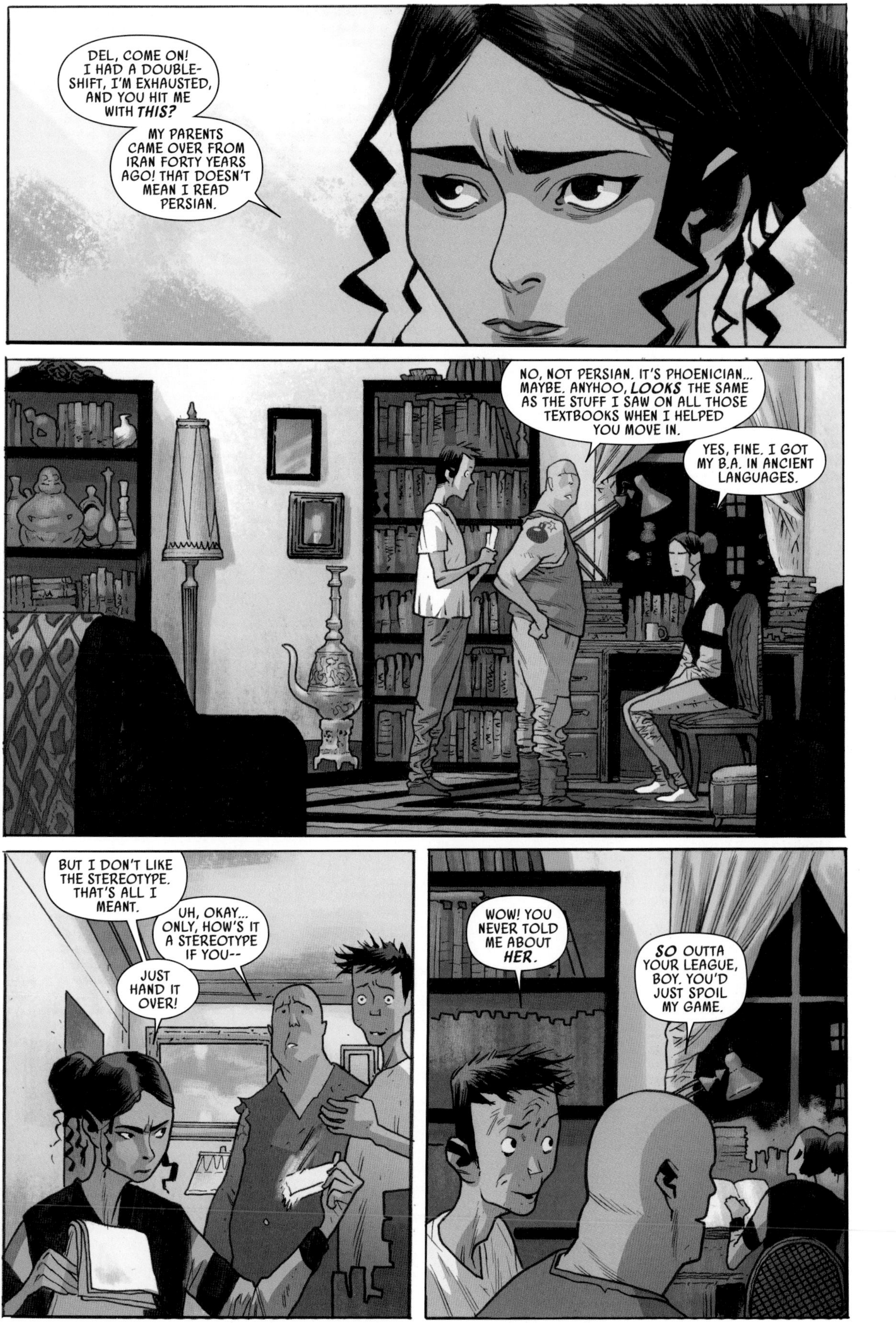
DEL, COME ON! I HAD A DOUBLE-SHIFT, I'M EXHAUSTED, AND YOU HIT ME WITH *THIS?*
MY PARENTS CAME OVER FROM IRAN FORTY YEARS AGO! THAT DOESN'T MEAN I READ PERSIAN.
NO, NOT PERSIAN. IT'S PHOENICIAN... MAYBE. ANYHOO, ***LOOKS*** THE SAME AS THE STUFF I SAW ON ALL THOSE TEXTBOOKS WHEN I HELPED YOU MOVE IN.
YES, FINE. I GOT MY B.A. IN ANCIENT LANGUAGES.
BUT I DON'T LIKE THE STEREOTYPE. THAT'S ALL I MEANT.
UH, OKAY... ONLY, HOW'S IT A STEREOTYPE IF YOU--
JUST HAND IT OVER!
WOW! YOU NEVER TOLD ME ABOUT ***HER.***
SO OUTTA YOUR LEAGUE, BOY. YOU'D JUST SPOIL MY GAME.

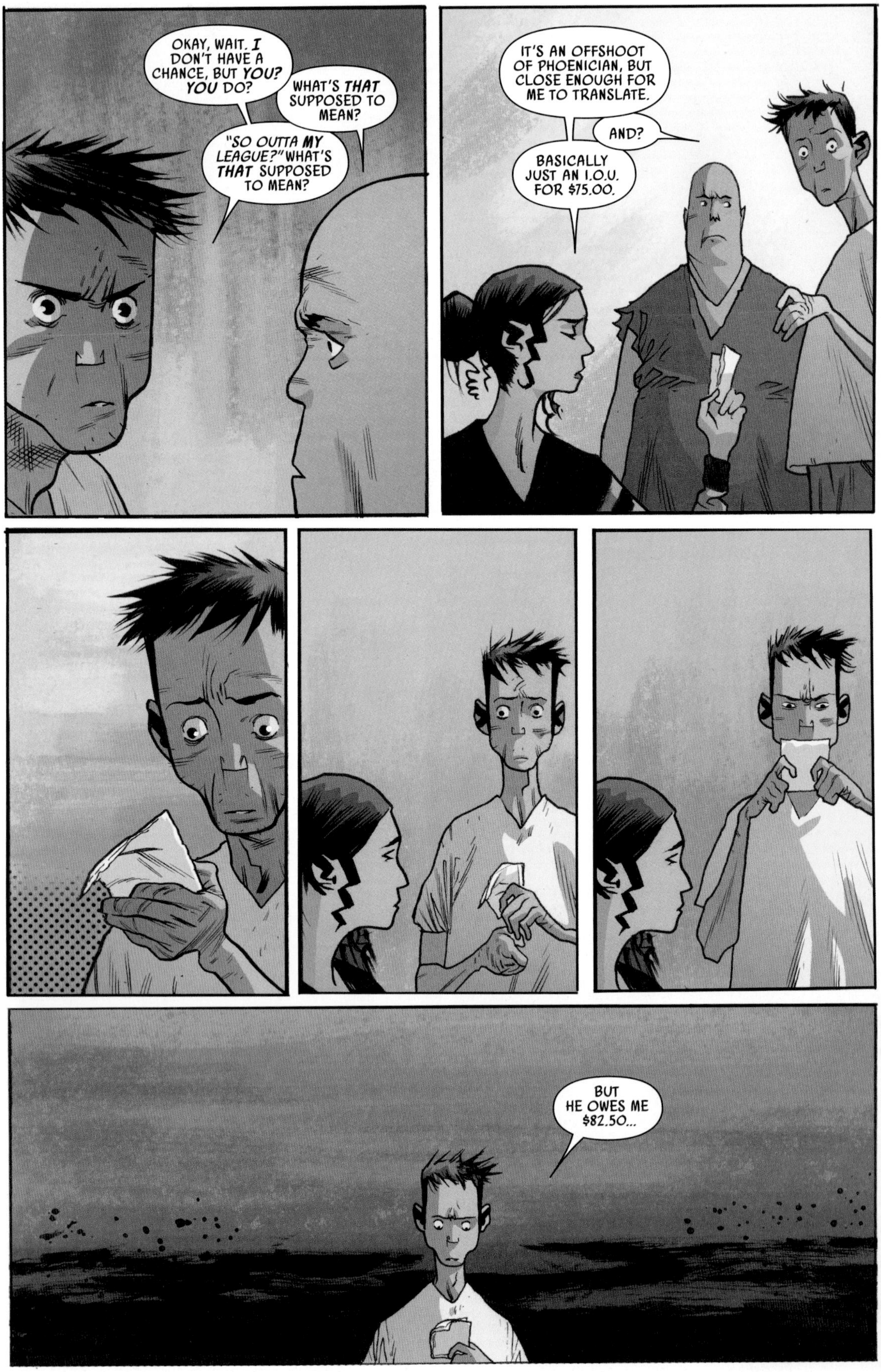
OKAY, WAIT. I DON'T HAVE A CHANCE, BUT YOU? YOU DO?
WHAT'S THAT SUPPOSED TO MEAN?
"SO OUTTA MY LEAGUE?" WHAT'S THAT SUPPOSED TO MEAN?
IT'S AN OFFSHOOT OF PHOENICIAN, BUT CLOSE ENOUGH FOR ME TO TRANSLATE.
AND?
BASICALLY JUST AN I.O.U. FOR $75.00.
BUT HE OWES ME $82.50...

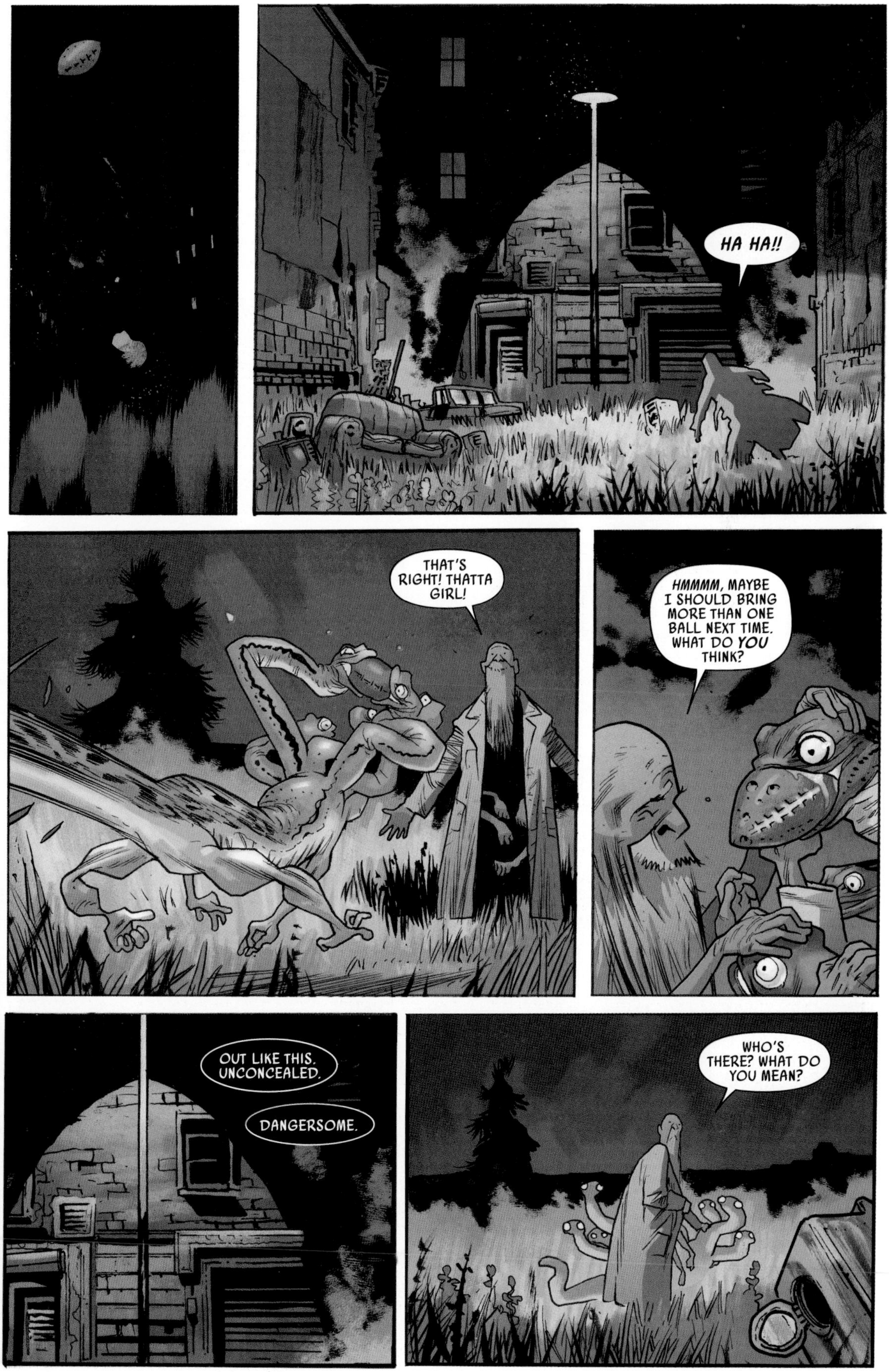
HA HA!!
THAT'S RIGHT! THATTA GIRL!
HMMMM, MAYBE I SHOULD BRING MORE THAN ONE BALL NEXT TIME. WHAT DO *YOU* THINK?
OUT LIKE THIS. UNCONCEALED.
DANGERSOME.
WHO'S THERE? WHAT DO YOU MEAN?

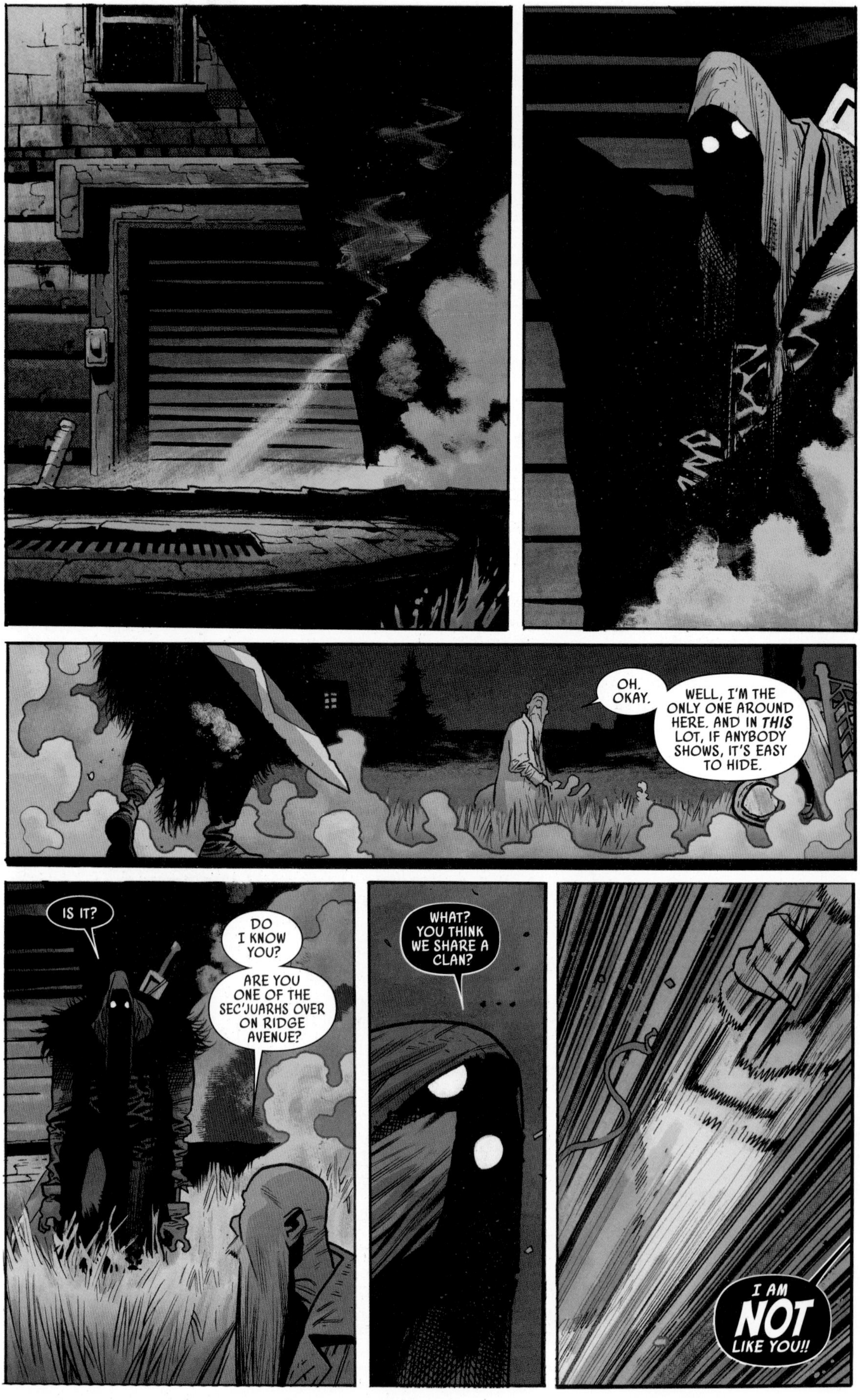
OH. OKAY.
WELL, I'M THE ONLY ONE AROUND HERE. AND IN THIS LOT, IF ANYBODY SHOWS, IT'S EASY TO HIDE.
IS IT?
DO I KNOW YOU?
ARE YOU ONE OF THE SEC'JUARHS OVER ON RIDGE AVENUE?
WHAT? YOU THINK WE SHARE A CLAN?
I AM NOT LIKE YOU!!

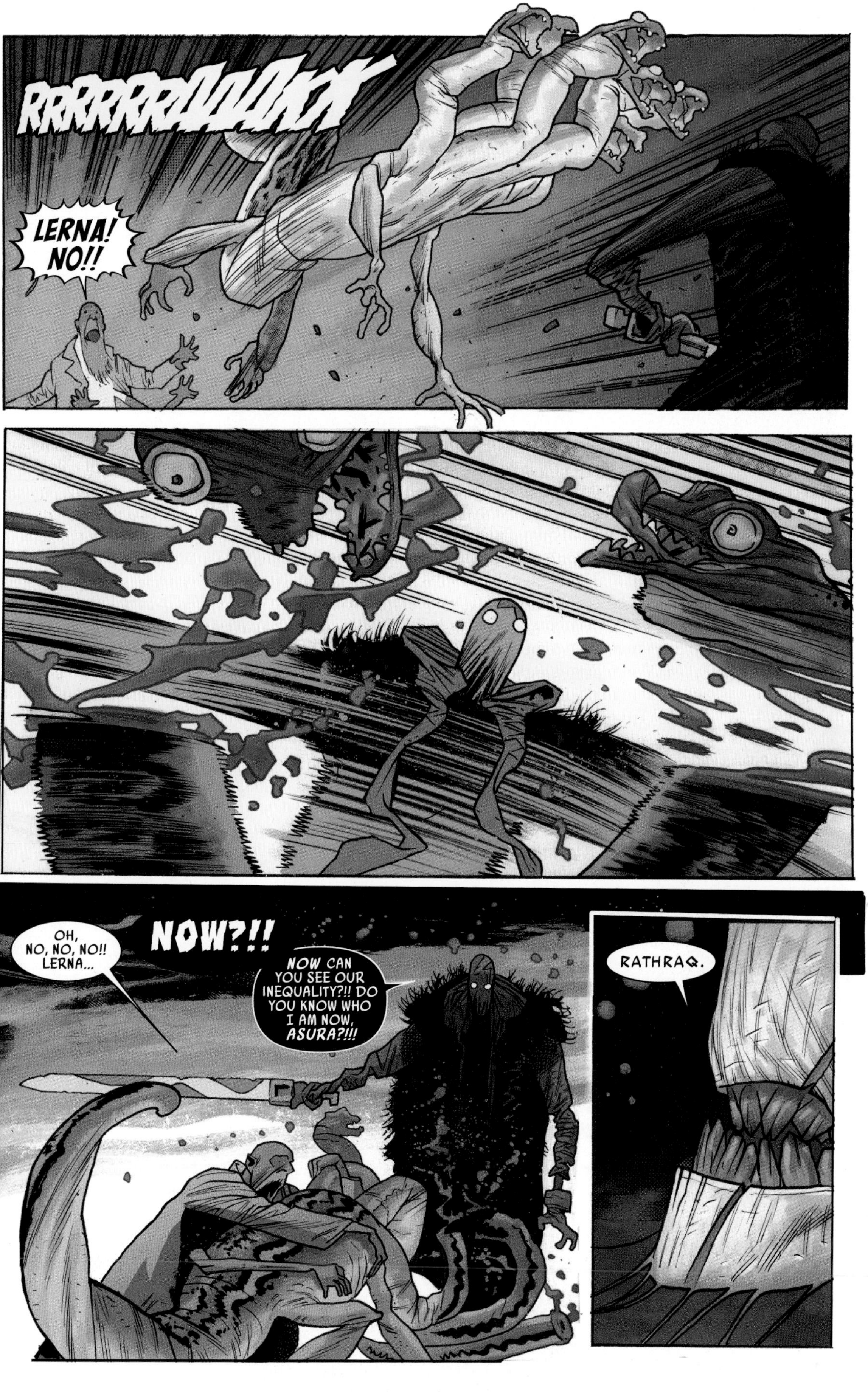
RRRRRRROOOOKK
LERNA! NO!!
OH, NO, NO, NO!! LERNA...
NOW?!!
NOW CAN YOU SEE OUR INEQUALITY?!! DO YOU KNOW WHO I AM NOW, ASURA?!!!
RATHRAQ.

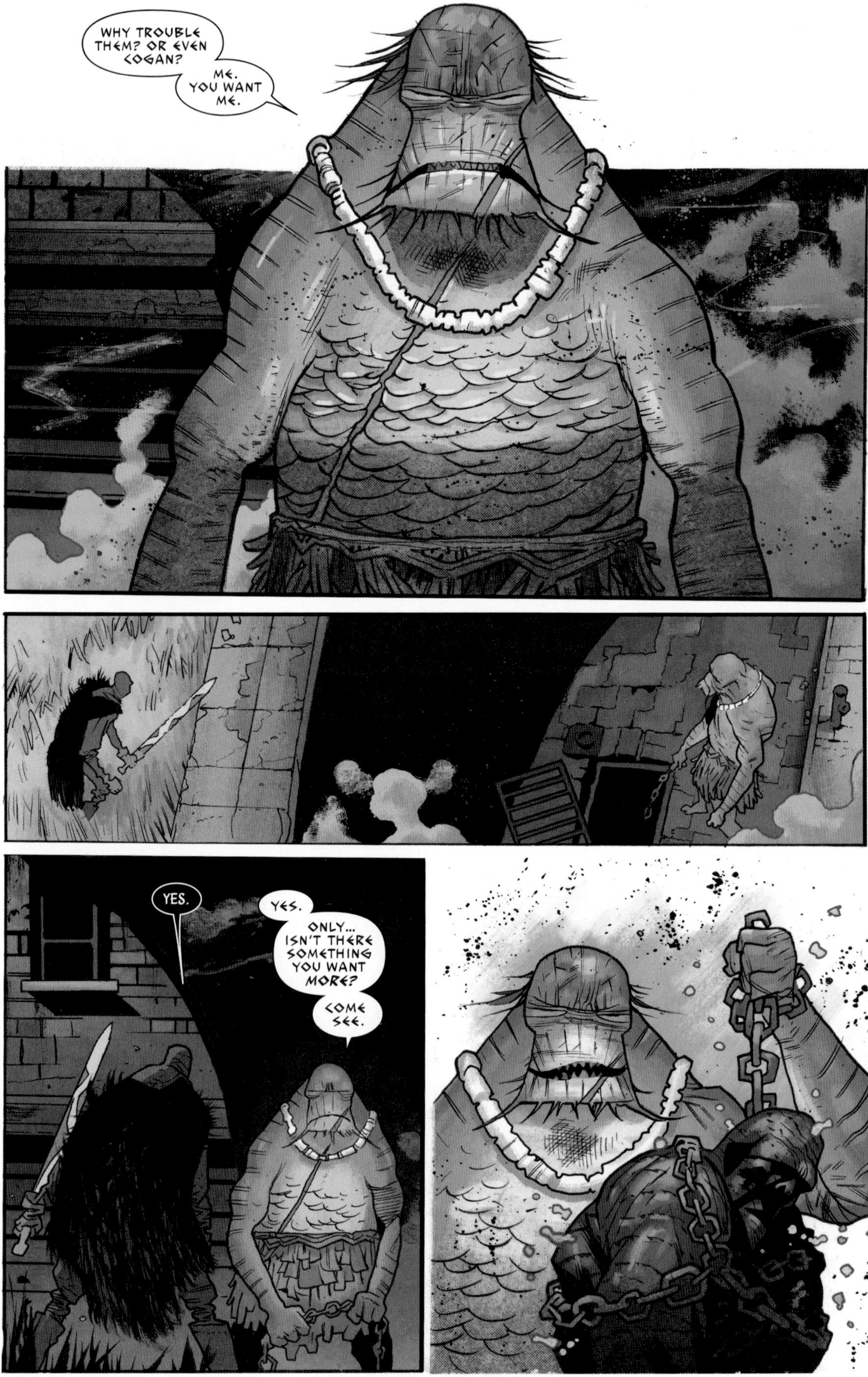
WHY TROUBLE THEM? OR EVEN COGAN?
ME. YOU WANT ME.
YES.
YES.
ONLY... ISN'T THERE SOMETHING YOU WANT MORE?
COME SEE.

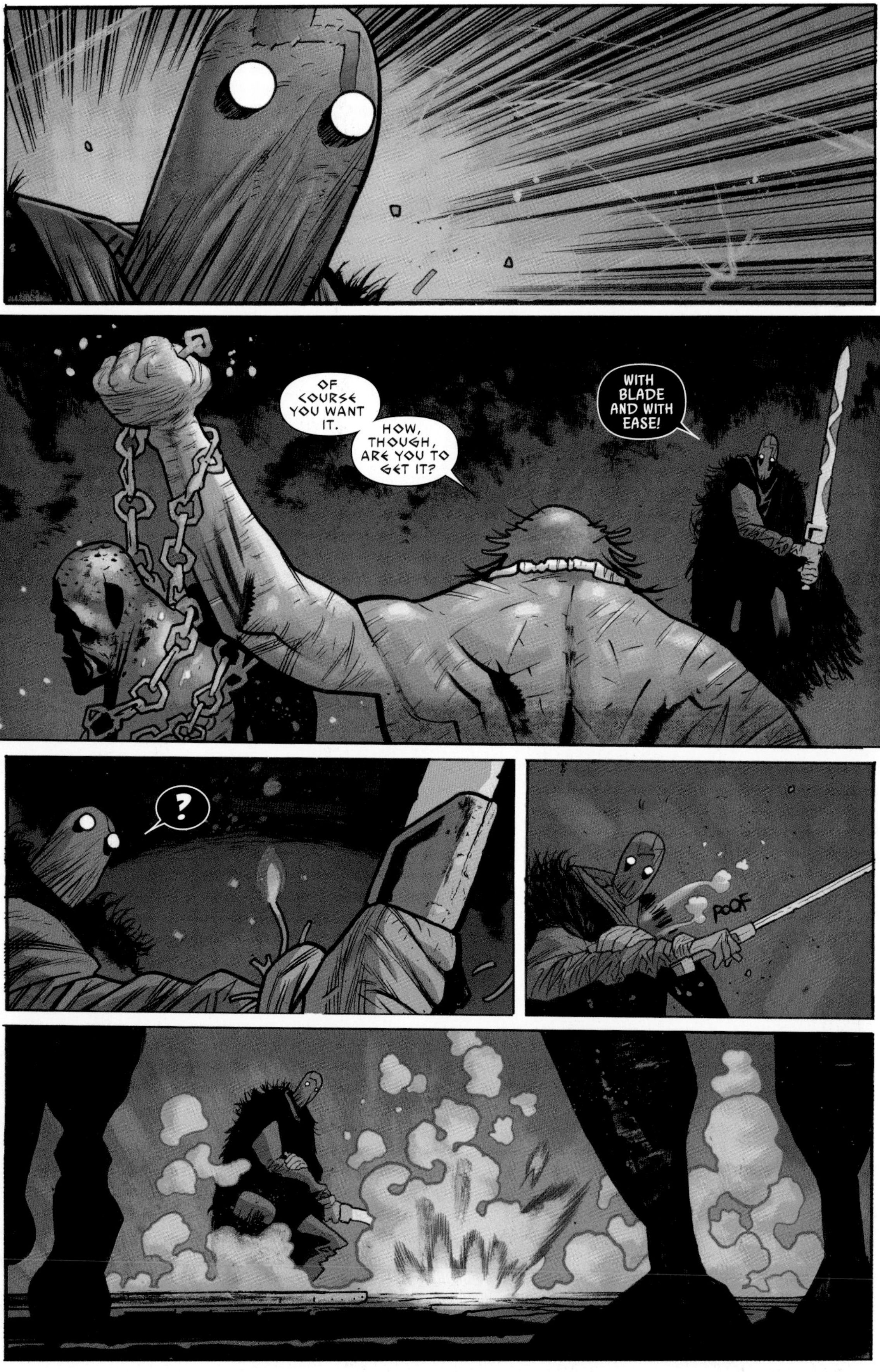

OF COURSE YOU WANT IT.
HOW, THOUGH, ARE YOU TO GET IT?
WITH BLADE AND WITH EASE!
?
POOF

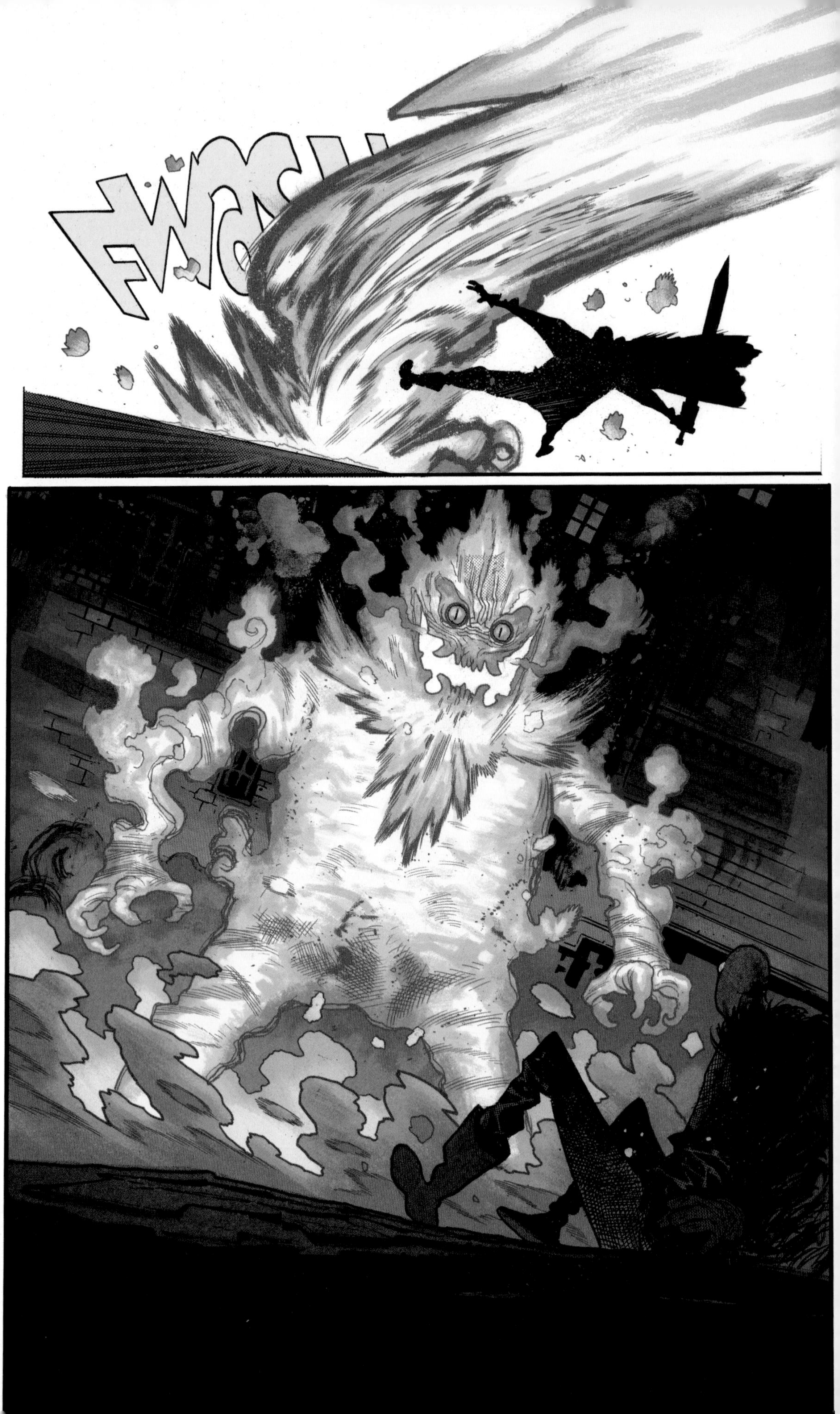
FWASH

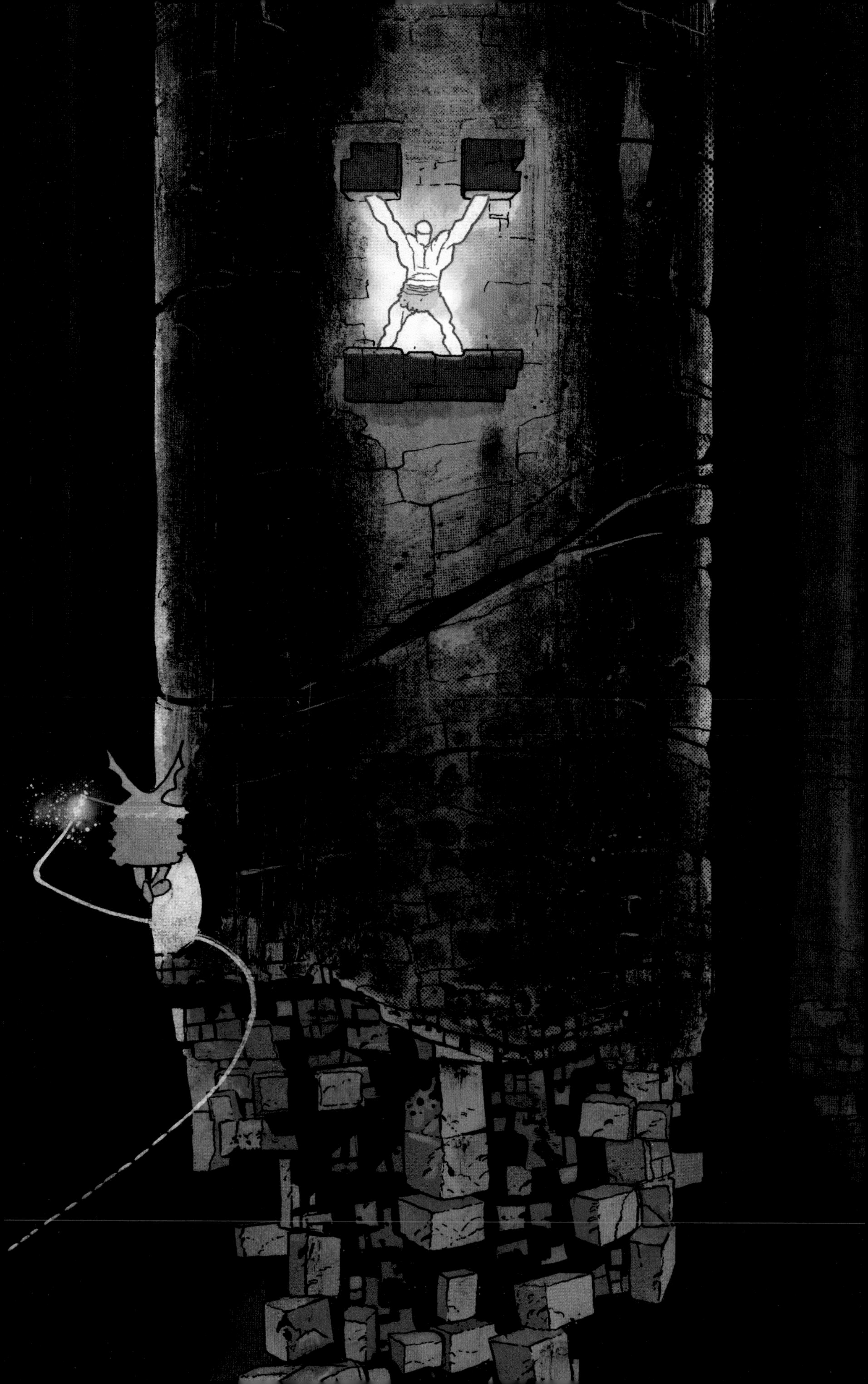

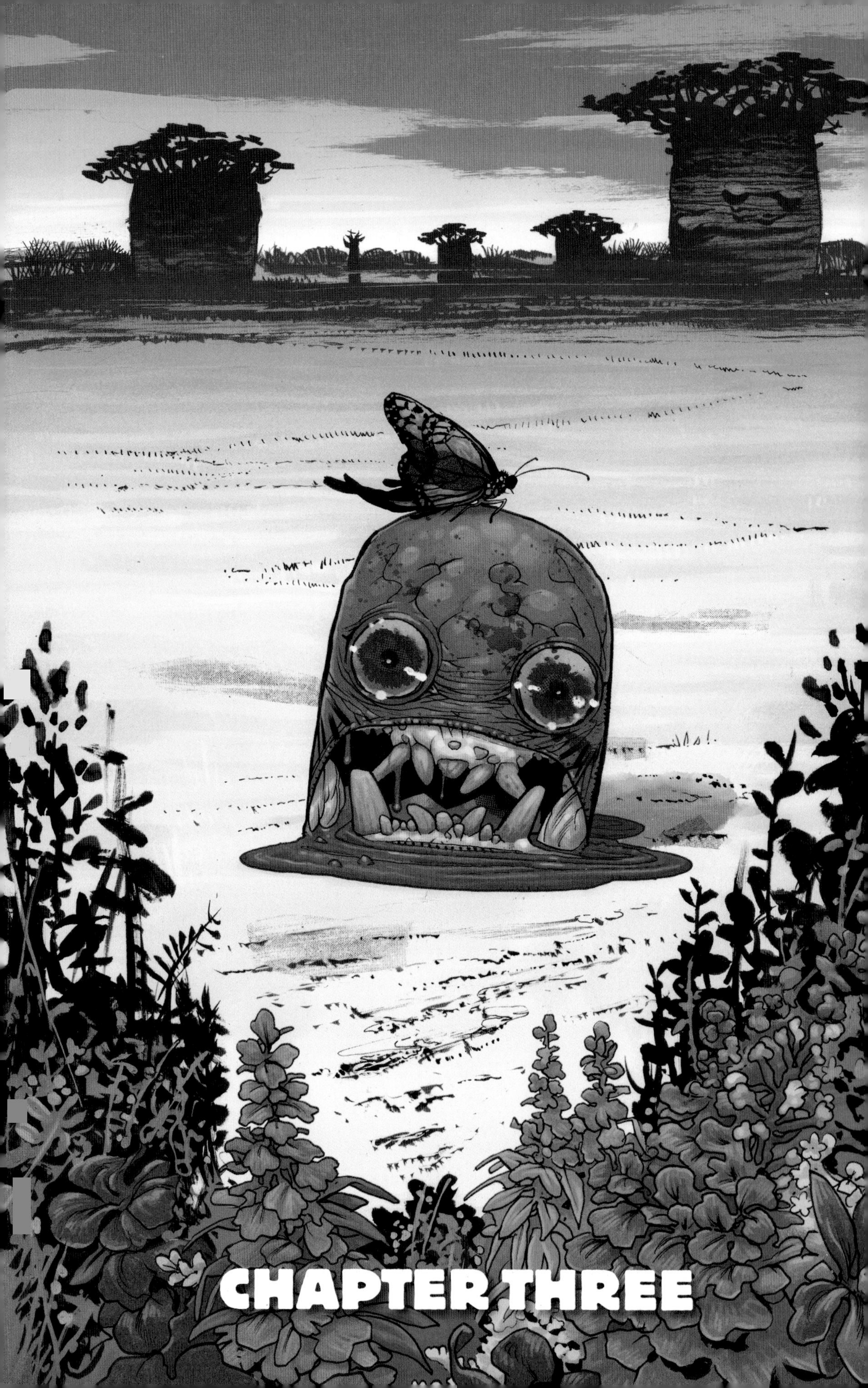
CHAPTER THREE

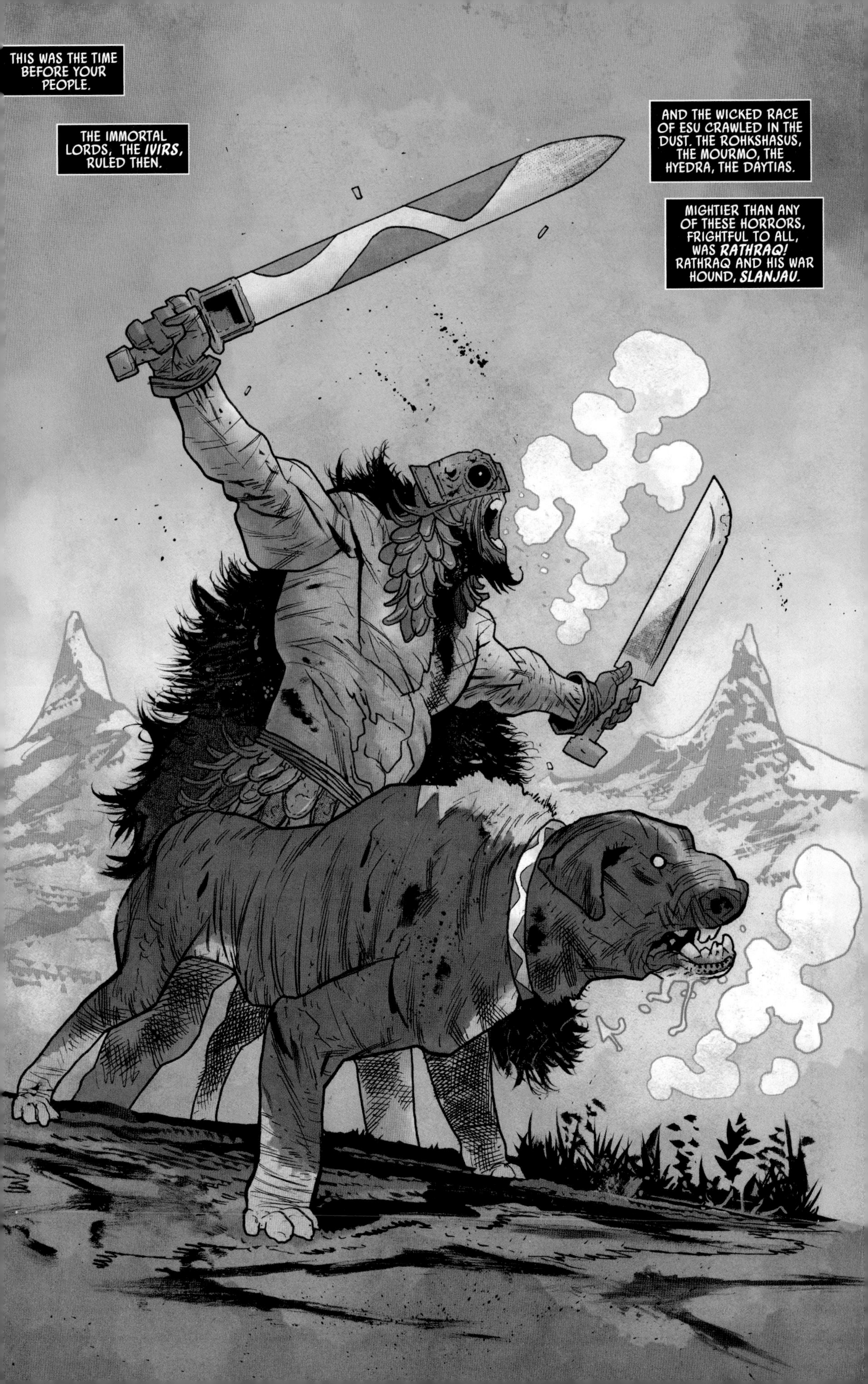
THIS WAS THE TIME BEFORE YOUR PEOPLE.
THE IMMORTAL LORDS, THE *IVIRS*, RULED THEN.
AND THE WICKED RACE OF ESU CRAWLED IN THE DUST. THE ROHKSHASUS, THE MOURMO, THE HYEDRA, THE DAYTIAS.
MIGHTIER THAN ANY OF THESE HORRORS, FRIGHTFUL TO ALL, WAS ***RATHRAQ!*** RATHRAQ AND HIS WAR HOUND, ***SLANJAU.***

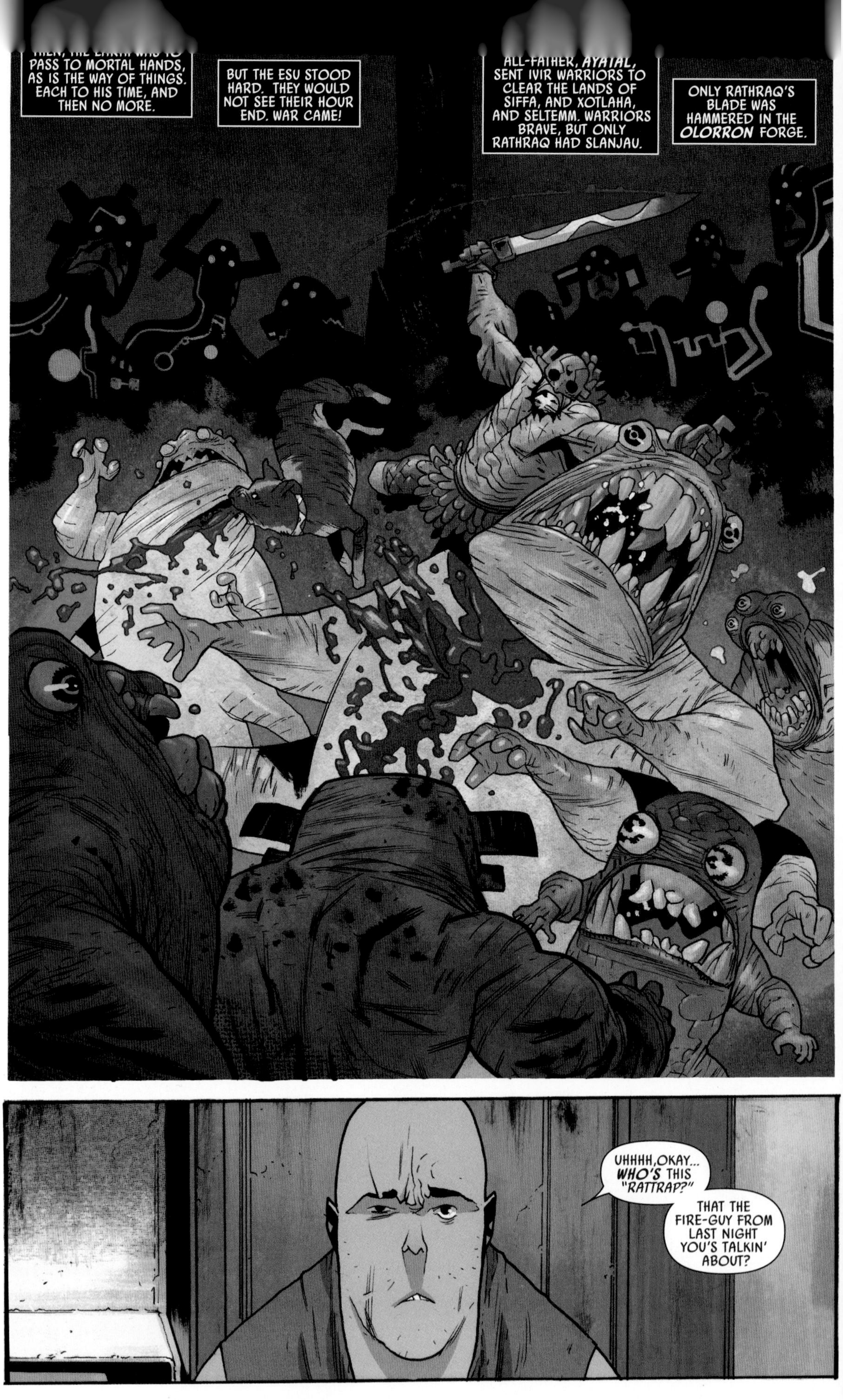

PASS TO MORTAL HANDS, AS IS THE WAY OF THINGS. EACH TO HIS TIME, AND THEN NO MORE.
BUT THE ESU STOOD HARD. THEY WOULD NOT SEE THEIR HOUR END. WAR CAME!
ALL-FATHER, *AYATAL*, SENT IVIR WARRIORS TO CLEAR THE LANDS OF SIFFA, AND XOTLAHA, AND SELTEMM. WARRIORS BRAVE, BUT ONLY RATHRAQ HAD SLANJAU.
ONLY RATHRAQ'S BLADE WAS HAMMERED IN THE *OLORRON* FORGE.
UHHHH,OKAY... *WHO'S* THIS *"RATTRAP?"*
THAT THE FIRE-GUY FROM LAST NIGHT YOU'S TALKIN' ABOUT?

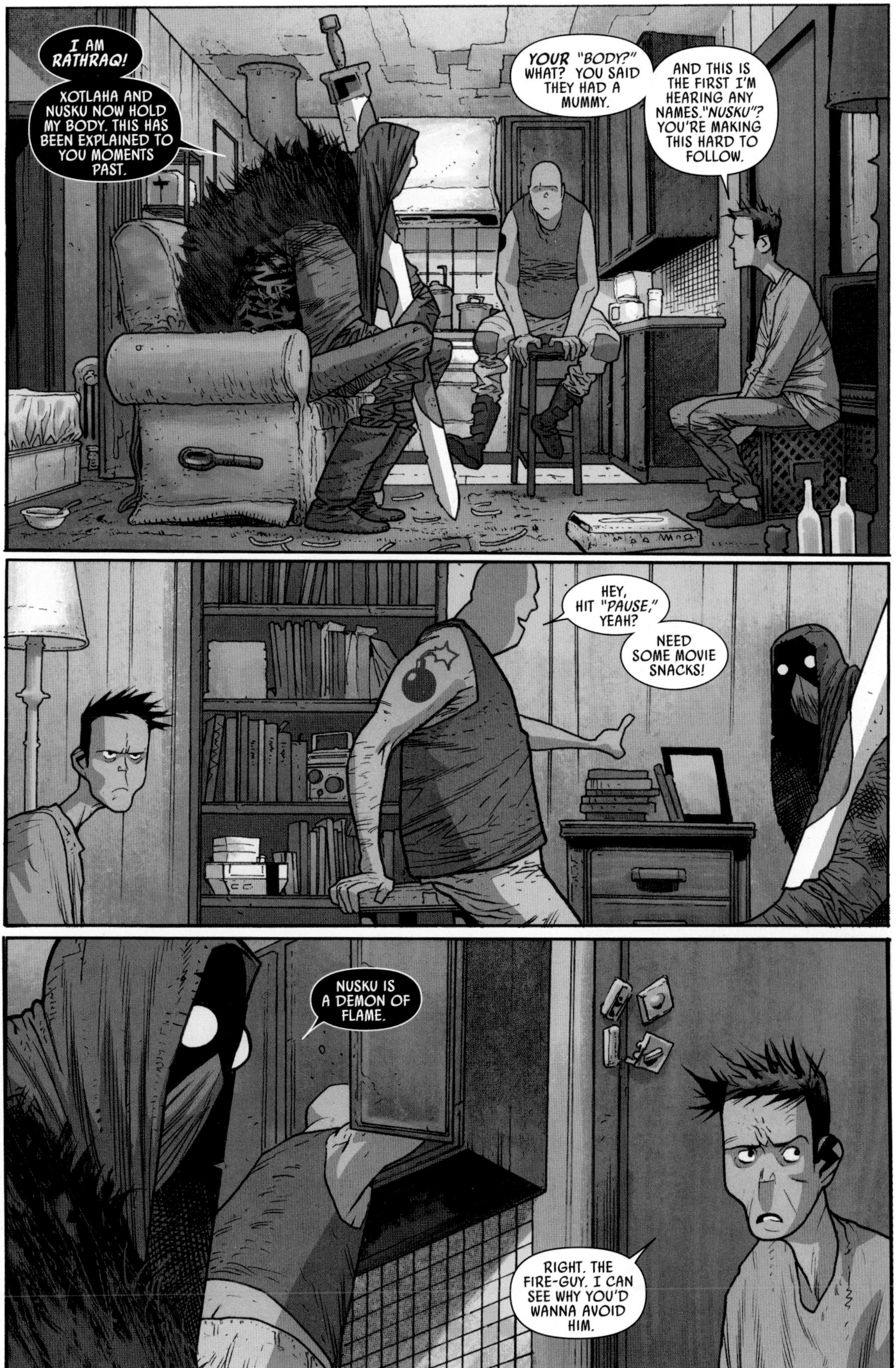
I AM RATHRAQ!
XOTLAHA AND NUSKU NOW HOLD MY BODY. THIS HAS BEEN EXPLAINED TO YOU MOMENTS PAST.
YOUR "BODY?" WHAT? YOU SAID THEY HAD A MUMMY.
AND THIS IS THE FIRST I'M HEARING ANY NAMES. "NUSKU"? YOU'RE MAKING THIS HARD TO FOLLOW.
HEY, HIT "PAUSE," YEAH?
NEED SOME MOVIE SNACKS!
NUSKU IS A DEMON OF FLAME.
RIGHT. THE FIRE-GUY. I CAN SEE WHY YOU'D WANNA AVOID HIM.

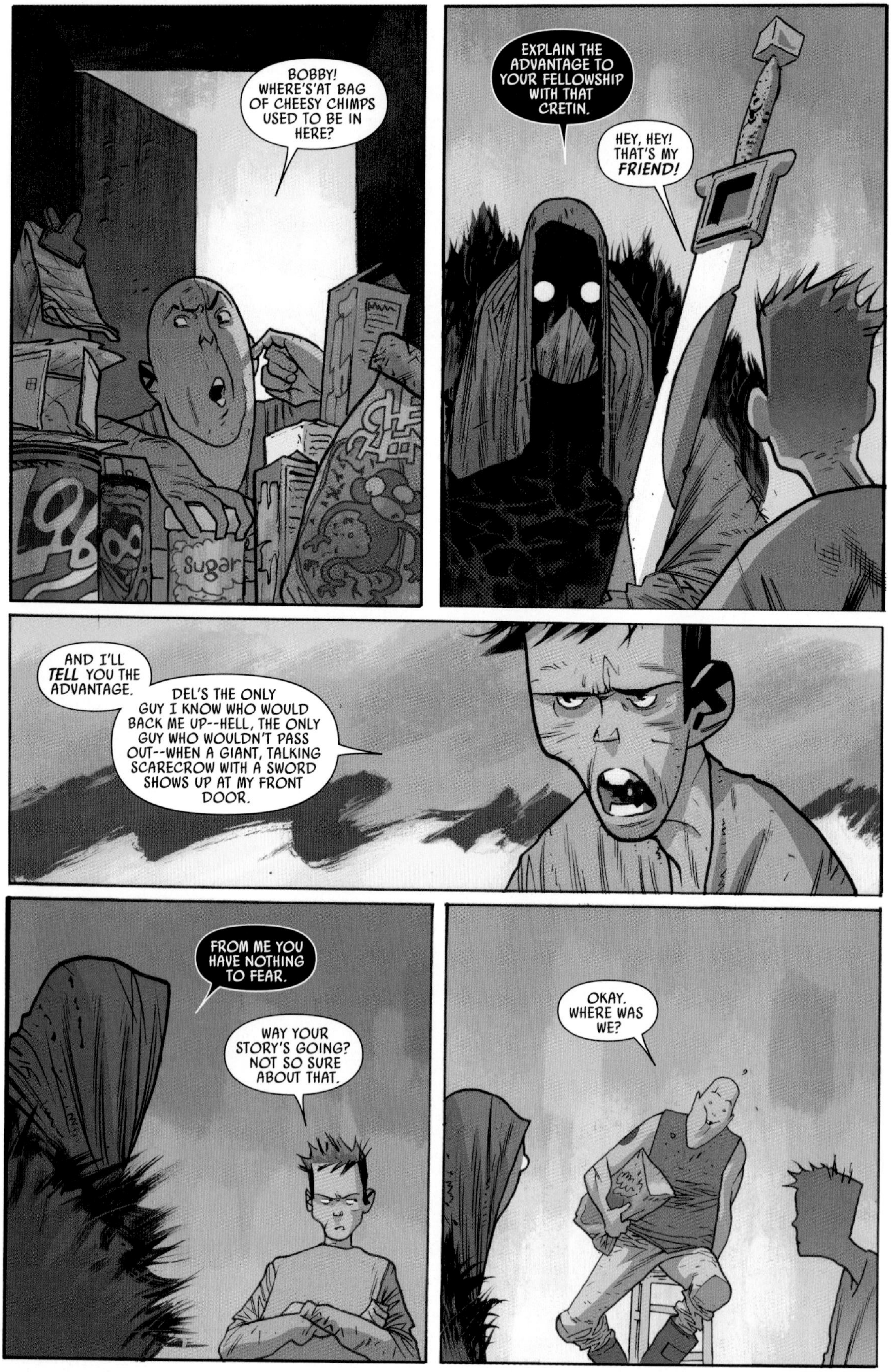
BOBBY! WHERE'S'AT BAG OF CHEESY CHIMPS USED TO BE IN HERE?
Sugar
EXPLAIN THE ADVANTAGE TO YOUR FELLOWSHIP WITH THAT CRETIN.
HEY, HEY! THAT'S MY FRIEND!
AND I'LL TELL YOU THE ADVANTAGE.
DEL'S THE ONLY GUY I KNOW WHO WOULD BACK ME UP--HELL, THE ONLY GUY WHO WOULDN'T PASS OUT--WHEN A GIANT, TALKING SCARECROW WITH A SWORD SHOWS UP AT MY FRONT DOOR.
FROM ME YOU HAVE NOTHING TO FEAR.
WAY YOUR STORY'S GOING? NOT SO SURE ABOUT THAT.
OKAY. WHERE WAS WE?

IN THE FACE OF MASSIVE LOSSES, ESU SOVEREIGN *XOTLAHA* CRIED OUT FOR A TRUCE TO BROKER TERMS OF SURRENDER.

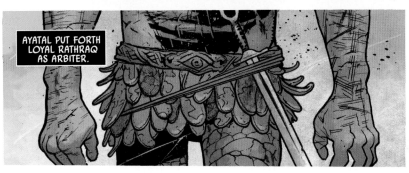

AYATAL PUT FORTH LOYAL RATHRAQ AS ARBITER.

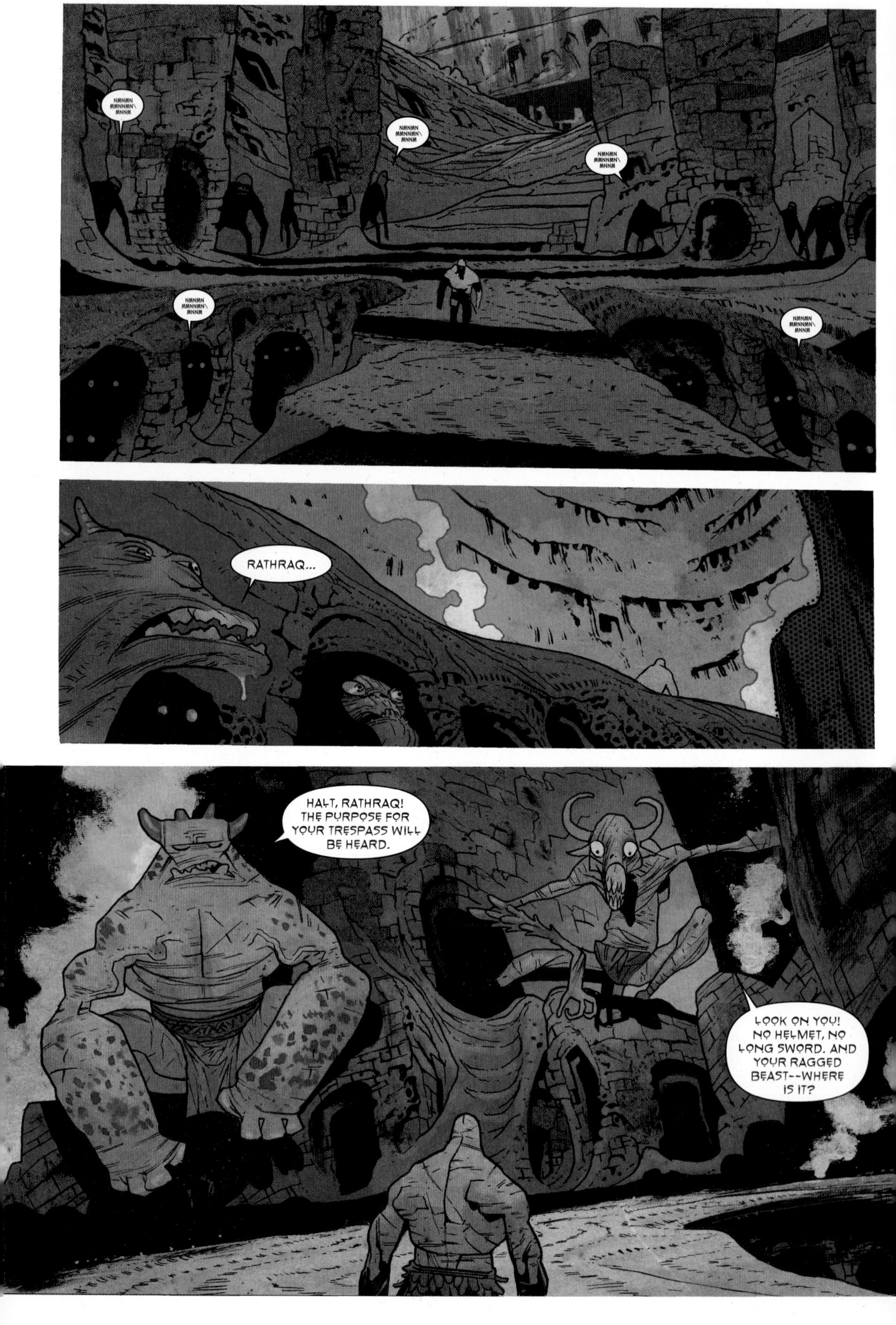
NMNMN MMNNMN\ MNNM
NMNMN MMNNMN\ MNNM
NMNMN MMNNMN\ MNNM
NMNMN MMNNMN\ MNNM
NMNMN MMNNMN\ MNNM
RATHRAQ...
HALT, RATHRAQ! THE PURPOSE FOR YOUR TRESPASS WILL BE HEARD.
LOOK ON YOU! NO HELMET, NO LONG SWORD. AND YOUR RAGGED BEAST--WHERE IS IT?

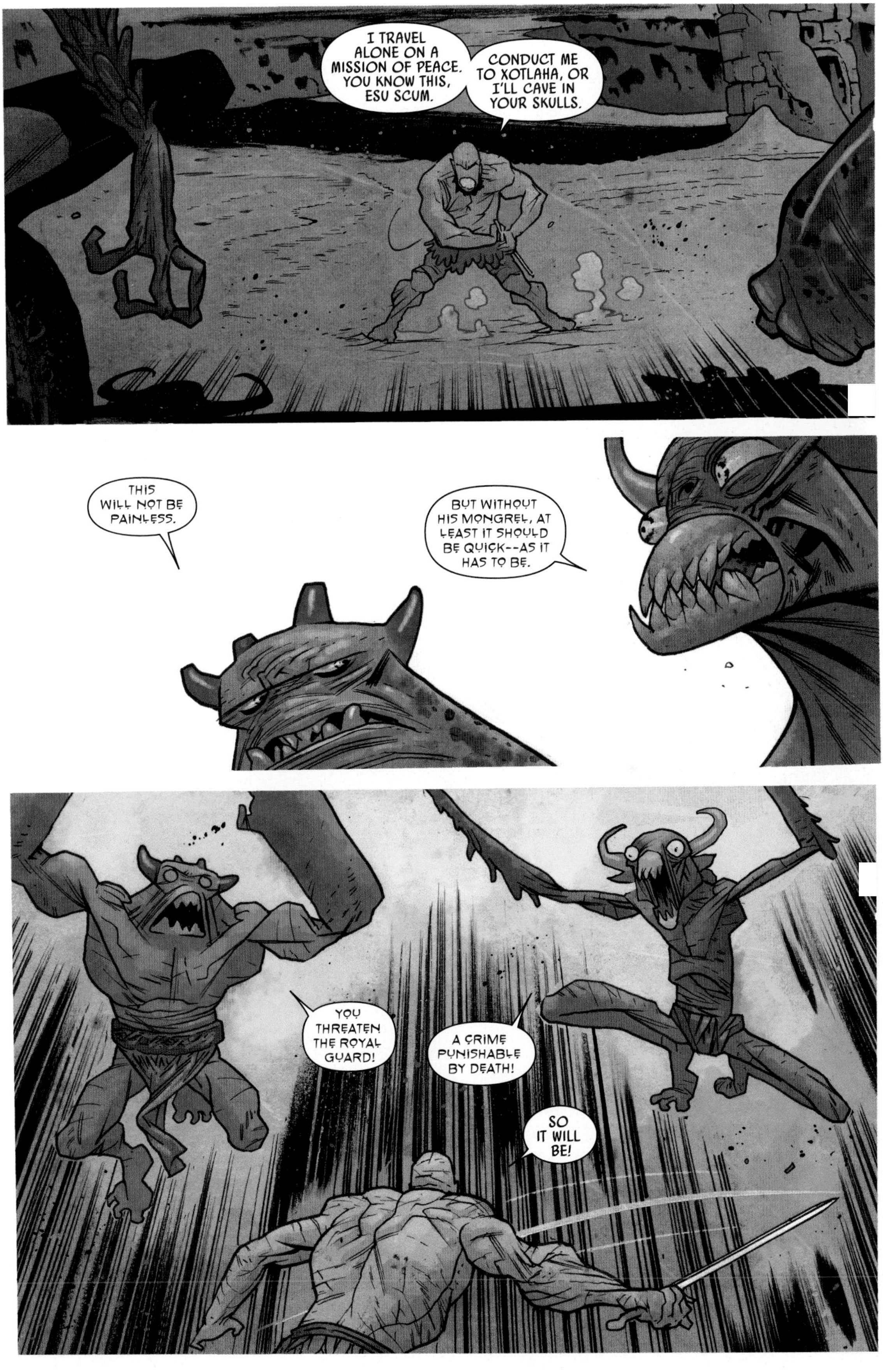
I TRAVEL ALONE ON A MISSION OF PEACE. YOU KNOW THIS, ESU SCUM.
CONDUCT ME TO XOTLAHA, OR I'LL CAVE IN YOUR SKULLS.
THIS WILL NOT BE PAINLESS.
BUT WITHOUT HIS MONGREL, AT LEAST IT SHOULD BE QUICK--AS IT HAS TO BE.
YOU THREATEN THE ROYAL GUARD!
A CRIME PUNISHABLE BY DEATH!
SO IT WILL BE!

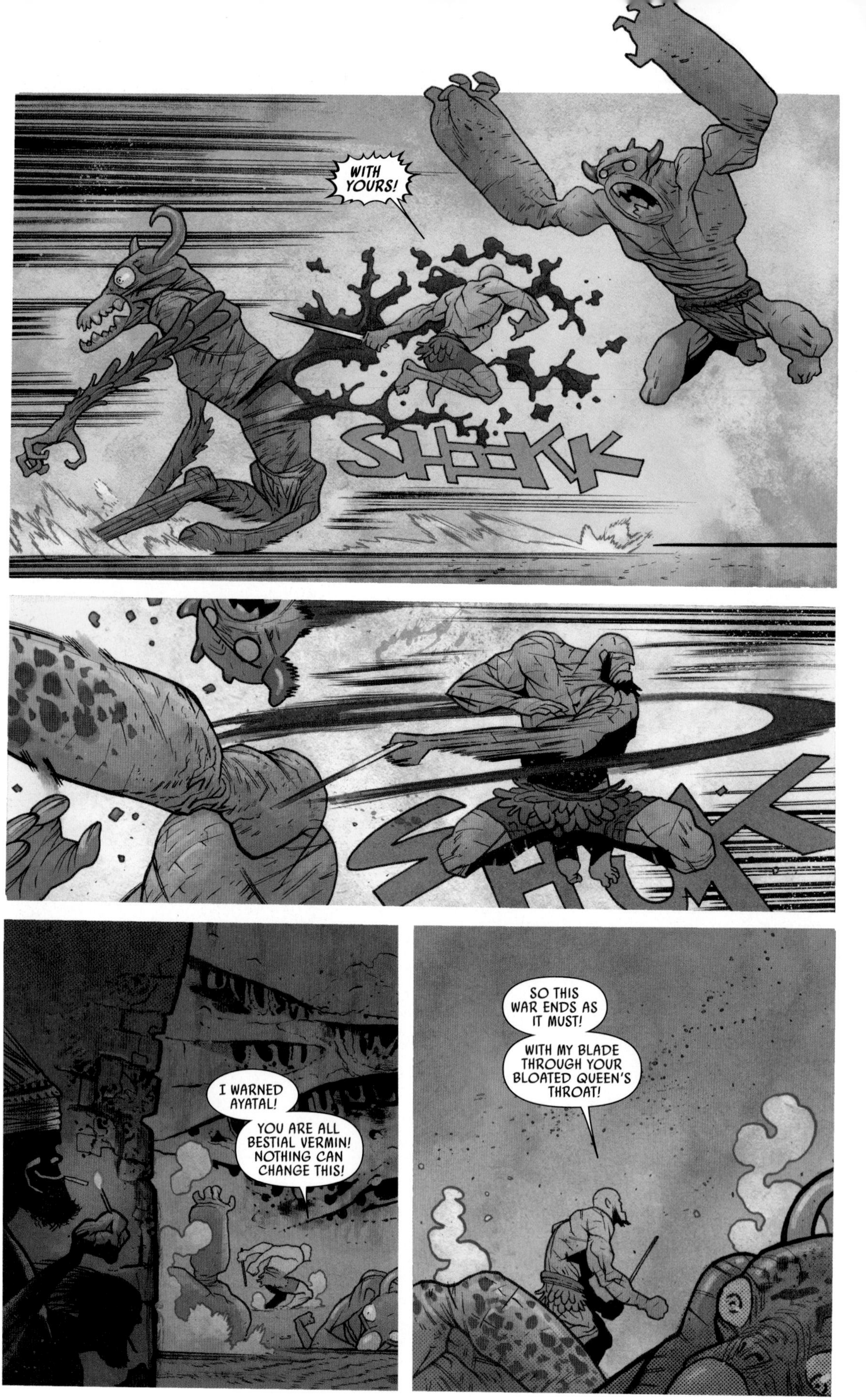
WITH YOURS!
SHEKK
SHOK
I WARNED AYATAL!
YOU ARE ALL BESTIAL VERMIN! NOTHING CAN CHANGE THIS!
SO THIS WAR ENDS AS IT MUST!
WITH MY BLADE THROUGH YOUR BLOATED QUEEN'S THROAT!

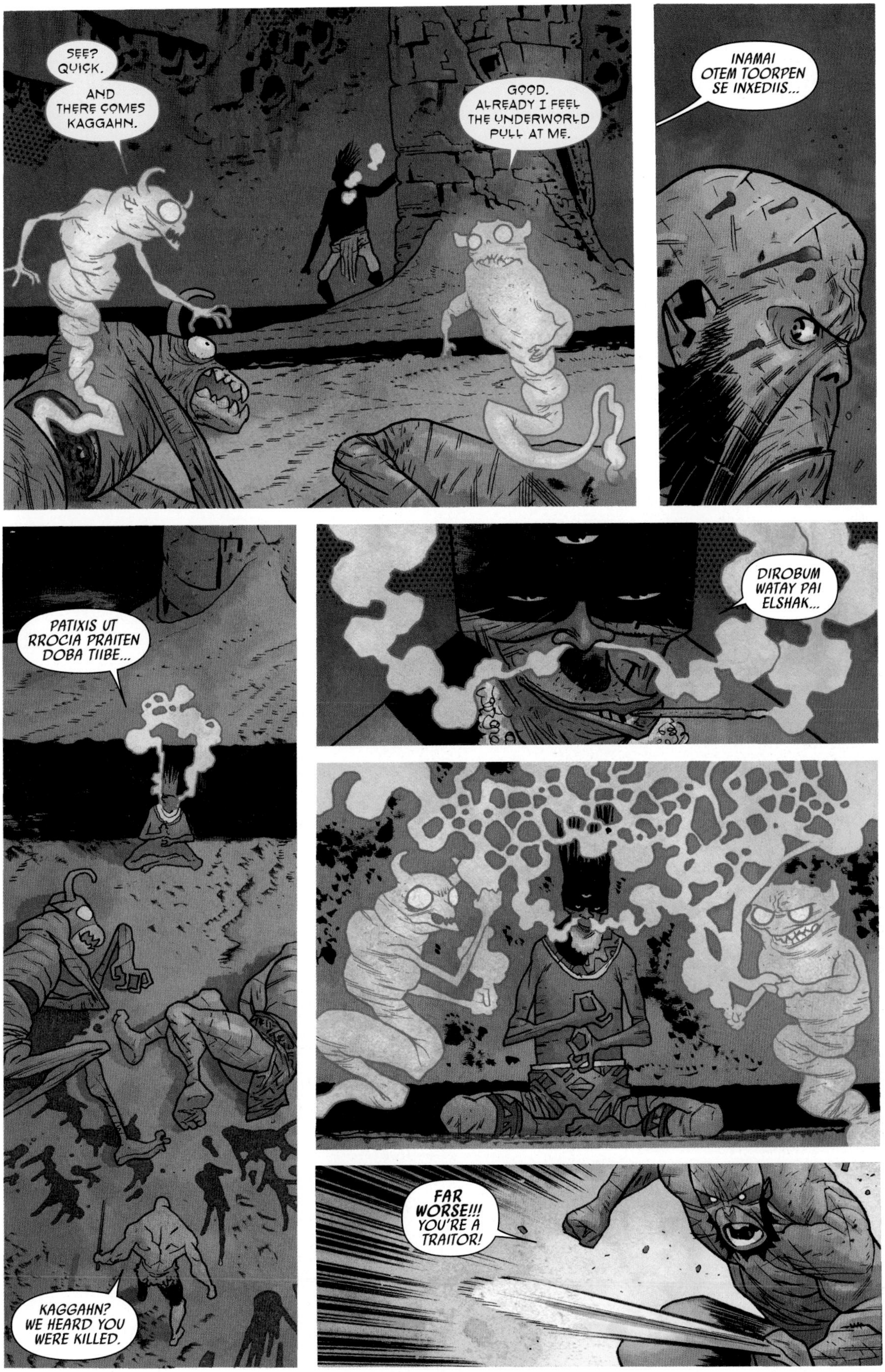
SEE? QUICK.
AND THERE COMES KAGGAHN.
GOOD. ALREADY I FEEL THE UNDERWORLD PULL AT ME.
INAMAI OTEM TOORPEN SE INXEDIIS...
PATIXIS UT RROCIA PRAITEN DOBA TIIBE...
DIROBUM WATAY PAI ELSHAK...
KAGGAHN? WE HEARD YOU WERE KILLED.
FAR WORSE!!! YOU'RE A TRAITOR!

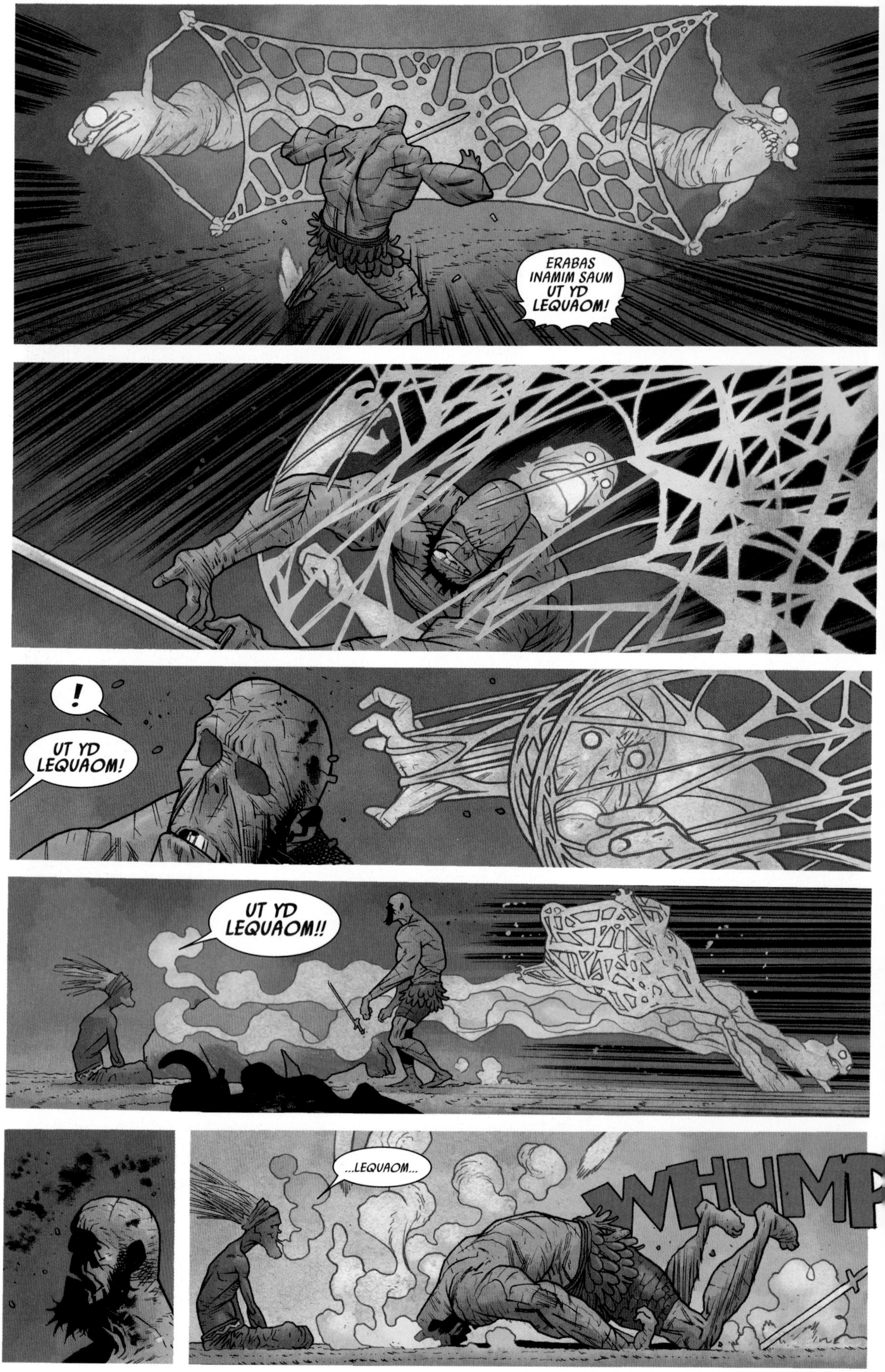
ERABAS INAMIM SAUM UT YD LEQUAOM!
!
UT YD LEQUAOM!
UT YD LEQUAOM!!
...LEQUAOM...
WHUMP

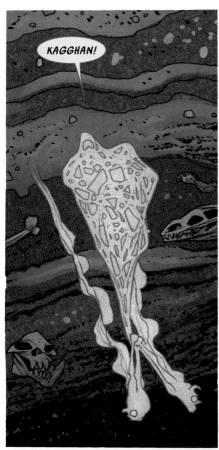

KAGGHAN!

WHAT BEFALLS ME?!! WHAT HAVE YOU DONE?!

KAGGHAAAAAN!

A SOUL NET! TRICKSTER, YOU ARE ALL SURPRISES!

A RETURN TO THE IVIRS FOR YOU NOW IS IMPOSSIBLE!

I LIKE IT HERE, XOTLAHA. I LIKE IT FULLY.

"KAGGHAN..." THAT OL' RUMMY ALWAYS HANGIN' AROUND THE BAR, HE'S GOT A NAME LIKE THAT.

...YYYYYEAH.

TREACHEROUSLY ACCOMPLISHED, MY SOUL WAS THEIR PRISONER.

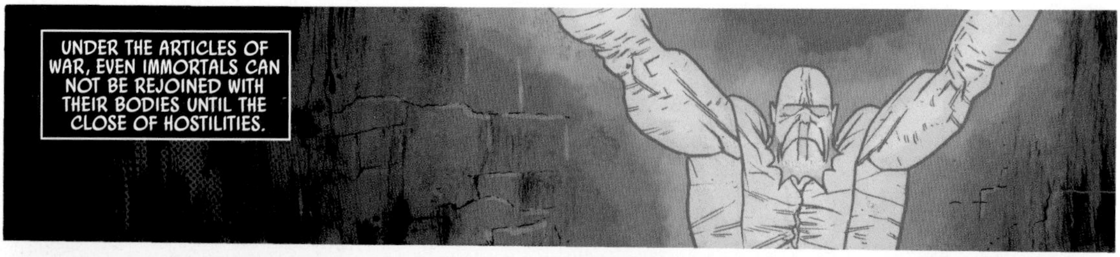
UNDER THE ARTICLES OF WAR, EVEN IMMORTALS CAN NOT BE REJOINED WITH THEIR BODIES UNTIL THE CLOSE OF HOSTILITIES.

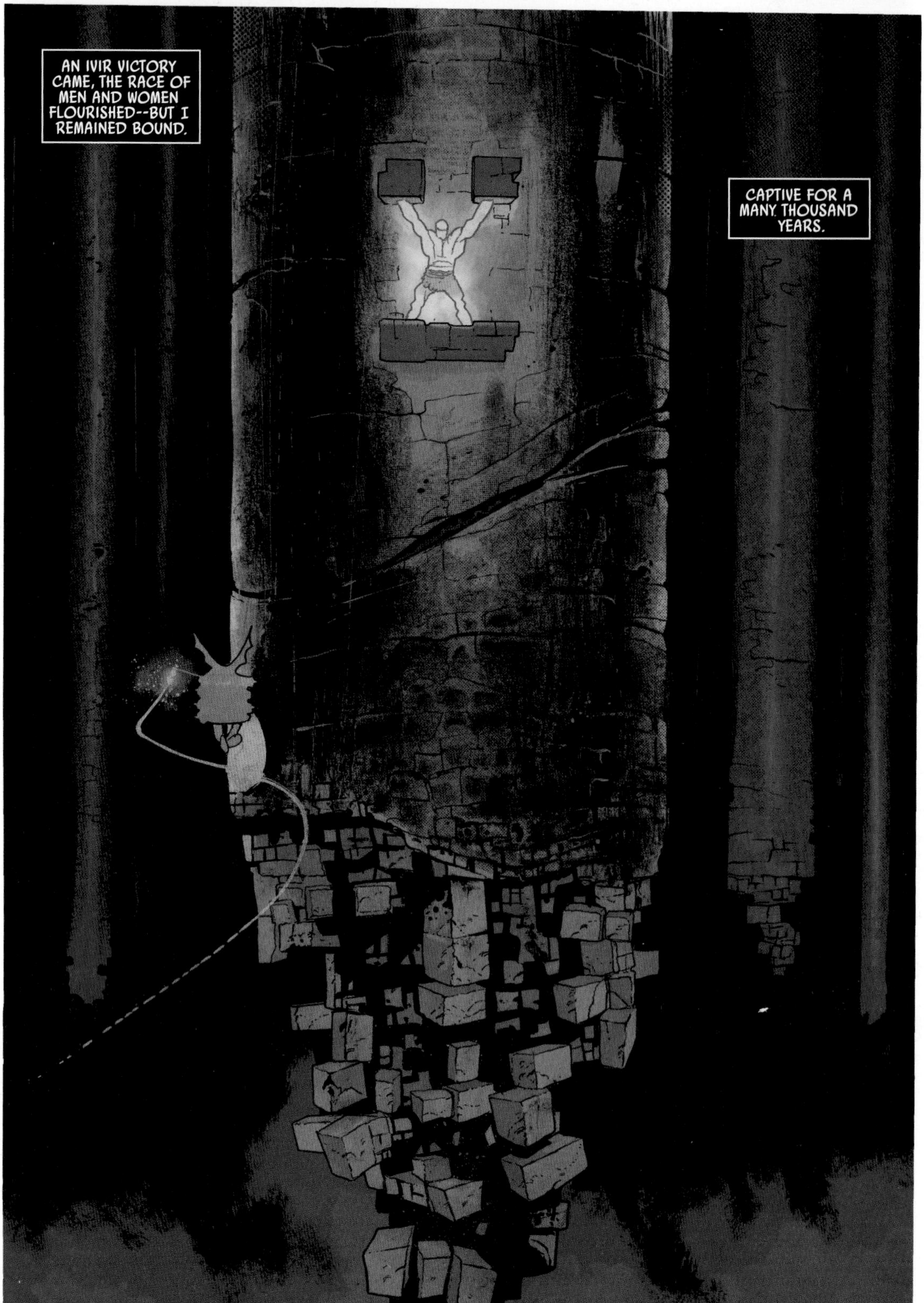
AN IVIR VICTORY CAME, THE RACE OF MEN AND WOMEN FLOURISHED--BUT I REMAINED BOUND.
CAPTIVE FOR A MANY THOUSAND YEARS.

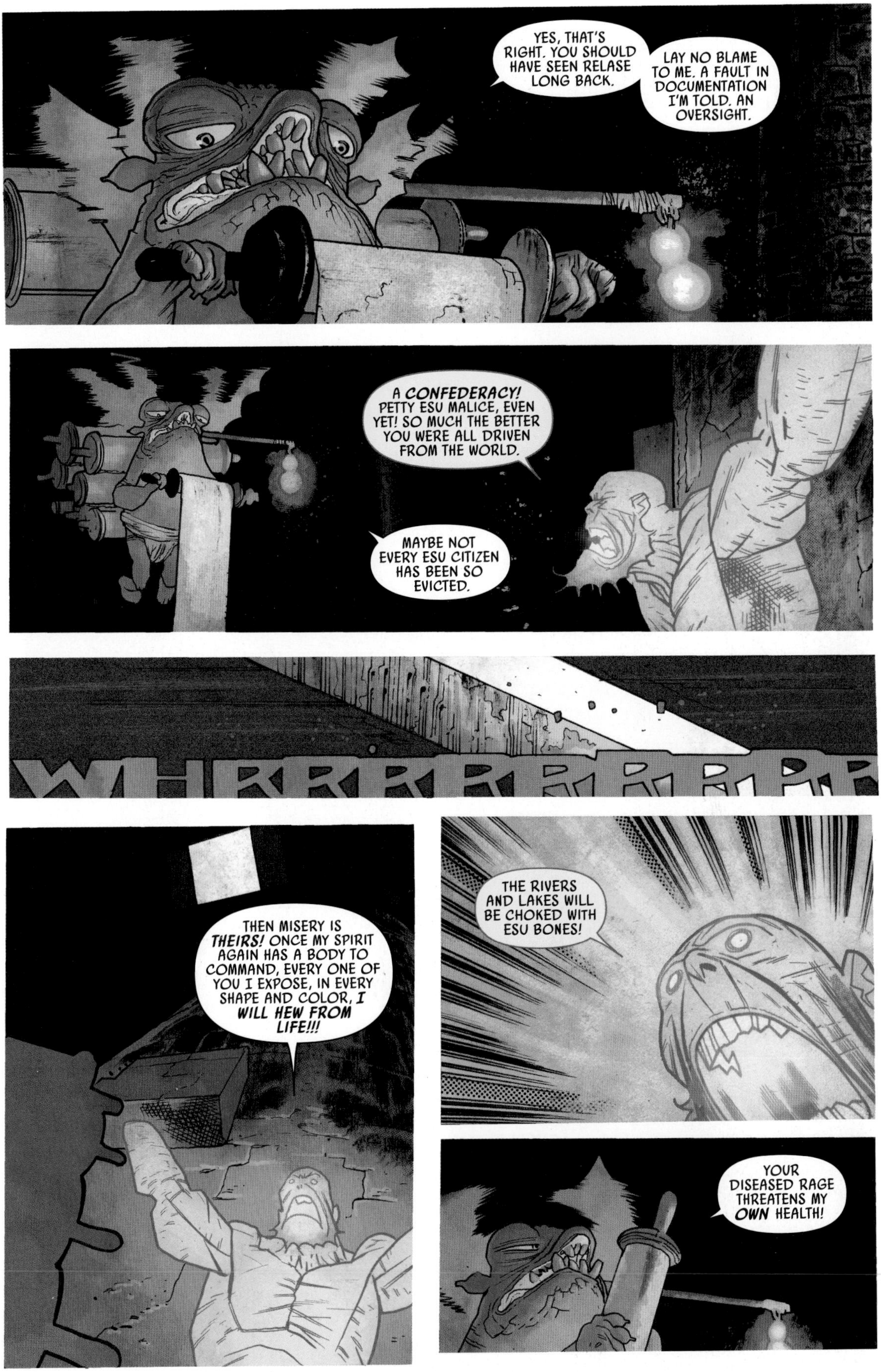
YES, THAT'S RIGHT. YOU SHOULD HAVE SEEN RELASE LONG BACK.
LAY NO BLAME TO ME. A FAULT IN DOCUMENTATION I'M TOLD. AN OVERSIGHT.
A *CONFEDERACY!* PETTY ESU MALICE, EVEN YET! SO MUCH THE BETTER YOU WERE ALL DRIVEN FROM THE WORLD.
MAYBE NOT EVERY ESU CITIZEN HAS BEEN SO EVICTED.
WHRRRRRRRRRR
THEN MISERY IS *THEIRS!* ONCE MY SPIRIT AGAIN HAS A BODY TO COMMAND, EVERY ONE OF YOU I EXPOSE, IN EVERY SHAPE AND COLOR, ***I WILL HEW FROM LIFE!!!***
THE RIVERS AND LAKES WILL BE CHOKED WITH ESU BONES!
YOUR DISEASED RAGE THREATENS MY ***OWN*** HEALTH!

YOUR MANDATED FREEDOM AWAITS.

?!?
...

"WHAT YOU ASK IS YOURS."

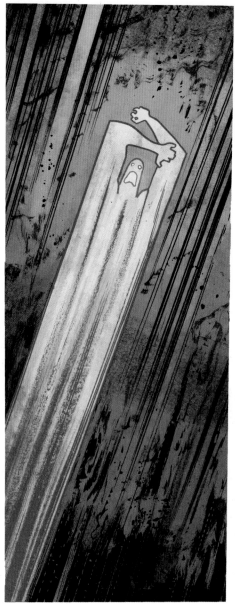

"A BODY TO COMMAND."

YAAAAAAAAAAAH!!

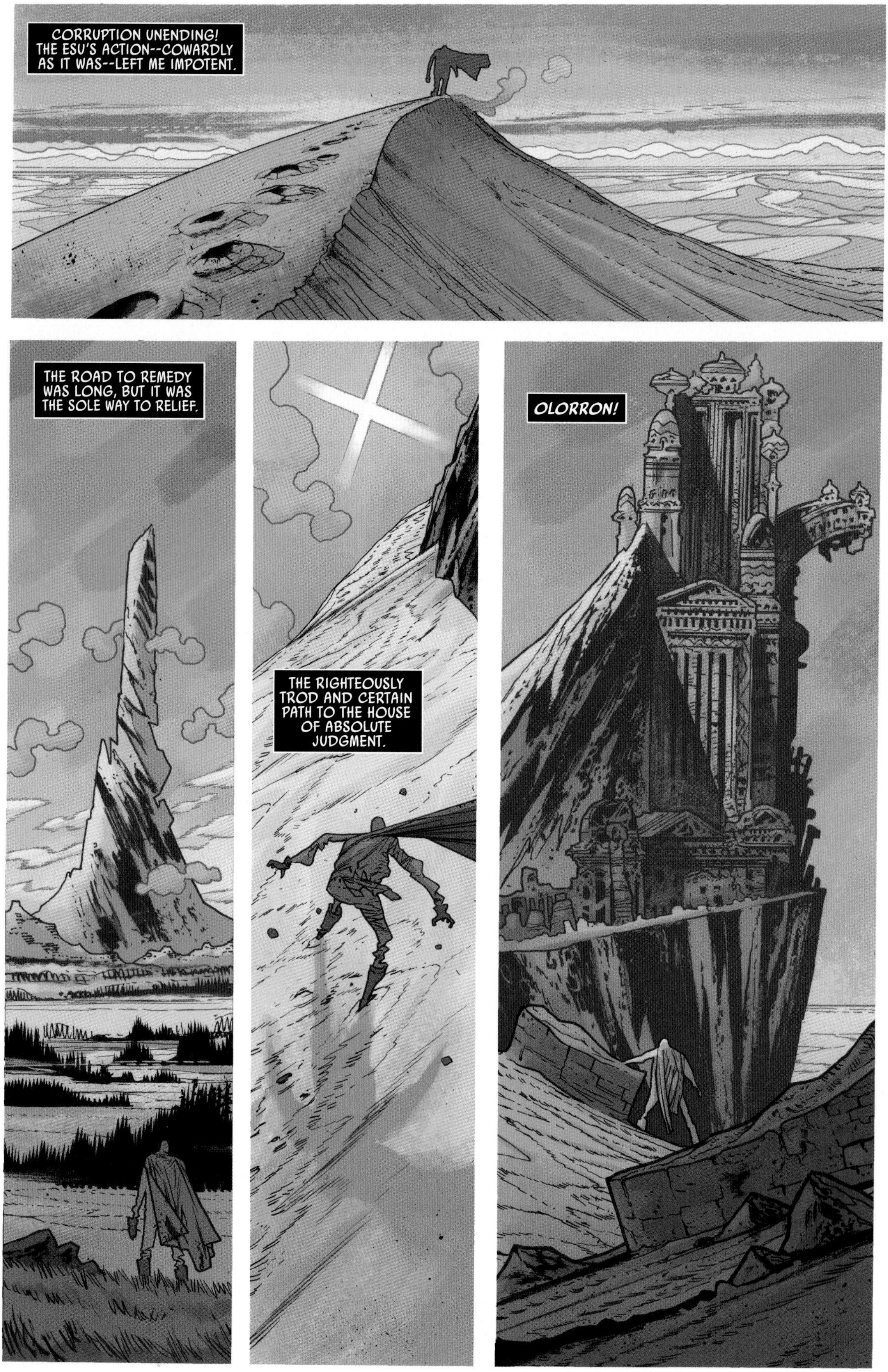
CORRUPTION UNENDING! THE ESU'S ACTION--COWARDLY AS IT WAS--LEFT ME IMPOTENT.
THE ROAD TO REMEDY WAS LONG, BUT IT WAS THE SOLE WAY TO RELIEF.
THE RIGHTEOUSLY TROD AND CERTAIN PATH TO THE HOUSE OF ABSOLUTE JUDGMENT.
OLORRON!

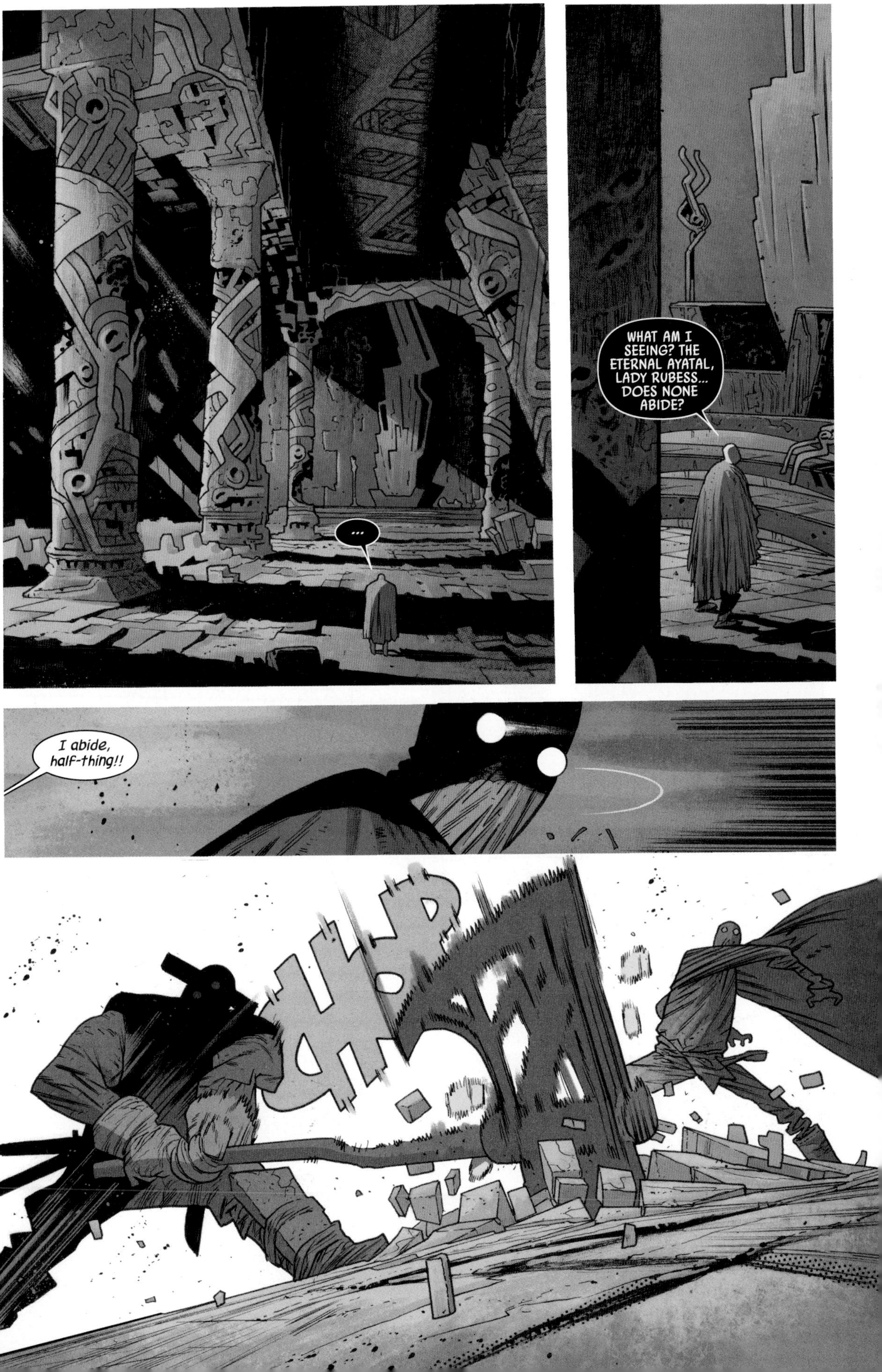
...
WHAT AM I SEEING? THE ETERNAL AYATAL, LADY RUBESS... DOES NONE ABIDE?
I abide, half-thing!!

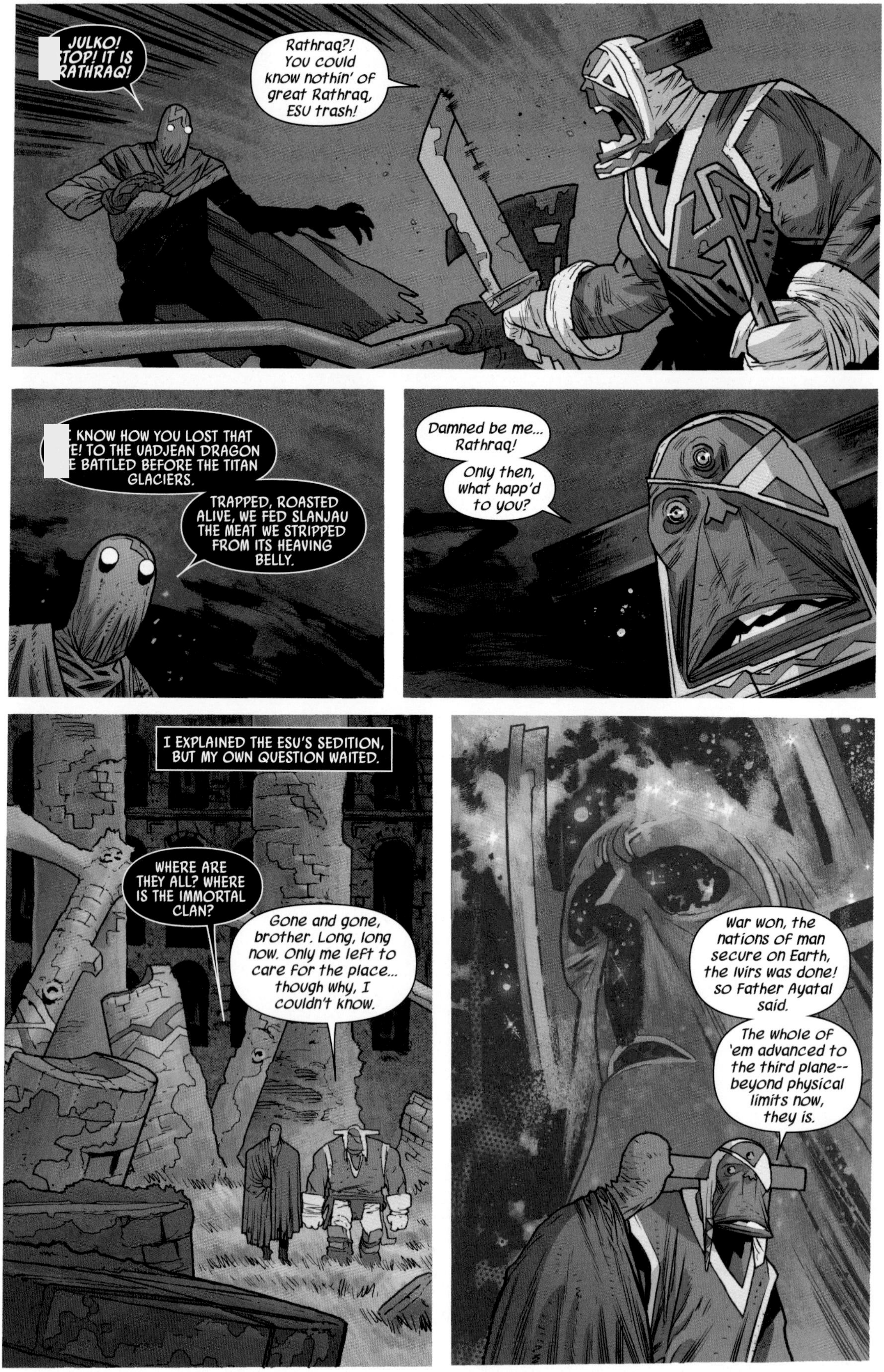
JULKO!
TOP! IT IS
ATHRAQ!
Rathraq?! You could know nothin' of great Rathraq, ESU trash!
KNOW HOW YOU LOST THAT
E! TO THE UADJEAN DRAGON
E BATTLED BEFORE THE TITAN
GLACIERS.
TRAPPED, ROASTED ALIVE, WE FED SLANJAU THE MEAT WE STRIPPED FROM ITS HEAVING BELLY.
Damned be me... Rathraq!
Only then, what happ'd to you?
I EXPLAINED THE ESU'S SEDITION, BUT MY OWN QUESTION WAITED.
WHERE ARE THEY ALL? WHERE IS THE IMMORTAL CLAN?
Gone and gone, brother. Long, long now. Only me left to care for the place... though why, I couldn't know.
War won, the nations of man secure on Earth, the Ivirs was done! so Father Ayatal said.
The whole of 'em advanced to the third plane-- beyond physical limits now, they is.

BUT I AM NOT!!

MY SERVICE FOR MILLENIA, AND THEY *FORGET* ME?! LEAVE ME WEAK, FRAIL, WITHOUT EVEN A WEAPON?!

Ah now, ol' Julko might be a little use there, brother.

Aye, and *he's* here, too.

Never left. couldn't chase him off.

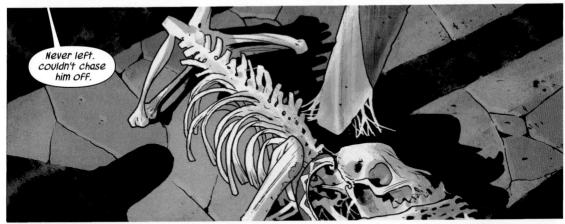

SLANJAU... FAITHFUL ONE.

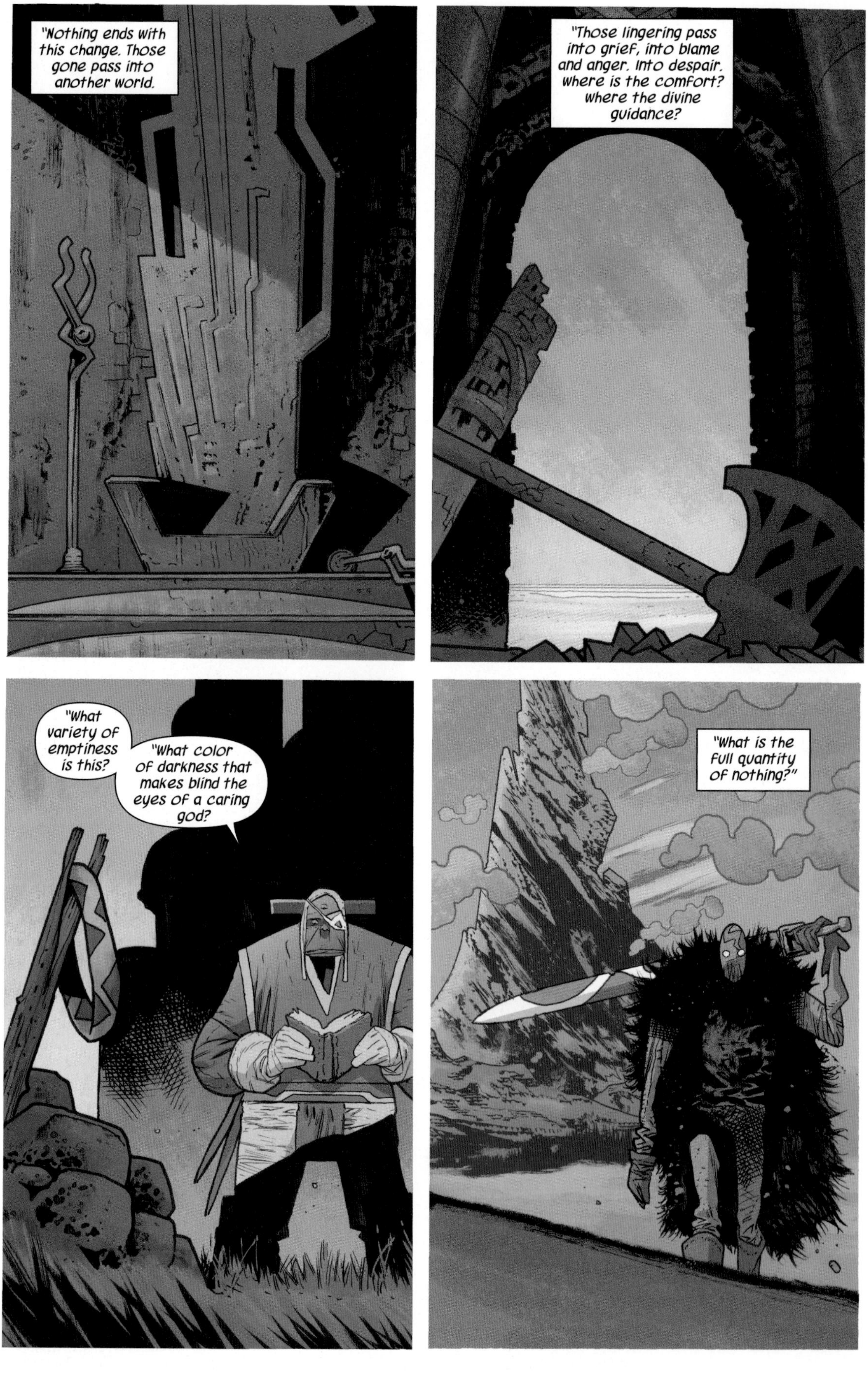
"Nothing ends with this change. Those gone pass into another world.
"Those lingering pass into grief, into blame and anger. Into despair. Where is the comfort? Where the divine guidance?
"What variety of emptiness is this?
"What color of darkness that makes blind the eyes of a caring god?
"What is the full quantity of nothing?"

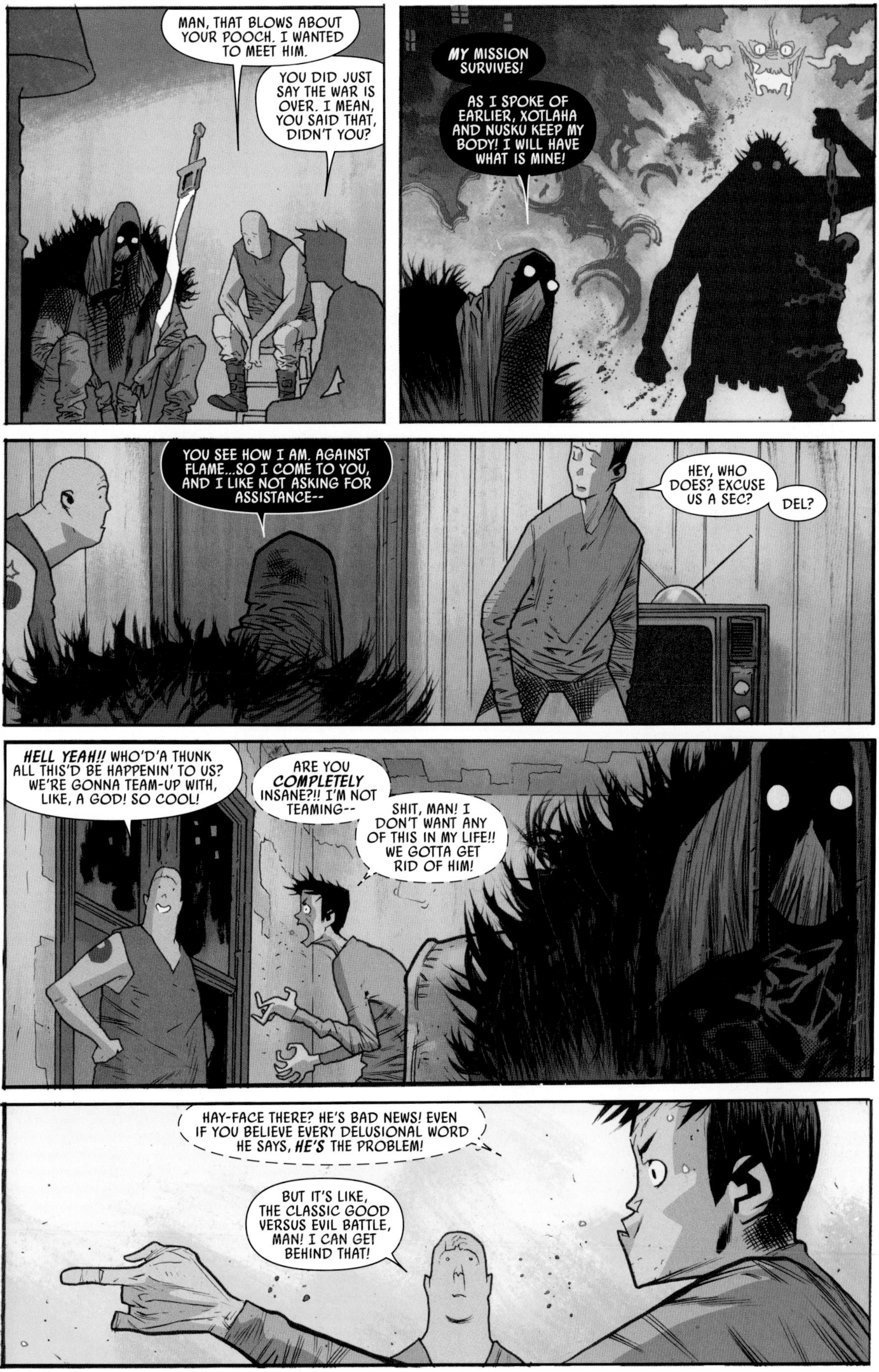
MAN, THAT BLOWS ABOUT YOUR POOCH. I WANTED TO MEET HIM.
YOU DID JUST SAY THE WAR IS OVER. I MEAN, YOU SAID THAT, DIDN'T YOU?
MY MISSION SURVIVES!
AS I SPOKE OF EARLIER, XOTLAHA AND NUSKU KEEP MY BODY! I WILL HAVE WHAT IS MINE!
YOU SEE HOW I AM. AGAINST FLAME...SO I COME TO YOU, AND I LIKE NOT ASKING FOR ASSISTANCE--
HEY, WHO DOES? EXCUSE US A SEC?
DEL?
HELL YEAH!! WHO'D'A THUNK ALL THIS'D BE HAPPENIN' TO US? WE'RE GONNA TEAM-UP WITH, LIKE, A GOD! SO COOL!
ARE YOU *COMPLETELY* INSANE?!! I'M NOT TEAMING--
SHIT, MAN! I DON'T WANT ANY OF THIS IN MY LIFE!! WE GOTTA GET RID OF HIM!
HAY-FACE THERE? HE'S BAD NEWS! EVEN IF YOU BELIEVE EVERY DELUSIONAL WORD HE SAYS, *HE'S* THE PROBLEM!
BUT IT'S LIKE, THE CLASSIC GOOD VERSUS EVIL BATTLE, MAN! I CAN GET BEHIND THAT!

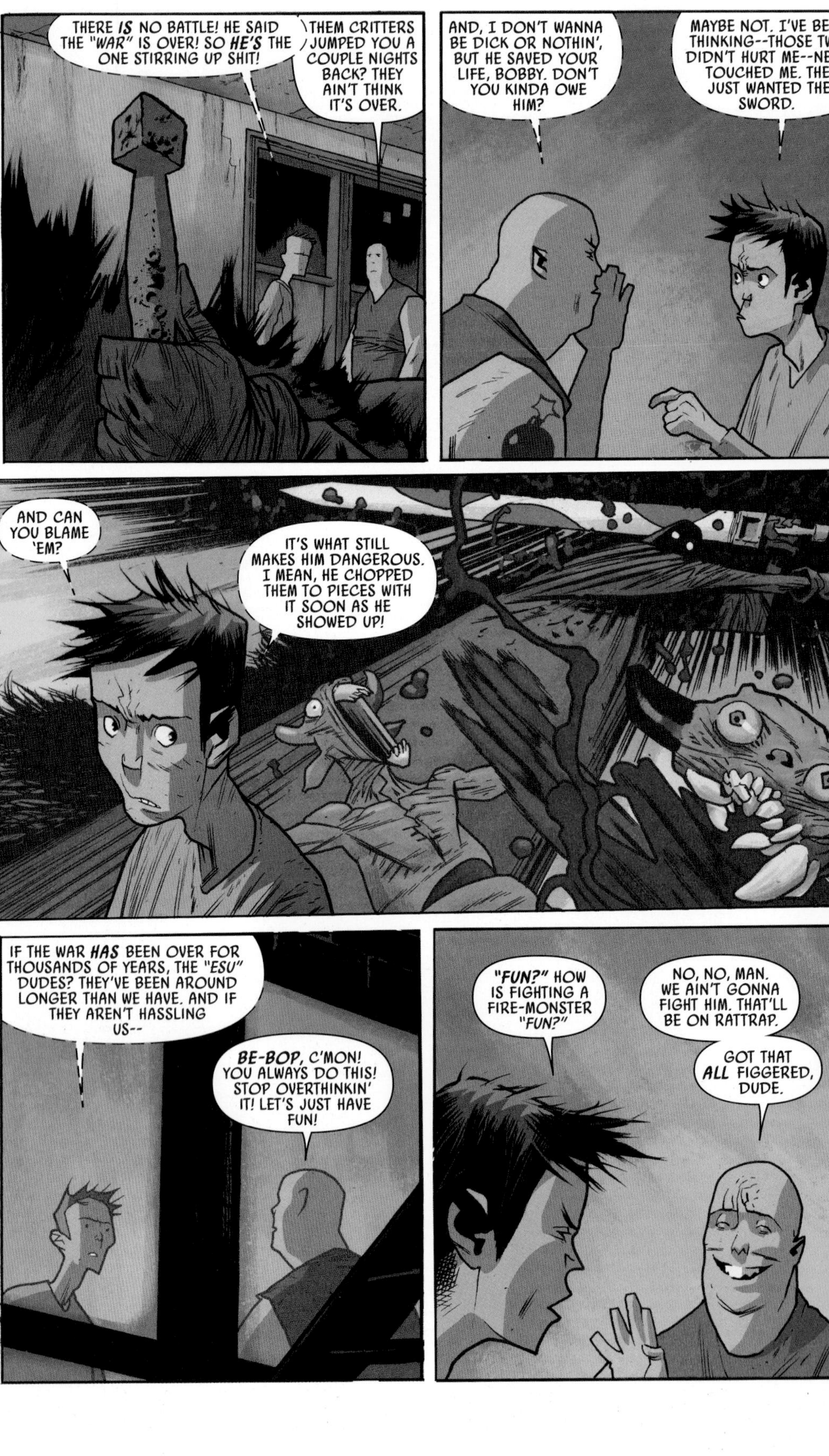

THERE IS NO BATTLE! HE SAID THE "WAR" IS OVER! SO HE'S THE ONE STIRRING UP SHIT!
THEM CRITTERS JUMPED YOU A COUPLE NIGHTS BACK? THEY AIN'T THINK IT'S OVER.
AND, I DON'T WANNA BE DICK OR NOTHIN', BUT HE SAVED YOUR LIFE, BOBBY. DON'T YOU KINDA OWE HIM?
MAYBE NOT. I'VE BEEN THINKING--THOSE TWO DIDN'T HURT ME--NEVER TOUCHED ME. THEY JUST WANTED THE SWORD.
AND CAN YOU BLAME 'EM?
IT'S WHAT STILL MAKES HIM DANGEROUS. I MEAN, HE CHOPPED THEM TO PIECES WITH IT SOON AS HE SHOWED UP!
IF THE WAR HAS BEEN OVER FOR THOUSANDS OF YEARS, THE "ESU" DUDES? THEY'VE BEEN AROUND LONGER THAN WE HAVE. AND IF THEY AREN'T HASSLING US--
BE-BOP, C'MON! YOU ALWAYS DO THIS! STOP OVERTHINKIN' IT! LET'S JUST HAVE FUN!
"FUN?" HOW IS FIGHTING A FIRE-MONSTER "FUN?"
NO, NO, MAN. WE AIN'T GONNA FIGHT HIM. THAT'LL BE ON RATTRAP.
GOT THAT ALL FIGGERED, DUDE.

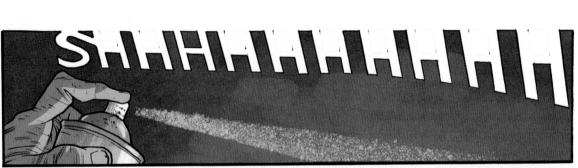

SHHHHHHHHHHHH

I'D SAY WE 'BOUT GOT YA' COVERED. MAYBE ONE LAST CAN TO JUST, Y'KNOW, BE SURE.

AND I'LL TELL YOU, BIG MAN, THIS FLAME RETARDANT *WORKS!!*

TWO CHRISTMASES AGO, I WENT OVER TO MY DAD'S PLACE WITH A GALLON OF GASOLINE AND--

RETARDANT

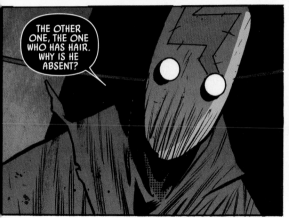

THE OTHER ONE, THE ONE WHO HAS HAIR. WHY IS HE ABSENT?

UHH, BOBBY? HE... HE HAD SOME STUFF HE HADDA DO.

KINDA SUCKS, I KNOW. I'D FEEL BETTER HE WAS HERE, TOO. STRENGTH IN NUMBERS, AND ALL THAT...

"BUT WE *GOT* THIS, BOSS. TRUST ME!"

GOD, LET THEM BE GONE WHEN I GET HOME...

THERE'S MY MAN! HOW YOU DOIN'?

TY, YOU DON'T GOT NEAR ENOUGH TIME FOR THAT ANSWER.

KNOW WHAT YOU MEAN.

NO YOU DON'T.

BE LIKE THAT, THEN. HEY, DON'T GUESS YOU'D LET ME TAKE YOUR SHIFT TONIGHT, *MMM?*

WHY WOULD YOU WANNA DO THAT?

NO REASON...

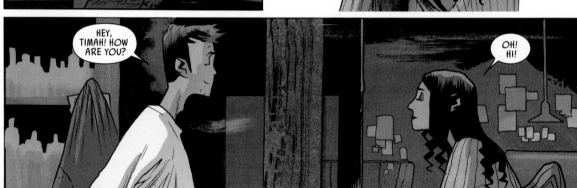

HEY, TIMAH! HOW ARE YOU?

OH! HI!

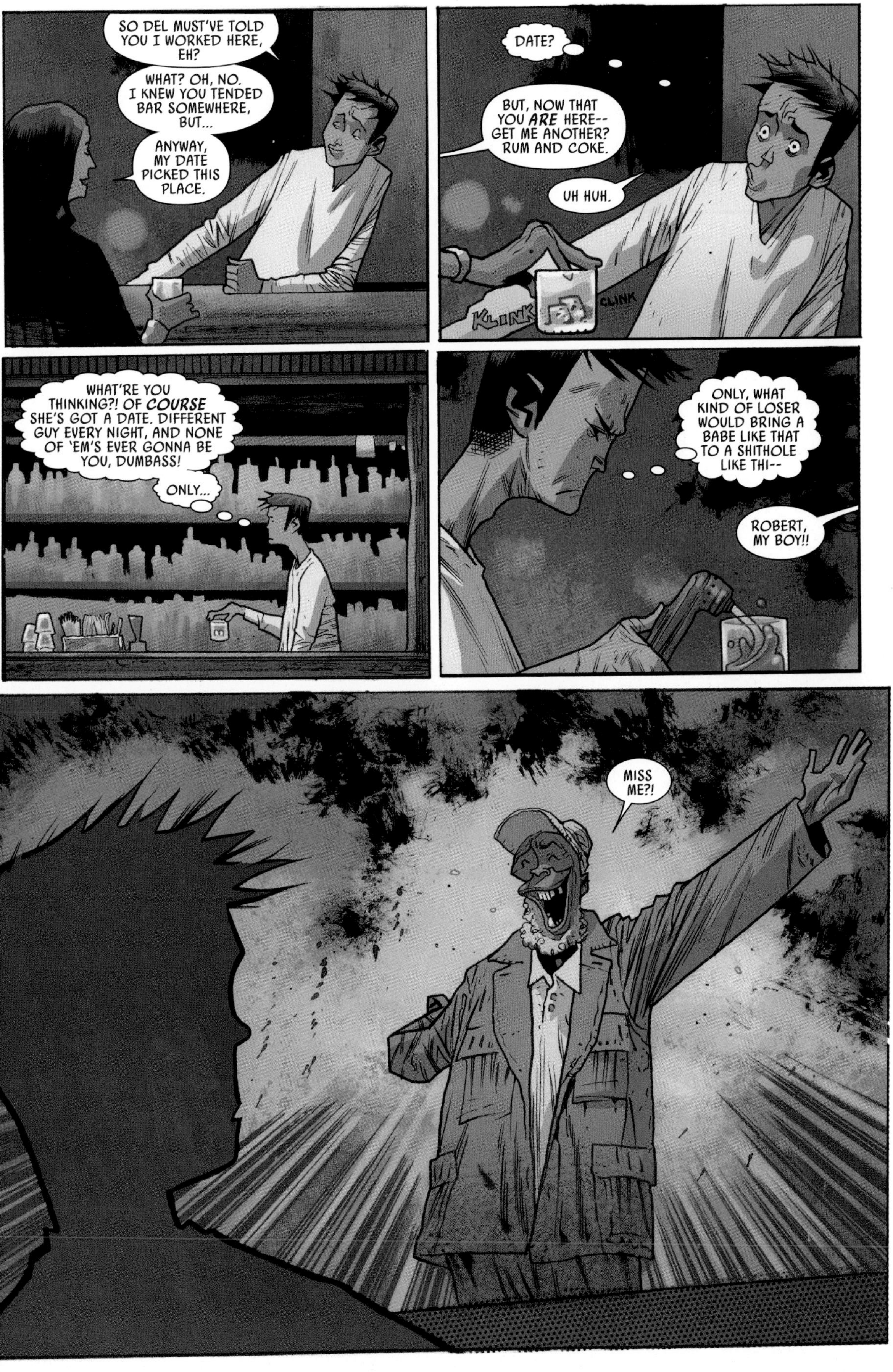
SO DEL MUST'VE TOLD YOU I WORKED HERE, EH?
WHAT? OH, NO. I KNEW YOU TENDED BAR SOMEWHERE, BUT...
ANYWAY, MY DATE PICKED THIS PLACE.
DATE?
BUT, NOW THAT YOU ARE HERE-- GET ME ANOTHER? RUM AND COKE.
UH HUH.
KLINK
CLINK
WHAT'RE YOU THINKING?! OF COURSE SHE'S GOT A DATE. DIFFERENT GUY EVERY NIGHT, AND NONE OF 'EM'S EVER GONNA BE YOU, DUMBASS!
ONLY...
ONLY, WHAT KIND OF LOSER WOULD BRING A BABE LIKE THAT TO A SHITHOLE LIKE THI--
ROBERT, MY BOY!!
MISS ME?!

CHAPTER FOUR

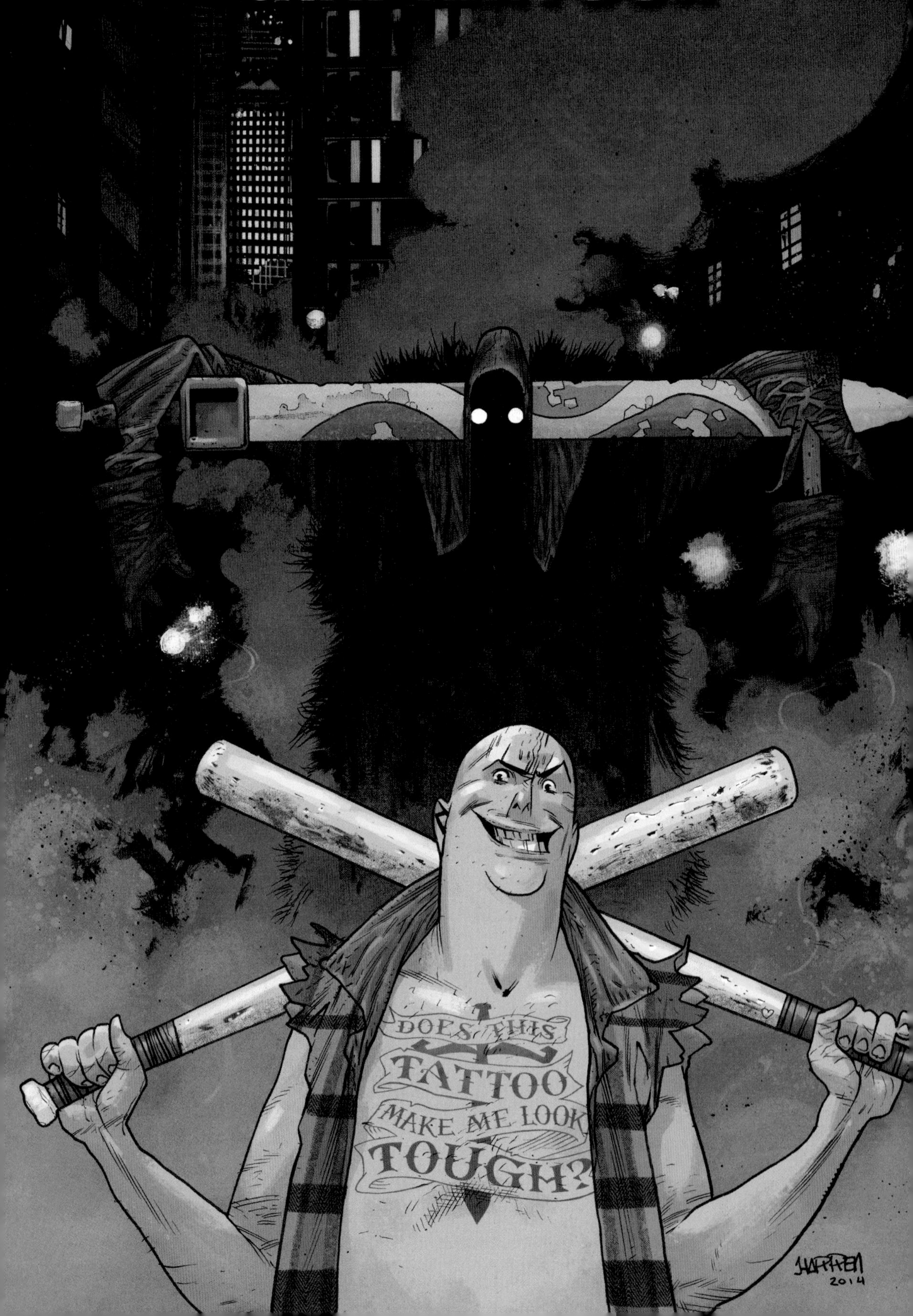
DOES THIS
TATTOO
MAKE ME LOOK
TOUGH?
HARREN
2014

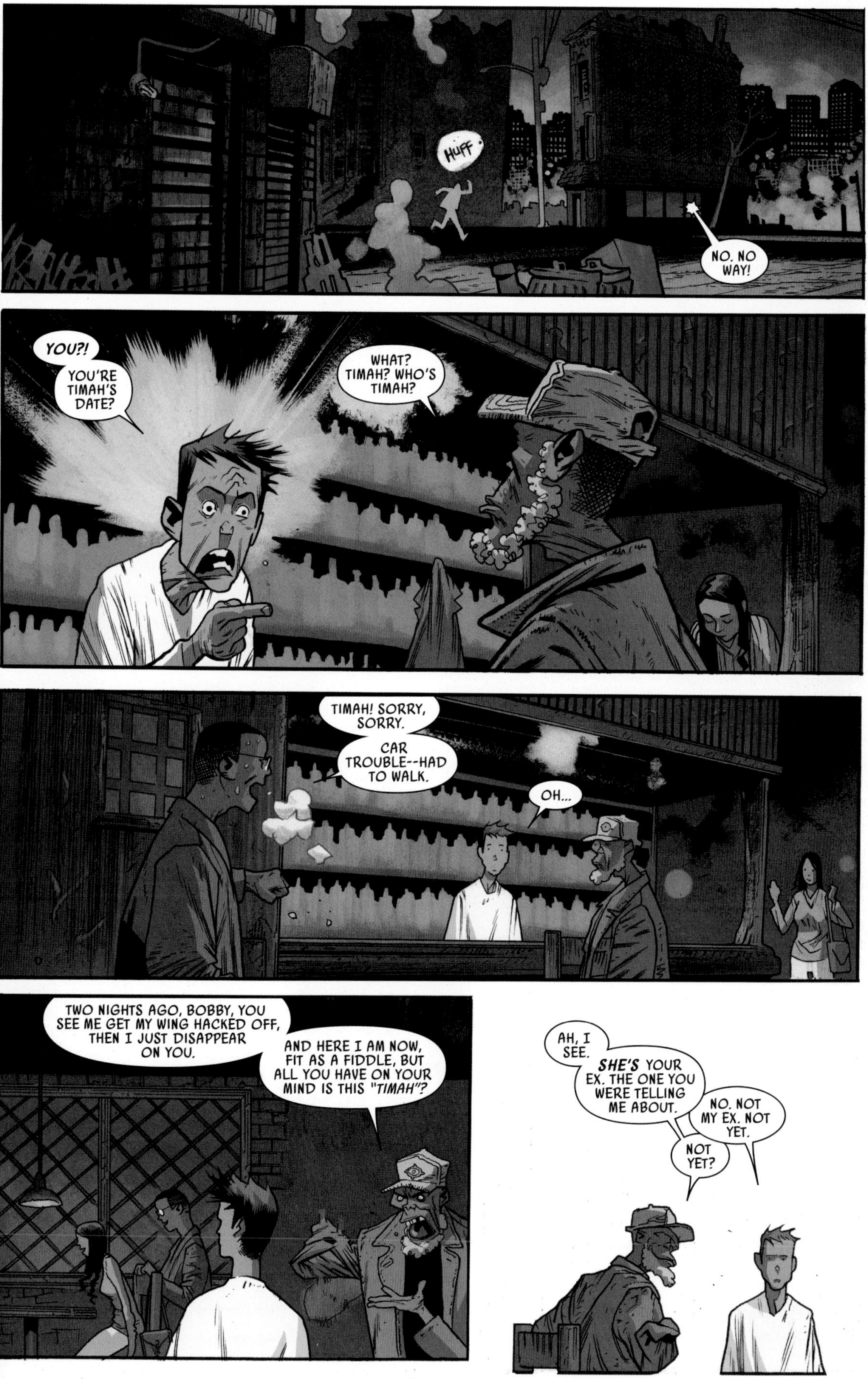
HUFF
NO. NO WAY!
YOU?!
YOU'RE TIMAH'S DATE?
WHAT? TIMAH? WHO'S TIMAH?
TIMAH! SORRY, SORRY.
CAR TROUBLE--HAD TO WALK.
OH...
TWO NIGHTS AGO, BOBBY, YOU SEE ME GET MY WING HACKED OFF, THEN I JUST DISAPPEAR ON YOU.
AND HERE I AM NOW, FIT AS A FIDDLE, BUT ALL YOU HAVE ON YOUR MIND IS THIS "TIMAH"?
AH, I SEE.
SHE'S YOUR EX. THE ONE YOU WERE TELLING ME ABOUT.
NO. NOT MY EX. NOT YET.
NOT YET?

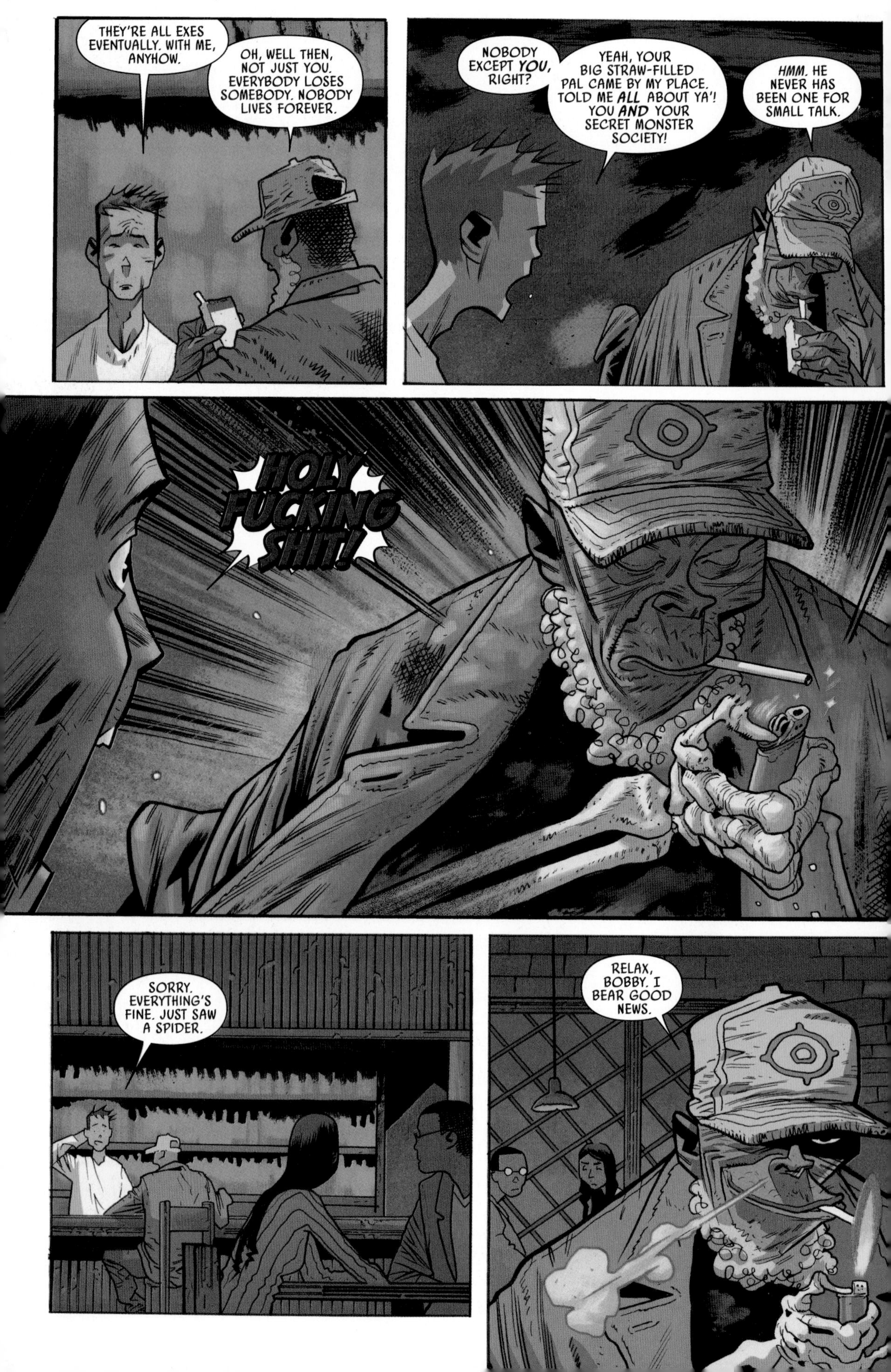
THEY'RE ALL EXES EVENTUALLY. WITH ME, ANYHOW.
OH, WELL THEN, NOT JUST YOU. EVERYBODY LOSES SOMEBODY. NOBODY LIVES FOREVER.
NOBODY EXCEPT *YOU*, RIGHT?
YEAH, YOUR BIG STRAW-FILLED PAL CAME BY MY PLACE. TOLD ME *ALL* ABOUT YA'! YOU *AND* YOUR SECRET MONSTER SOCIETY!
HMM. HE NEVER HAS BEEN ONE FOR SMALL TALK.
HOLY FUCKING SHIT!
SORRY. EVERYTHING'S FINE. JUST SAW A SPIDER.
RELAX, BOBBY. I BEAR GOOD NEWS.

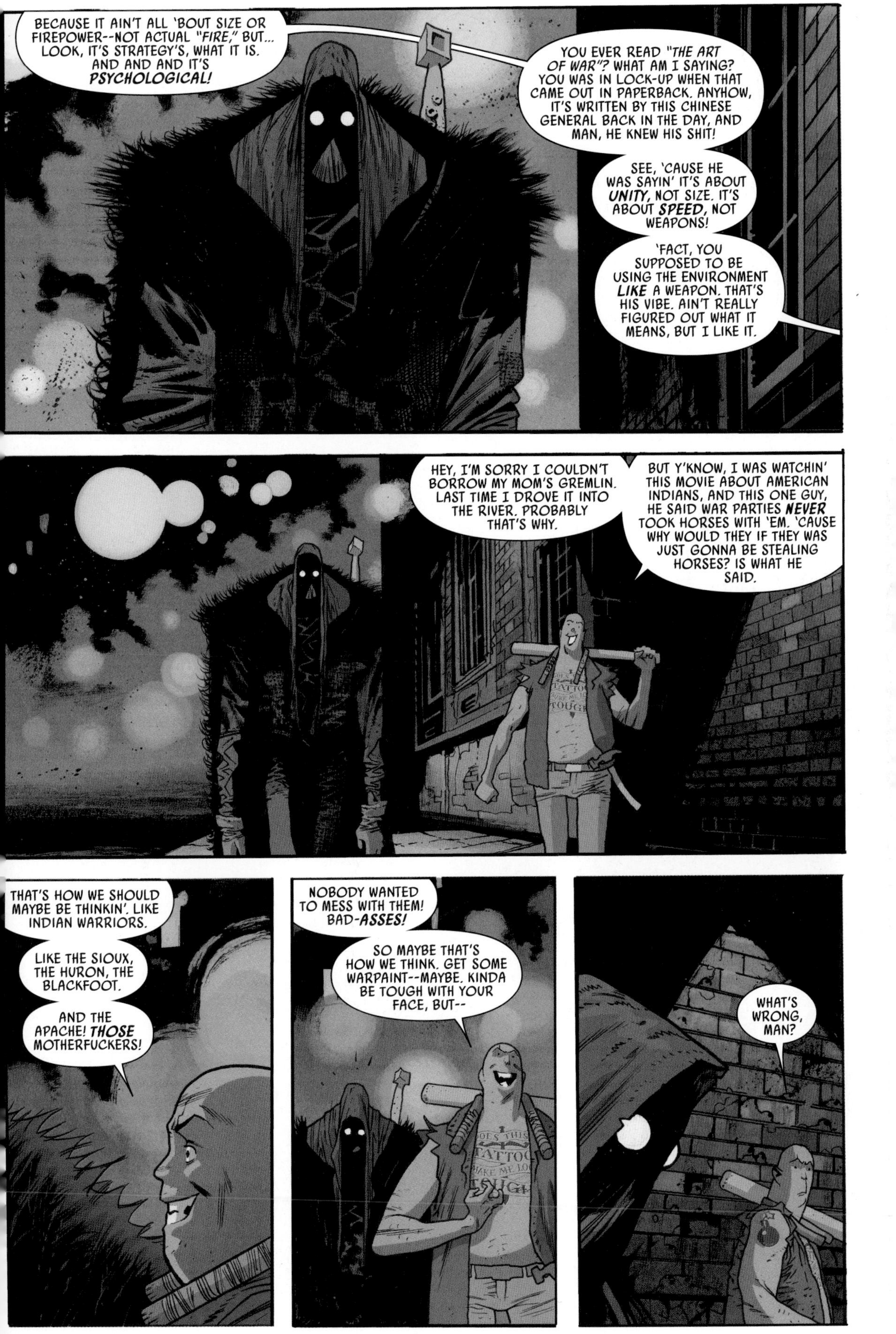
BECAUSE IT AIN'T ALL 'BOUT SIZE OR FIREPOWER--NOT ACTUAL "FIRE," BUT... LOOK, IT'S STRATEGY'S, WHAT IT IS. AND AND AND IT'S PSYCHOLOGICAL!
YOU EVER READ "THE ART OF WAR"? WHAT AM I SAYING? YOU WAS IN LOCK-UP WHEN THAT CAME OUT IN PAPERBACK. ANYHOW, IT'S WRITTEN BY THIS CHINESE GENERAL BACK IN THE DAY, AND MAN, HE KNEW HIS SHIT!
SEE, 'CAUSE HE WAS SAYIN' IT'S ABOUT UNITY, NOT SIZE. IT'S ABOUT SPEED, NOT WEAPONS!
'FACT, YOU SUPPOSED TO BE USING THE ENVIRONMENT LIKE A WEAPON. THAT'S HIS VIBE. AIN'T REALLY FIGURED OUT WHAT IT MEANS, BUT I LIKE IT.
HEY, I'M SORRY I COULDN'T BORROW MY MOM'S GREMLIN. LAST TIME I DROVE IT INTO THE RIVER. PROBABLY THAT'S WHY.
BUT Y'KNOW, I WAS WATCHIN' THIS MOVIE ABOUT AMERICAN INDIANS, AND THIS ONE GUY, HE SAID WAR PARTIES NEVER TOOK HORSES WITH 'EM. 'CAUSE WHY WOULD THEY IF THEY WAS JUST GONNA BE STEALING HORSES? IS WHAT HE SAID.
THAT'S HOW WE SHOULD MAYBE BE THINKIN'. LIKE INDIAN WARRIORS.
LIKE THE SIOUX, THE HURON, THE BLACKFOOT.
AND THE APACHE! THOSE MOTHERFUCKERS!
NOBODY WANTED TO MESS WITH THEM! BAD-ASSES!
SO MAYBE THAT'S HOW WE THINK. GET SOME WARPAINT--MAYBE. KINDA BE TOUGH WITH YOUR FACE, BUT--
WHAT'S WRONG, MAN?

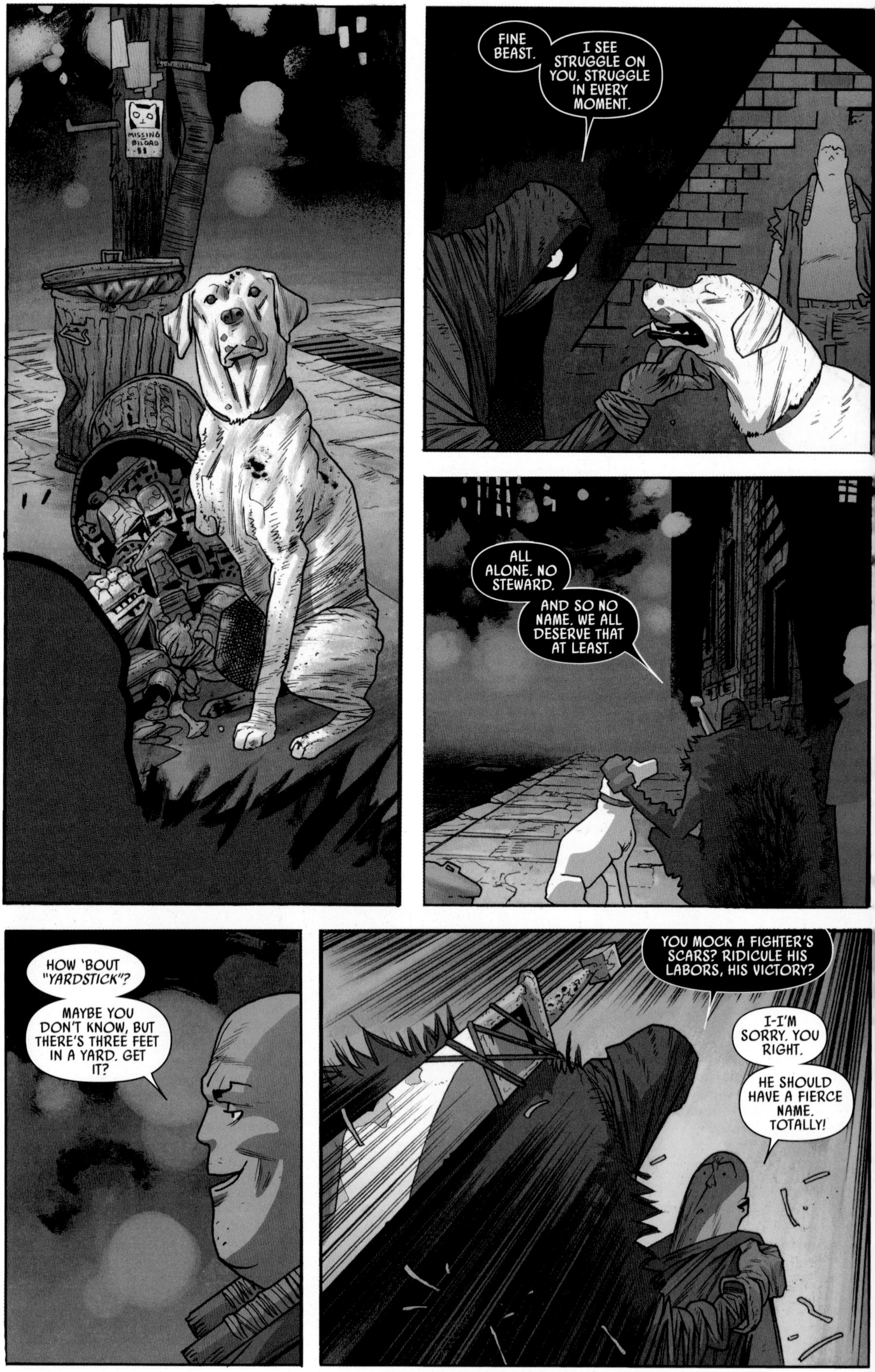
MISSING
BILOAD
FINE BEAST.
I SEE STRUGGLE ON YOU. STRUGGLE IN EVERY MOMENT.
ALL ALONE. NO STEWARD.
AND SO NO NAME. WE ALL DESERVE THAT AT LEAST.
HOW 'BOUT "YARDSTICK"?
MAYBE YOU DON'T KNOW, BUT THERE'S THREE FEET IN A YARD. GET IT?
YOU MOCK A FIGHTER'S SCARS? RIDICULE HIS LABORS, HIS VICTORY?
I-I'M SORRY. YOU RIGHT.
HE SHOULD HAVE A FIERCE NAME. TOTALLY!

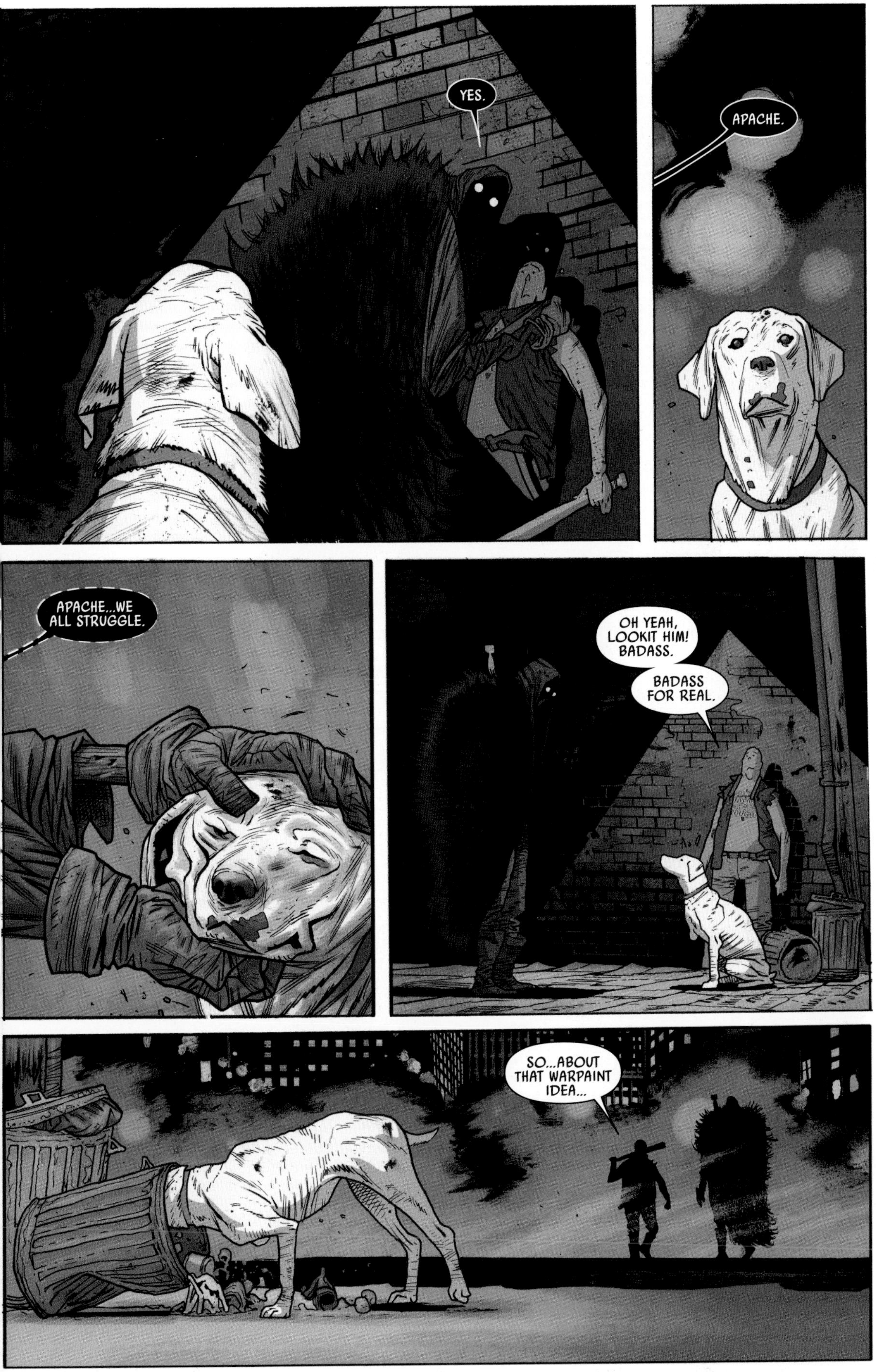
YES.
APACHE.
APACHE...WE ALL STRUGGLE.
OH YEAH, LOOKIT HIM! BADASS.
BADASS FOR REAL.
SO...ABOUT THAT WARPAINT IDEA...

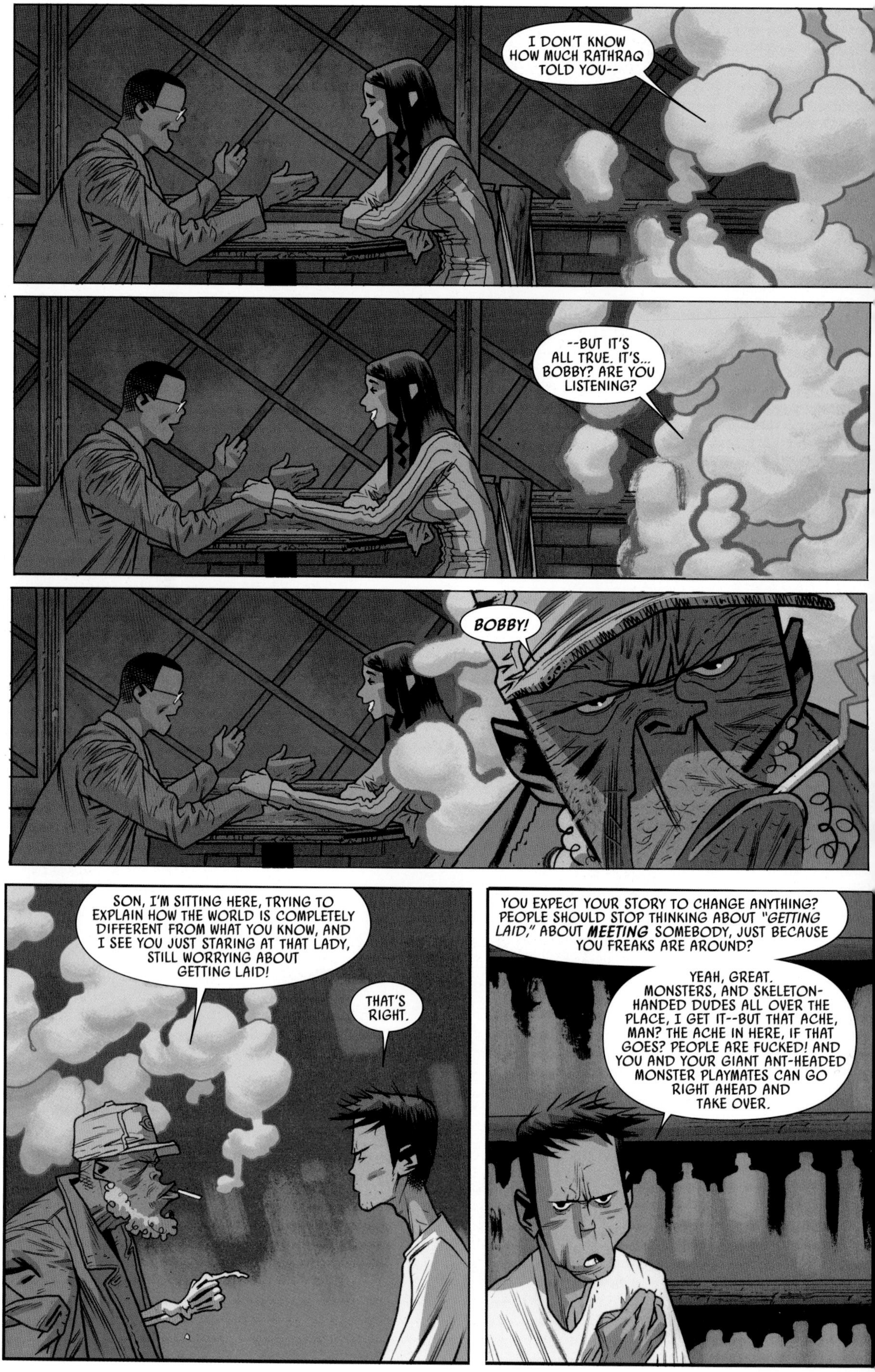
I DON'T KNOW HOW MUCH RATHRAQ TOLD YOU--
--BUT IT'S ALL TRUE. IT'S... BOBBY? ARE YOU LISTENING?
BOBBY!
SON, I'M SITTING HERE, TRYING TO EXPLAIN HOW THE WORLD IS COMPLETELY DIFFERENT FROM WHAT YOU KNOW, AND I SEE YOU JUST STARING AT THAT LADY, STILL WORRYING ABOUT GETTING LAID!
THAT'S RIGHT.
YOU EXPECT YOUR STORY TO CHANGE ANYTHING? PEOPLE SHOULD STOP THINKING ABOUT "GETTING LAID," ABOUT MEETING SOMEBODY, JUST BECAUSE YOU FREAKS ARE AROUND?
YEAH, GREAT. MONSTERS, AND SKELETON-HANDED DUDES ALL OVER THE PLACE, I GET IT--BUT THAT ACHE, MAN? THE ACHE IN HERE, IF THAT GOES? PEOPLE ARE FUCKED! AND YOU AND YOUR GIANT ANT-HEADED MONSTER PLAYMATES CAN GO RIGHT AHEAD AND TAKE OVER.

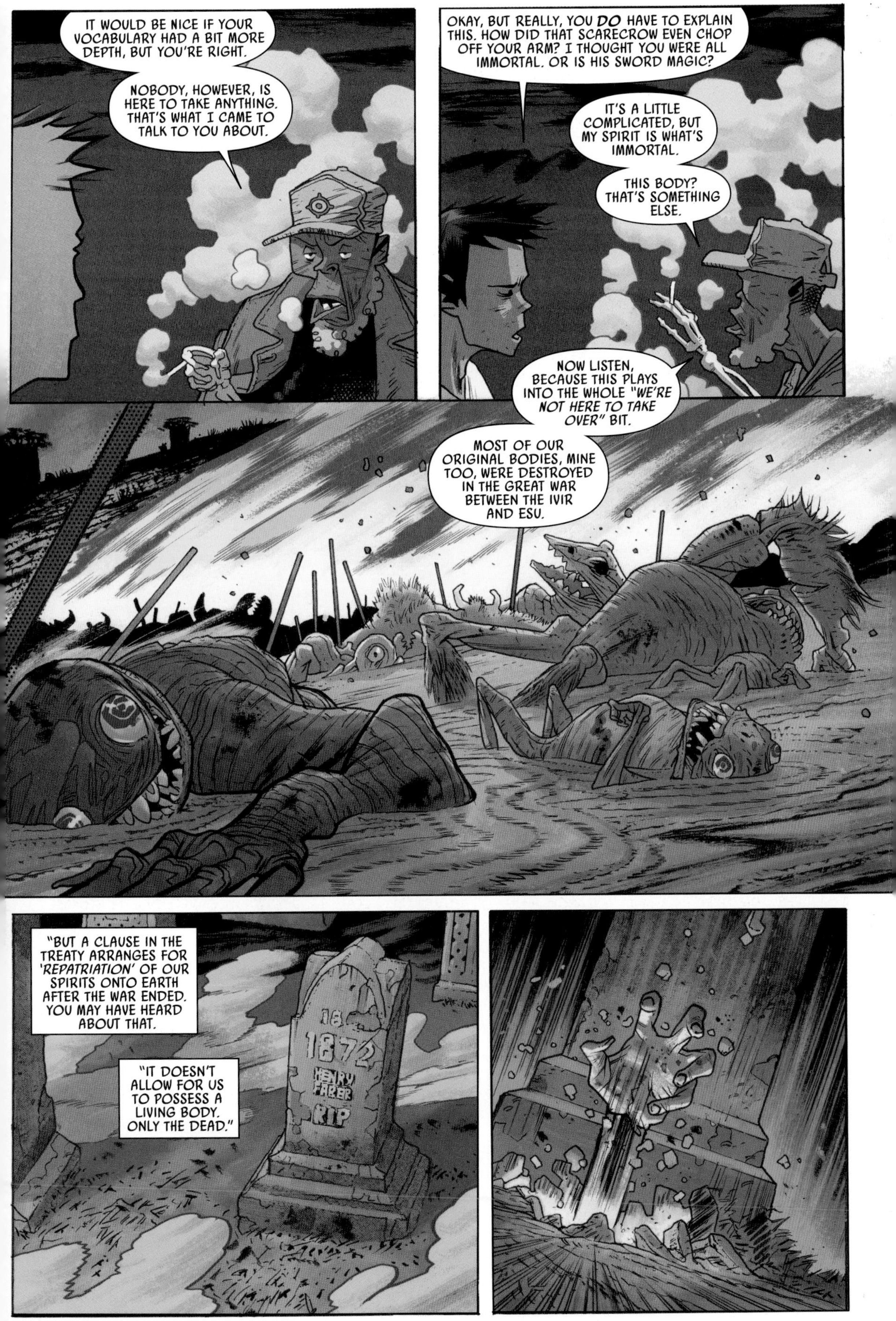
IT WOULD BE NICE IF YOUR VOCABULARY HAD A BIT MORE DEPTH, BUT YOU'RE RIGHT.
NOBODY, HOWEVER, IS HERE TO TAKE ANYTHING. THAT'S WHAT I CAME TO TALK TO YOU ABOUT.
OKAY, BUT REALLY, YOU *DO* HAVE TO EXPLAIN THIS. HOW DID THAT SCARECROW EVEN CHOP OFF YOUR ARM? I THOUGHT YOU WERE ALL IMMORTAL. OR IS HIS SWORD MAGIC?
IT'S A LITTLE COMPLICATED, BUT MY SPIRIT IS WHAT'S IMMORTAL.
THIS BODY? THAT'S SOMETHING ELSE.
NOW LISTEN, BECAUSE THIS PLAYS INTO THE WHOLE *"WE'RE NOT HERE TO TAKE OVER"* BIT.
MOST OF OUR ORIGINAL BODIES, MINE TOO, WERE DESTROYED IN THE GREAT WAR BETWEEN THE IVIR AND ESU.
"BUT A CLAUSE IN THE TREATY ARRANGES FOR *'REPATRIATION'* OF OUR SPIRITS ONTO EARTH AFTER THE WAR ENDED. YOU MAY HAVE HEARD ABOUT THAT.
18
1872
HENRY FABER
RIP
"IT DOESN'T ALLOW FOR US TO POSSESS A LIVING BODY. ONLY THE DEAD."

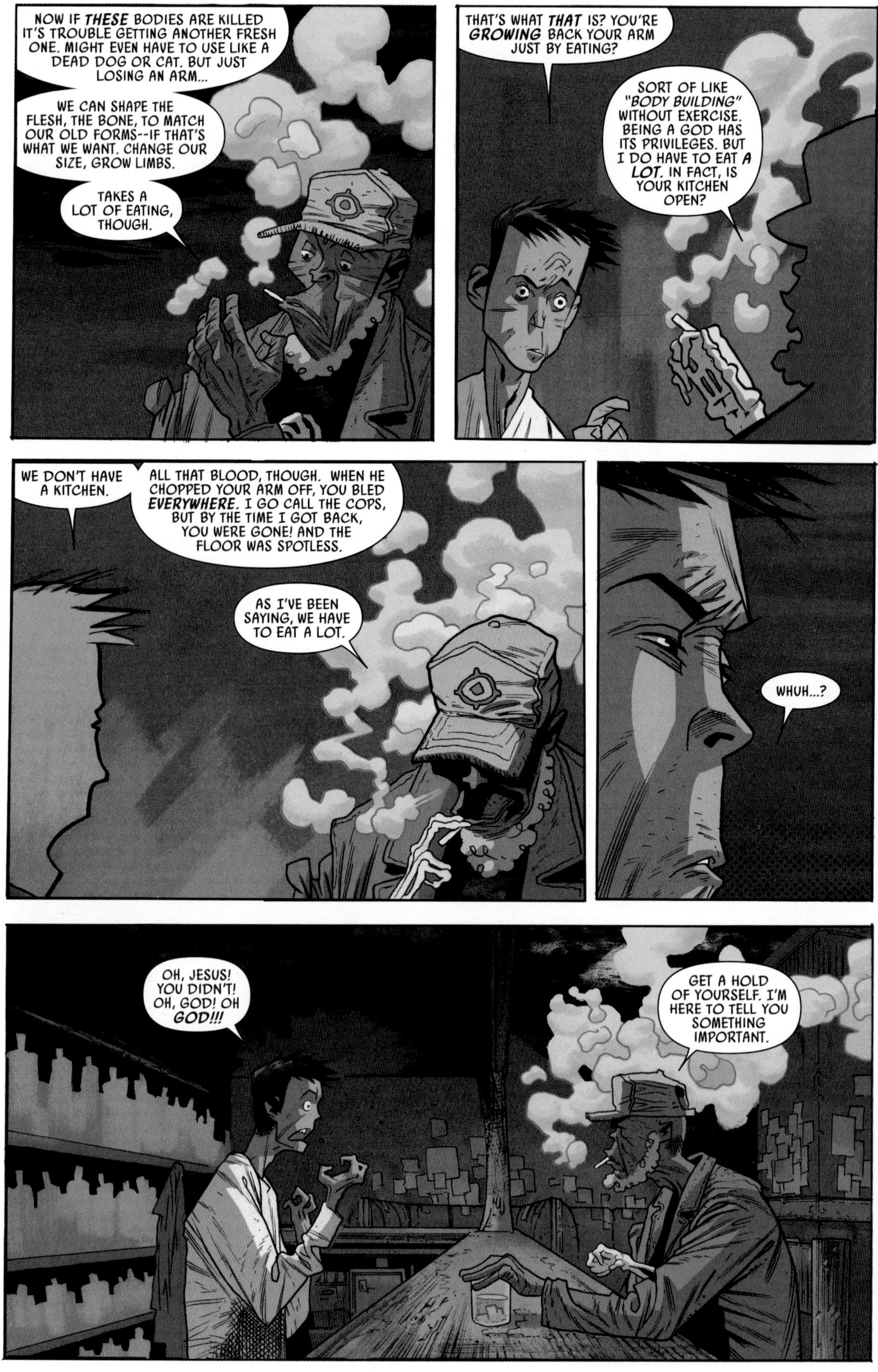
NOW IF *THESE* BODIES ARE KILLED IT'S TROUBLE GETTING ANOTHER FRESH ONE. MIGHT EVEN HAVE TO USE LIKE A DEAD DOG OR CAT. BUT JUST LOSING AN ARM...
WE CAN SHAPE THE FLESH, THE BONE, TO MATCH OUR OLD FORMS--IF THAT'S WHAT WE WANT. CHANGE OUR SIZE, GROW LIMBS.
TAKES A LOT OF EATING, THOUGH.
THAT'S WHAT *THAT* IS? YOU'RE *GROWING* BACK YOUR ARM JUST BY EATING?
SORT OF LIKE "*BODY BUILDING*" WITHOUT EXERCISE. BEING A GOD HAS ITS PRIVILEGES. BUT I DO HAVE TO EAT *A LOT*. IN FACT, IS YOUR KITCHEN OPEN?
WE DON'T HAVE A KITCHEN.
ALL THAT BLOOD, THOUGH. WHEN HE CHOPPED YOUR ARM OFF, YOU BLED *EVERYWHERE*. I GO CALL THE COPS, BUT BY THE TIME I GOT BACK, YOU WERE GONE! AND THE FLOOR WAS SPOTLESS.
AS I'VE BEEN SAYING, WE HAVE TO EAT A LOT.
WHUH...?
OH, JESUS! YOU DIDN'T! OH, GOD! OH *GOD!!!*
GET A HOLD OF YOURSELF. I'M HERE TO TELL YOU SOMETHING IMPORTANT.

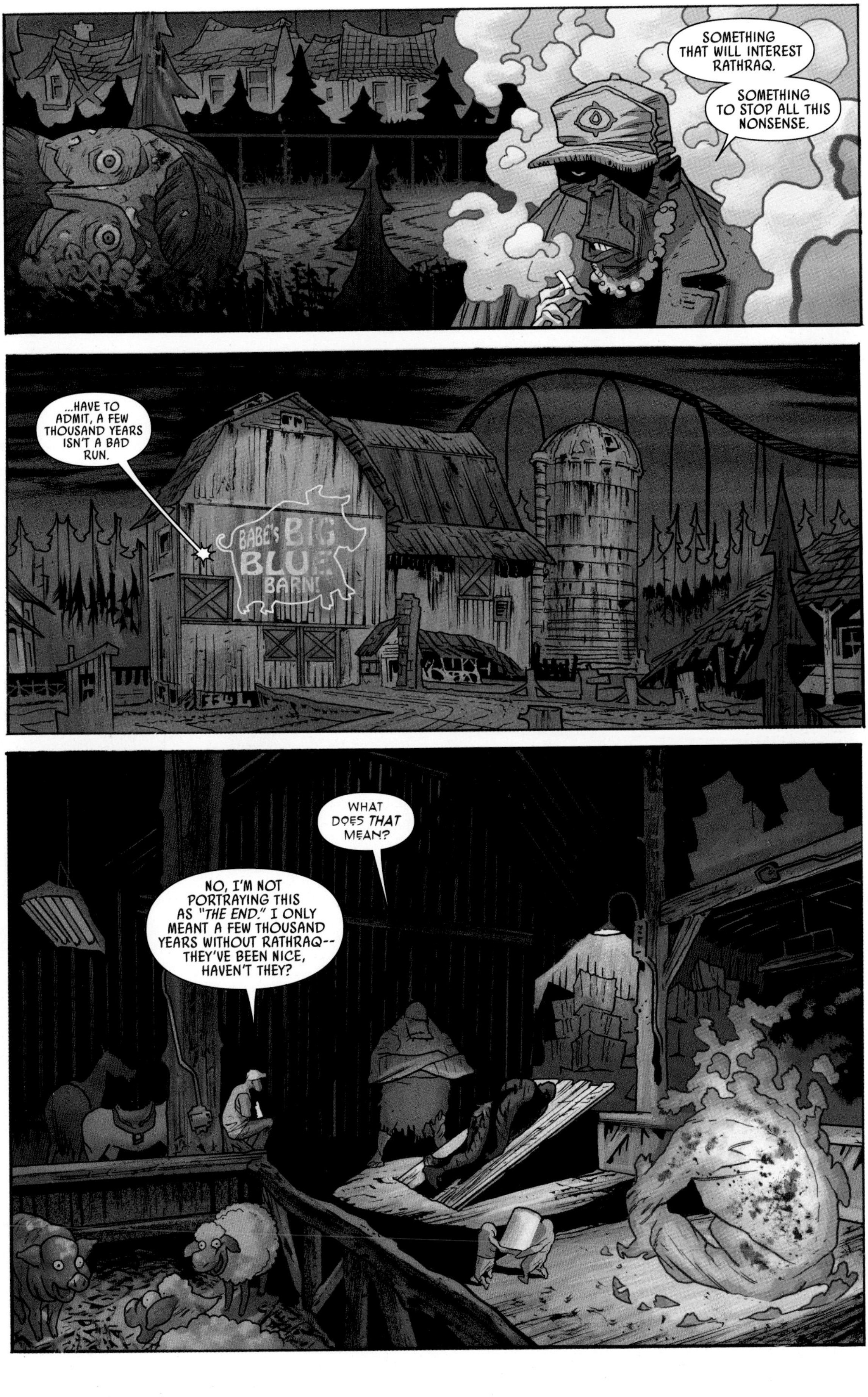
SOMETHING THAT WILL INTEREST RATHRAQ.
SOMETHING TO STOP ALL THIS NONSENSE.
...HAVE TO ADMIT, A FEW THOUSAND YEARS ISN'T A BAD RUN.
BABE'S BIG BLUE BARN!
WHAT DOES THAT MEAN?
NO, I'M NOT PORTRAYING THIS AS "THE END." I ONLY MEANT A FEW THOUSAND YEARS WITHOUT RATHRAQ-- THEY'VE BEEN NICE, HAVEN'T THEY?

YES, BUT NOW THAT HE IS BACK, HE SEEMS... THE LONG IMPRISONMENT HAS POSSIBLY UNHINGED HIM. HE CHARGED ME WHEN HE SAW HIS BODY.

CHARGED *ME!* AND HE'S JUST A SCARECROW!

BUT HE STOPPED WHEN NUSKU SHOWED. AND RAN AWAY. NO, HE'S RATIONAL ENOUGH. JUST ANGRY.

COGAN, HE'S BEEN SEEN STARTING TO TALK TO THE PEOPLE. THROUGH THEM, IF HE FINDS A WAY TO FIGHT NUSKU...

OR WORSE, A WAY BACK INTO HIS *OWN BODY!* SO TELL ME, WHY SHOULDN'T I DESTROY IT FIRST?

THAT OLD BOG MUMMY THERE IS THE ONLY THING YOU HAVE THAT MAY KEEP HIM AT BAY. THAT'S WHY I ADVISED YOU TO RETRIEVE IT.

DESTROY IT, YOU LOSE ALL YOUR LEVERAGE.

YOU WANT TO SEE ANGRY? *NOTHING* WILL STOP HIM THEN.

OLD MOTHER HUBBARD'S SHOP TALLOW

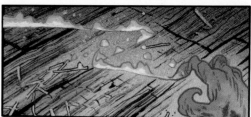

I CAN STOP HIM.

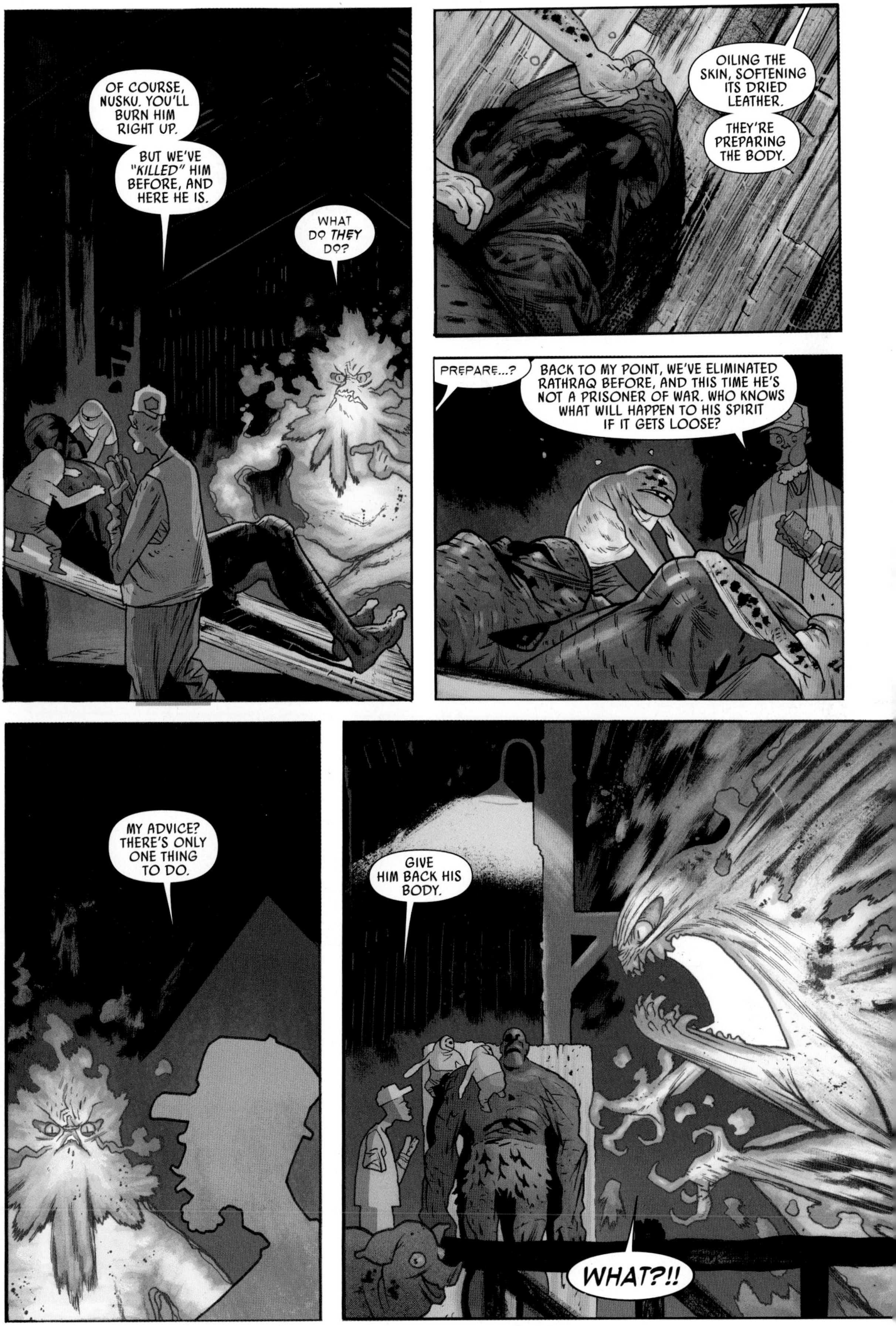
OF COURSE, NUSKU. YOU'LL BURN HIM RIGHT UP.
BUT WE'VE "KILLED" HIM BEFORE, AND HERE HE IS.
WHAT DO THEY DO?
OILING THE SKIN, SOFTENING ITS DRIED LEATHER.
THEY'RE PREPARING THE BODY.
PREPARE...?
BACK TO MY POINT, WE'VE ELIMINATED RATHRAQ BEFORE, AND THIS TIME HE'S NOT A PRISONER OF WAR. WHO KNOWS WHAT WILL HAPPEN TO HIS SPIRIT IF IT GETS LOOSE?
MY ADVICE? THERE'S ONLY ONE THING TO DO.
GIVE HIM BACK HIS BODY.
WHAT?!!

NO!! NO!!
I'LL DESTROY IT RIGHT NOW!
YOU WILL NOT!
I FORBID IT!
AAAAAAAHHHHHH!!
DIDN'T I SAY HE WOULD BE TROUBLE?
NOW LET'S TALK ABOUT THIS EXCHANGE.

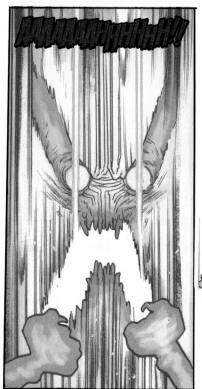

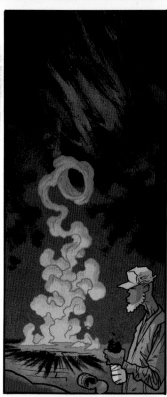

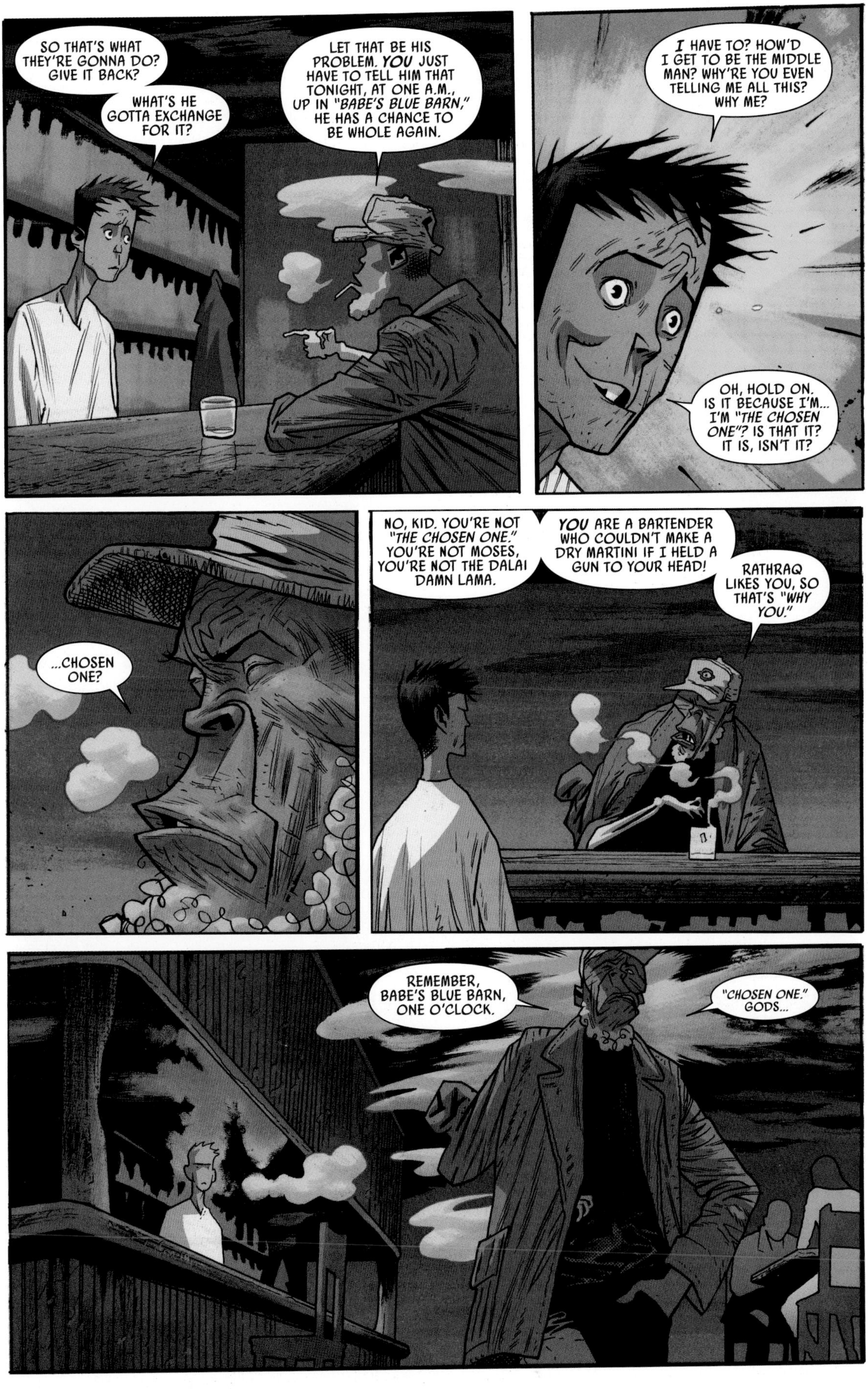
SO THAT'S WHAT THEY'RE GONNA DO? GIVE IT BACK?
WHAT'S HE GOTTA EXCHANGE FOR IT?
LET THAT BE HIS PROBLEM. YOU JUST HAVE TO TELL HIM THAT TONIGHT, AT ONE A.M., UP IN "BABE'S BLUE BARN," HE HAS A CHANCE TO BE WHOLE AGAIN.
I HAVE TO? HOW'D I GET TO BE THE MIDDLE MAN? WHY'RE YOU EVEN TELLING ME ALL THIS? WHY ME?
OH, HOLD ON. IS IT BECAUSE I'M... I'M "THE CHOSEN ONE"? IS THAT IT? IT IS, ISN'T IT?
...CHOSEN ONE?
NO, KID. YOU'RE NOT "THE CHOSEN ONE." YOU'RE NOT MOSES, YOU'RE NOT THE DALAI DAMN LAMA.
YOU ARE A BARTENDER WHO COULDN'T MAKE A DRY MARTINI IF I HELD A GUN TO YOUR HEAD!
RATHRAQ LIKES YOU, SO THAT'S "WHY YOU."
REMEMBER, BABE'S BLUE BARN, ONE O'CLOCK.
"CHOSEN ONE." GODS...

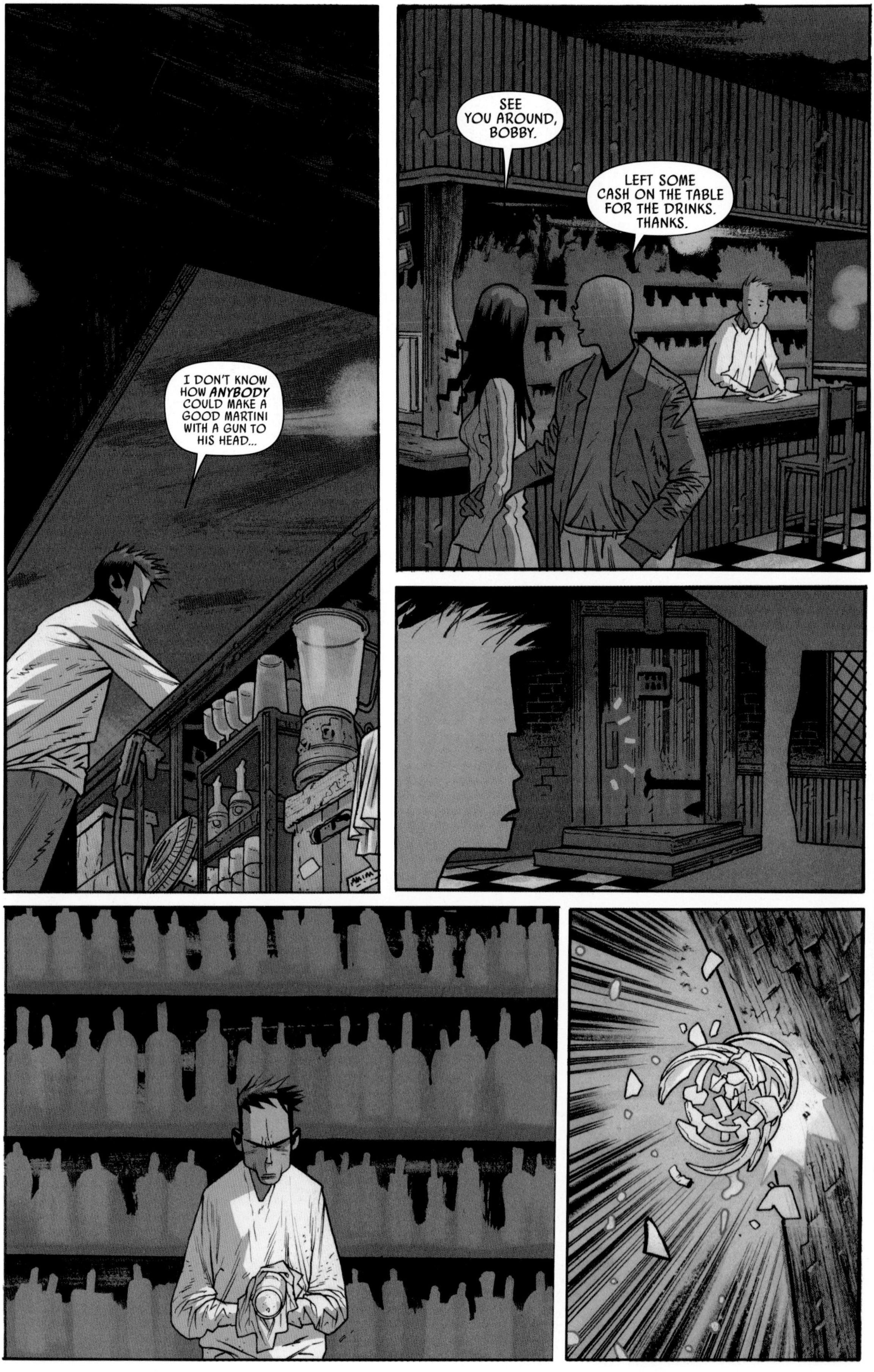
I DON'T KNOW HOW ANYBODY COULD MAKE A GOOD MARTINI WITH A GUN TO HIS HEAD...
SEE YOU AROUND, BOBBY.
LEFT SOME CASH ON THE TABLE FOR THE DRINKS. THANKS.

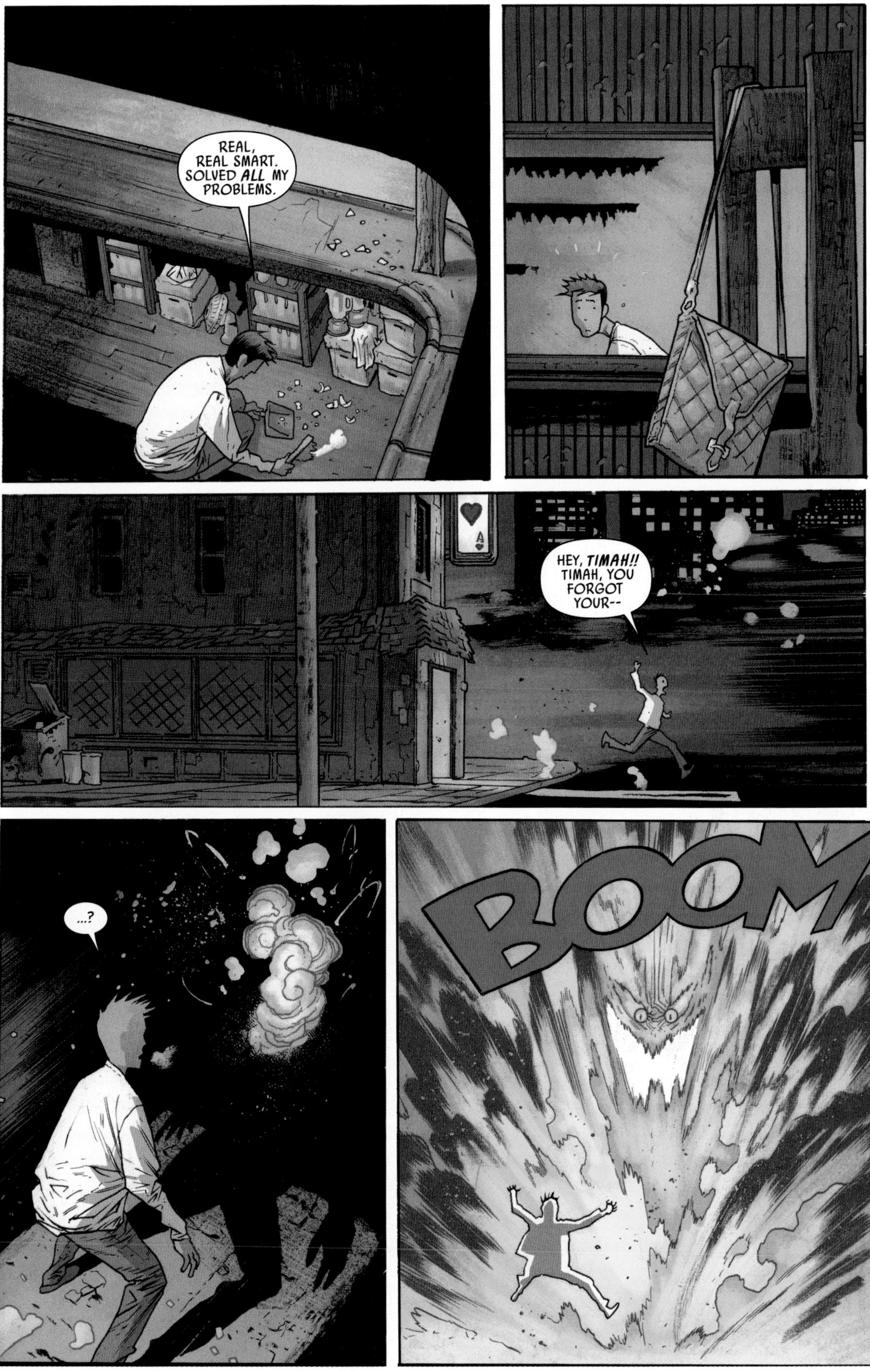
REAL, REAL SMART. SOLVED ALL MY PROBLEMS.
HEY, TIMAH!! TIMAH, YOU FORGOT YOUR--
...?
BOOM

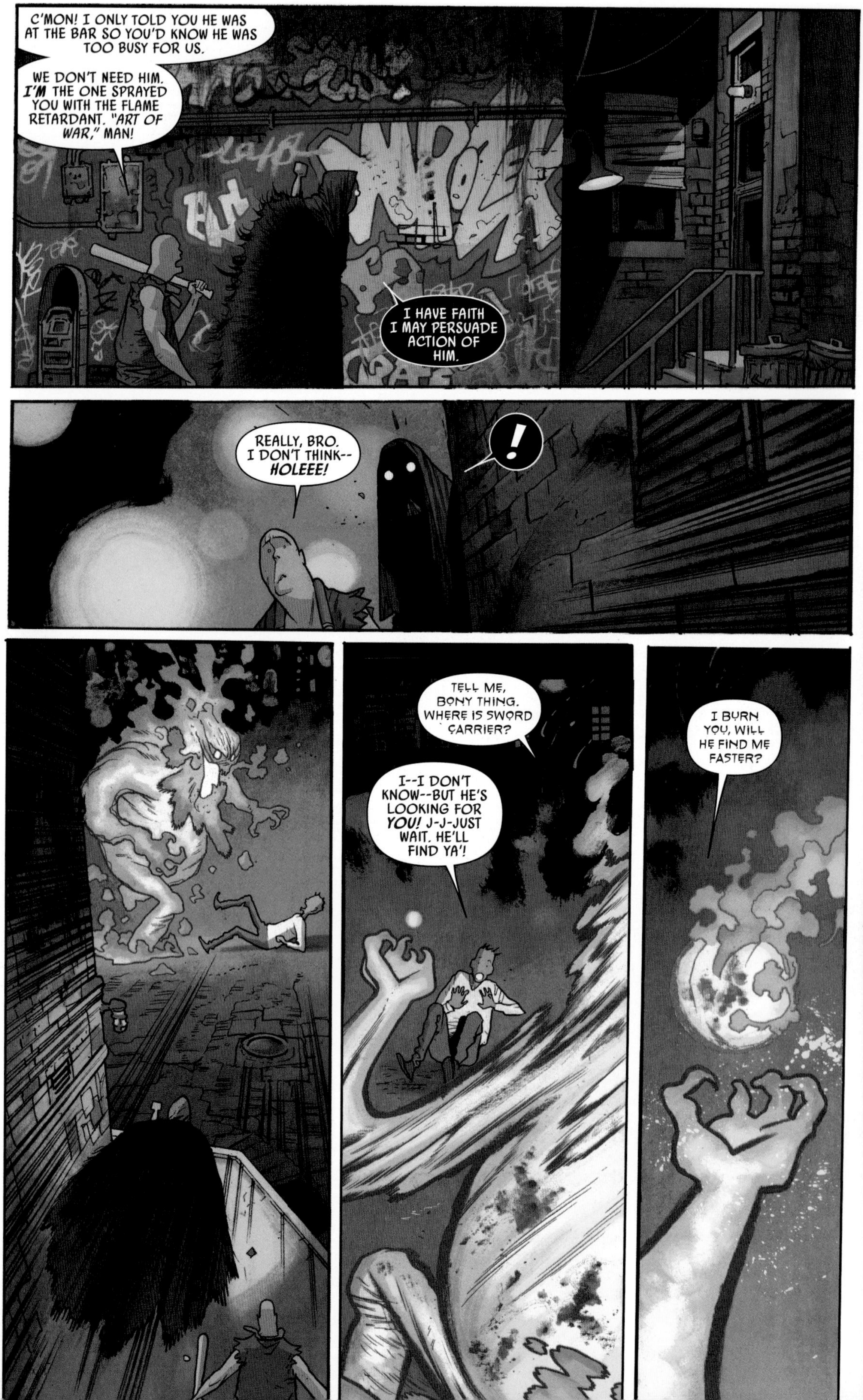
C'MON! I ONLY TOLD YOU HE WAS AT THE BAR SO YOU'D KNOW HE WAS TOO BUSY FOR US.
WE DON'T NEED HIM. I'M THE ONE SPRAYED YOU WITH THE FLAME RETARDANT. "ART OF WAR," MAN!
I HAVE FAITH I MAY PERSUADE ACTION OF HIM.
REALLY, BRO. I DON'T THINK-- HOLEEE!
!
TELL ME, BONY THING. WHERE IS SWORD CARRIER?
I--I DON'T KNOW--BUT HE'S LOOKING FOR YOU! J-J-JUST WAIT. HE'LL FIND YA'!
I BURN YOU, WILL HE FIND ME FASTER?

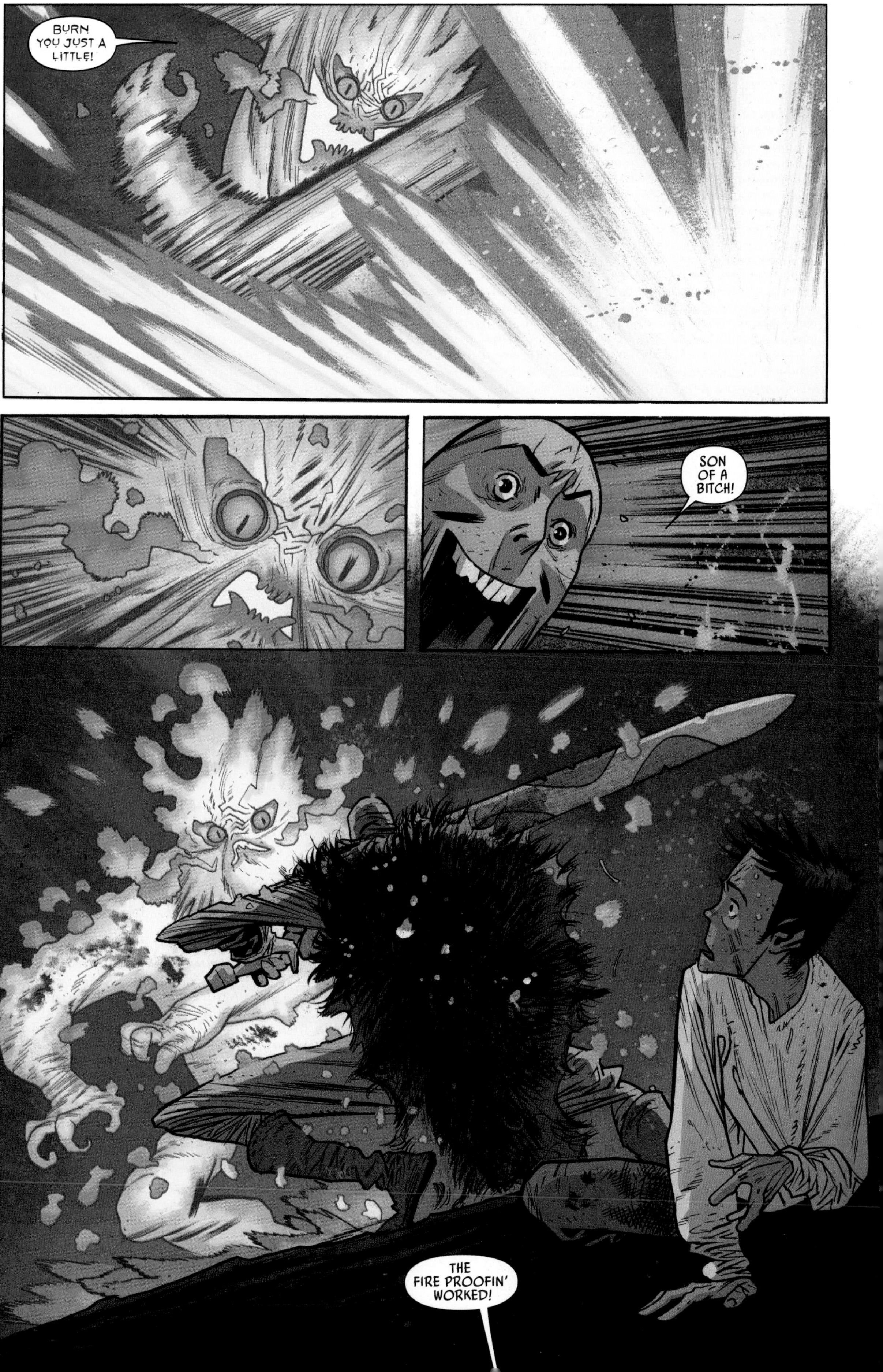
BURN YOU JUST A LITTLE!
SON OF A BITCH!
THE FIRE PROOFIN' WORKED!

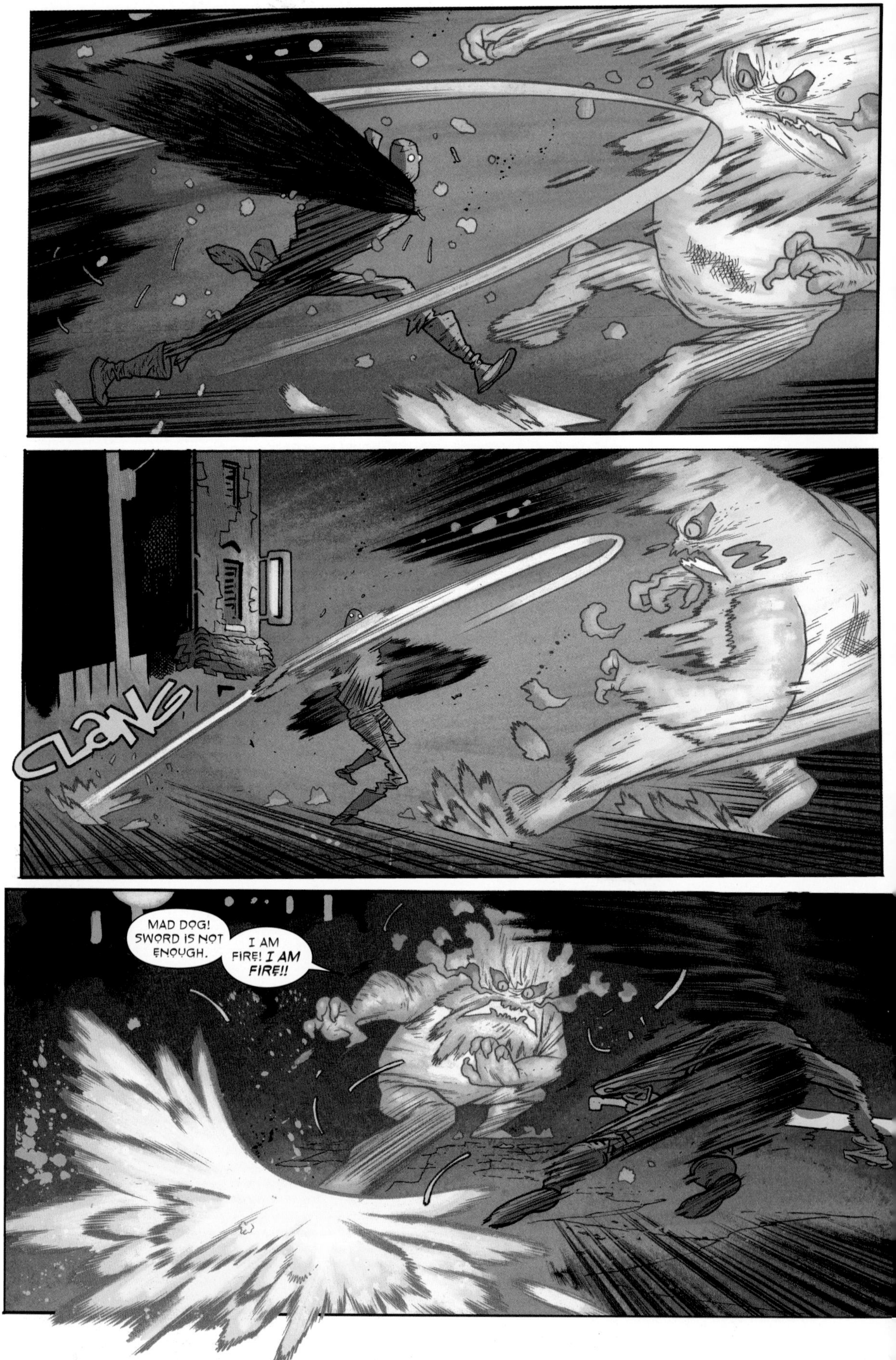
CLANG
MAD DOG! SWORD IS NOT ENOUGH.
I AM FIRE! I AM FIRE!!

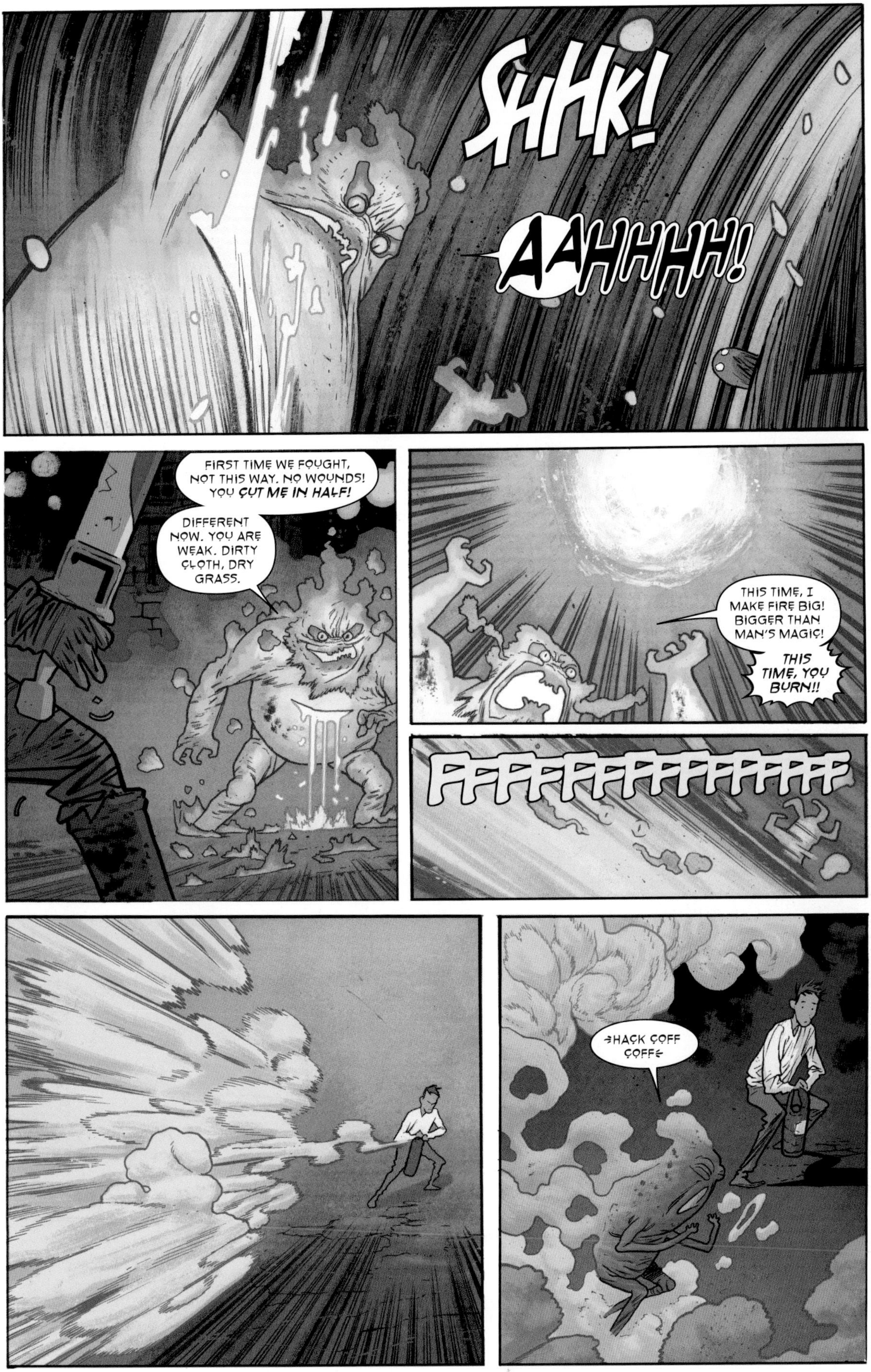
SHHK!
AAHHHH!
FIRST TIME WE FOUGHT, NOT THIS WAY. NO WOUNDS! YOU CUT ME IN HALF!
DIFFERENT NOW. YOU ARE WEAK. DIRTY CLOTH, DRY GRASS.
THIS TIME, I MAKE FIRE BIG! BIGGER THAN MAN'S MAGIC!
THIS TIME, YOU BURN!!
FFFFFFFFFFFFFFFFFFF
=HACK COFF COFF=

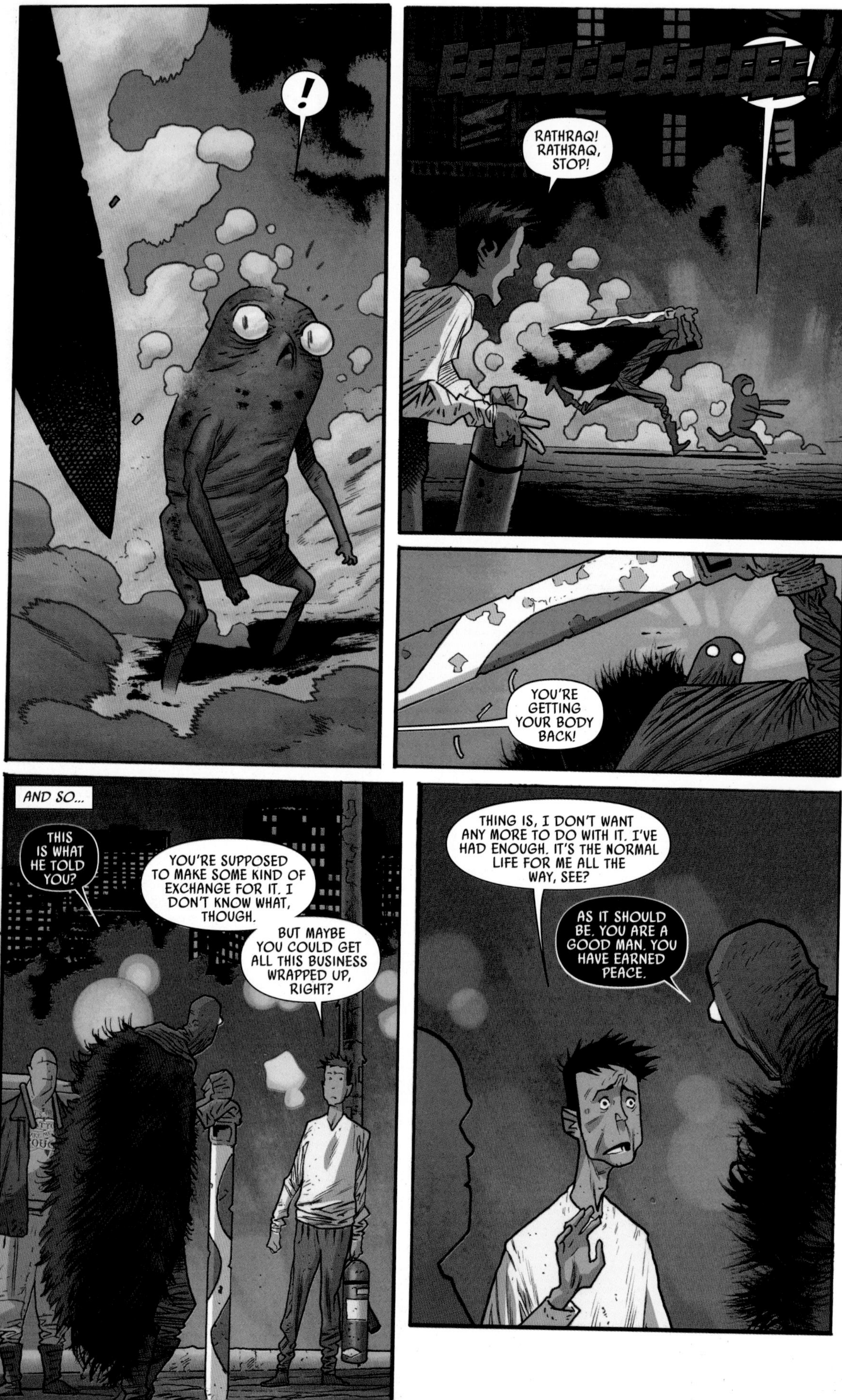
!
EEEEEEEEEEEEEEEE!
RATHRAQ! RATHRAQ, STOP!
YOU'RE GETTING YOUR BODY BACK!
AND SO...
THIS IS WHAT HE TOLD YOU?
YOU'RE SUPPOSED TO MAKE SOME KIND OF EXCHANGE FOR IT. I DON'T KNOW WHAT, THOUGH.
BUT MAYBE YOU COULD GET ALL THIS BUSINESS WRAPPED UP, RIGHT?
THING IS, I DON'T WANT ANY MORE TO DO WITH IT. I'VE HAD ENOUGH. IT'S THE NORMAL LIFE FOR ME ALL THE WAY, SEE?
AS IT SHOULD BE. YOU ARE A GOOD MAN. YOU HAVE EARNED PEACE.

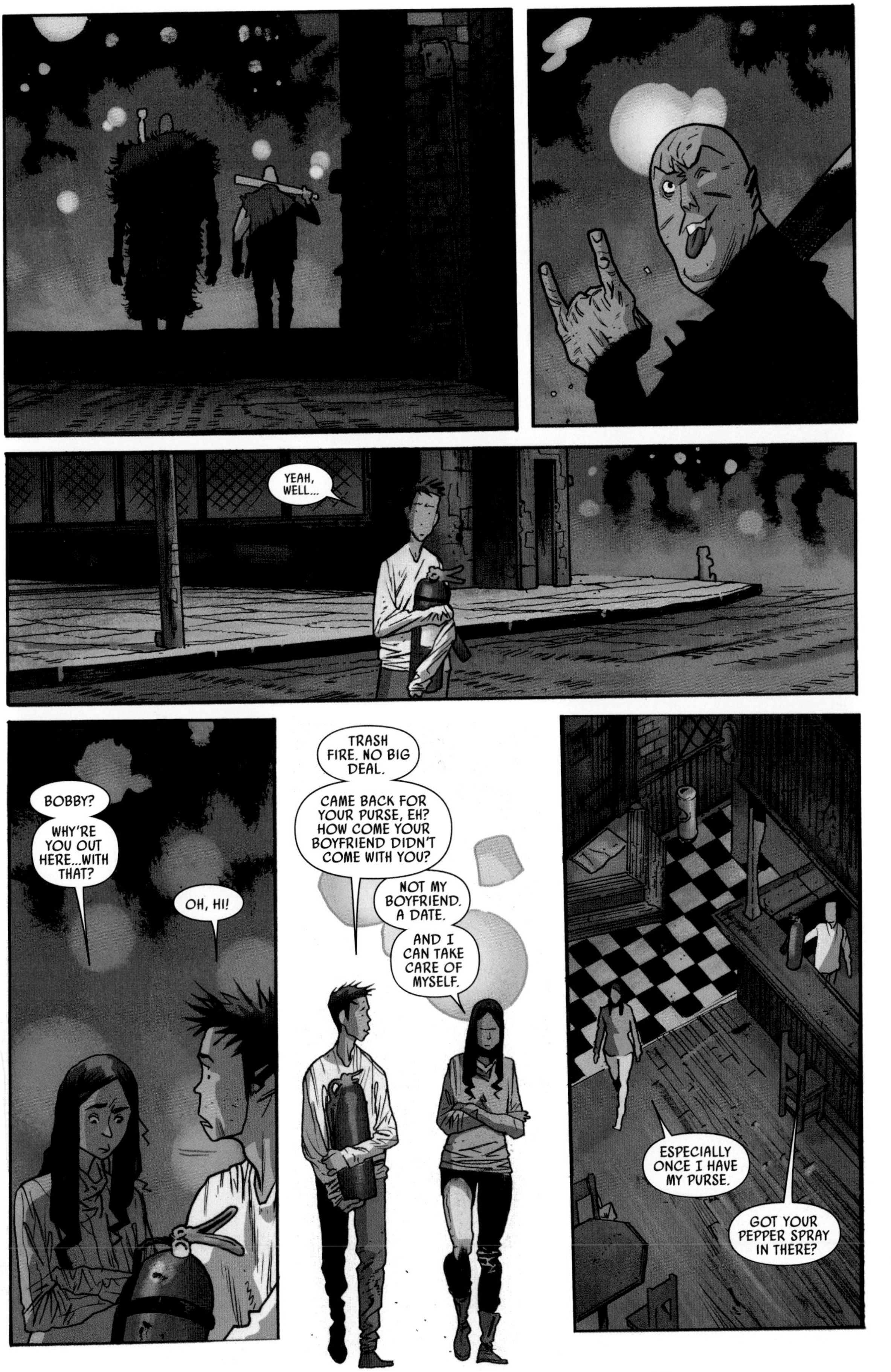
YEAH, WELL...
BOBBY?
WHY'RE YOU OUT HERE...WITH THAT?
OH, HI!
TRASH FIRE. NO BIG DEAL.
CAME BACK FOR YOUR PURSE, EH? HOW COME YOUR BOYFRIEND DIDN'T COME WITH YOU?
NOT MY BOYFRIEND. A DATE.
AND I CAN TAKE CARE OF MYSELF.
ESPECIALLY ONCE I HAVE MY PURSE.
GOT YOUR PEPPER SPRAY IN THERE?

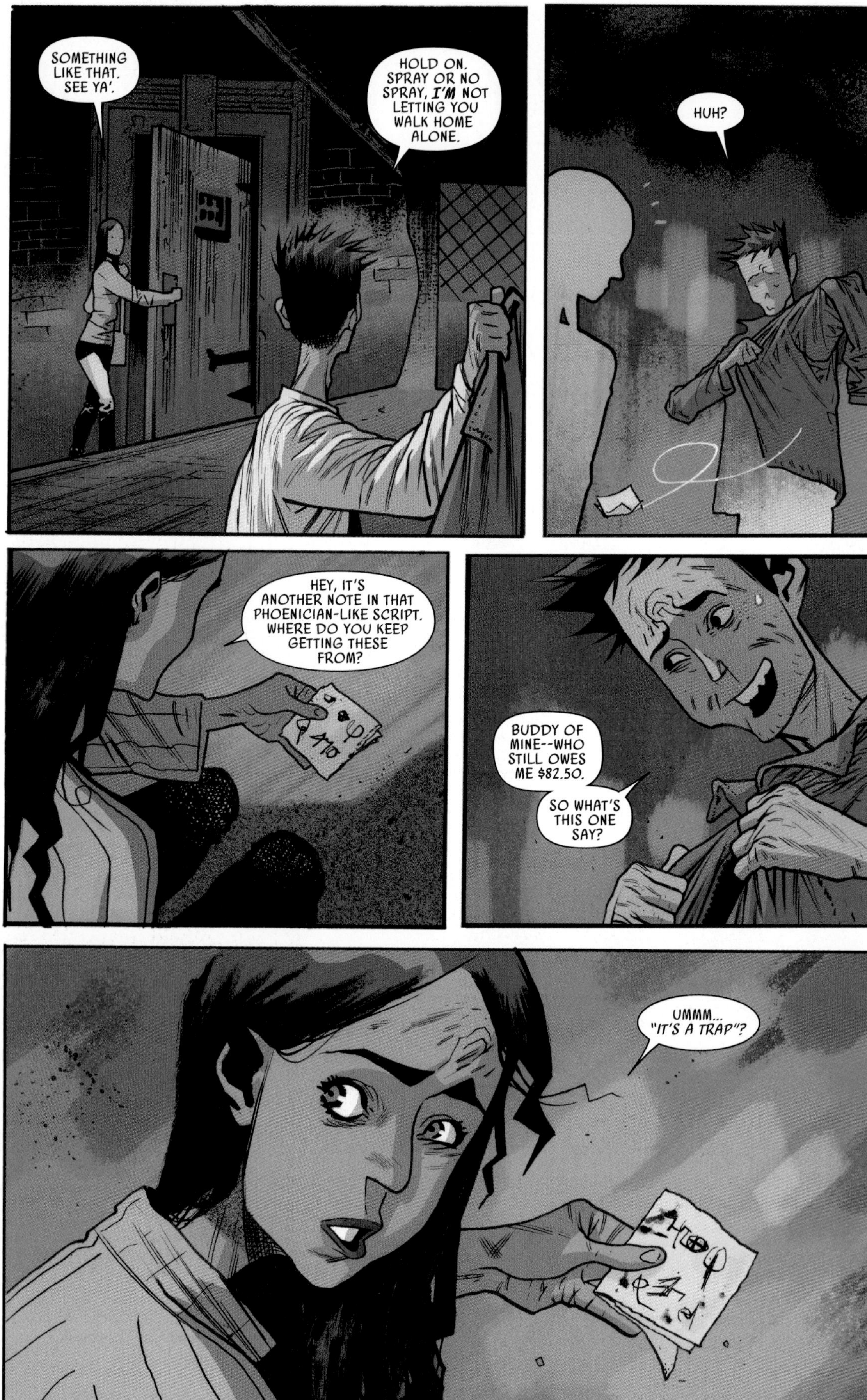
SOMETHING LIKE THAT. SEE YA'.
HOLD ON. SPRAY OR NO SPRAY, I'M NOT LETTING YOU WALK HOME ALONE.
HUH?
HEY, IT'S ANOTHER NOTE IN THAT PHOENICIAN-LIKE SCRIPT. WHERE DO YOU KEEP GETTING THESE FROM?
BUDDY OF MINE--WHO STILL OWES ME $82.50.
SO WHAT'S THIS ONE SAY?
UMMM... "IT'S A TRAP"?

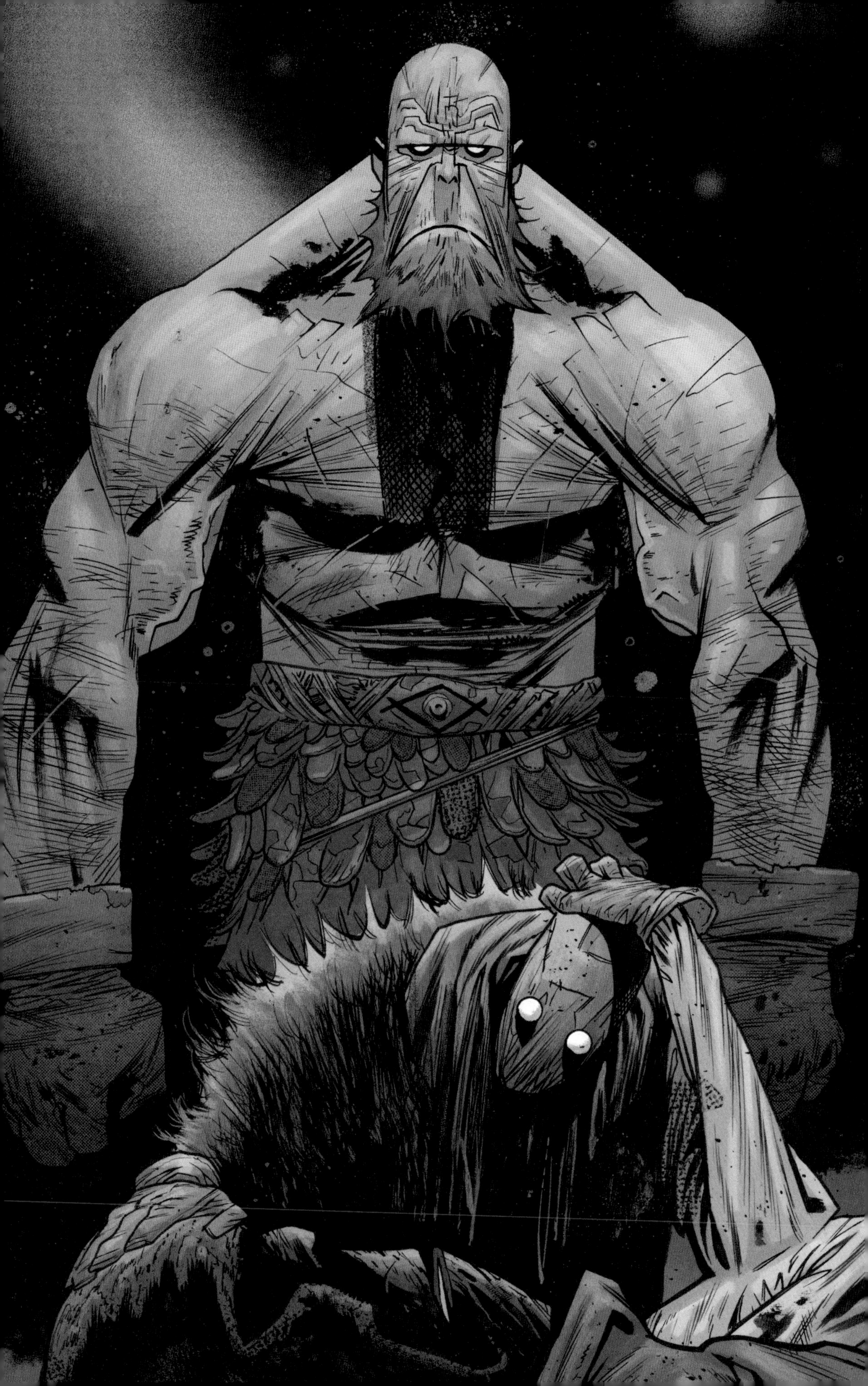

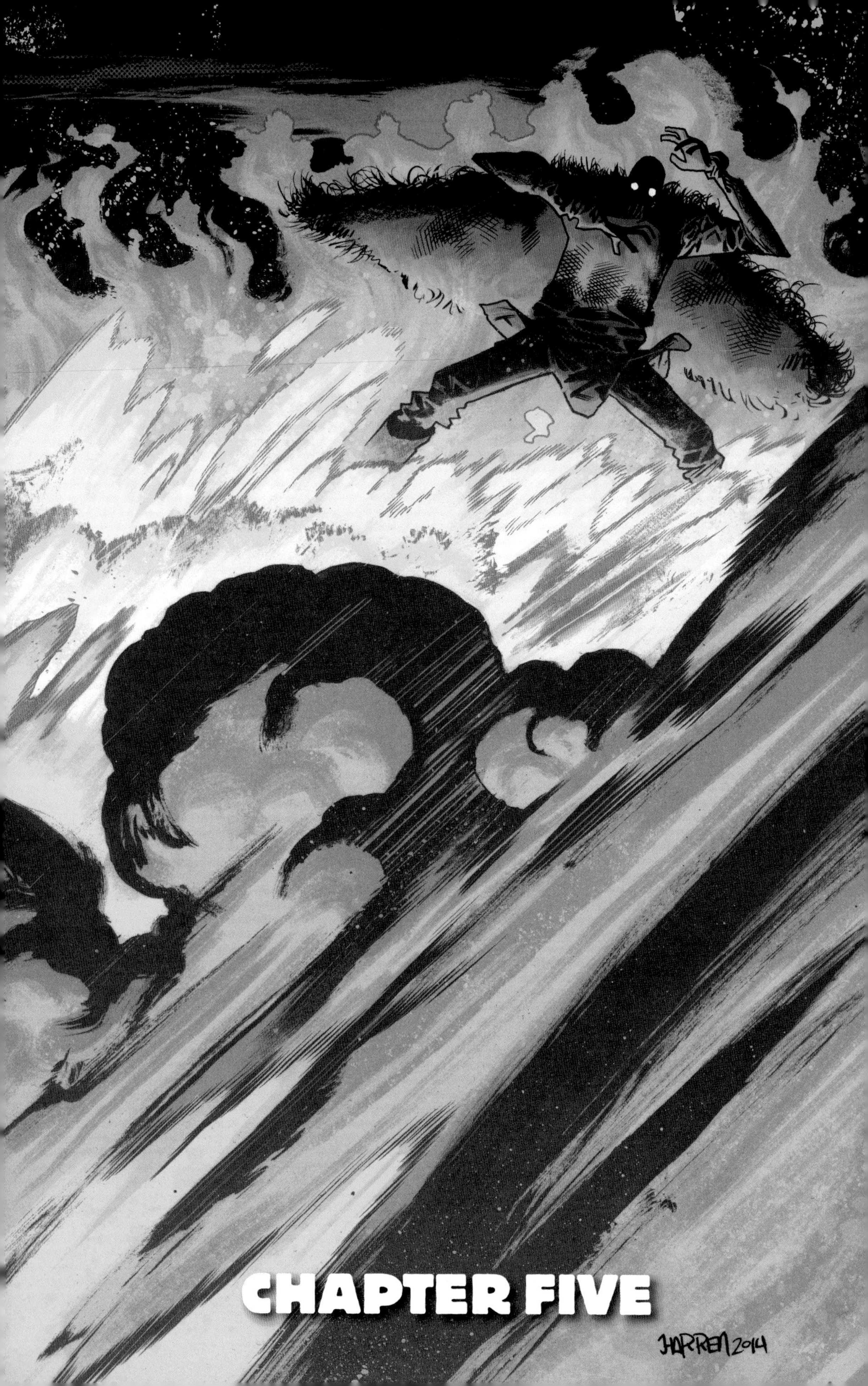
HARREN 2014

CHAPTER FIVE

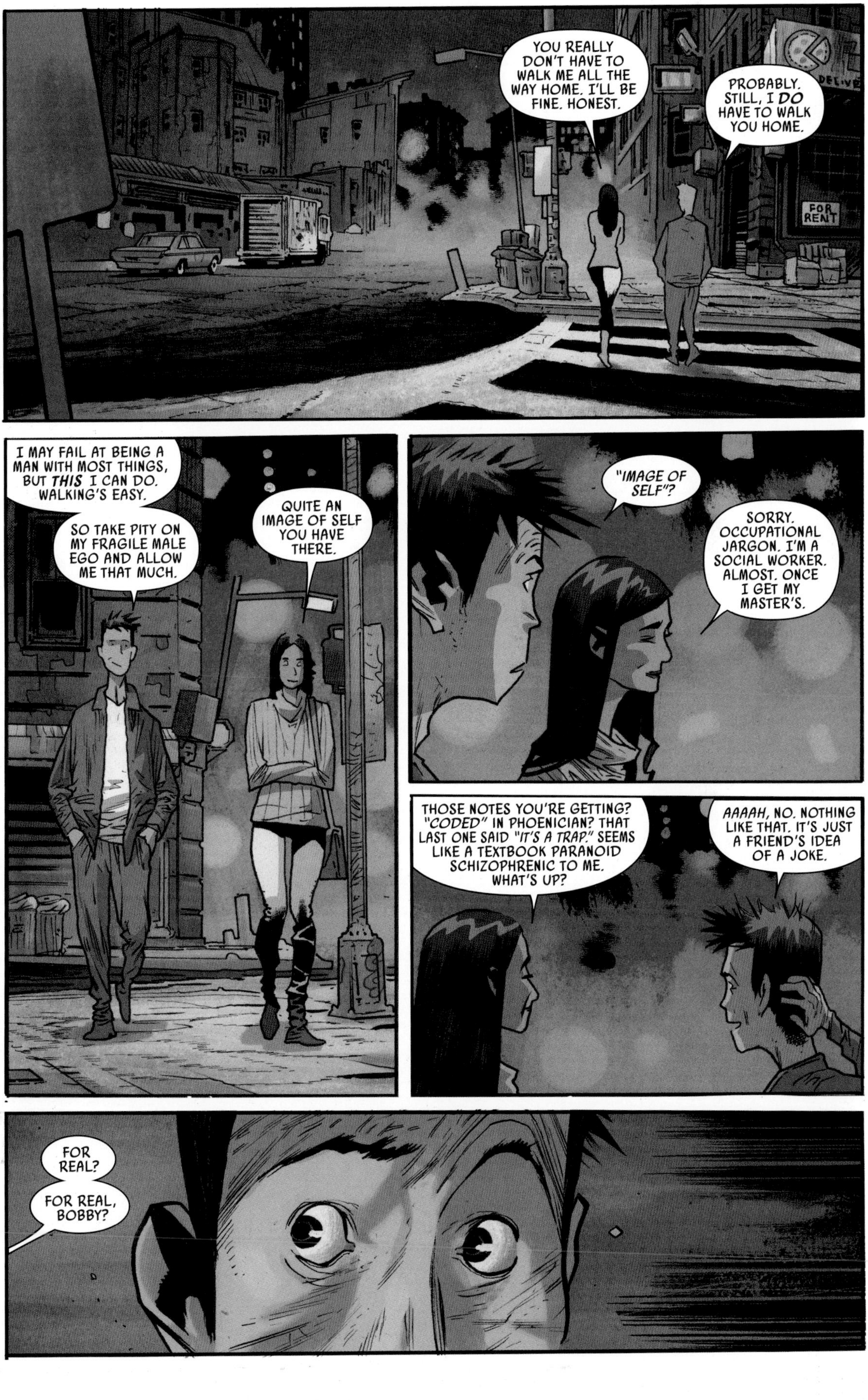
YOU REALLY DON'T HAVE TO WALK ME ALL THE WAY HOME. I'LL BE FINE. HONEST.
PROBABLY. STILL, I *DO* HAVE TO WALK YOU HOME.
FOR RENT
I MAY FAIL AT BEING A MAN WITH MOST THINGS, BUT *THIS* I CAN DO. WALKING'S EASY.
SO TAKE PITY ON MY FRAGILE MALE EGO AND ALLOW ME THAT MUCH.
QUITE AN IMAGE OF SELF YOU HAVE THERE.
"IMAGE OF SELF"?
SORRY. OCCUPATIONAL JARGON. I'M A SOCIAL WORKER. ALMOST. ONCE I GET MY MASTER'S.
THOSE NOTES YOU'RE GETTING? *"CODED"* IN PHOENICIAN? THAT LAST ONE SAID *"IT'S A TRAP."* SEEMS LIKE A TEXTBOOK PARANOID SCHIZOPHRENIC TO ME. WHAT'S UP?
AAAAH, NO. NOTHING LIKE THAT. IT'S JUST A FRIEND'S IDEA OF A JOKE.
FOR REAL?
FOR REAL, BOBBY?

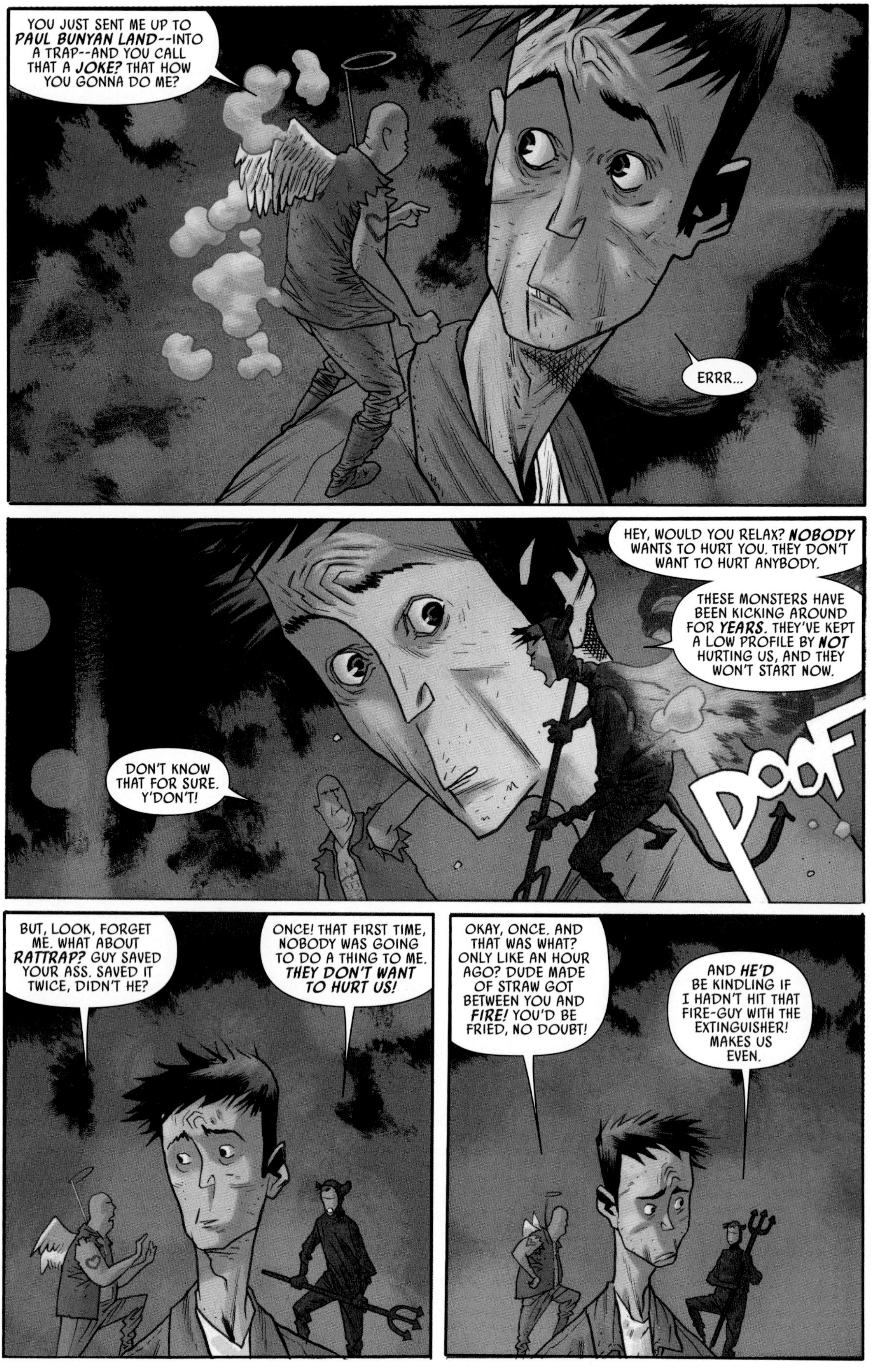
YOU JUST SENT ME UP TO PAUL BUNYAN LAND--INTO A TRAP--AND YOU CALL THAT A JOKE? THAT HOW YOU GONNA DO ME?
ERRR...
HEY, WOULD YOU RELAX? NOBODY WANTS TO HURT YOU. THEY DON'T WANT TO HURT ANYBODY.
THESE MONSTERS HAVE BEEN KICKING AROUND FOR YEARS. THEY'VE KEPT A LOW PROFILE BY NOT HURTING US, AND THEY WON'T START NOW.
POOF
DON'T KNOW THAT FOR SURE. Y'DON'T!
BUT, LOOK, FORGET ME. WHAT ABOUT RATTRAP? GUY SAVED YOUR ASS. SAVED IT TWICE, DIDN'T HE?
ONCE! THAT FIRST TIME, NOBODY WAS GOING TO DO A THING TO ME. THEY DON'T WANT TO HURT US!
OKAY, ONCE. AND THAT WAS WHAT? ONLY LIKE AN HOUR AGO? DUDE MADE OF STRAW GOT BETWEEN YOU AND FIRE! YOU'D BE FRIED, NO DOUBT!
AND HE'D BE KINDLING IF I HADN'T HIT THAT FIRE-GUY WITH THE EXTINGUISHER! MAKES US EVEN.

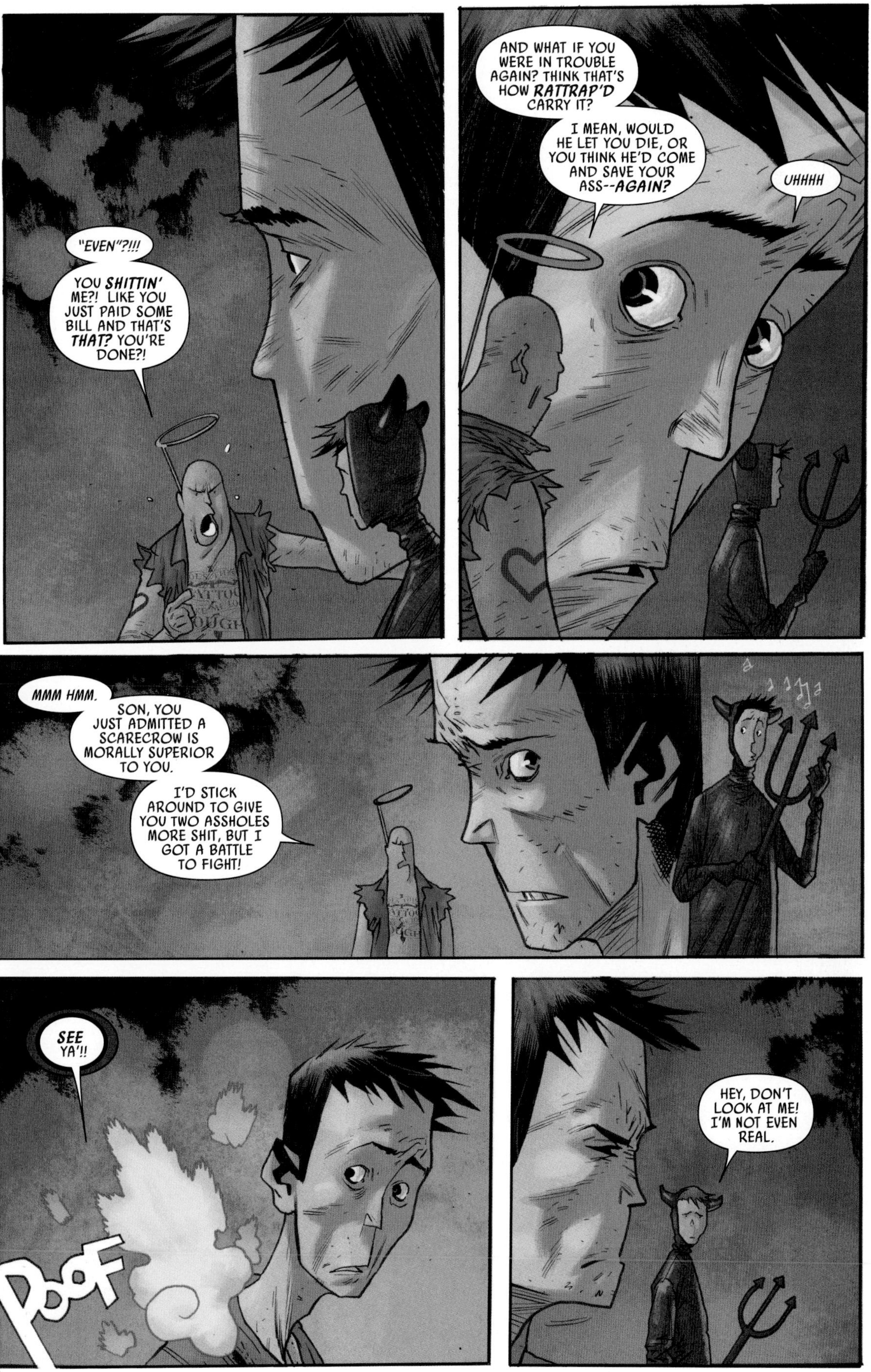
"EVEN"?!!!
YOU SHITTIN' ME?! LIKE YOU JUST PAID SOME BILL AND THAT'S THAT? YOU'RE DONE?!
AND WHAT IF YOU WERE IN TROUBLE AGAIN? THINK THAT'S HOW RATTRAP'D CARRY IT?
I MEAN, WOULD HE LET YOU DIE, OR YOU THINK HE'D COME AND SAVE YOUR ASS--AGAIN?
UHHHH
MMM HMM.
SON, YOU JUST ADMITTED A SCARECROW IS MORALLY SUPERIOR TO YOU.
I'D STICK AROUND TO GIVE YOU TWO ASSHOLES MORE SHIT, BUT I GOT A BATTLE TO FIGHT!
SEE YA'!!
POOF
HEY, DON'T LOOK AT ME! I'M NOT EVEN REAL.

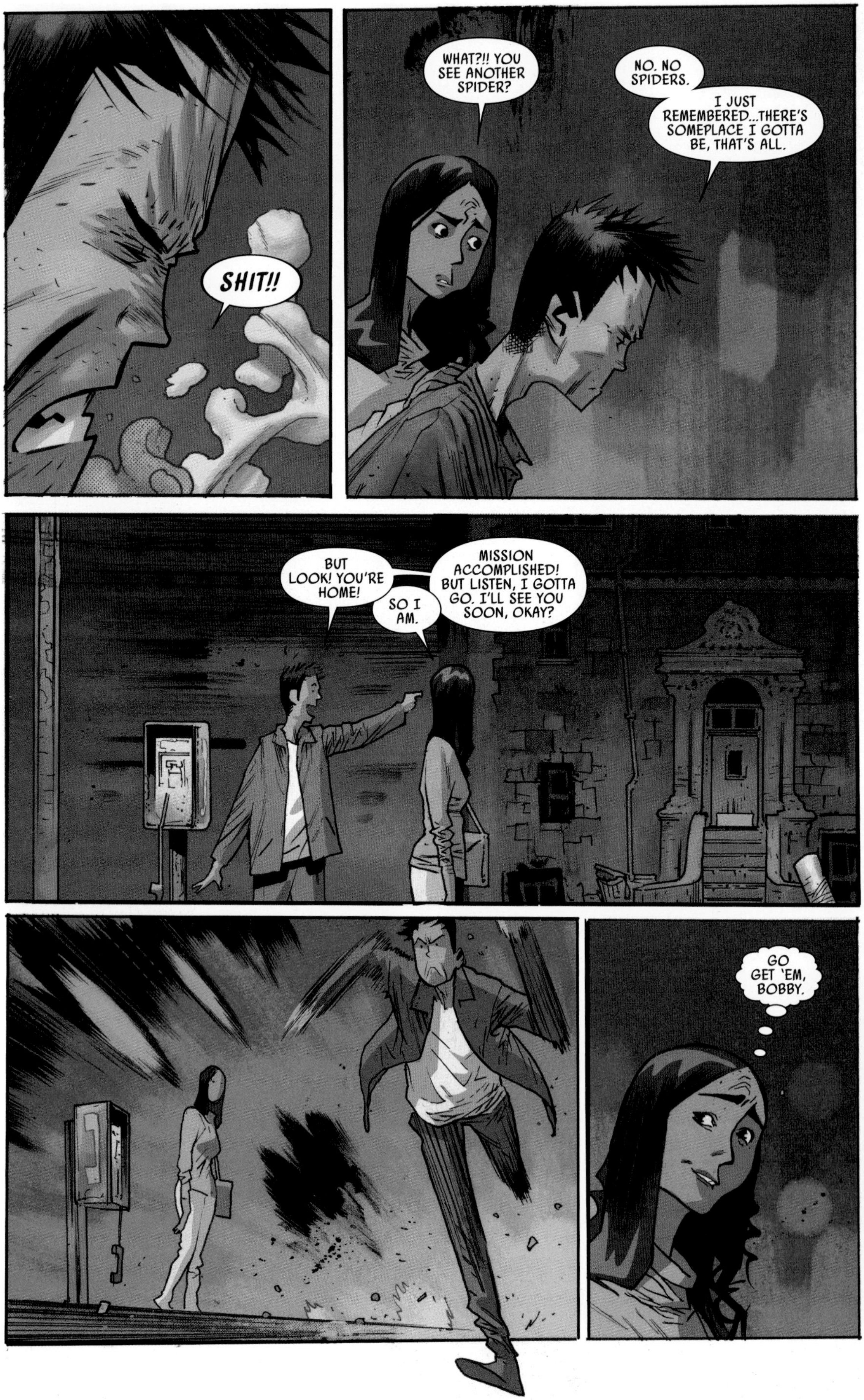
SHIT!!
WHAT?!! YOU SEE ANOTHER SPIDER?
NO. NO SPIDERS.
I JUST REMEMBERED...THERE'S SOMEPLACE I GOTTA BE, THAT'S ALL.
BUT LOOK! YOU'RE HOME!
SO I AM.
MISSION ACCOMPLISHED! BUT LISTEN, I GOTTA GO. I'LL SEE YOU SOON, OKAY?
GO GET 'EM, BOBBY.

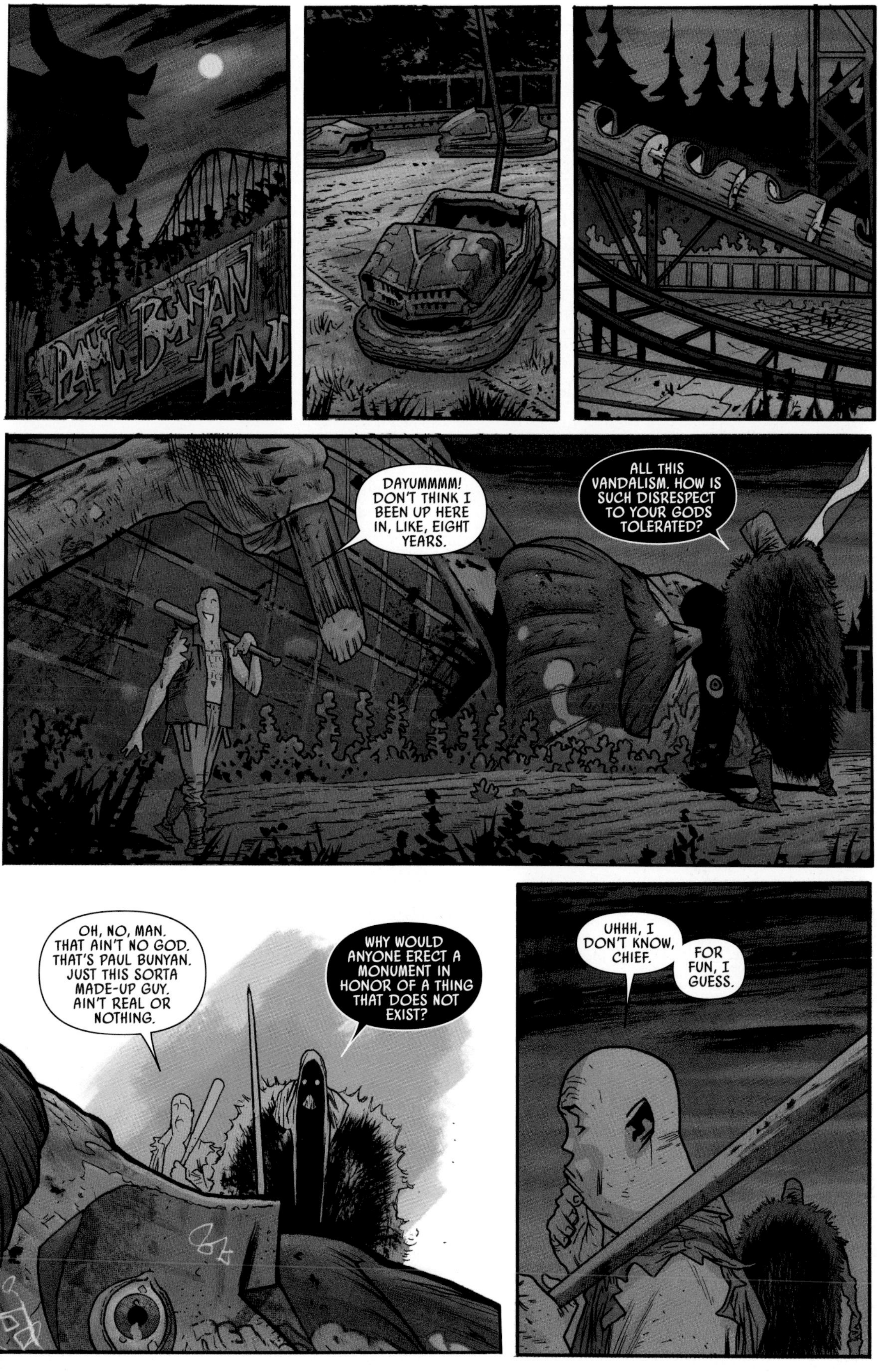
PAUL BUNYAN LAND
DAYUMMMM! DON'T THINK I BEEN UP HERE IN, LIKE, EIGHT YEARS.
ALL THIS VANDALISM. HOW IS SUCH DISRESPECT TO YOUR GODS TOLERATED?
OH, NO, MAN. THAT AIN'T NO GOD. THAT'S PAUL BUNYAN. JUST THIS SORTA MADE-UP GUY. AIN'T REAL OR NOTHING.
WHY WOULD ANYONE ERECT A MONUMENT IN HONOR OF A THING THAT DOES NOT EXIST?
UHHH, I DON'T KNOW, CHIEF.
FOR FUN, I GUESS.

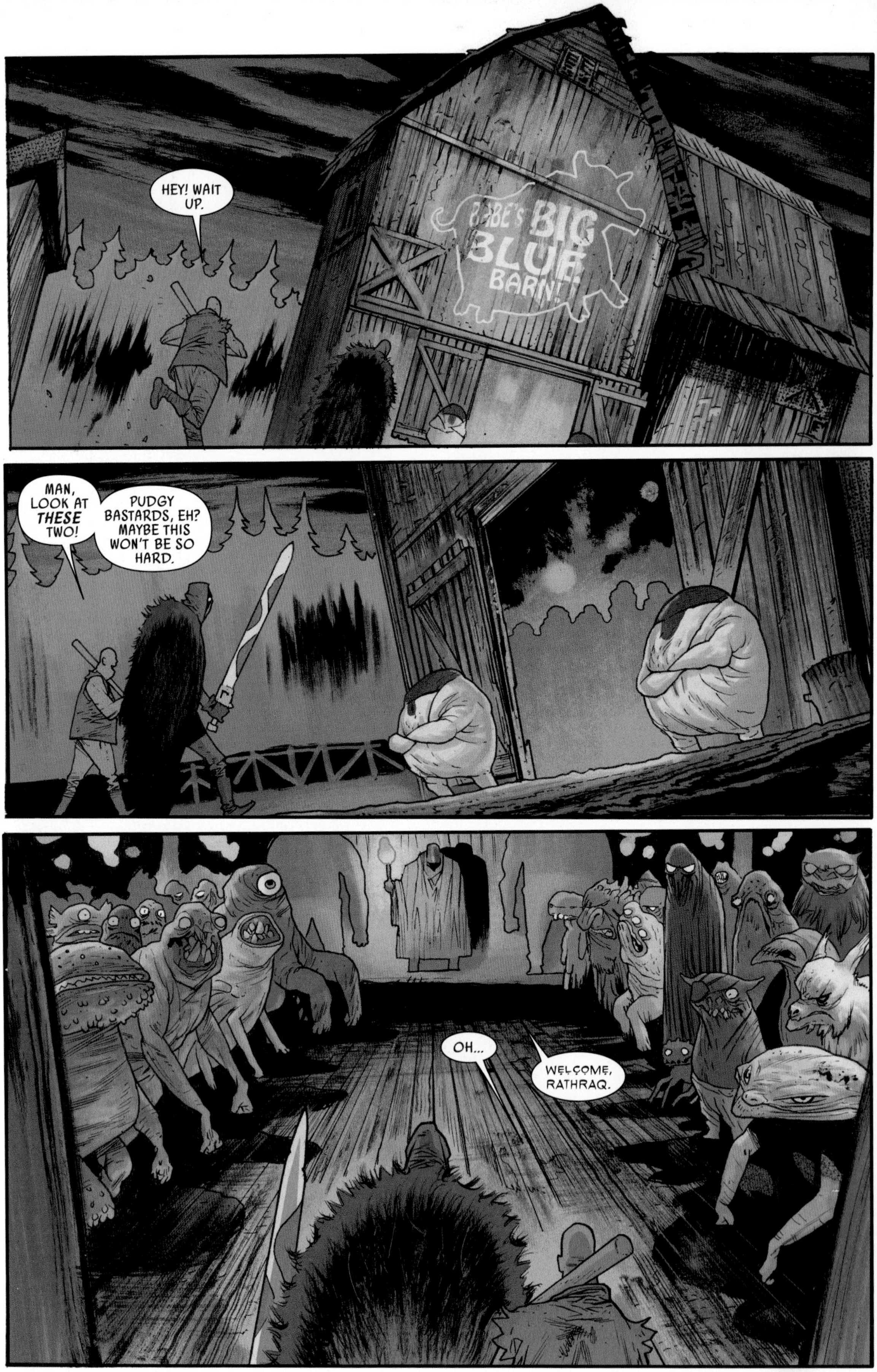
HEY! WAIT UP.
BABE'S BIG BLUE BARN!
MAN, LOOK AT *THESE* TWO!
PUDGY BASTARDS, EH? MAYBE THIS WON'T BE SO HARD.
OH...
WELÇOME, RATHRAQ.

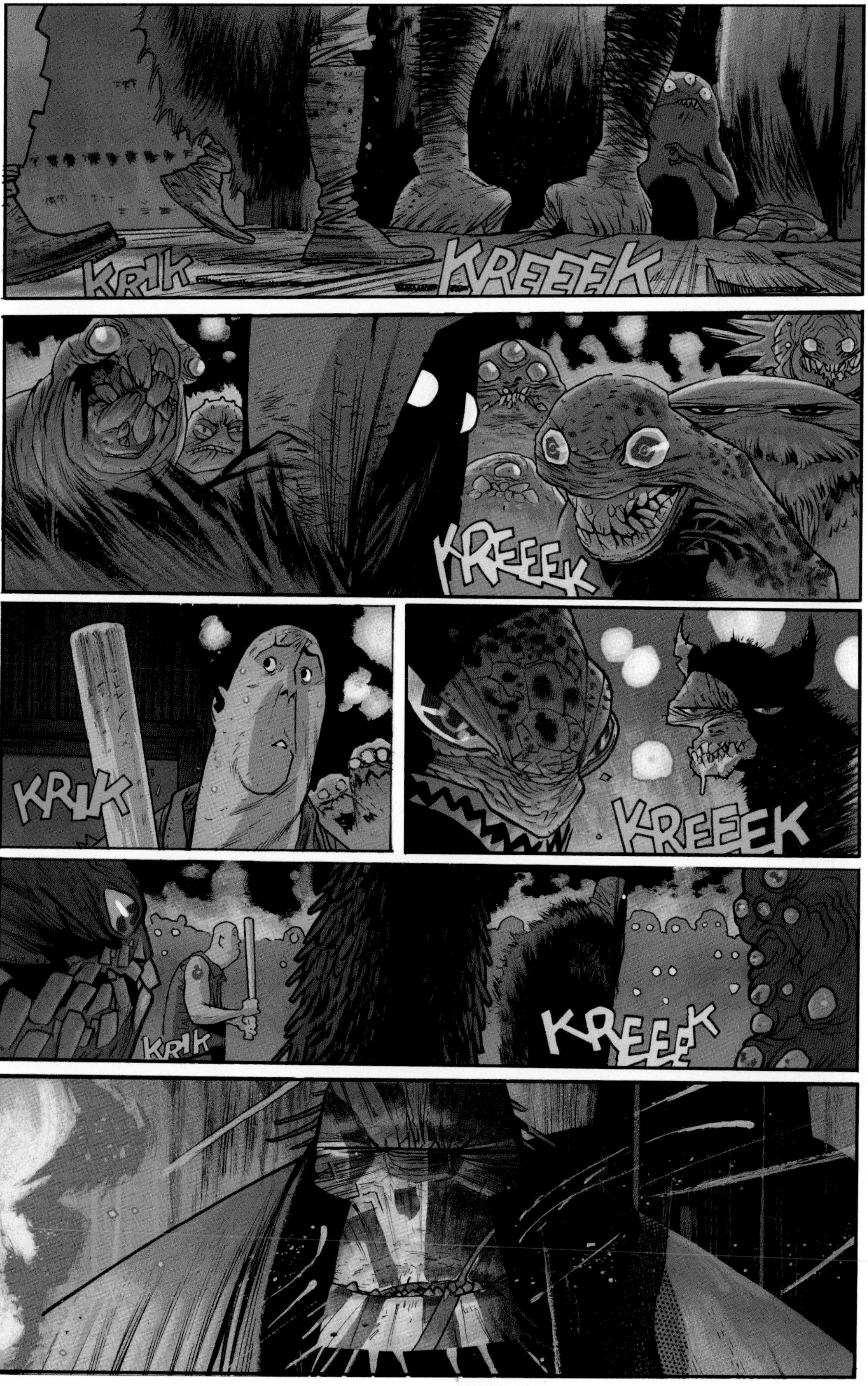
KRIK
KREEEK
KREEEK
KRIK
KREEEK
KRIK
KREEEK

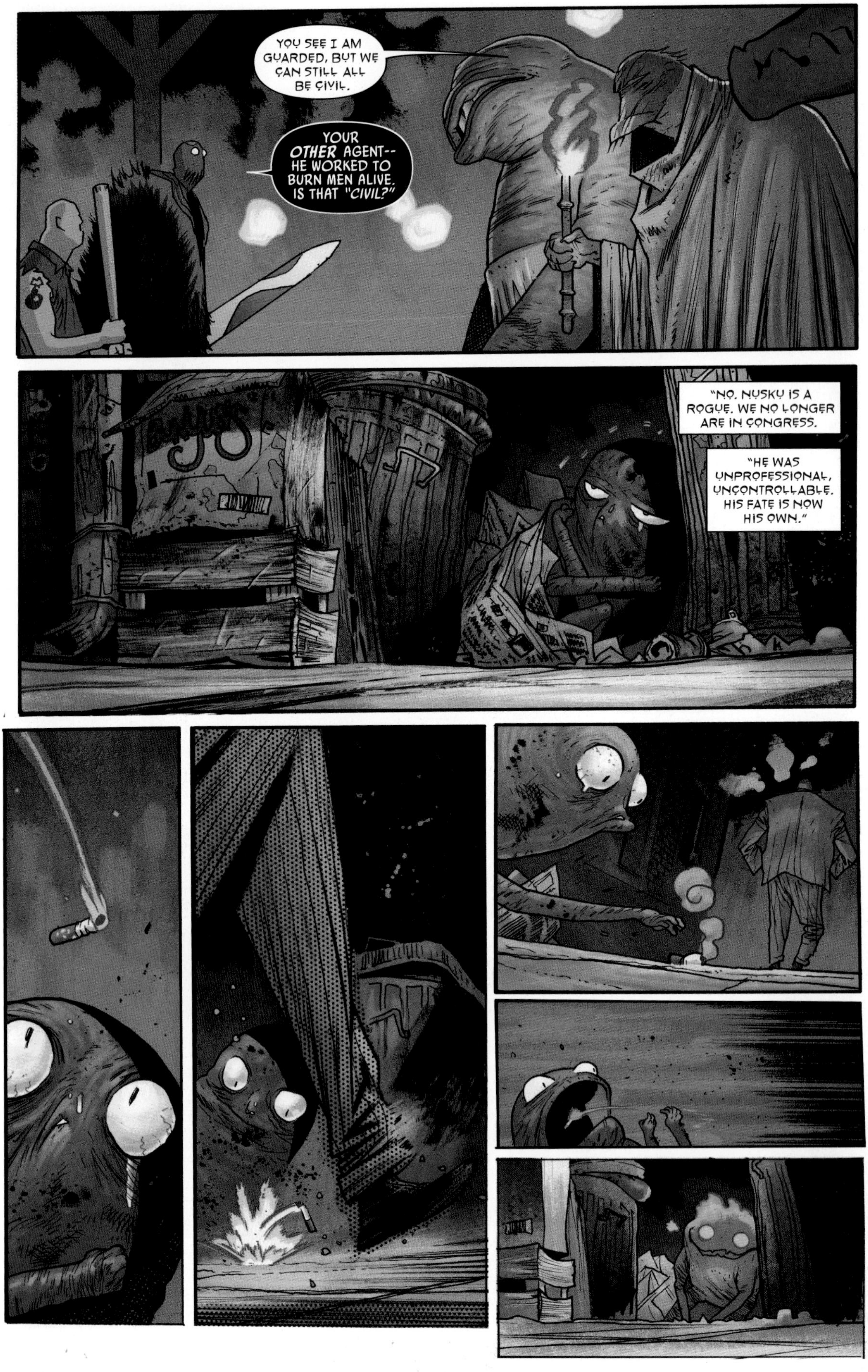
YOU SEE I AM GUARDED, BUT WE CAN STILL ALL BE CIVIL.
YOUR *OTHER* AGENT-- HE WORKED TO BURN MEN ALIVE. IS THAT *"CIVIL?"*
"NO. NUSKU IS A ROGUE. WE NO LONGER ARE IN CONGRESS.
"HE WAS UNPROFESSIONAL, UNCONTROLLABLE. HIS FATE IS NOW HIS OWN."

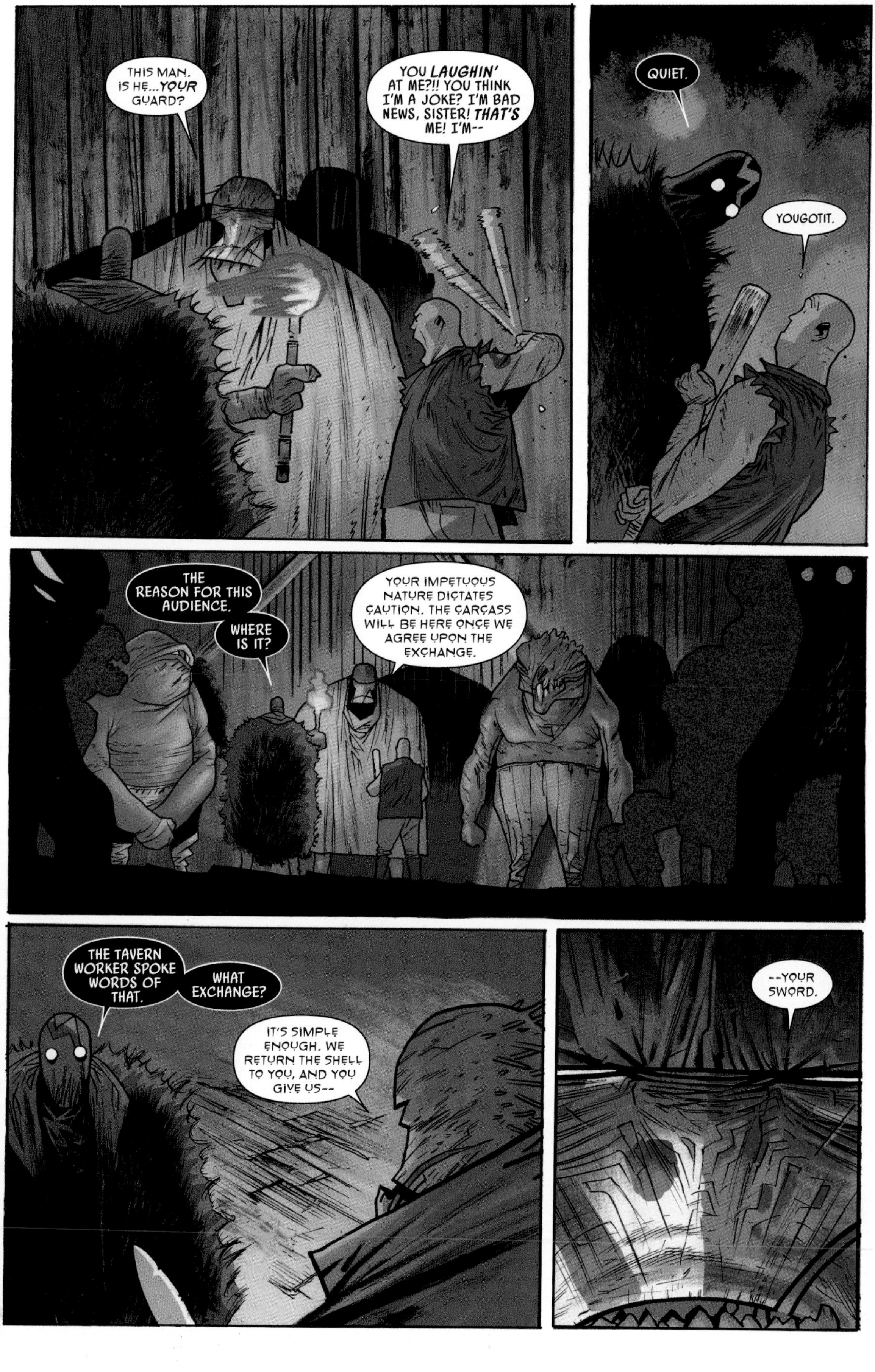
THIS MAN. IS HE...YOUR GUARD?
YOU LAUGHIN' AT ME?!! YOU THINK I'M A JOKE? I'M BAD NEWS, SISTER! THAT'S ME! I'M--
QUIET.
YOUGOTIT.
THE REASON FOR THIS AUDIENCE.
WHERE IS IT?
YOUR IMPETUOUS NATURE DICTATES CAUTION. THE CARCASS WILL BE HERE ONCE WE AGREE UPON THE EXCHANGE.
THE TAVERN WORKER SPOKE WORDS OF THAT.
WHAT EXCHANGE?
IT'S SIMPLE ENOUGH. WE RETURN THE SHELL TO YOU, AND YOU GIVE US--
--YOUR SWORD.

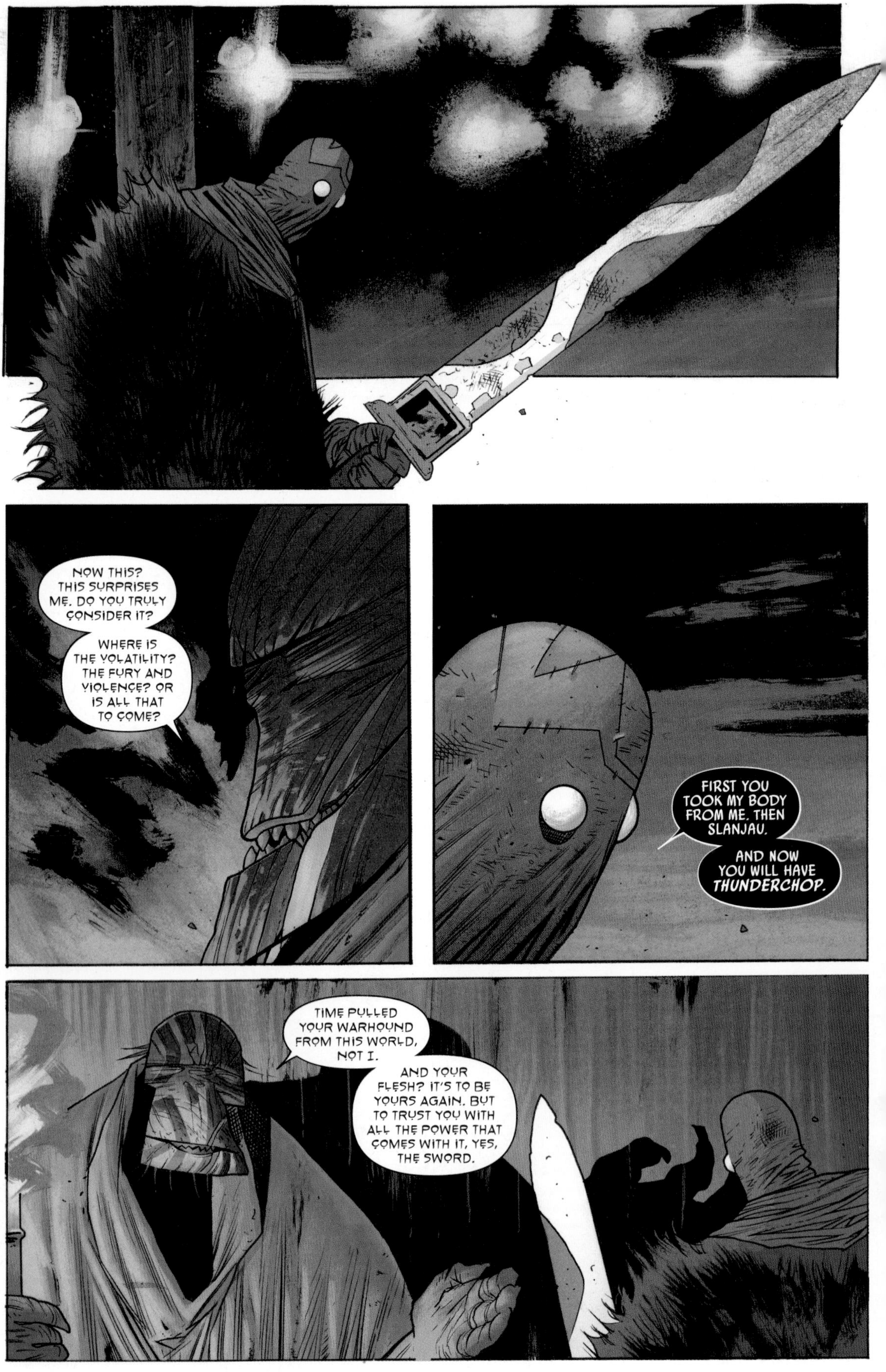
NOW THIS? THIS SURPRISES ME. DO YOU TRULY CONSIDER IT?
WHERE IS THE VOLATILITY? THE FURY AND VIOLENCE? OR IS ALL THAT TO COME?
FIRST YOU TOOK MY BODY FROM ME. THEN SLANJAU.
AND NOW YOU WILL HAVE THUNDERCHOP.
TIME PULLED YOUR WARHOUND FROM THIS WORLD, NOT I.
AND YOUR FLESH? IT'S TO BE YOURS AGAIN. BUT TO TRUST YOU WITH ALL THE POWER THAT COMES WITH IT, YES, THE SWORD.

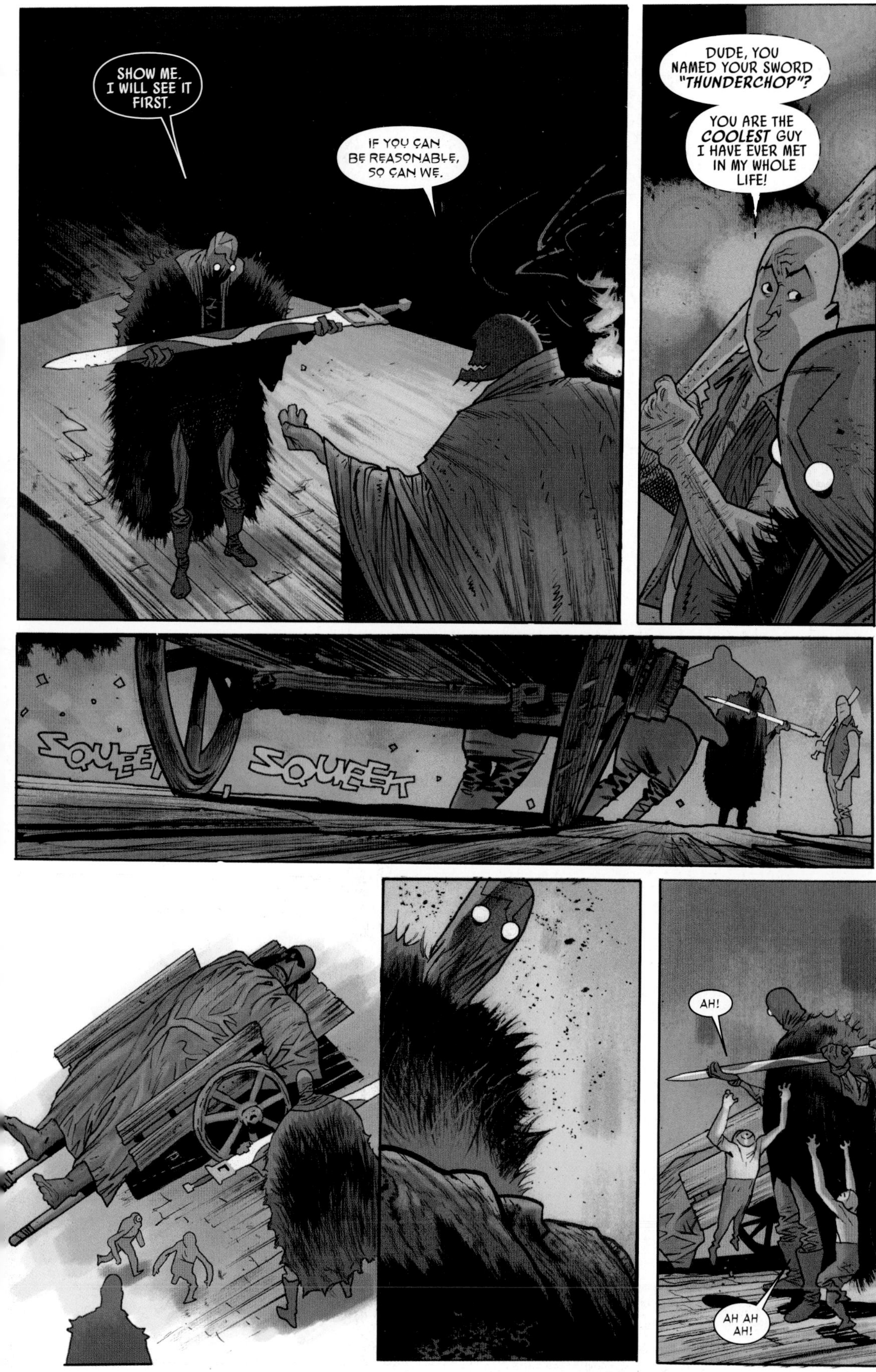
SHOW ME. I WILL SEE IT FIRST.
IF YOU CAN BE REASONABLE, SO CAN WE.
DUDE, YOU NAMED YOUR SWORD "THUNDERCHOP"?
YOU ARE THE COOLEST GUY I HAVE EVER MET IN MY WHOLE LIFE!
SQUEEEK
SQUEEEK
AH!
AH AH AH!

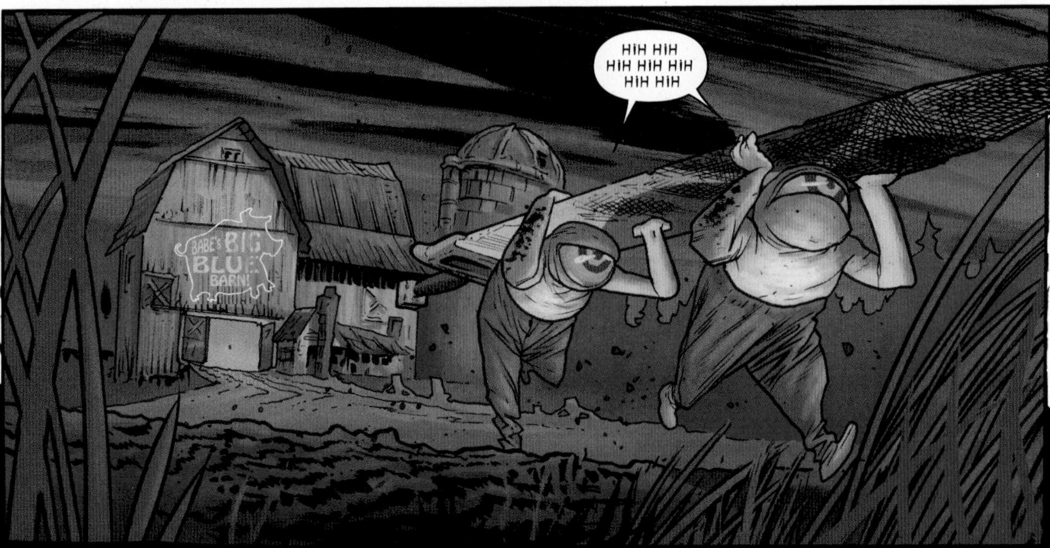
HIH HIH
HIH HIH HIH
HIH HIH
BABE'S BIG BLUE BARN!
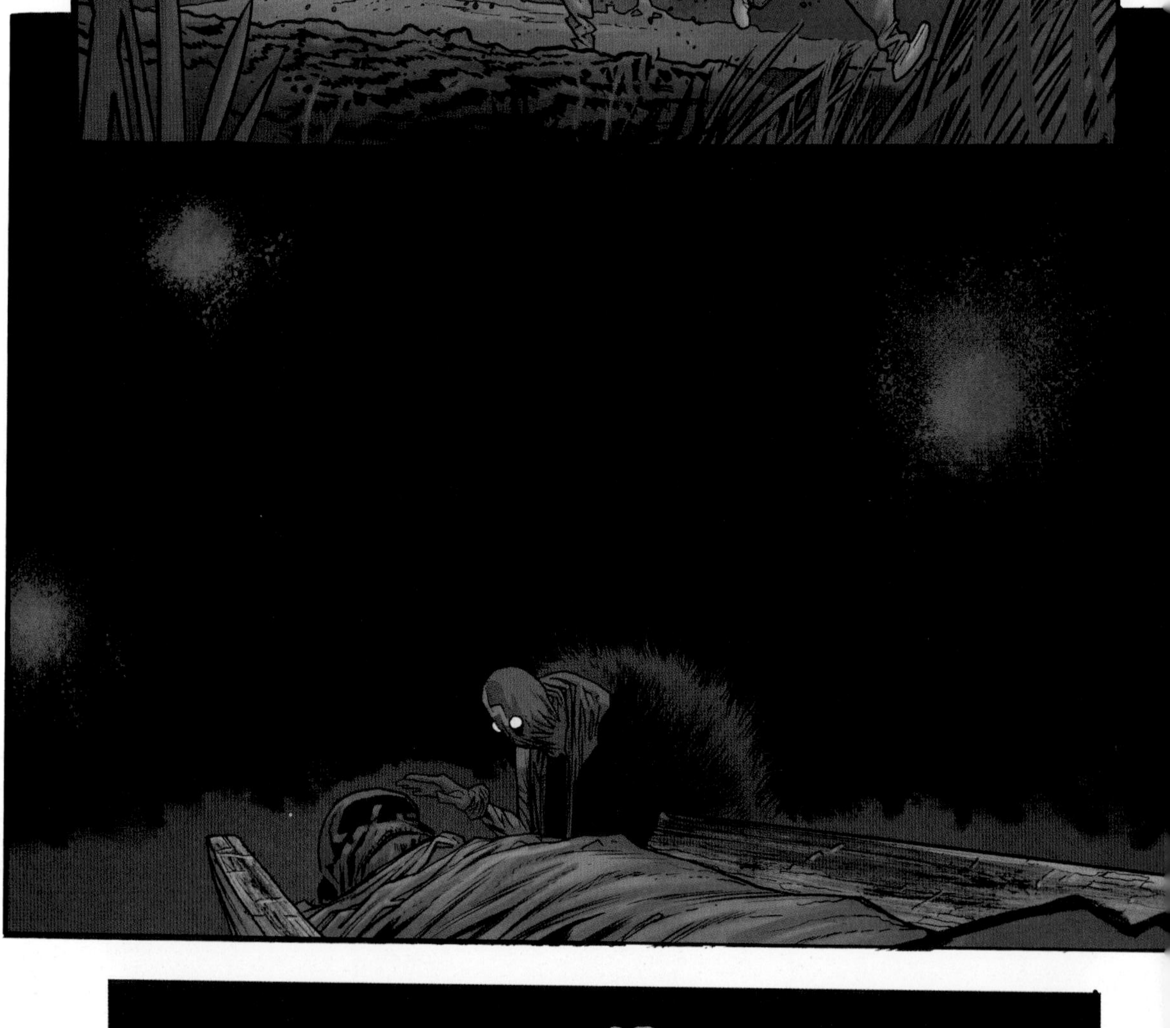
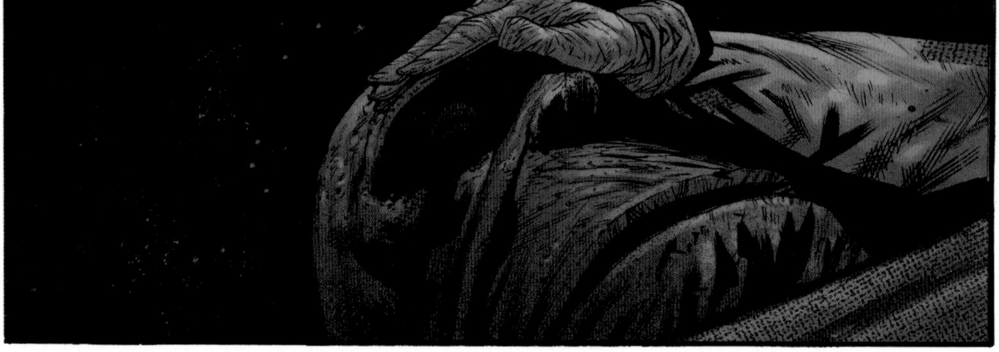

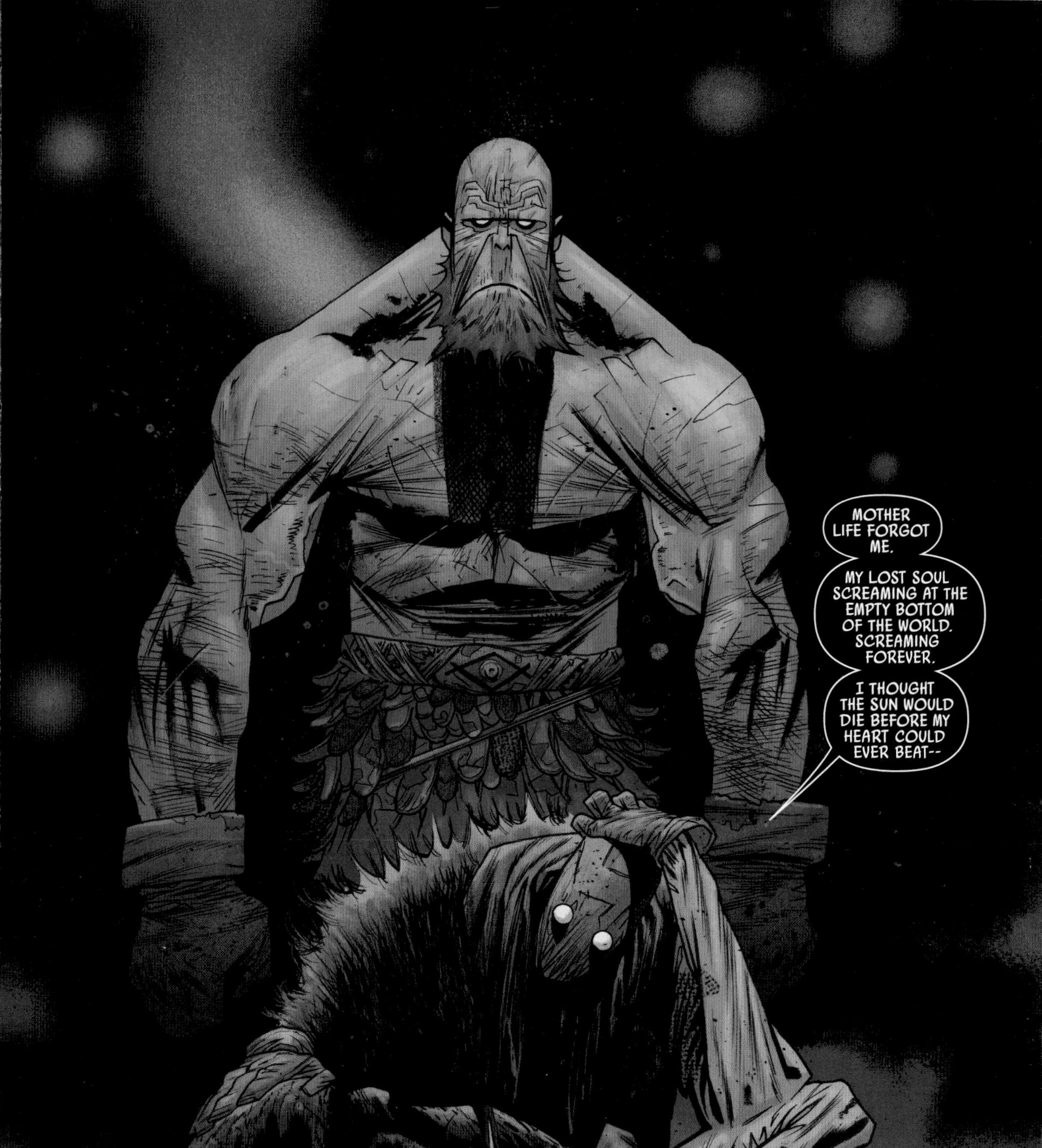
MOTHER LIFE FORGOT ME.
MY LOST SOUL SCREAMING AT THE EMPTY BOTTOM OF THE WORLD. SCREAMING FOREVER.
I THOUGHT THE SUN WOULD DIE BEFORE MY HEART COULD EVER BEAT--

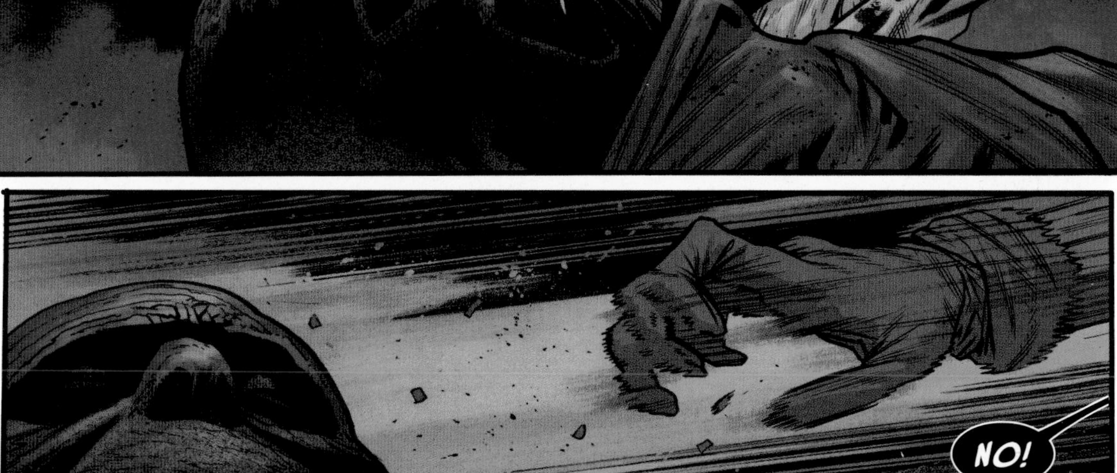
NO!

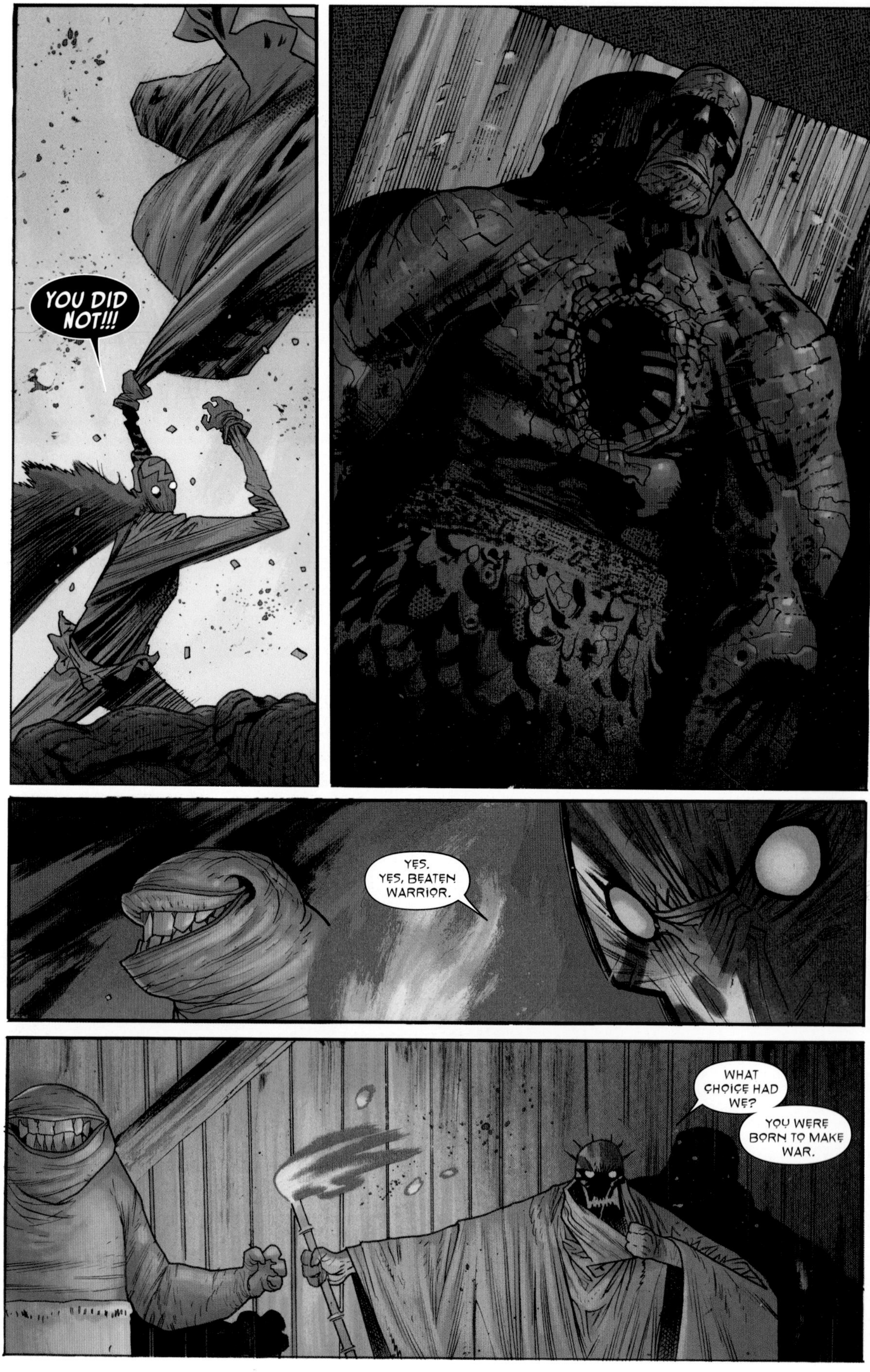
YOU DID NOT!!!
YES. YES, BEATEN WARRIOR.
WHAT CHOICE HAD WE?
YOU WERE BORN TO MAKE WAR.

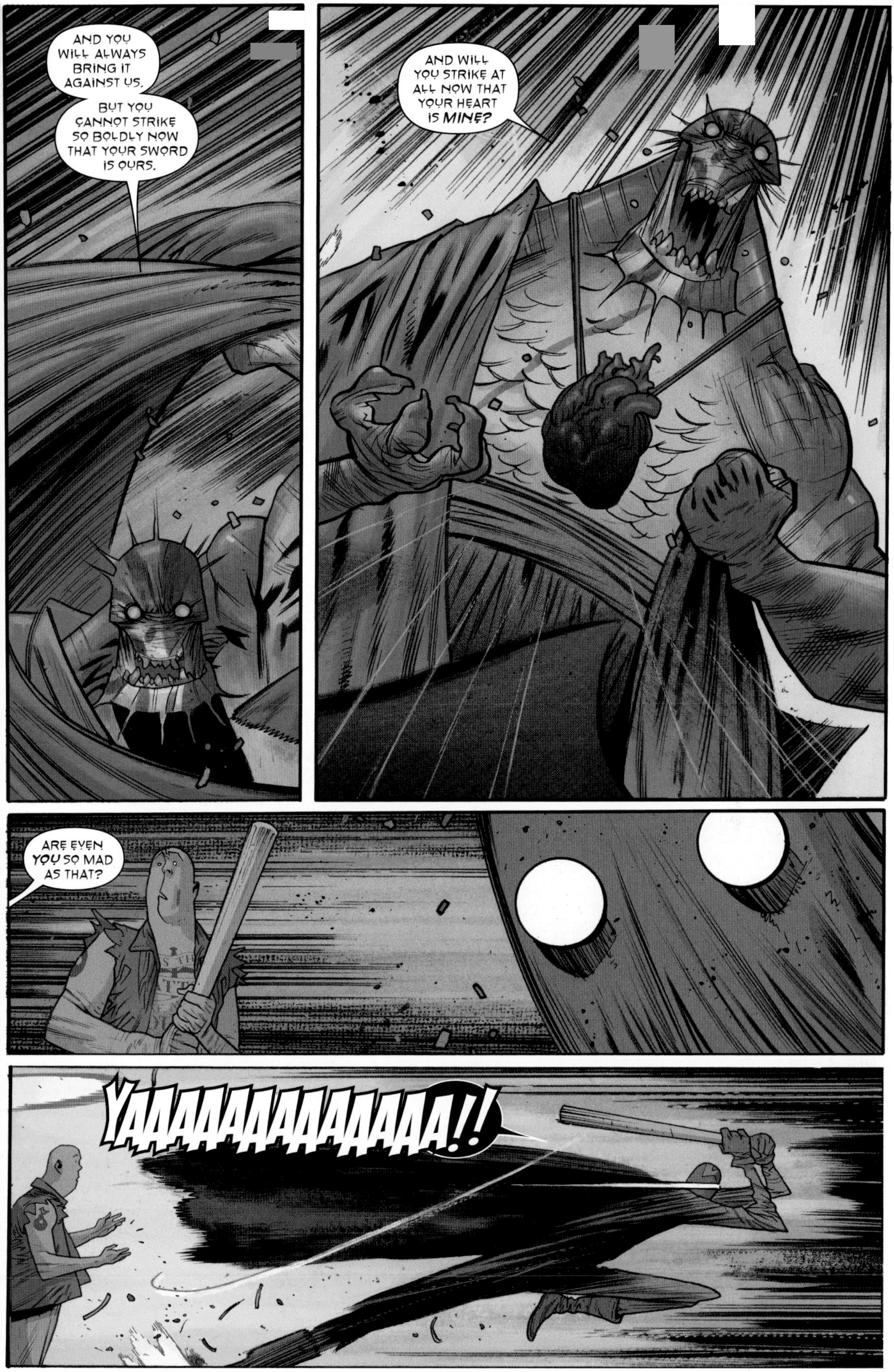
AND YOU WILL ALWAYS BRING IT AGAINST US.
BUT YOU CANNOT STRIKE SO BOLDLY NOW THAT YOUR SWORD IS OURS.
AND WILL YOU STRIKE AT ALL NOW THAT YOUR HEART IS MINE?
ARE EVEN YOU SO MAD AS THAT?
YAAAAAAAAAAAAA!!

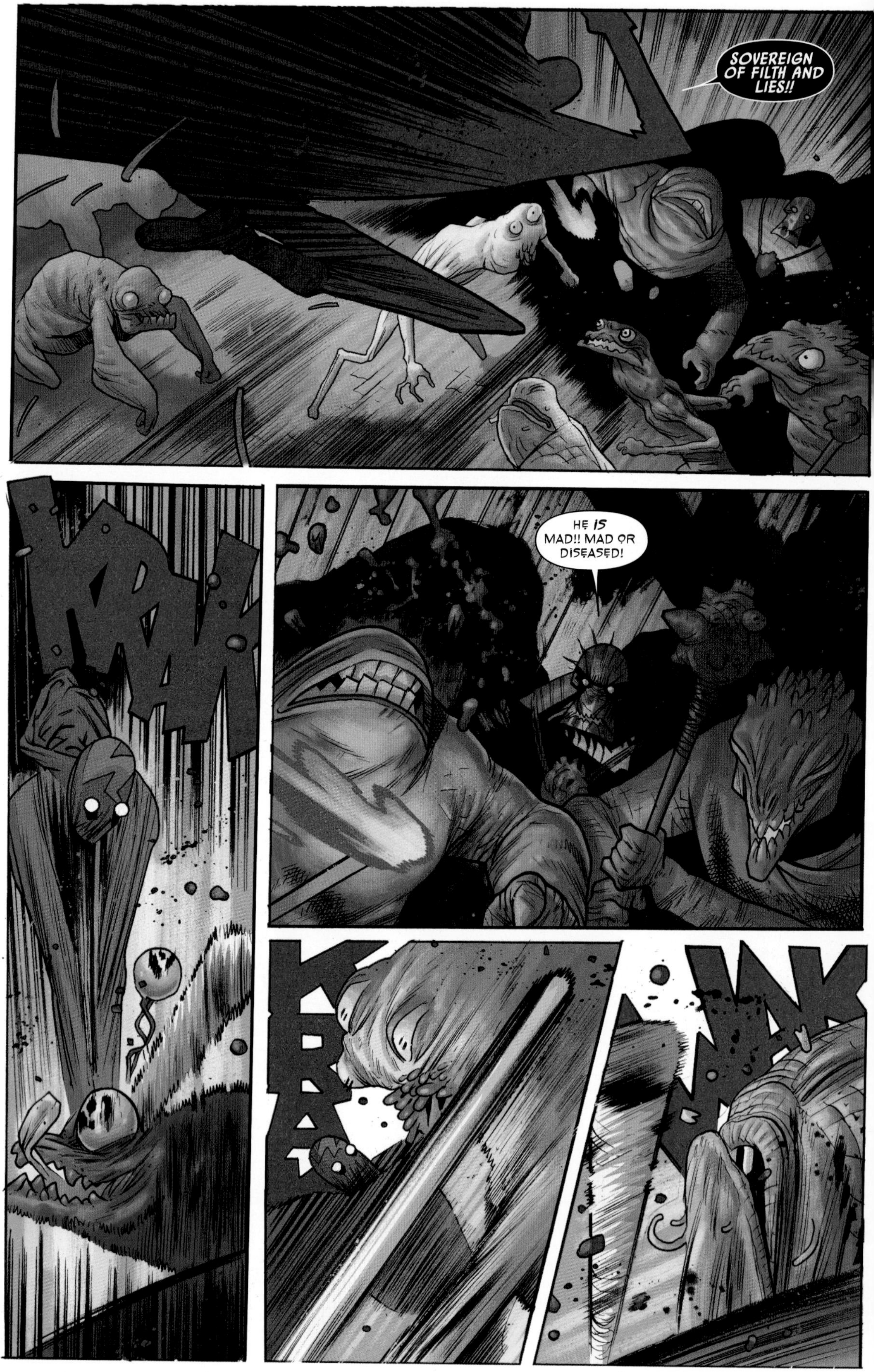
SOVEREIGN OF FILTH AND LIES!!
HE *IS* MAD!! MAD OR DISEASED!

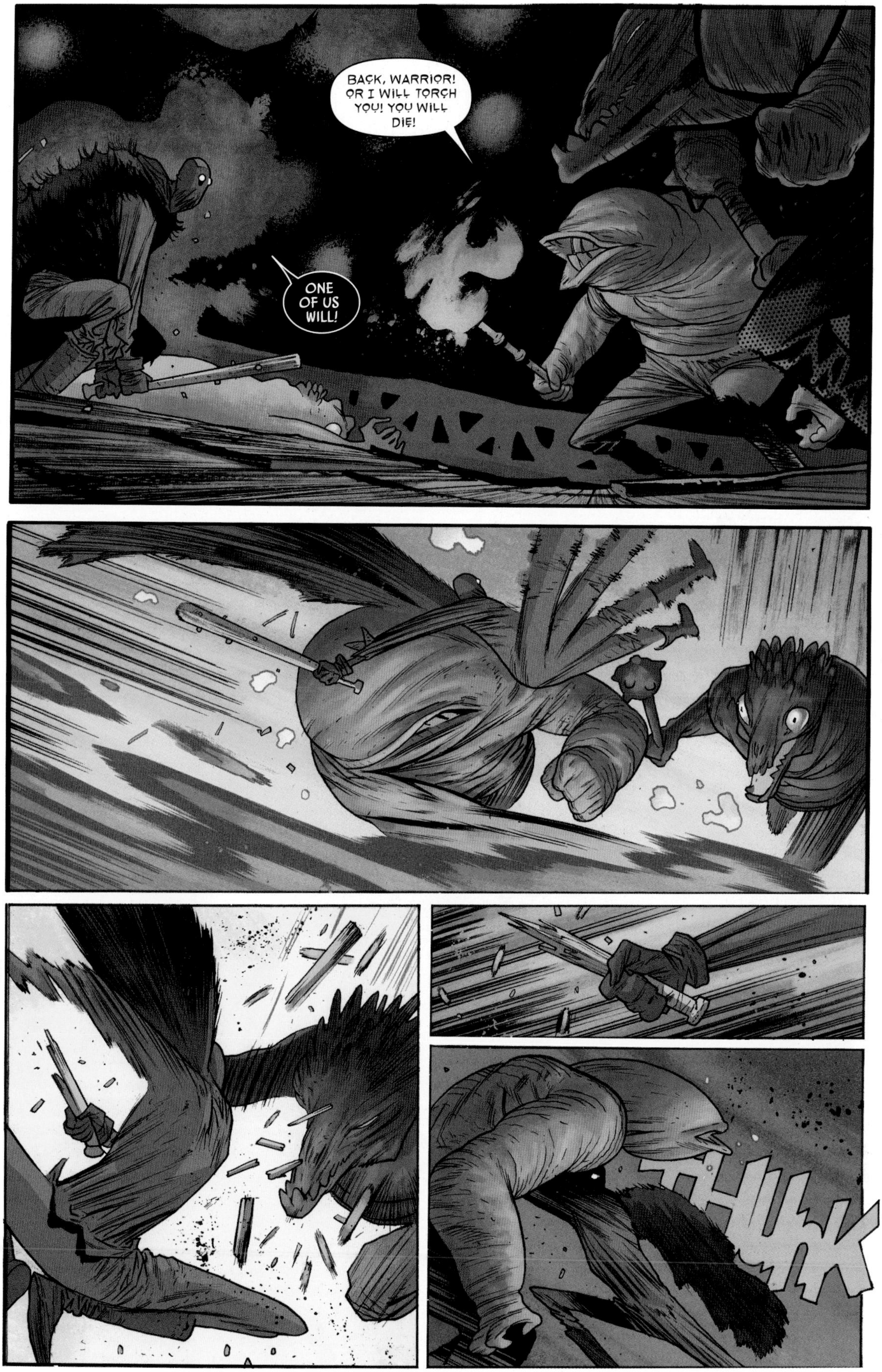
BACK, WARRIOR! OR I WILL TORCH YOU! YOU WILL DIE!
ONE OF US WILL!
THUNK

I MUST BE CRAZY COMING HERE. WHAT AM I SUPPOSED TO DO? WHAT *CAN* I DO?

JRNK, GRAAA KRAK WHAK ROOOARR

OH, GOD! *LISTEN* TO THAT! IT'S A MONSTER FIGHT!

NO *WAY* I CAN LIVE THROUGH THAT! I GO IN THERE, I'M DEAD!

?

WHHOOOM!

YEEEE!!

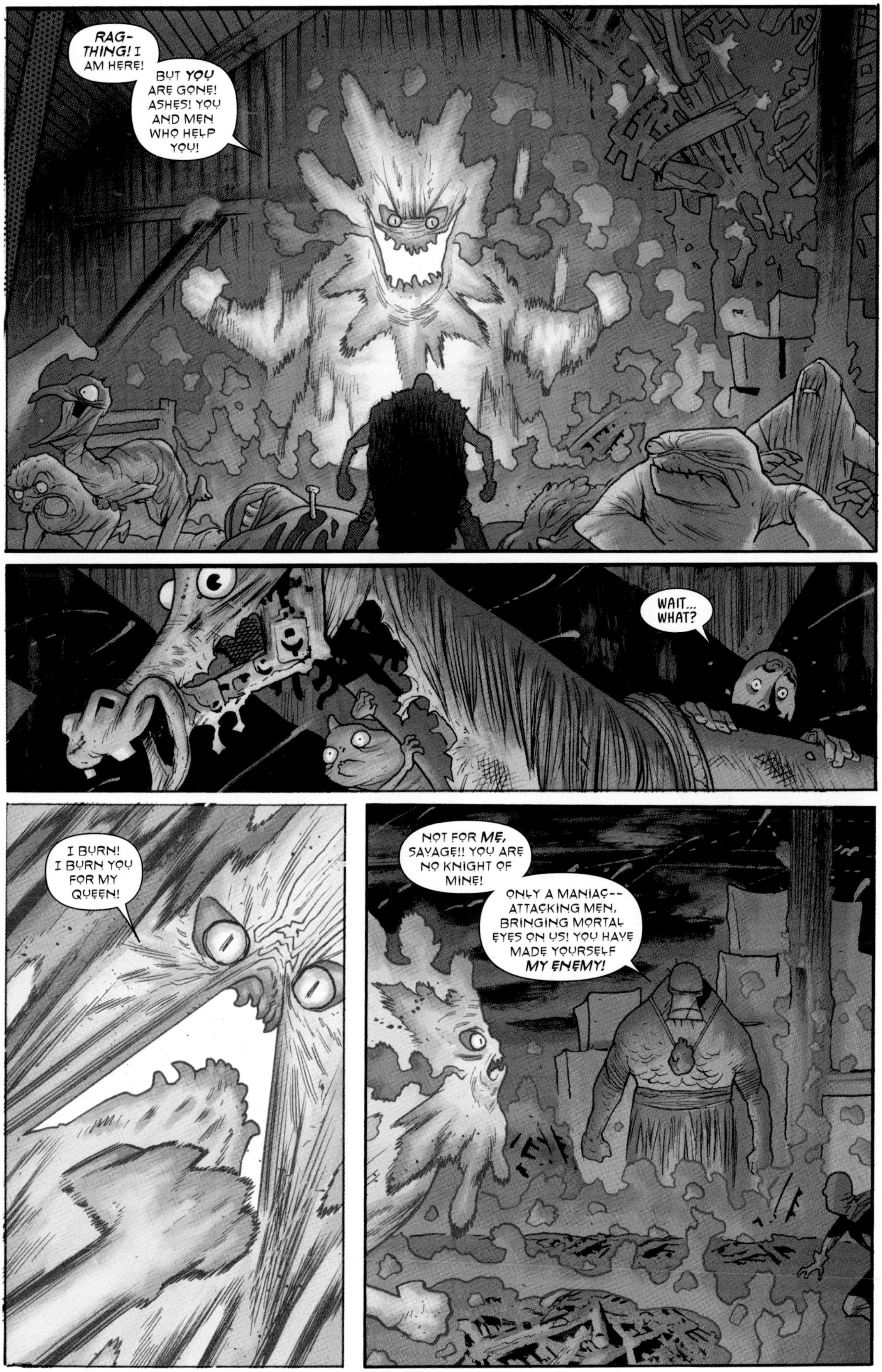
RAG-THING! I AM HERE!
BUT YOU ARE GONE! ASHES! YOU AND MEN WHO HELP YOU!
WAIT... WHAT?
I BURN! I BURN YOU FOR MY QUEEN!
NOT FOR ME, SAVAGE!! YOU ARE NO KNIGHT OF MINE!
ONLY A MANIAC-- ATTACKING MEN, BRINGING MORTAL EYES ON US! YOU HAVE MADE YOURSELF MY ENEMY!

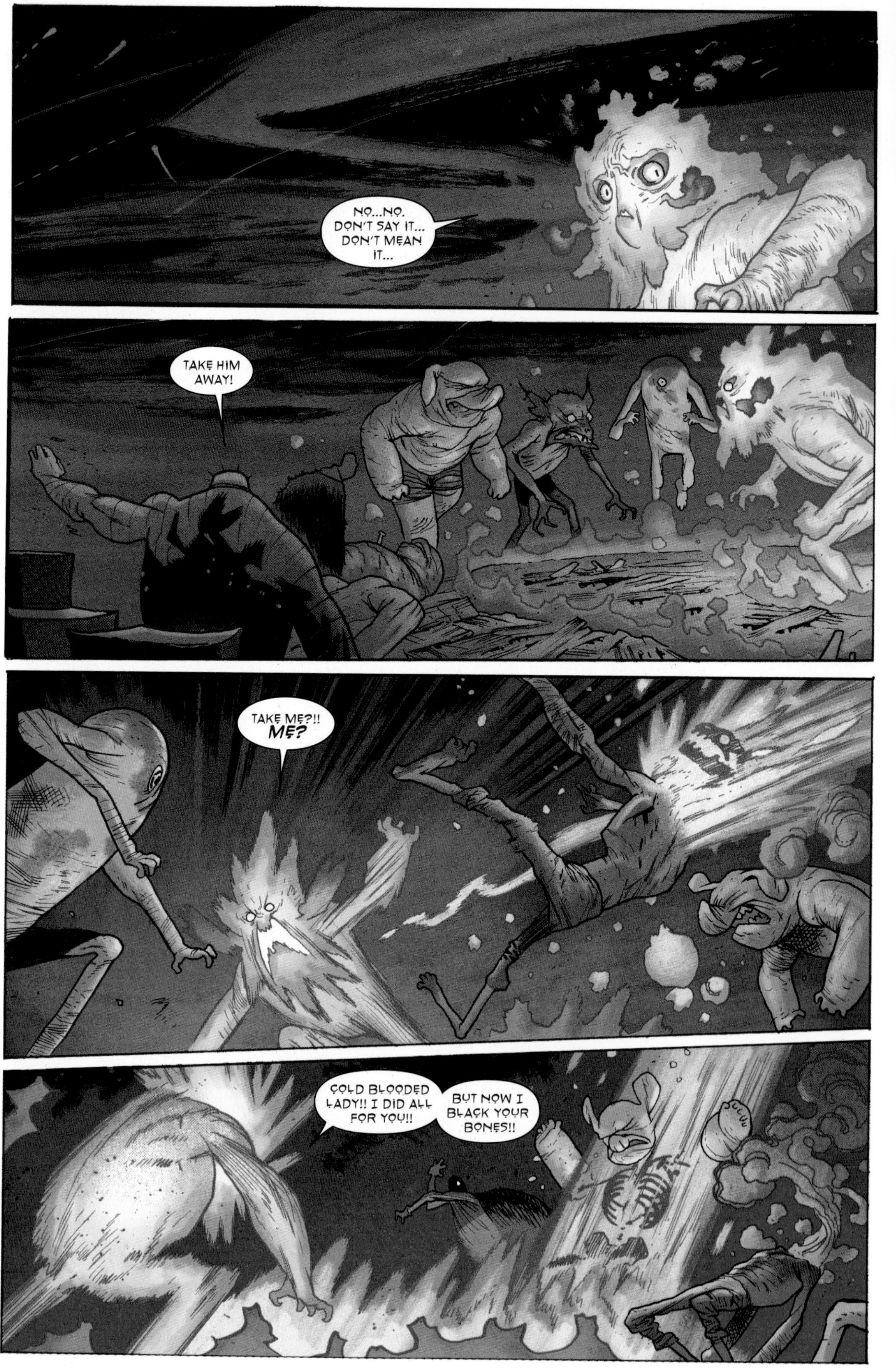
NO...NO. DON'T SAY IT... DON'T MEAN IT...
TAKE HIM AWAY!
TAKE ME?!! ME?
COLD BLOODED LADY!! I DID ALL FOR YOU!!
BUT NOW I BLACK YOUR BONES!!

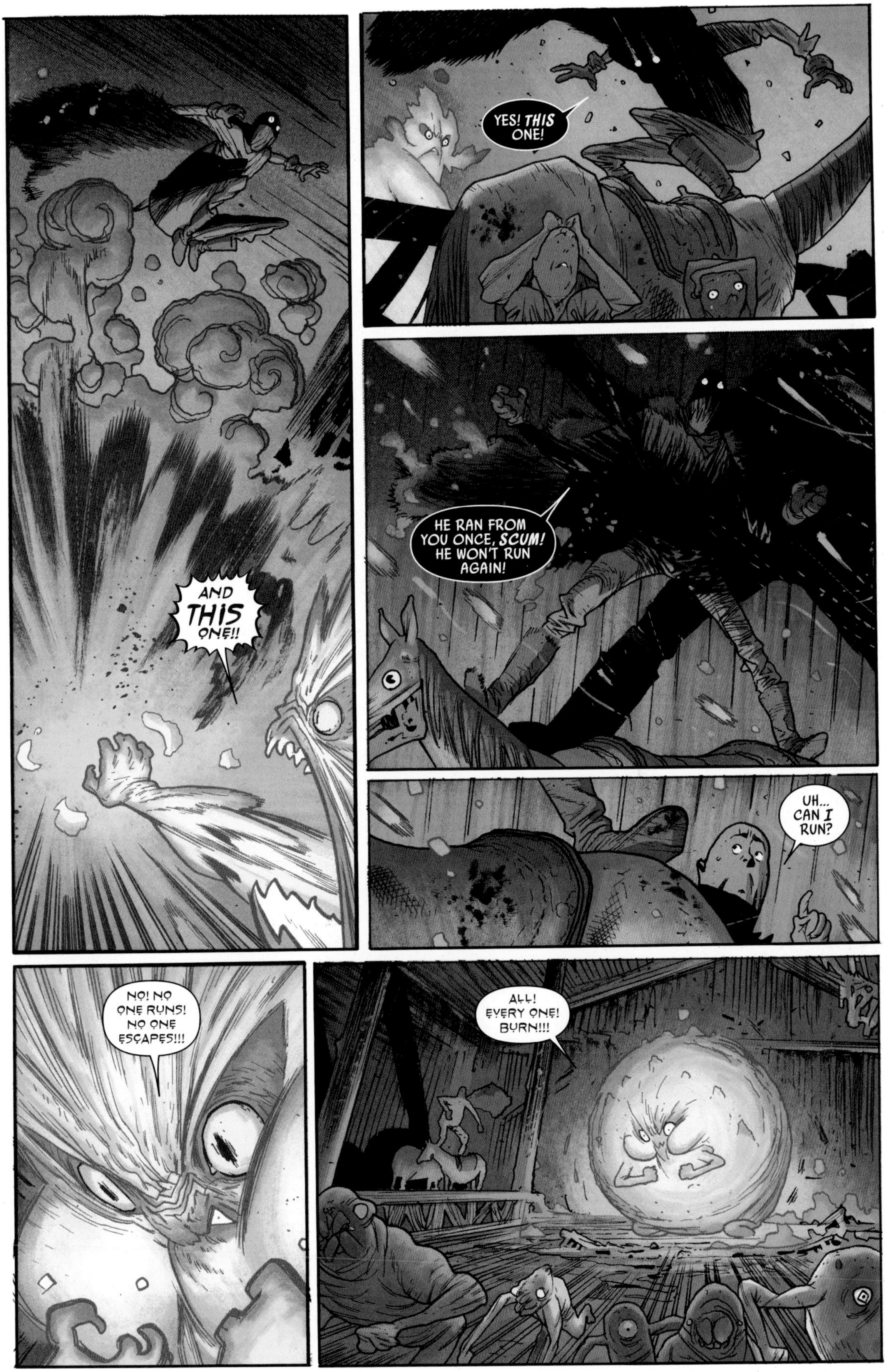
AND THIS ONE!!
YES! THIS ONE!
HE RAN FROM YOU ONCE, SCUM! HE WON'T RUN AGAIN!
UH... CAN I RUN?
NO! NO ONE RUNS! NO ONE ESCAPES!!!
ALL! EVERY ONE! BURN!!!

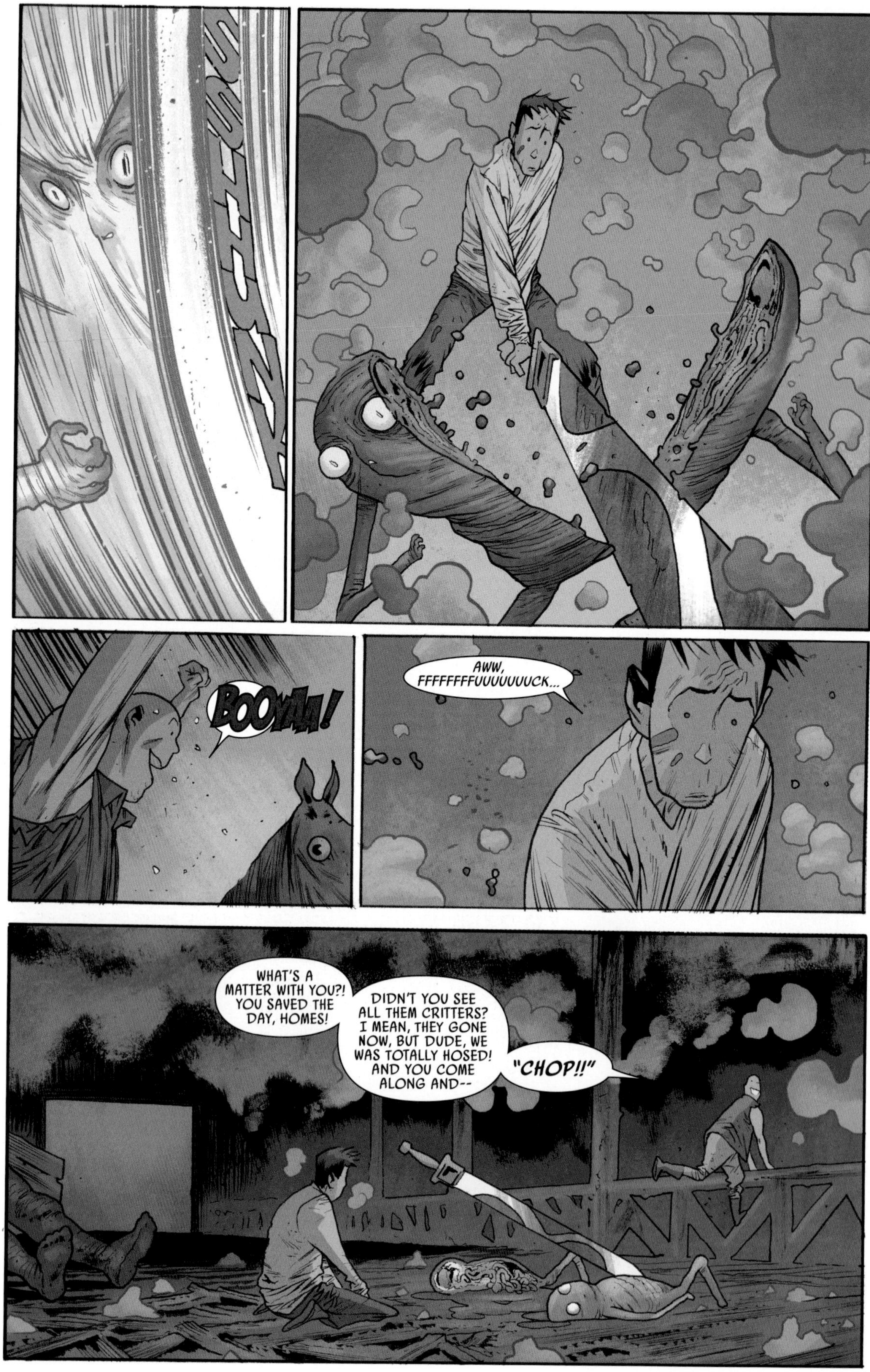
BOOYAA!
AWW, FFFFFFFFUUUUUUUCK...
WHAT'S A MATTER WITH YOU?! YOU SAVED THE DAY, HOMES!
DIDN'T YOU SEE ALL THEM CRITTERS? I MEAN, THEY GONE NOW, BUT DUDE, WE WAS TOTALLY HOSED! AND YOU COME ALONG AND--
"CHOP!!"

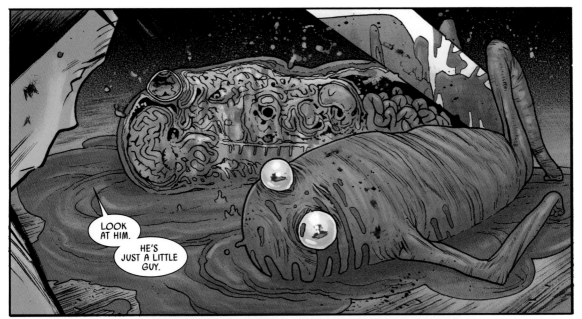

LOOK AT HIM.

HE'S JUST A LITTLE GUY.

NOW, MAYBE. BUT HE WAS 'BOUT TO WASTE EVERYBODY IN THIS PLACE! YOU'RE LIKE GODDAMN RAMBO OVER HERE!

I--THINK I'M GONNA PUKE.

THE FIRST TIME YOU TAKE LIFE, IT IS TORMENT.

"FIRST TIME"?!! WHAT ARE YOU TALKING ABOUT?! THERE'S NEVER GONNA BE A SECOND TIME! NEVER!

NEVER EVER!!

YO, BIG DADDY! WHAT WE DO WITH THIS GUY? GUTS STARTING TO LEAK ALL OVER.

URP!

THE ESU HAVE TAKEN THEIR DEAD WITH THEM, BUT ABANDONED NUSKU AS OFFAL.

NO SOLDIER DESERVES THAT.

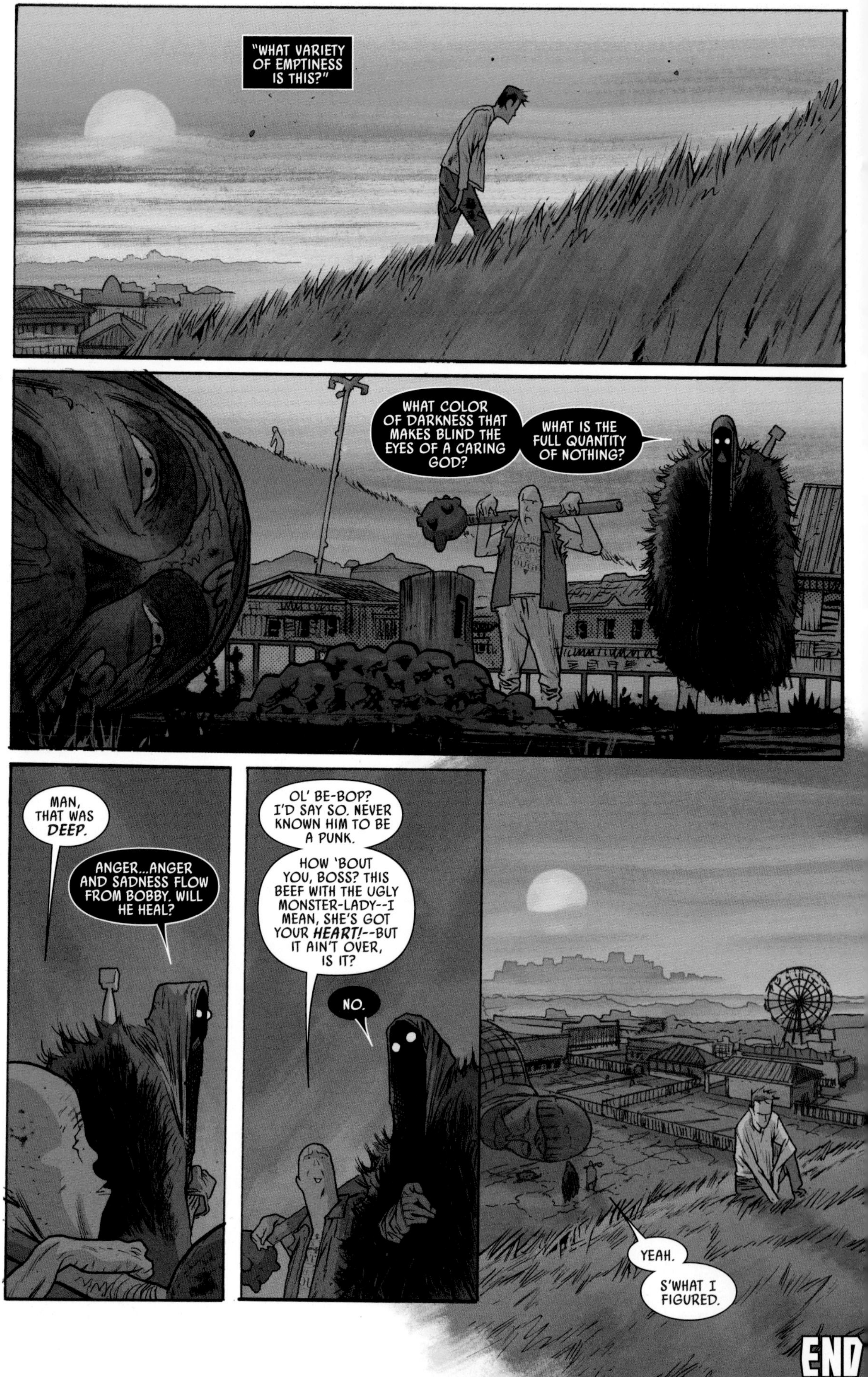
"WHAT VARIETY OF EMPTINESS IS THIS?"
WHAT COLOR OF DARKNESS THAT MAKES BLIND THE EYES OF A CARING GOD?
WHAT IS THE FULL QUANTITY OF NOTHING?
MAN, THAT WAS *DEEP.*
ANGER...ANGER AND SADNESS FLOW FROM BOBBY. WILL HE HEAL?
OL' BE-BOP? I'D SAY SO. NEVER KNOWN HIM TO BE A PUNK.
HOW 'BOUT YOU, BOSS? THIS BEEF WITH THE UGLY MONSTER-LADY--I MEAN, SHE'S GOT YOUR *HEART!*--BUT IT AIN'T OVER, IS IT?
NO.
YEAH.
S'WHAT I FIGURED.
END

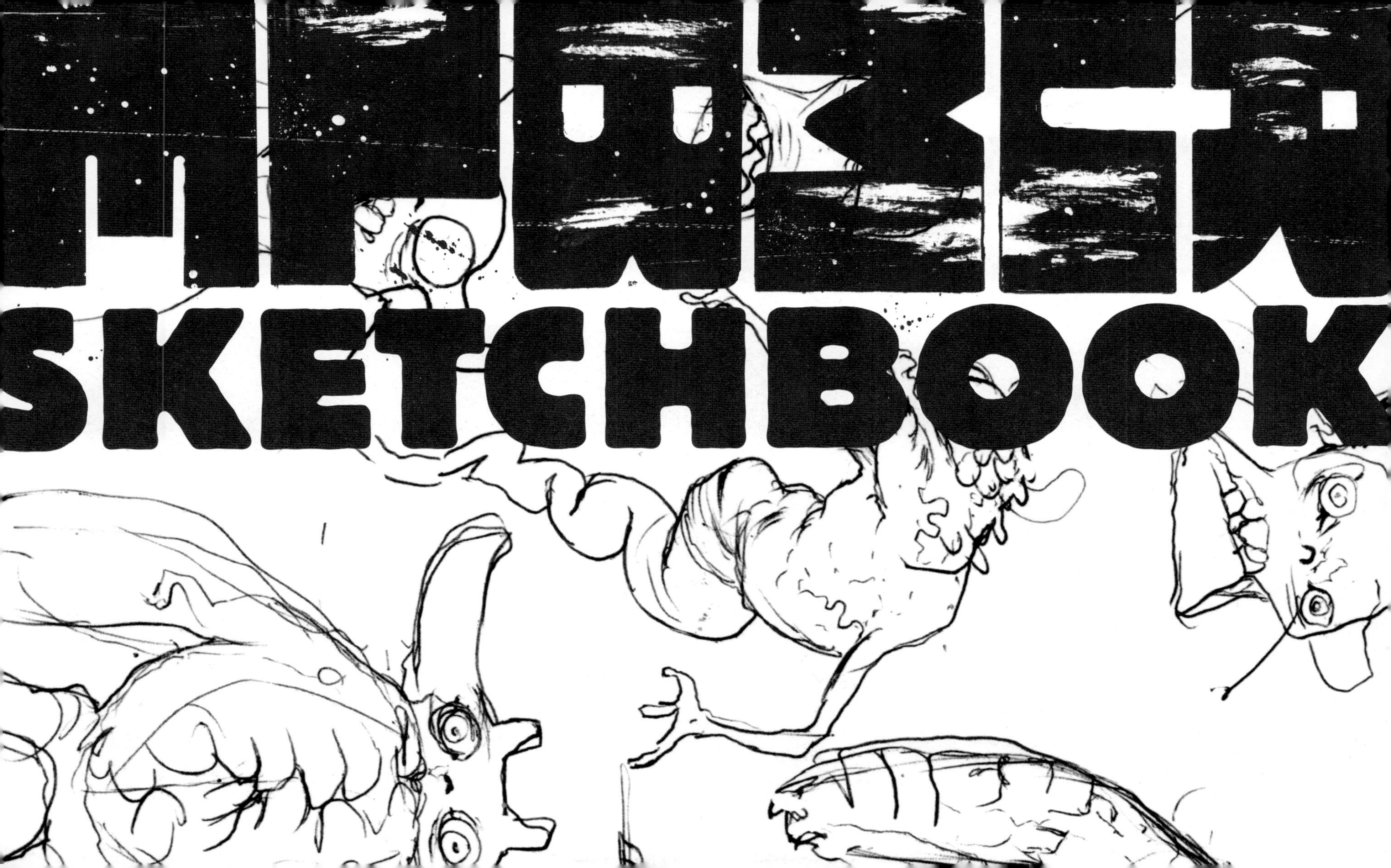
SKETCHBOOK

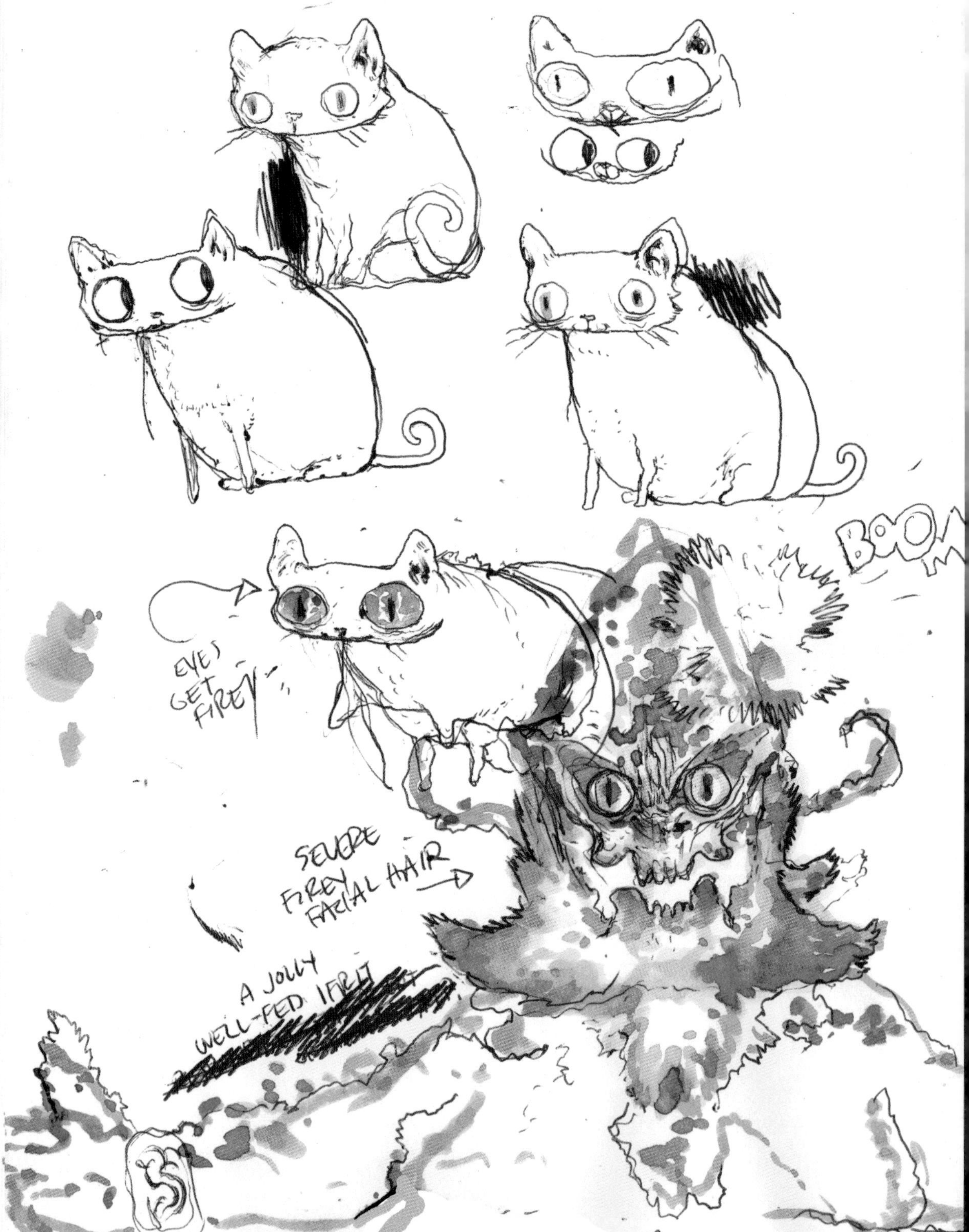
BOOM
EYES GET FIREY
SEVERE FIREY FACIAL HAIR
A JOLLY WELL-FED IFRIT

NUSKU

Nusku! I believe this was my first and only pass with designing him. When John described an ancient fire demon I immediately imagined a big-bellied moustachioed fella.

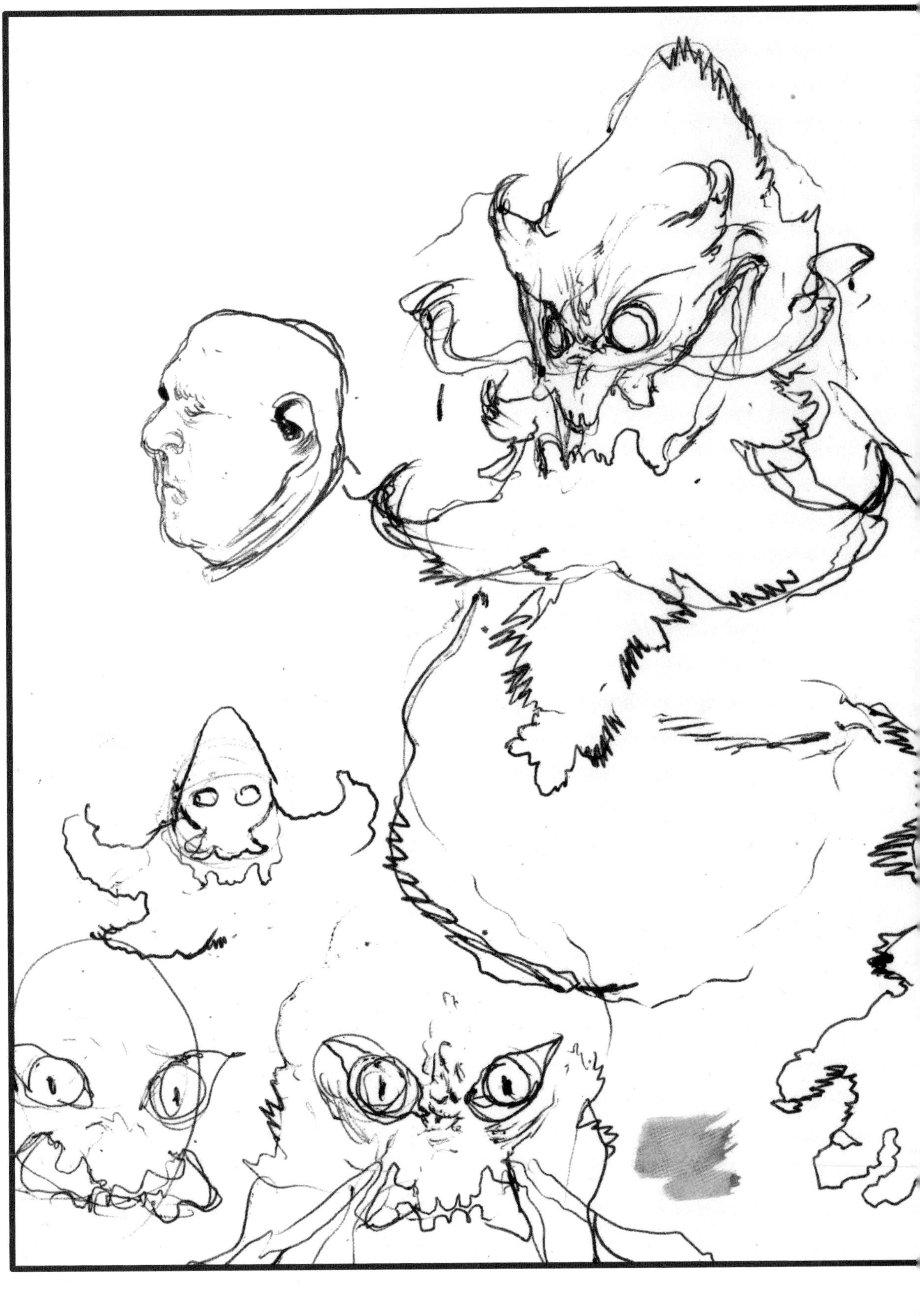

THE BAR

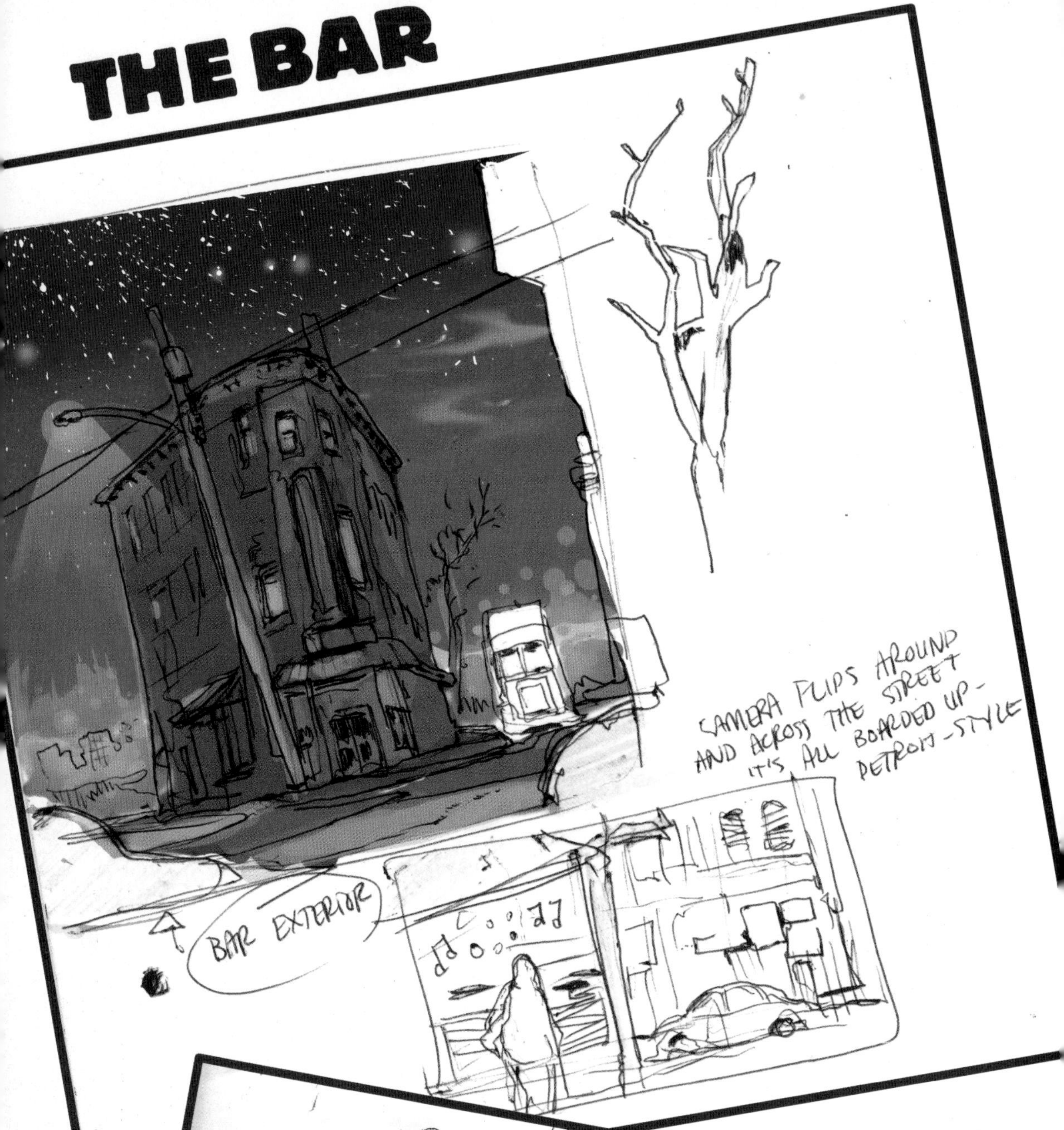
CAMERA FLIPS AROUND AND ACROSS THE STREET
IT'S ALL BOARDED UP - PETRON-STYLE
BAR EXTERIOR

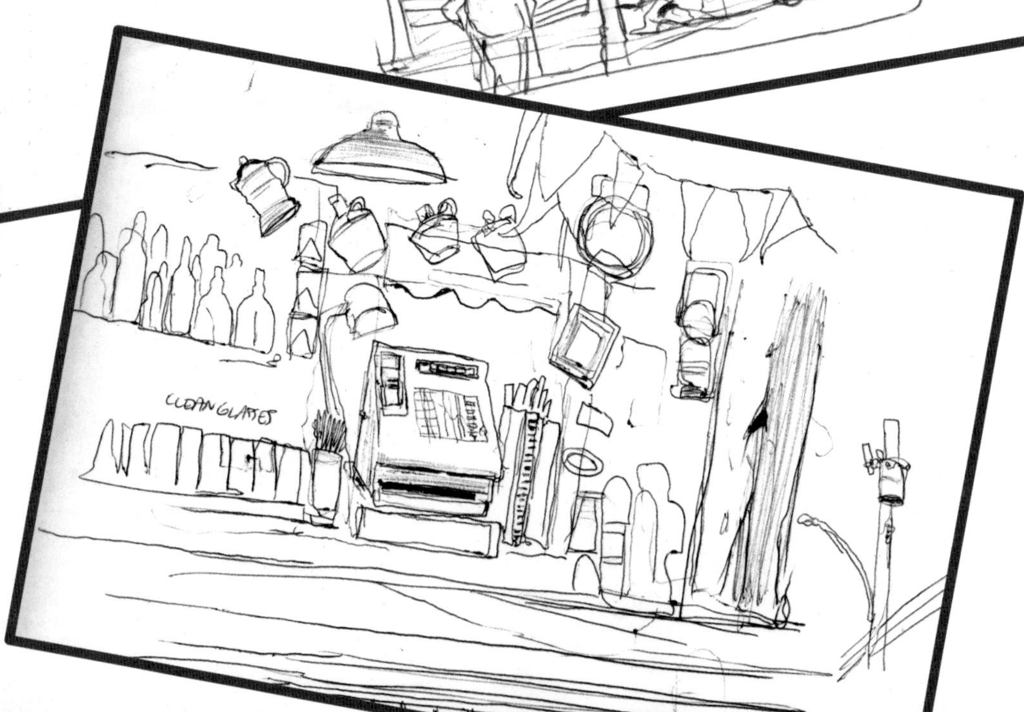
CLEAN GLASSES

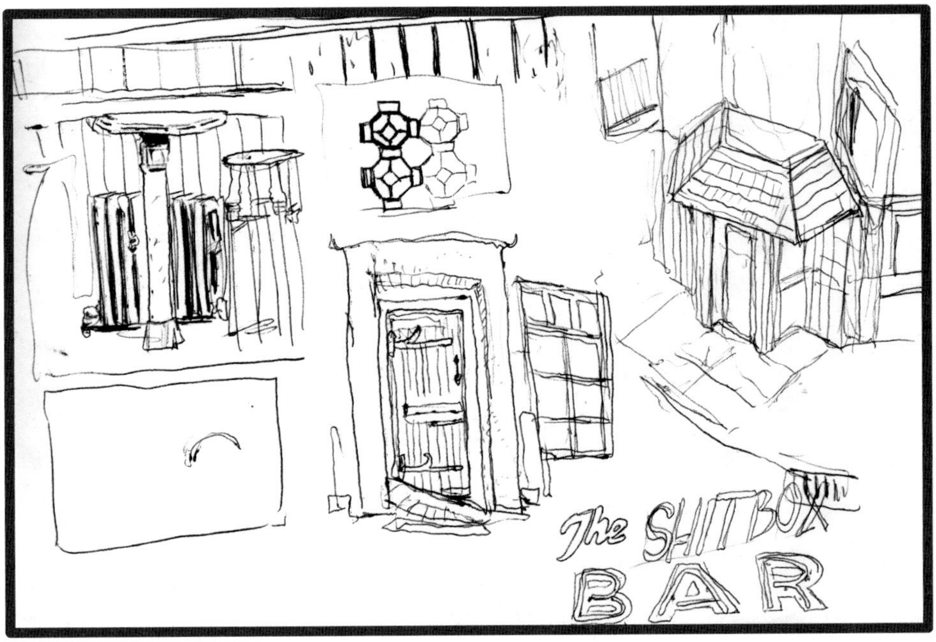
The SHITBOX
BAR

As a lifelong tee-totaler I didn't have the greatest mental reference for bar interiors. So, I remember doing a lot of studies of cool Irish pubs and all the crazy crap that litter them. Most of this didn't wind up in the pages because little details are time consuming and monthly books are hard to draw.

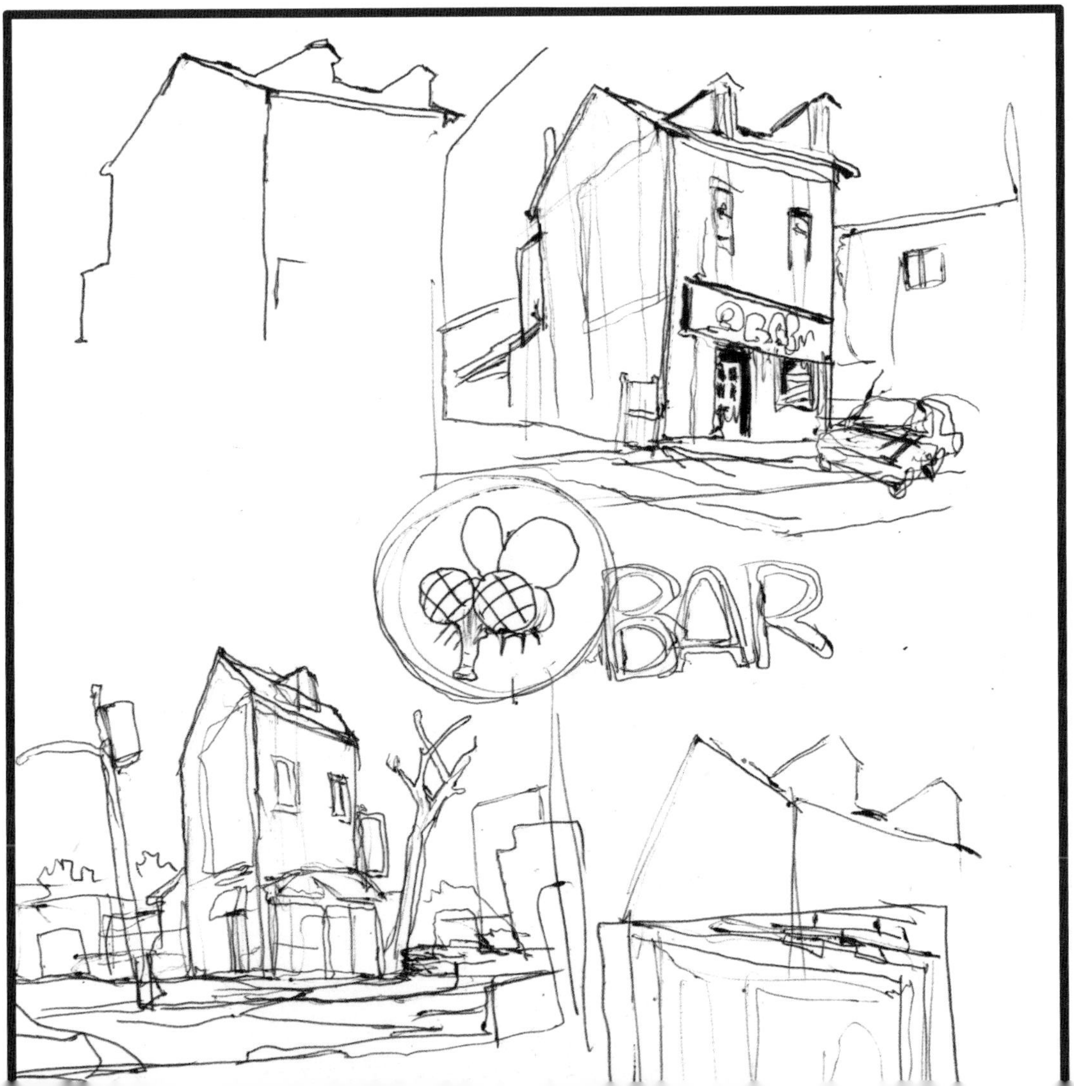
BAR

XOTLAHA

The road to designing her was a really, really difficult one. John's description of Xotlaha was vague at the beginning, which prompted me to look in every dank corner I could for inspiraton, trying to find shapes, texture, character. I wanted to do something no one had seen before. I wound up in some strange places before being yanked back to what would serve the story. Sure would be fun to revisit this stuff later on though.

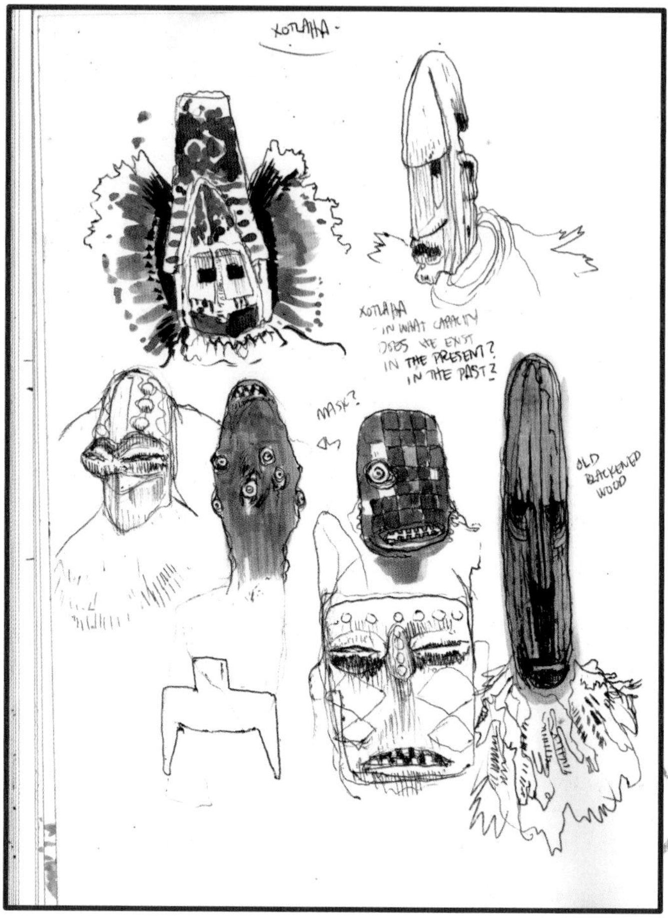
XOTLAHA -
XOTLAHA
- IN WHAT CAPACITY
DOES SHE EXIST
IN THE PRESENT?
IN THE PAST?
MASK?
OLD BLACKENED WOOD

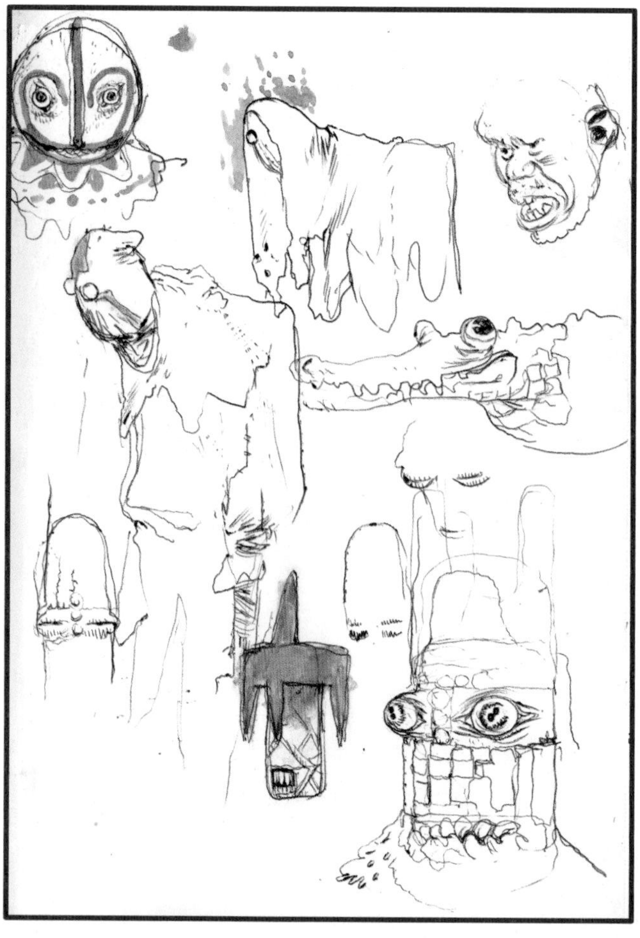

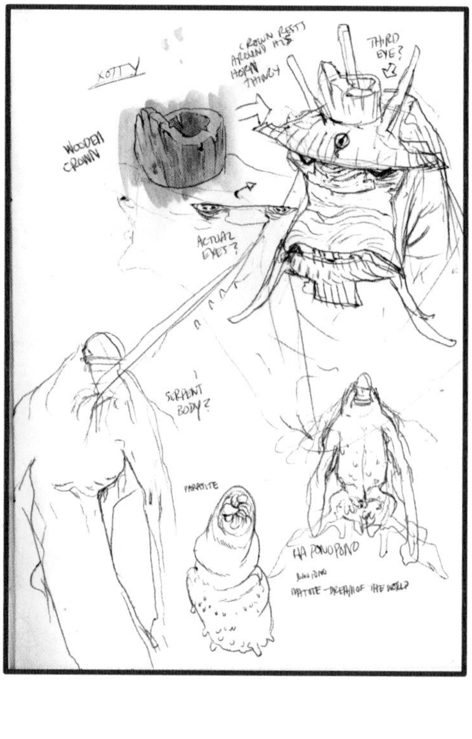
XOTTY
CROWN RESTS AROUND ITS HORN THINGY
THIRD EYE?
WOODEN CROWN
ACTUAL EYES?
SERPENT BODY?
PARASITE
HA PONOPONO

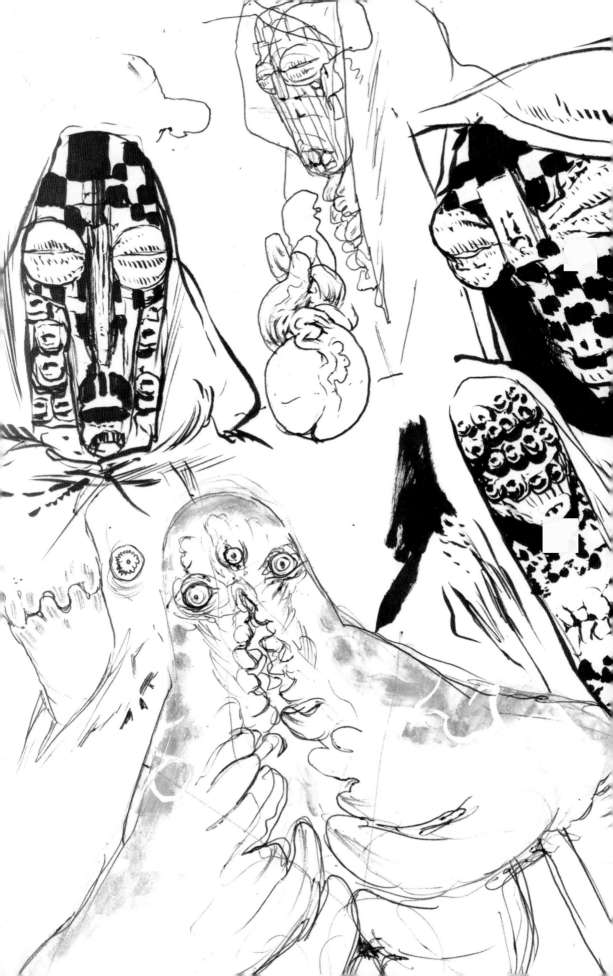

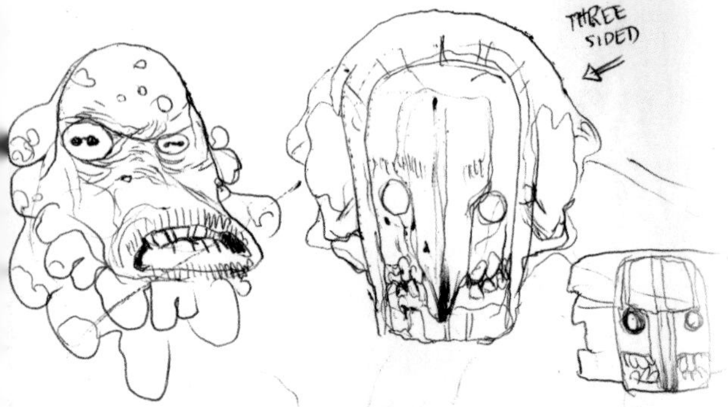
THREE SIDED

For about a week I was positive this was going to be her.

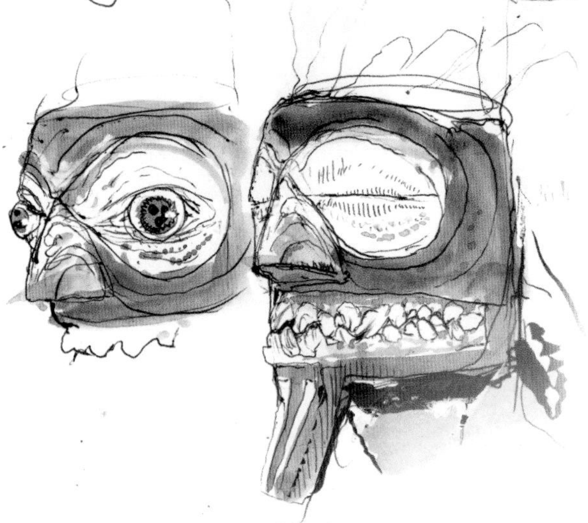

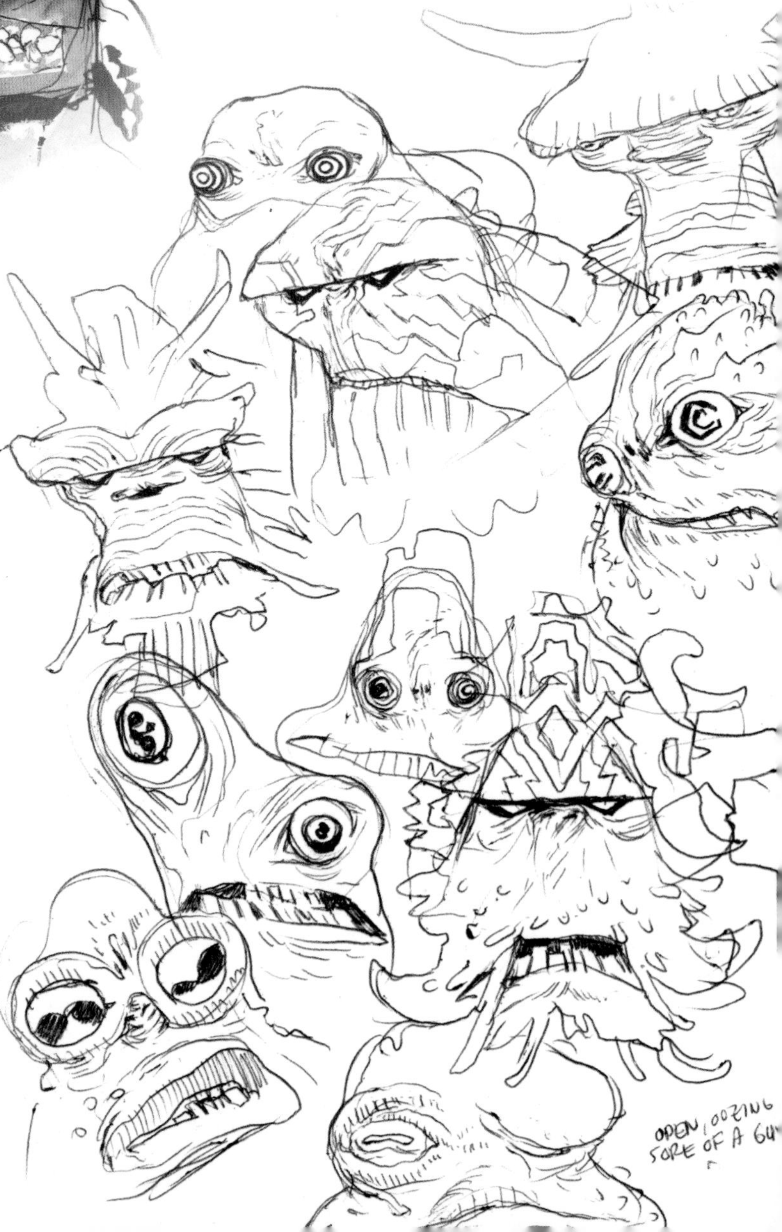
OPEN, OOZING
SORE OF A GU

More digging for that elusive Xotlaha design.

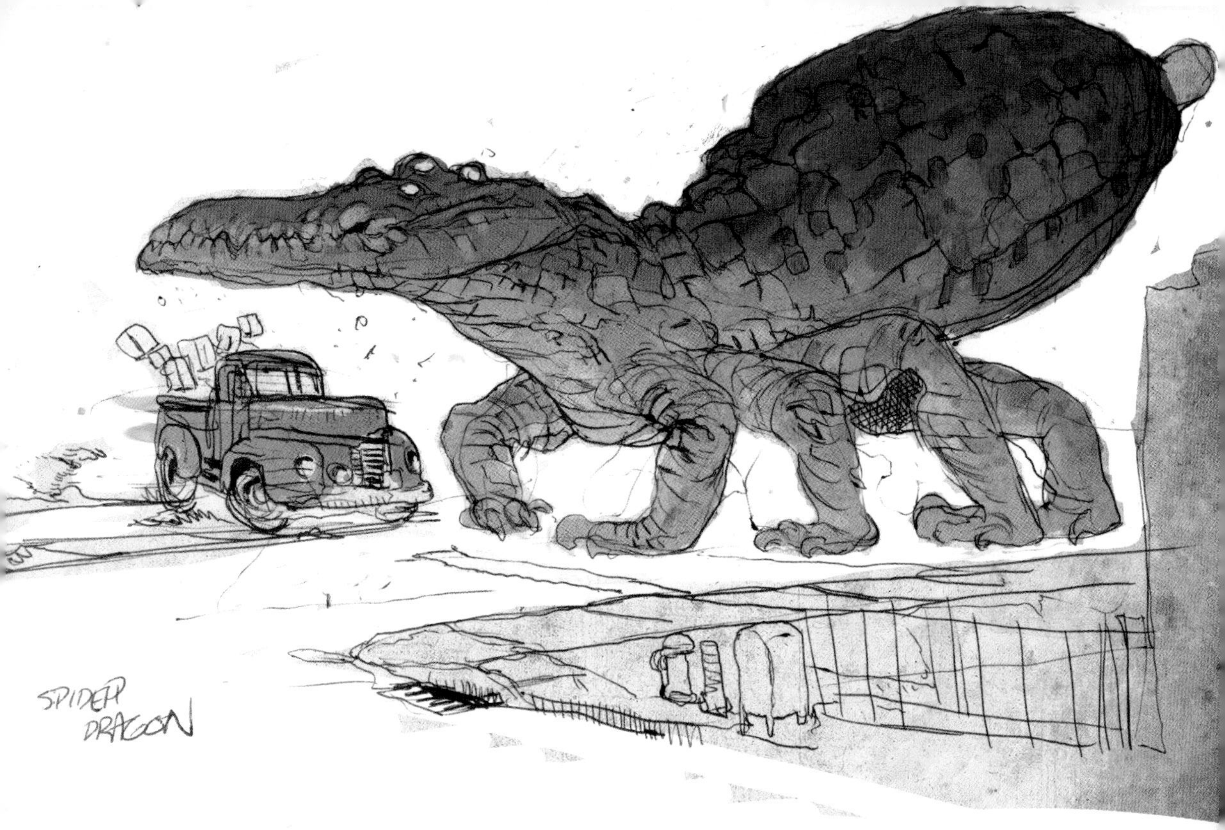
SPIDER
DRAGON

John told me to draw a Spider-Dragon. So, I did. I kinda love this guy. I didn't realize how much fun it could be to draw period cars and dragons in the same doodle.

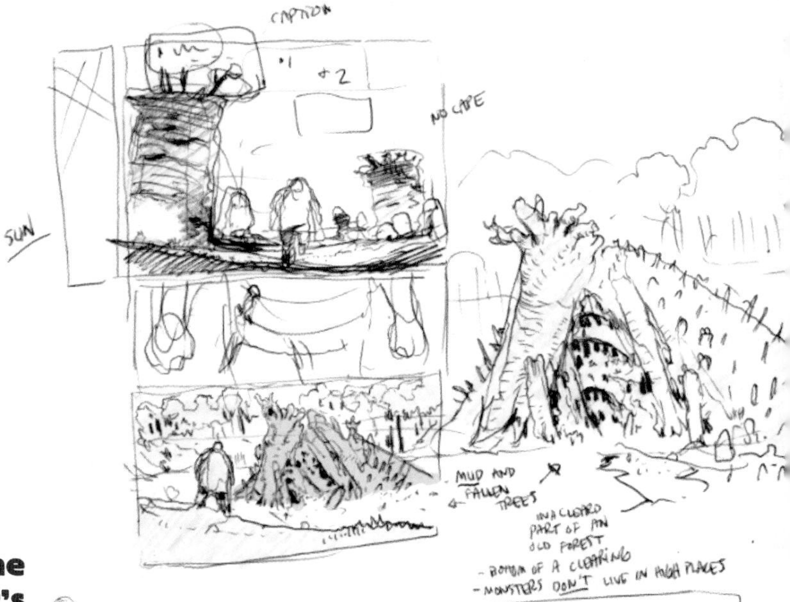
CAPTION
1
2
NO CAPE
SUN
MUD AND FALLEN TREES
IN A CLEARED PART OF AN OLD FOREST
- BOTTOM OF A CLEARING
- MONSTERS DON'T LIVE IN HIGH PLACES

Some sketches for the Pangea monster's dwelling. I think John mentioned an above ground structure of some kind, but it felt right to put them below ground, burrowed into the rock. Living in all that stone might help explain how they could take to living in the city later on.

6

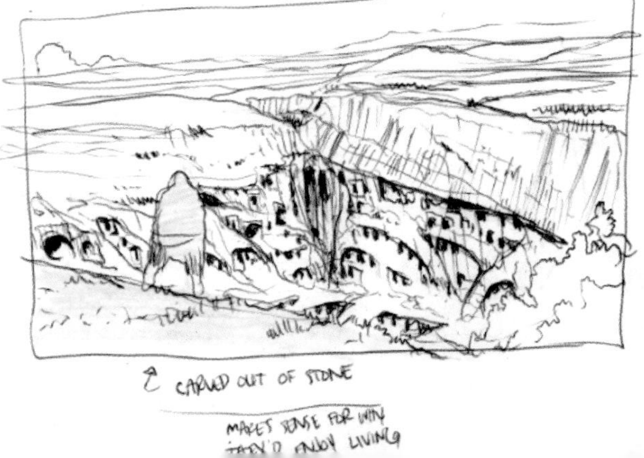
2 CARVED OUT OF STONE
MAKES SENSE FOR WHY
THEY'D ENJOY LIVING

DEL

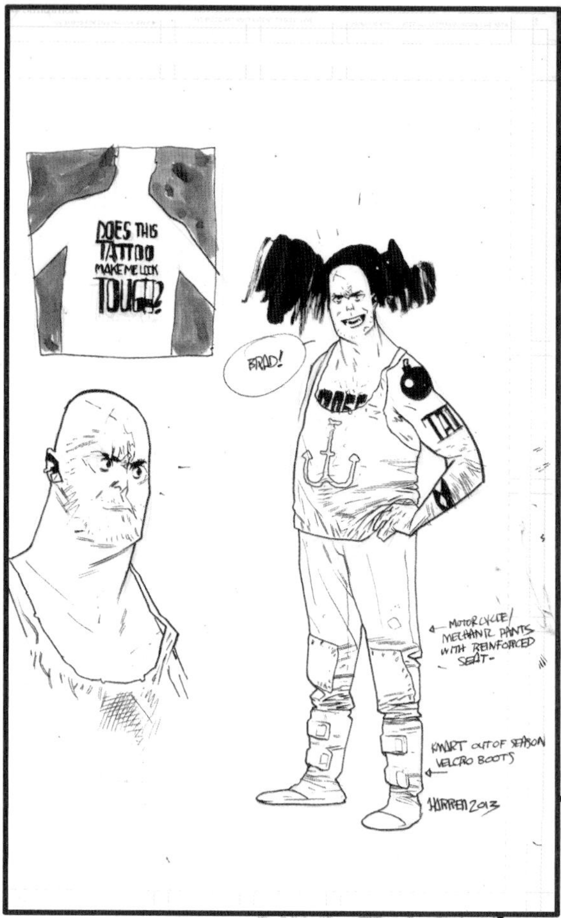
DOES THIS TATTOO MAKE ME LOOK TOUGH?!
BRAD!
MOTORCYCLE/ MECHANIC PANTS WITH REINFORCED SEAT-
KMART OUT OF SEASON VELCRO BOOTS
J.HARREN 2013

BOBBY

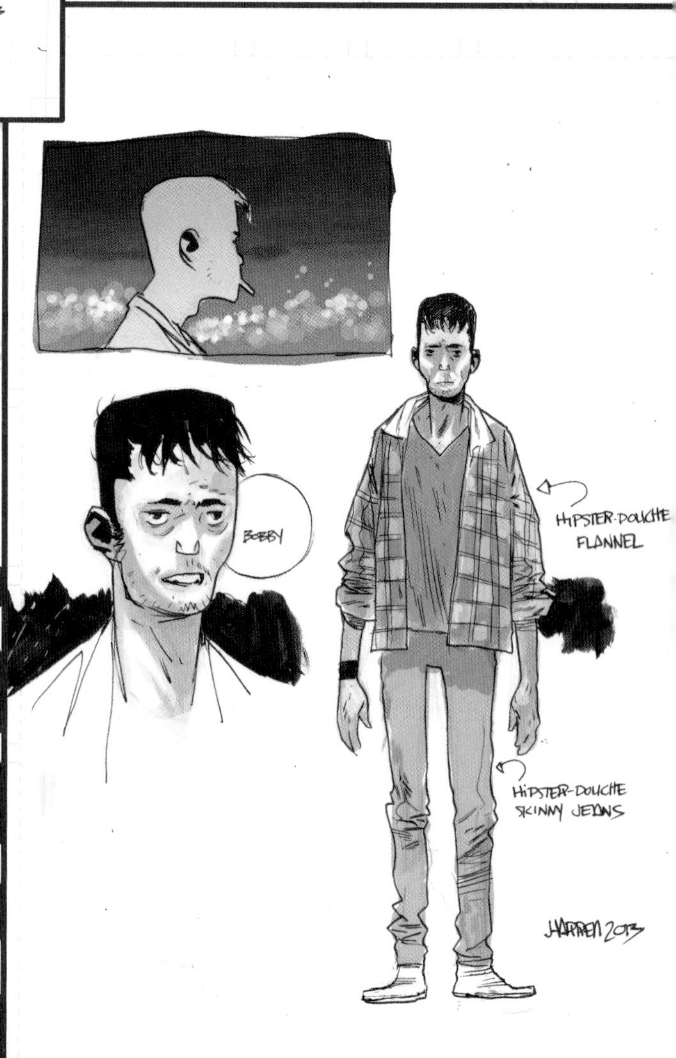
BOBBY
HIPSTER-DOUCHE FLANNEL
HIPSTER-DOUCHE SKINNY JEANS
J.HARREN 2013

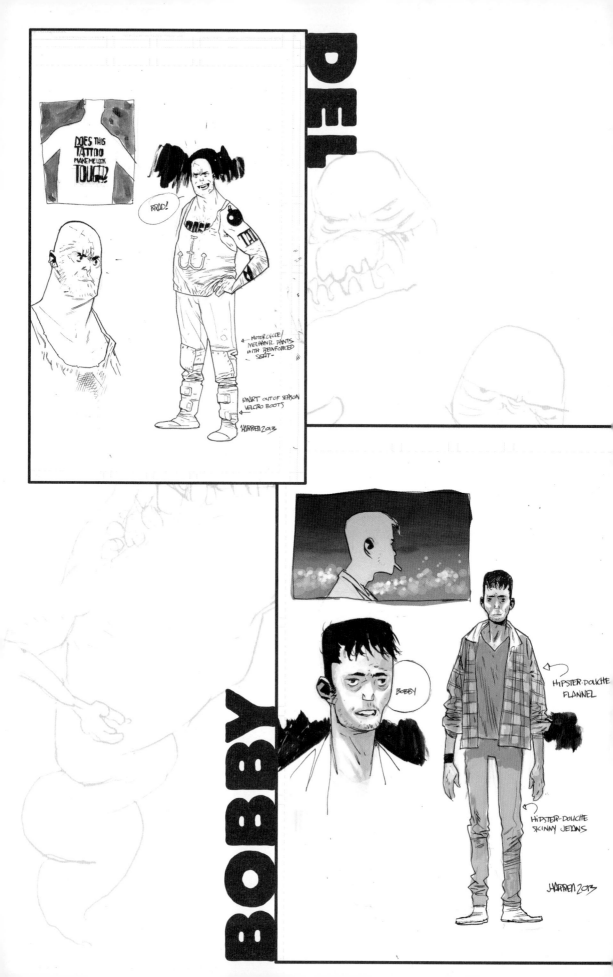

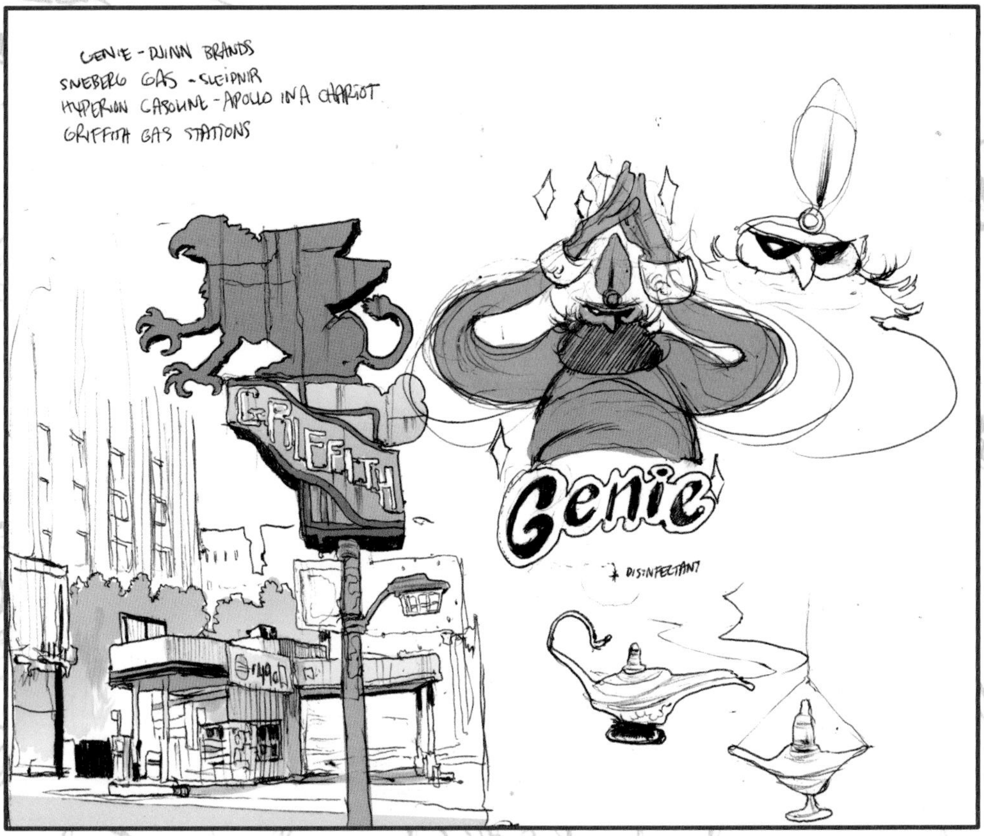
GENIE - DJINN BRANDS
SNEBERG GAS - SLEIPNIR
HYPERION GASOLINE - APOLLO IN A CHARIOT
GRIFFITH GAS STATIONS
GRIFFITH
Genie
+ DISINFECTANT

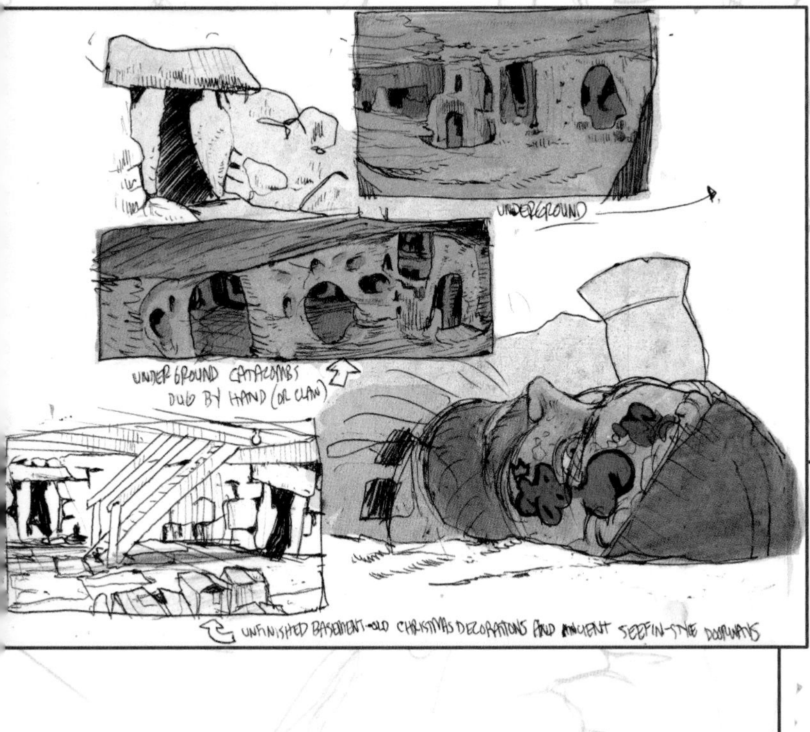
UNDERGROUND
UNDERGROUND CATACOMBS DUG BY HAND (OR CLAW)
UNFINISHED BASEMENT - OLD CHRISTMAS DECORATIONS AND ANCIENT SEEFIN-STYLE DOORWAYS

MORE PLACES & THINGS

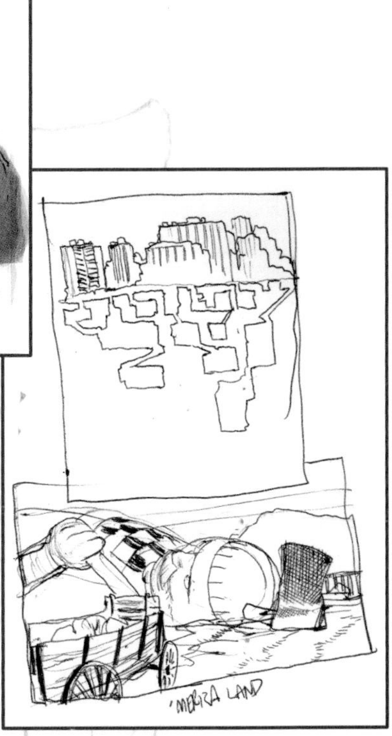
'MERICA LAND

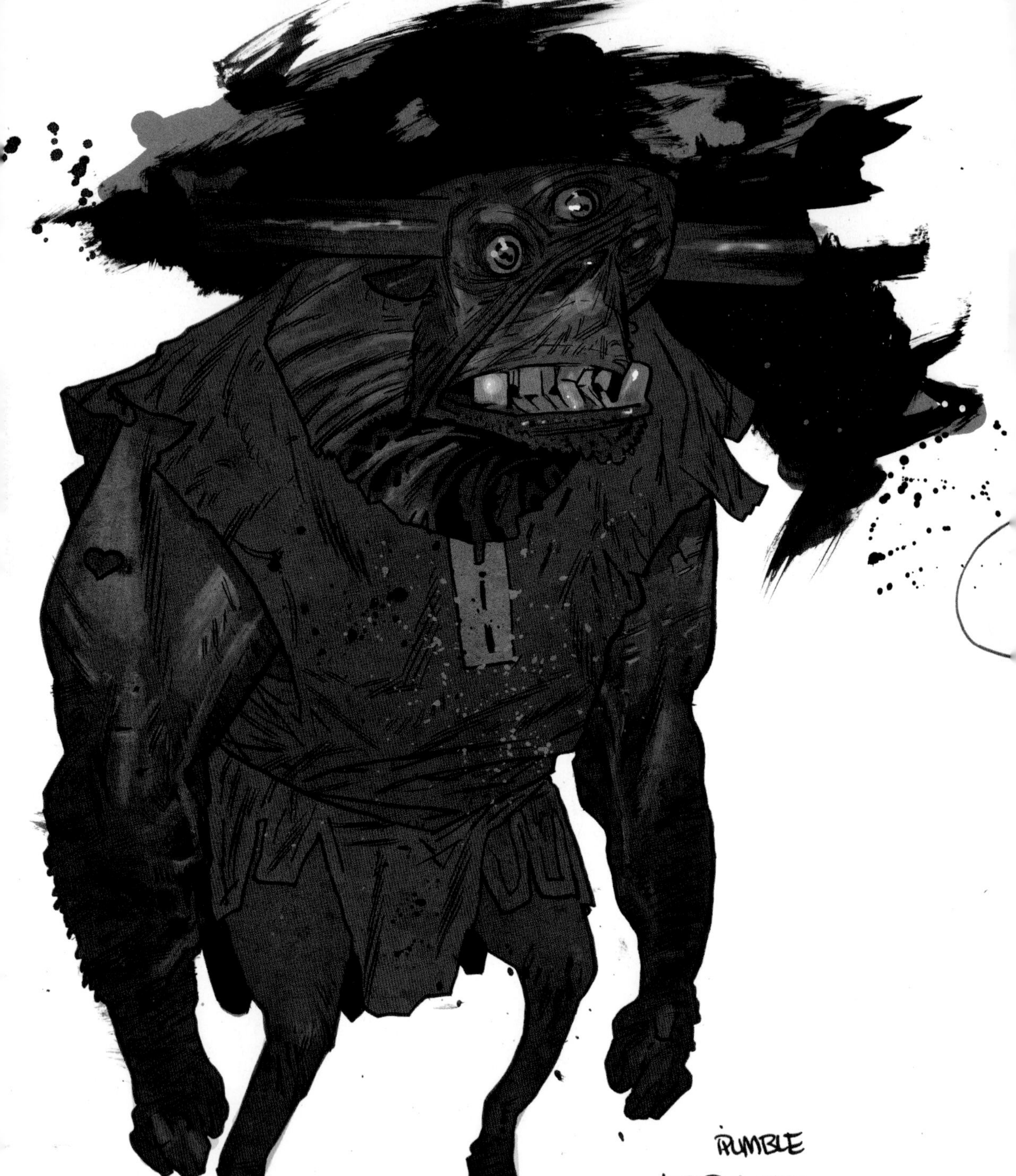
RUMBLE
HARREN 2013

I named this guy Stewart. He was the very first non-scarecrow drawing I did for Rumble in an attempt to find out what the hell a book could look like. This was back when I thought I could color the book as well.

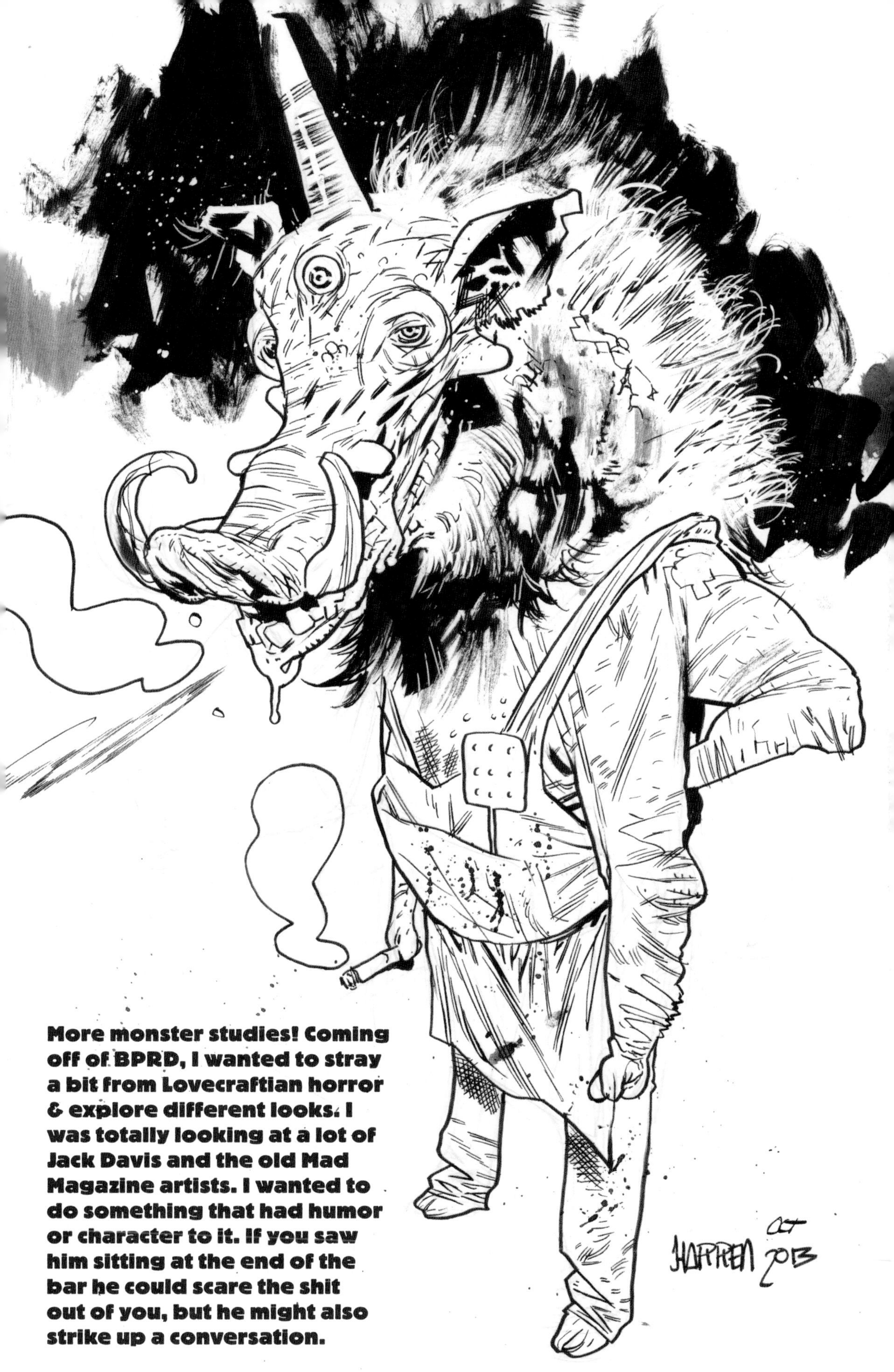

JHARREN
OCT
2013

More monster studies! Coming off of BPRD, I wanted to stray a bit from Lovecraftian horror & explore different looks. I was totally looking at a lot of Jack Davis and the old Mad Magazine artists. I wanted to do something that had humor or character to it. If you saw him sitting at the end of the bar he could scare the shit out of you, but he might also strike up a conversation.

TEASER PAGES

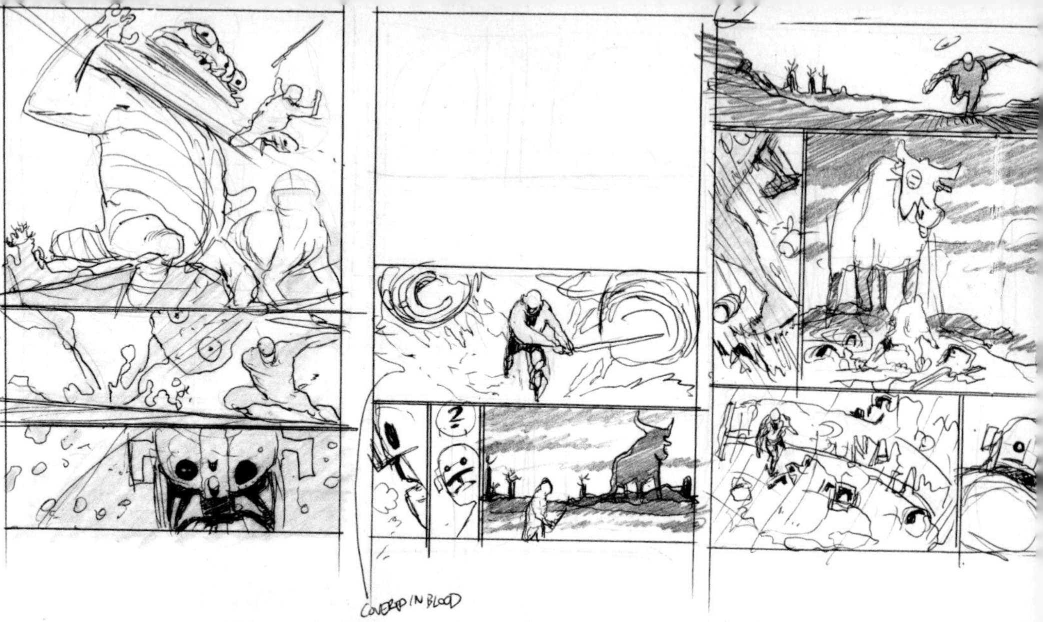
COVERED IN BLOOD

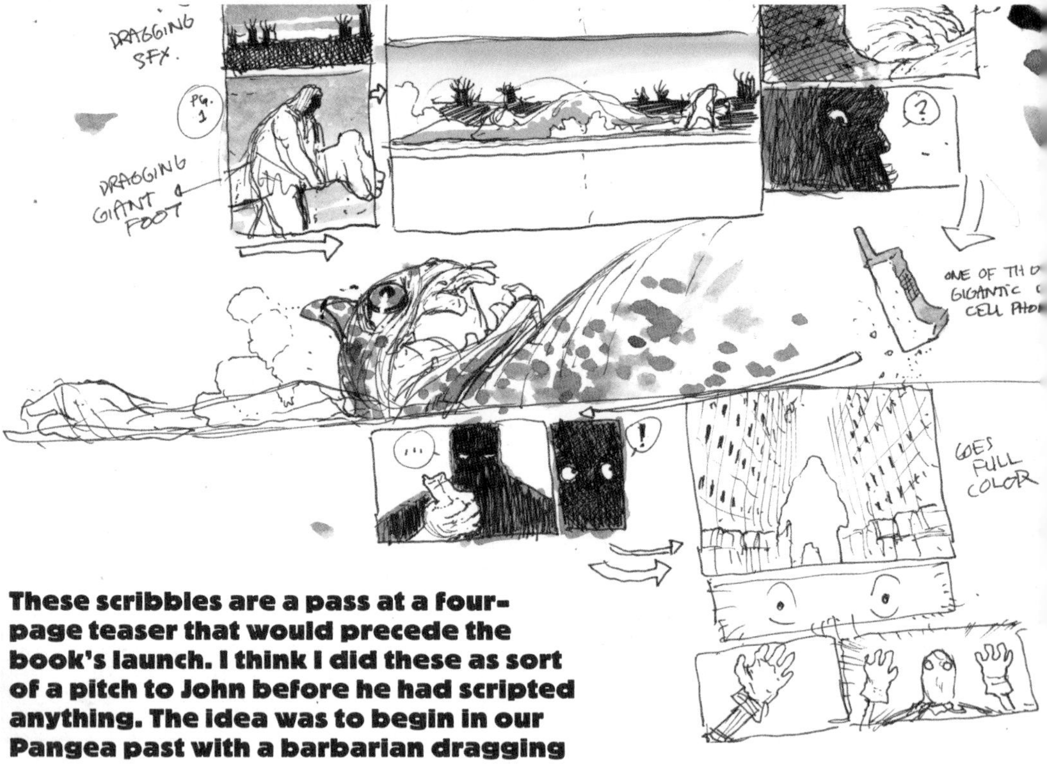
DRAGGING SFX.
PG. 1
DRAGGING GIANT FOOT
GOES FULL COLOR

These scribbles are a pass at a four-page teaser that would precede the book's launch. I think I did these as sort of a pitch to John before he had scripted anything. The idea was to begin in our Pangea past with a barbarian dragging a giant monster carcass across the desert and he stumbles upon an old 80's cell phone. When he looks up again, he's in a dizzying metropolis as a scarecrow; no dialogue or narration. I think John's complaint was that it was too on-the-nose. It gave away the whole story too early. I still like the images quite a bit though. Would love to recycle it later.

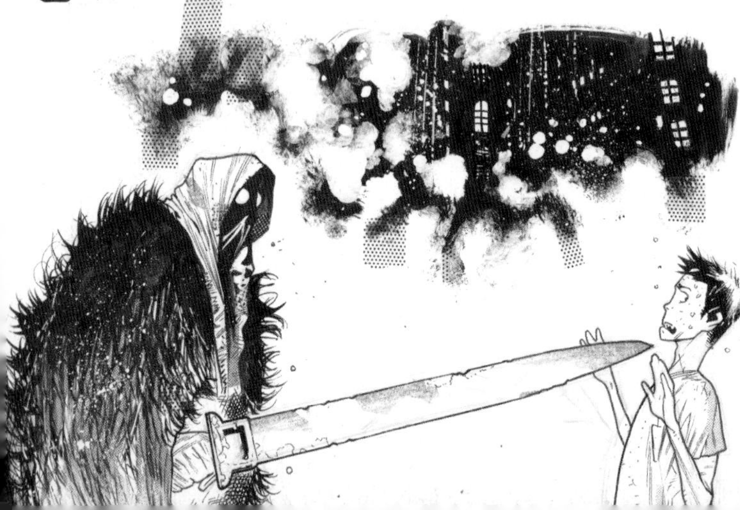

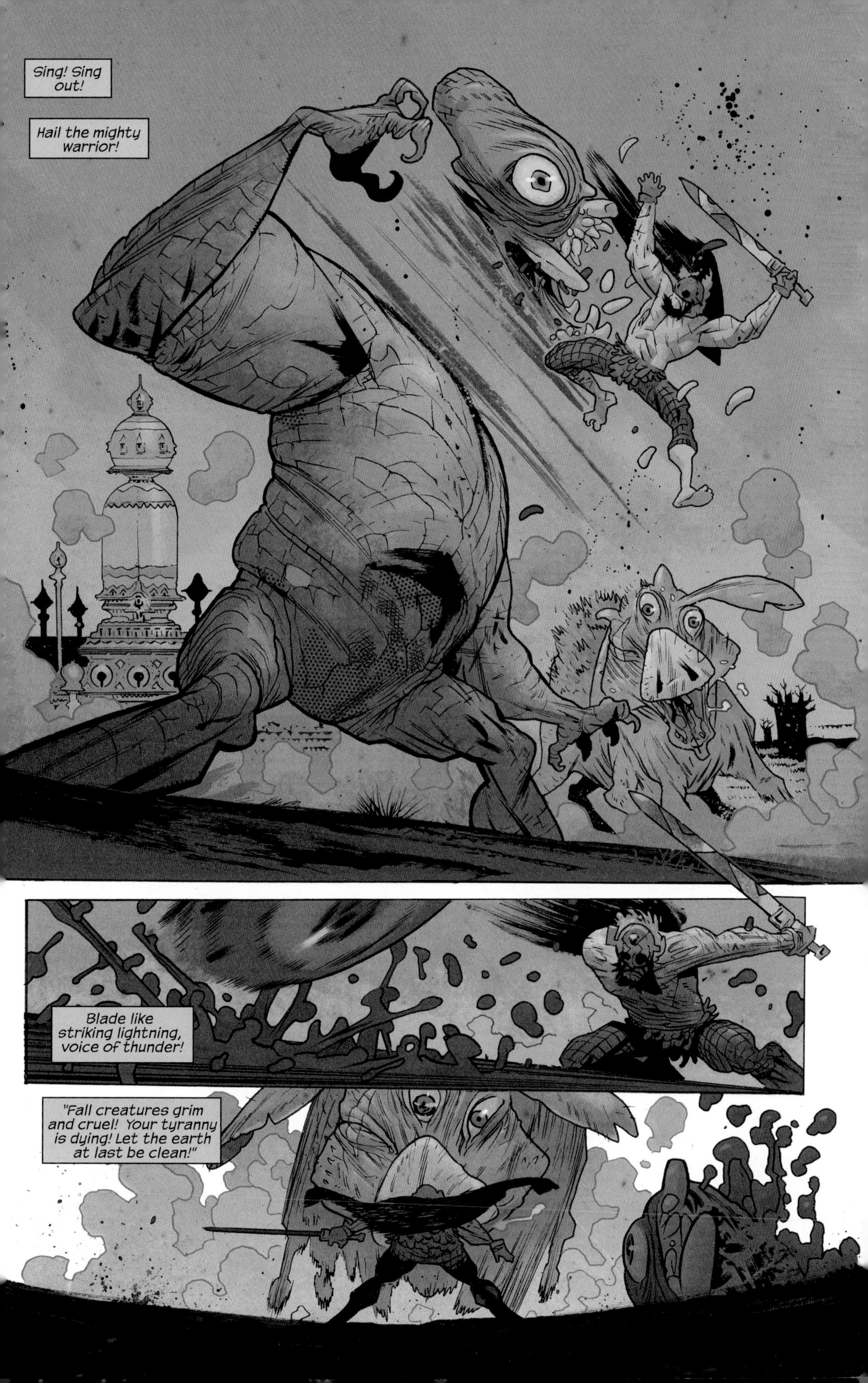
Sing! Sing out!
Hail the mighty warrior!
Blade like striking lightning, voice of thunder!
"Fall creatures grim and cruel! Your tyranny is dying! Let the earth at last be clean!"

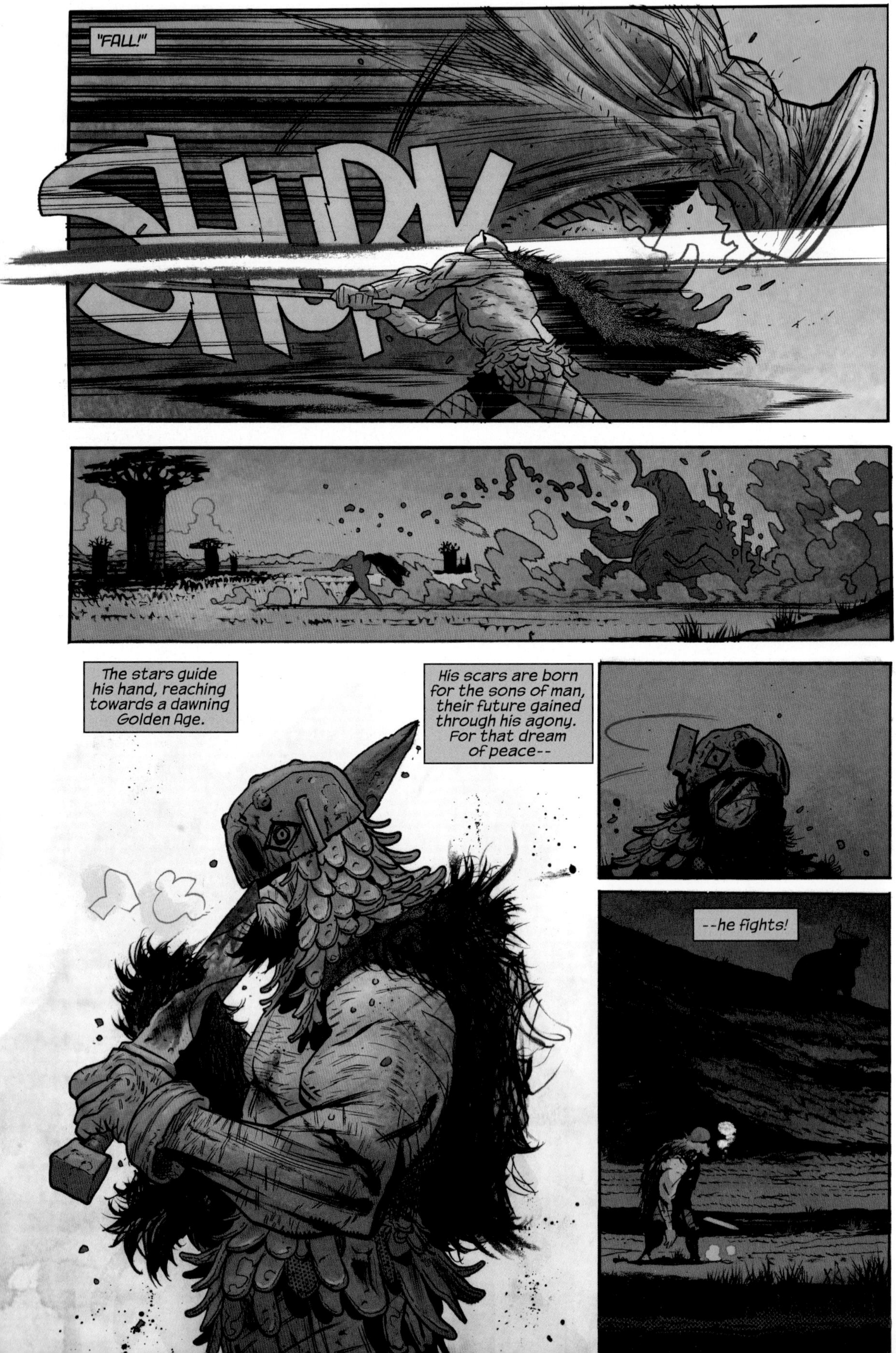
"FALL!"
The stars guide his hand, reaching towards a dawning Golden Age.
His scars are born for the sons of man, their future gained through his agony. For that dream of peace--
--he fights!

He fights for the new world.

For the paradise to come.

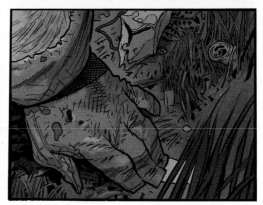

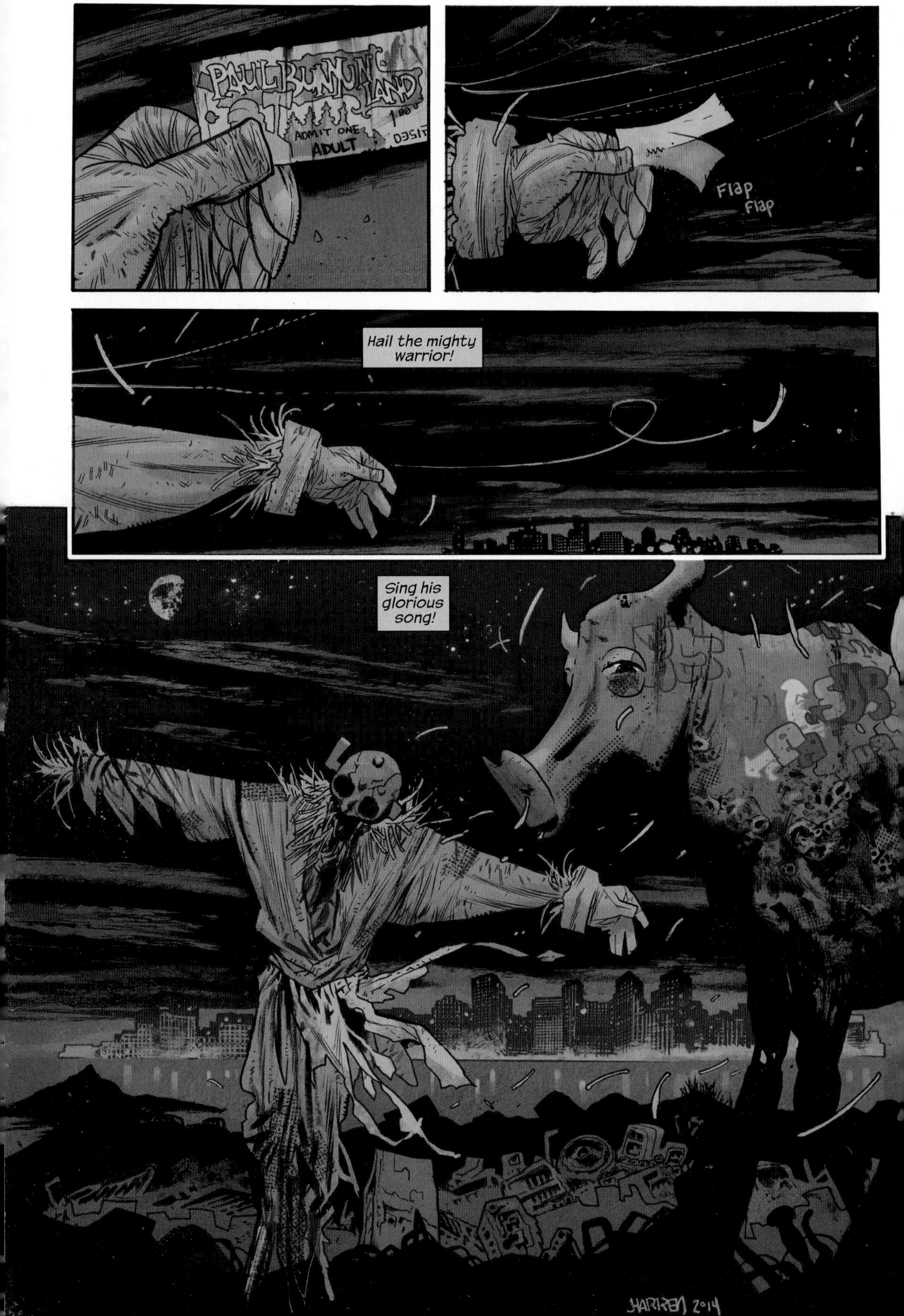
PAUL BUNYUN LAND
1.00
ADMIT ONE
ADULT
Flap flap
Hail the mighty warrior!
Sing his glorious song!
HARREN 2014